JACK KETCHUM

PEACEABLE KINGDOM

LEISURE BOOKS NEW YORK CITY

A LEISURE BOOK®

August 2003

Published by

Dorchester Publishing Co., Inc.
200 Madison Avenue, Suite 2000
New York, NY 10016

Peaceable Kingdom copyright © 2003 by Dallas Mayr

For individual story copyrights, see page 416.

ISBN 0-8439-5216-4

The name "Leisure Books" and the stylized "L" with design are trademarks of Dorchester Publishing Co., Inc.

Printed in the United States of America.

Visit us on the web at www.dorchesterpub.com.

CONTENTS

Introduction

I don't know why you put up with me.

It's a matter of consistency. Or in my case, inconsistency. As a writer I'm all over the place.

Take the books. Suppose you came to my stuff through *Off Season* way back when and you kinda liked its violent streak and its extreme stance so you're looking for more of the same. You have to wait a while—four whole years—and then when you finally do find a new Ketchum title on the racks what do you get? *Hide and Seek*. A quiet little first-person suspense story, a *love* story no less with, yeah, some nasty low-ball curves thrown at you at the end but compared to the first book, practically good-natured.

Or here's another scenario. Suppose the first book of mine you read is *Hide and Seek*, and you miss *Cover* completely—hell, almost everybody did—and the next thing you find is *The Girl Next Door*. Now I'm going to do a *lot* of supposing here and assume that you ignore the ditsy skullheaded cheerleader on the cover, you assume it's *not* Ketchum doing an R.L. Stine ripoff and actually buy the thing and sit down to read it and at first it's another quiet little first-person memoir-type novel so you're comfortable with that from having read *Hide and Seek*, so you get a little into it and then a little more into it and finally you say . . .

. . . what the hell *is* this shit! Has he gone totally out of his fucking *mind*?

Then maybe your first Ketchum book's *She Wakes*. Ancient Greek Gods and Goddesses, zombies and cats and snakes all chasing one another all over the Aegean. Then you pick up *Red*.

Hmmm. That's interesting.

This one seems to be about an old guy and his dog.

Has he gone totally out of his *mind*?

You get the point.

Still, should you need any further proof of my inconsistency, that's what this volume is about—to rid you of any notion other than that once and for all. And I welcome it wholeheartedly. The short-fiction form is where a writer gets to move around most anyway. Unlike a novel you don't have to live with an idea or a set of ideas for six months or a year, so as long as you obey whatever idea you do have you can zig and zag to your heart's delight. Experiment. Float like a butterfly, sting like a bee. Get in, get out, go on to something else.

So there's stuff in here like "To Suit the Crime" that's as ice-cold heartless as anything I've ever done and stuff like "Firedance" which is almost cuddly. Surreal stories like "The Holding Cell" and "Chain Letter" and the odd black comedy like "The Haunt" or "The Business." You even get my one and only vampire story in "The Turning" and an honest-to-God UFO yarn in "Amid the Walking Wounded."

There's even a Western.

As I say, I'm all over the place. And I think that I've been very fortunate in that most of my readers seem to expect that of me by now and apparently have no real urge to pin me down. Peter Straub once paid me the compliment of saying that he thought a lot of people came to my writing for the wrong reasons but stuck with me for the right ones. I suspect there's some truth in that.

But there's also the fact that in my experience most of my readers are first and foremost plain old-fashioned *readers*. *Good* readers. They're not looking for cozy brand-name output and that means I don't have to give it to 'em. They're not lazy and have little patience with pre-fab beach-bag books or Oprah's opine du jour. They're questers.

They know that every now and then you're gonna get lucky and pure gold like King and Straub's *Black House* will simply drop into your lap at the local supermarket but after that, if your bent is horror and suspense fiction, you're gonna have to get your hands dirty and root around for more. Find a Ramsey Campbell or an Edward Lee. They *expect* diversity and search it out. They want what all good readers want—to be taken somewhere in a book or a story that's really worth visiting for a while. Maybe even worth thinking about after.

If that place happens to scare the hell out of you all the better.

Some of the stories collected here try to do exactly that and some don't. Sure, they all tend to proceed from some dark place—it's me after all—but sometimes they've got something else on their mind too. And that's one of the reasons this book is called *Peaceable Kingdom*.

I wasn't just being ironic, honest.

The title comes from the final story in the book, "Firedance."

Yep, the *almost cuddly* one. Keep in mind that I said almost.

For those of you who might be a little rusty on your Old Testament or art history the phrase derives from a passage in Isaiah 11:6–9, which a number of nineteenth-century *naif* painters favored, often rendering the scene beautifully and using *Peaceable Kingdom* as the title for their works. I

3

reference the paintings in my story. But here's an excerpt from the biblical passage:

The wolf also shall dwell with the lamb, and the leopard shall lie down with the kid; and the calf and the young lion and the fatling together; and a little child shall lead them . . . and they shall not hurt or destroy on all my holy mountain . . .

Wolf and lamb. Leopard and goat-kid. Calf and lion, little piggy and little child.

Diversity, union, harmony. Hopes I have for this collection.

With the predators among them all defanged for good.

And that, finally, is my wish for us all, concealed or obvious somewhere in each of these stories—*they shall not hurt or destroy.*

Not on my damn mountain.

Jack Ketchum
December, 2001

The Rifle

She found the rifle standing on its stock in the back of his cluttered closet.

Unexpected as a snake in there.

Not that he'd made very much attempt to hide it.

It was leaning in the corner behind the twenty-pound fiberglass bow and the quiver of target arrows his father had bought him for Christmas—over her objections. His winter jacket hung in front of it. She'd moved the jacket aside. And there it was.

He'd complained in the past about her going in his closet and for a long time she'd obliged him. Privacy, she knew, was important to a ten-year-old—it was especially important to Danny. But when you noticed dustballs rolling out from under the door somebody was going to have to get in there and clean and obviously it wasn't going to be him.

She was only planning to vacuum.

Now this.

She reached around behind her and turned off the Electrolux. For a moment she just knelt there staring at the rifle in the heavy summer silence.

A slim black barrel lurking in the shadows.

A *secret*, she thought.

Yet another.

She reached inside and grasped the cool metal. Drew it out into the light.

The rifle was an old bolt-action .22. Her brother had owned one very much like it when he was fifteen—took it down to the VFW target range on Saturdays for a while. Then he discovered girls.

Danny was only ten.

Where in God's name had he got it?

Richard wouldn't have bought it for him. Not even her ex-husband was fool enough to think for one minute that she'd allow a weapon in the house. No, it had to be . . .

. . . *her father's.*

Which meant that Danny had also stolen it.

They'd visited his farm the weekend before last. She was struck again by how empty the house seemed now that her mother was gone and had sat in the kitchen with her father drinking cup after cup of black coffee, knowing how starved for conversation he was now. So that Danny was on his own most of the day. Through the big bay window she saw him go into the barn where her father kept his two remaining horses. A little later noticed him walking through the field of long dry grass toward the woods and stream beyond. And then she'd forgotten all about him until what must have been over an hour had passed and he came slamming in through the screen door with a big box turtle in his hand, Danny all excited until she told him to put it back by the stream where he'd found it, that they weren't taking a turtle all the way back to Connecticut with them and that was that.

Her father kept his newer guns behind glass on a rack in the living room.

6

The older ones, the ones he never used anymore, were stacked in the workshop of the cellar.

She examined the stock. It was scratched and pitted. Her sinuses were giving her hell this summer and she could barely smell a thing but she sniffed it anyway. It smelled of earth and mold. It was her father's, all right. She sniffed again, the scent of old gun oil on her hands. Probably he hadn't used it in years.

It would be months before her father noticed it was missing. If then.

She threw the bolt. Inside a brass shell casing gleamed.

She felt a sudden mix of shock and fury.

My God.

He'd *loaded* the Goddamn thing.

Her father would never have left it loaded. That meant that Danny had searched around the basement for shells as well. And found some. *How many more did he have? Where were they?*

She resisted the urge to go tearing through his drawers, rummaging through his closet.

That could wait.

What she needed to do now was find him and confront him. One more confrontation. More and more as he got older.

She wondered how he'd explain *this* away.

It was not going to be like stealing Milky Ways from the Pathmark Store.

It was not going to be like the fire he and Billy Berendt had set, yet denied they'd set, in the field behind the Catholic Church last year.

He couldn't say that he'd meant to pay for the candy bars but didn't because he got to looking at the comic books and forgot they were in his pocket. He couldn't claim that the two eyewitnesses—kids from the rougher part of town who'd seen Billy and Danny go into the field and then come out running and laughing just before smoke appeared on the horizon—had it in for him.

7

The rifle was concrete. The bullet even more so.

They did not lend themselves to easy explanation.

It was not going to be like the jackknife from Nowhere or the brand-new Sega Genesis computer game from Nowhere or the Bic cigarette lighters that kept cropping up which he'd always *found on the street*. What a lucky kid.

She was angry. She was scared.

Angry and scared enough so that her hands were shaking as she removed the shell from the breech and put it in her jeans pocket. She felt a by-now all-too-familiar access of what could only be called grief, a feeling that even though her son was only ten she'd already lost him somehow, as though there were something in him she could no longer touch or speak to and for which mourning was easily as justifiable and as appropriate as her father's grief over the loss of her mother.

She knew it was important to push that feeling aside. To let the anger flow freely instead. She needed the anger. Otherwise too much love and loss, too much sympathy and—*let's face it*—too much plain old-fashioned self-pity would only weaken her.

Tough love, she thought. That's what's left.

She'd tried the shrinks. Tried the counselors. She'd tried to understand him.

Taking things away from him, privileges—the computer, TV, the movies—was the only thing that seemed to work anymore.

Well, they're all going out the window today. Everything.

She slid the black bolt of the rifle back into position and marched on out of the room. She knew where to find him.

At the clubhouse.

The grass in her back yard tickled her ankles. It was time to cut the lawn again. Humidity made the stock of the rifle feel sticky in her hand. She slid between the two pine trees in back of the lawn out onto the well-worn path into the woods.

The path belonged to the boys. Billy Berendt, Danny, Charlie Haas and the others. She never came back this way. Hardly ever. Only when she was calling him for supper and he was late and didn't answer. Even then she rarely had to venture this far. The path was only two feet wide at most through thick, waist-high brush, dry brown grass and briars as tall as she was. A path the width of a boy's body— not the width of hers. She was glad of the jeans—already studded with burrs—and unhappy with the short-sleeve blouse. A thorn bush scored two thin lines of blood along her upper arm. She used the barrel of the rifle to part another. She heard the stream rushing over its rocky bed through a line of trees to her left. The path split ahead of her. She took it to the right, away from the stream.

All these woods would one day be developed, bulldozed into oblivion. But in the three years they'd lived here that hadn't happened yet—and Danny was getting to the age where soon it wouldn't matter. In the meantime the woods and stream were part of the reason she'd wanted the place for him.

Nature, she believed, was a teacher. She'd grown up on a farm and thought that most of what she knew about life she'd glimpsed there first and then had come to understand more fully later. Birth, death, sex, the renewal of the land, its fragility and its power, the chaos inside the order, the changes in people that came with the change of seasons. The implacability of the natural world and how important it was simply to accept that.

She wanted all this for Danny.

What she'd had. And what now sustained her.

She knew that many women would have been bitter about a broken marriage that they hadn't chosen to end. But she wasn't. Not really. Unhappy, yes, of course—but there had never really been any bitterness. Love, she thought, was a contract you signed knowing that someday the signatures might fade. Richard had fallen out of love with her and gotten involved with someone else. A simple change of seasons. Hard as winter, but bearable and some-how even understandable. It was no longer necessary to the scheme of things that people mate for life. Reality was what it was and couldn't be changed by her own distress in the face of it. She thought Richard's choice of second partners was one he someday might live to regret. But that was his affair. She'd let him go.

And she might have been bitter about Danny too. Instead she simply kept plugging away. Though the boy was far from easy. He'd *never* been easy. But since the breakup four years ago he always seemed, if not actually in trouble, al-ways on the verge of it. Sliding grades. Clowning, fighting in class. Bad language around the girls at school. Once he'd been caught throwing stones at Charlie Haas on the play-ground. And of course there were the stealing and brushfire incidents.

Beyond paying child-support his father was no help at all. Richard thought it was all typical boy behavior. It would pass, he said. She'd never been a boy and it was possible he was right.

But Richard didn't have to live with him.

Didn't have to endure the tantrums when he didn't get his way or the hostile silences.

She felt exhausted by him sometimes.

What more could a kid get into?

He could get into firearms, obviously.

At age ten.

Great. Just great.

She wondered how he'd smuggled it home in the first place and then remembered the blanket she kept in back of the station wagon. He could have hidden a box of dy-namite back there and she'd never have known it.

Very cute, Danny. Very sneaky. Very neat.

Her arms felt sticky with sweat, itchy from the pollen and dust in the air and the warm brush of leaves. She could barely breathe for all the damn pollen.

But she was nearly there now.

She could see its location in the distance to the right of the path, up a hill through a tall thin stand of birch.

His clubhouse. His personal sanctuary.

Aside from the occasional visit from Billy Berendt, inviolate to the world.

Until today.

Once, perhaps a hundred years ago, there had been a house here but it had long since burned to the ground—leaving only the root cellar—and whoever the owners were they'd never rebuilt it. He'd taken her up to look at it, all excited, shortly after they moved in and he first discovered it. At that time it was nothing but a hole in the ground five feet by eight feet wide and four feet deep, overgrown with weeds. But he'd cleared the weeds to expose the fieldstone walls and raw earth floor within and, with her permission, begged a pair of old double doors from her father's barn, and he and Richard had spent one uncommonly ambitious afternoon painting the two doors green and sinking hinges into the walls and then attaching the doors so that they covered the hole and could be secured together by a combination padlock from the outside and a simple hook and eye from the inside.

Total privacy.

He called it his clubhouse.

His private little gathering of one.

She had always thought it was kind of sad. Possibly not even good for him.

But Danny had always been a loner. She guessed that was his nature. He always seemed to tolerate the other neighborhood boys more than he actually befriended them—though for some reason they all seemed to like him well enough and were eager to get him out to play even though they were excluded from the clubhouse and were probably jealous that Danny'd discovered it first. For some reason that didn't seem to matter. Maybe the place imparted status of some kind. She didn't know. *Boys*, she thought.

11

All she knew was that he spent a lot of time here. More than she'd have liked.

She'd bought him a battery-powered lantern. Not much light got in through the doors, he said. A step-ladder for going up and down. Toys and books and games would disappear and then reappear in his room as well as mason jars from the kitchen and hammers and boxes of nails from the toolbox so she knew he was bringing them out here and then returning them according to some private agenda.

She never pried.

But now she was going to have to take all this away from him too for a while.

She leaned on the rifle, catching her breath before starting in on the remaining trek up the slope of the hill. She heard bees buzzing in the grass beside her.

Her sinuses were killing her.

Warm wind ruffled her hair. She steeled herself for what was to come and headed on.

The doors had weathered considerably since last she'd seen them. They could seriously use another paint job. She saw that the combination lock was gone. That meant he had it with him. He was inside.

"Danny."

No answer. She listened. No movement either.

"Danny. I know you're in there."

She reached down for the door handles and rattled the doors.

"Come out of here. Now."

She was starting to get seriously angry again. *Good*, she thought. You damn well *should* be angry.

"I said now. Did you hear me?"

"You're not supposed to be here."

"What?"

"I said you're not supposed to be here. You never come out here."

"Well that's too bad because I'm here now. Do I have to kick these doors apart or what?"

12

She heard a click and the rattle of glass and then steps on the ladder. She heard him unfasten the hook and the door creak open.

He slid through the doors, out of the dark below, and let the doors fall shut behind him. There was something furtive about him. Something she didn't like. He knelt and took the padlock out of his pocket.

"Leave it," she said. "Stand up. Look at me."

He did as he was told. And saw the rifle. Glanced at it once and then turned away.

"Where did you get this?"

He didn't answer. He just kept staring down the hill, arms folded across his skinny chest.

"It's your grampa's, isn't it?"

No answer to that one either.

"You stole it, didn't you."

"I was going to put it back," he said. *Sullen. Caught.* "Next time we went there."

"Oh, really? Were you going to put this back, too?"

She took the bullet from her pocket and held it out to him.

"Or were you planning to use it?"

He sighed, staring down the hill.

"You have more of these?"

He nodded.

"Where?"

"My drawer."

"You're in big trouble. You know that, don't you."

He sighed again and then bent down with the padlock in his hand to secure the double doors.

She remembered the way he'd opened them, just wide enough to slide through and no further.

"Leave it," she said. "What's down there?"

"Just my stuff."

"What stuff? You have some more surprises for me?"

"No."

"Open it up. I want to see."

"Mom . . . it's *my* stuff."

"As of today you don't have any stuff. Not until I say you do. Do you understand me? Now open it."

"Mom!"

"Open it!"

He stood there. *He isn't going to move*, she thought.

Why you little sonova . . .

"God dammit!"

She reached down and threw open one door and then the other and the first thing that hit her was the smell even with her sinus problem, the smell was rank and old and horrible beyond belief, and the second thing was the incredible clutter of rags and jars and buckets on the floor and the third was what she saw on the walls, hanging there from masonry nails pounded into the fieldstone, hung like decorations, like trophies, like the galleries she'd seen in castles in Scotland and England on her honeymoon and which were hunter's galleries. A boy's awful parody of that.

His stuff . . .

She gagged and put her hand to her mouth and dropped the bullet. She stooped reflexively to pick it up again.

She looked at him, hoping that her knees wouldn't buckle.

Hoping crazily in a way that he wouldn't even be there.

He was staring directly at her. The first time since he'd climbed out of the root cellar. The expression on his face was neutral but the look in his eyes was not. The eyes were examining her coldly, intent on her reaction.

As perhaps they had examined coldly what was down below.

Adult eyes. But not the eyes of any adult she'd ever seen or ever dreamt to see.

Was this her son?

For a moment she felt a stunning terror of him. Of this little boy who didn't even weigh ninety pounds yet. Who still balked at showering every day and washing his hair on schedule. It was a terror that skittered suddenly inside

14

her and seemed to awaken all her memories of him at once, memories like claps of thunder—the stealing, the stone-throwing, the fire, the dark half-hidden glances, the bullying tantrums—terror that suddenly gave pattern to all this, all the interstices of understanding and seeing suddenly closing together for her to compose a black seamless wall of events and behavior which defined him.

And *she knew*.

She looked into his eyes and saw what he was.

And knew what he would become.

She reeled under the weight of it. Ten years of life.

When had it begun? At the breast?

In the womb?

She needed to know the whole of it, needed to embrace the horror of this as she had always needed his embrace. However cold. However distant.

She had always needed to embrace her son.

"You have a light . . . down there?" she murmured.

He nodded.

Her voice faltered. Then, "*Go turn it on*," she said.

He preceded her down the ladder and switched on the lantern. The room was suddenly very bright.

She stood in his chamber and looked at the walls.

The box turtle—*had he smuggled it here from her father's house too or was this a different one and how many others? What about before he found the clubhouse? What about . . . ?* The turtle was nailed to the wall by its feet. Its shriveled head lolled back onto its greying shell. The frogs were impaled by a single nail through roughly the center of their bodies and there were six of them. Some belly-up, some not. She saw a pair of withered garter snakes, three crayfish. And a salamander.

Like the turtle the cats were nailed through all fours. He had eviscerated both of them and looped their entrails around them and nailed the entrails to the wall at intervals so that the cats were at the center of a kind of crude bull's eye. She saw that he had strangled them with some sort of rope or twine. He had nearly taken off the head of the larger one in doing so. Its black-and-white fur was caked with old dried blood.

The other was just a kitten.

A tabby.

She was aware of him watching her.

She was aware too of the tears in her eyes and knew what he didn't know—that the tears were for her. Not him. Not this time. She wiped them away.

She had heard of people like this. Read about them. Saw them on the evening news. It seemed they were everywhere these days.

She knew what they were. And what they were not.

She had not expected her son to be one of them.

Her son was ten. Only ten. She saw all the years of his life ahead of him. So many years.

So much death to come.

Treatment, she thought. He needs treatment. He needs help.

But they did not respond to treatment.

"I'm going back up," she murmured. Her voice sounded flat and strange to her and she wondered if it did to him and then wondered if it was the fieldstone walls and earthen floor that made her voice sound the way it did or if it was something inside her, some seachange in her that was expressing itself now in this new strange voice.

She thought, *implacable*.

She moved up the stepladder and stepped out into the field and heard him snap off the lantern below as she threw the bolt on the rifle and inserted the bullet into the chamber. He looked up at her once just as he was near the top and she saw that no, there was nothing to save in his nature and she fired into his left eye and he fell back into the root cellar. She closed the double doors.

She would have to return the rifle to her father's. She would have to distract him somehow and put it back in his workshop where it belonged.

And then she would call . . . whoever.

Another missing boy.

Sooner or later they'd find him, the combination padlock in his pocket and they'd wonder. Who would do such a thing?

Such things.

Those things on the walls.

My God.

How had it happened?

It was a question she would ask herself, she thought, for a great many seasons after, as spring plunged into sweltering summer, as fall turned to winter again and the coldness of heart and mind set in for its long terrible duration.

The Box

"What's in the box?" my son said.

"Danny," I said, "Leave the man alone."

It was two Sundays before Christmas and the Stamford local was packed—shoppers lined the aisles and we were lucky to have found seats. The man sat facing my daughters Clarissa and Jenny and me, the three of us squeezed together across from him and Danny in the seat beside him.

I could understand my son's curiosity. The man was holding the red square gift box in his lap as though afraid that the Harrison stop, coming up next, might jolt it from his grasp. He'd been clutching it that way for three stops now—since he got on.

He was tall, perhaps six feet or more and maybe twenty pounds overweight and he was perspiring heavily despite the cold dry air rushing over us each time the train's double doors opened behind our backs. He had a black walrus mustache and sparse thinning hair and wore a tan Burbury raincoat that had not been new for many years now over a rumpled grey business suit. I judged the pant-legs to be an inch too short for him. The socks were grey nylon, a much lighter shade than the suit, and the elastic in the left one was shot so that it bunched up over his ankle like the skin of one of those ugly pug-nosed pedigree dogs that are so trendy nowadays. The man smiled at Danny and looked down at the box, shiny red paper over cardboard about two feet square.

"Present," he said. Looking not at Danny but at me.

His voice had the wet phlegmy sound of a heavy smoker. Or maybe he had a cold.

"Can I see?" Danny said.

I knew exactly where all of this was coming from. It's not easy spending a day in New York with two nine-year-old girls and a seven-year-old boy around Christmas time when they know there is such a thing as F.A.O. Schwartz only a few blocks away. Even if you *have* taken them to the matinee at Radio City and then skating at Rockefeller Center. Even if all their presents had been bought weeks ago and were sitting under our bed waiting to be put beneath the tree. There was always something they hadn't thought of yet that Schwartz *had* thought of and they knew that perfectly well. I'd had to fight with them—with Danny in particular—to get them aboard the 3:55 back to Rye in time for dinner.

But presents were still on his mind.

"Danny . . ."

"It's okay," said the man. "No problem." He glanced out the window. We were just pulling in to the Harrison station.

He opened the lid of the box on Danny's side, not all the way open but only about three inches—enough for him to see but not the rest of us, excluding us three—and I watched my son's face brighten at that, smiling, as he looked first at Clarissa and Jenny as if to say *nyah nyah* and then looked down into the box.

The smile was slow to vanish. But it did vanish, fading into a kind of puzzlement. I had the feeling that there was something in there that my son did not understand—not at all. The man let him look a while but his bewildered expression did not change and then he closed the box.

"Gotta go," the man said. "My stop."

He walked past us and his seat was taken immediately by a middle-aged woman carrying a pair of heavy shopping bags which she placed on the floor between her feet—and then I felt the cold December wind at my back as the double-doors slid open and closed again. Presumably the man was gone. Danny looked at the woman's bags and said shyly, "Presents?"

The woman looked at him and nodded, smiling.

He elected to question her no further.

The train rumbled on.

Our own stop was next. We walked out into the wind on the Rye platform and headed clanging down the metal steps.

"What did he have?" asked Clarissa.

"Who?" said Danny.

"The man, dummy," said Jenny. "The man with the box! What was in the *box*?"

"Oh. Nothing."

"Nothing? What? It was *empty*?"

And then they were running along ahead of me toward our car off to the left in the second row of the parking lot.

I couldn't hear his answer. If he answered her at all.

And by the time I unlocked the car I'd forgotten all about the guy.

That night Danny wouldn't eat.

It happened sometimes. It happened with each of the kids. Other things to do or too much snacking during the day. Both my wife Susan and I had been raised in homes where a depression-era mentality still prevailed. If you didn't like or didn't want to finish your dinner that was just too bad. You sat there at the table, your food getting colder and colder, until you pretty much cleaned the plate.

We'd agreed that we weren't going to lay that on our kids. And most of the experts these days seemed to agree with us that skipping the occasional meal didn't matter. And certainly wasn't worth fighting over.

So we excused him from the table.

The next night—Monday night—same thing.

"What'd you do," my wife asked him, "have six desserts for lunch?" She was probably half serious. Desserts and pizza were pretty much all our kids could stomach on the menu at the school cafeteria.

"Nope. Just not hungry, that's all."

We let it go at that.

I kept an eye on him during the night though—figuring he'd be up in the middle of a commercial break in one of our Monday-night sitcoms, headed for the kitchen and a bag of pretzels or a jar of honey-roasted peanuts or some dry fruit loops out of the box. But it never happened. He went to bed without so much as a glass of water. Not that he looked sick or anything. His color was good and he laughed at the jokes right along with the rest of us.

I figured he was coming down with something. So did Susan. He almost had to be. Our son normally had the appetite of a Sumo wrestler.

I fully expected him to beg off school in the morning, pleading headache or upset stomach.

He didn't.

And he didn't want his breakfast, either.

And the next night, same thing.

Now this was particularly strange because Susan had cooked spaghetti and meat sauce that night and there was nothing in her considerable repertoire that the kids liked better. Even though—or maybe because of the fact—that it was one of the simplest dishes she ever threw together. But Danny just sat there and said he wasn't hungry, contented to watch while everybody else heaped it on. I'd come home late after a particularly grueling day—I work for a brokerage firm in the City—and personally I was famished.

And not a little unnerved by my son's repeated refusals to eat.

"Listen," I said. "You've got to have something. We're talking *three days* now."

"Did you eat lunch?" Susan asked.

Danny doesn't lie. "I didn't feel like it," he said.

Even Clarissa and Jenny were looking at him like he had two heads by now.

"But you *love* spaghetti," Susan said.

"Try some garlic bread," said Clarissa.

"No thanks."

"Do you *feel* okay, guy?" I asked him.

"I feel fine. I'm just not hungry's all."

So he sat there.

Wednesday night Susan went all out, making him his personal favorite—roast leg of lemon-spiced lamb with mint sauce, baked potato and red wine gravy, and green snap-peas on the side.

He sat there. Though he seemed to enjoy watching *us* eat.

Thursday night we tried take-out—chinese food from his favorite Szechuan restaurant. Ginger beef, shrimp fried rice, fried won ton and sweet-and-sour ribs.

He said it smelled good. And sat there.

By Friday night whatever remnants of depression-era mentality lingered in my own personal psyche kicked in with a vengeance and I found myself standing there yelling at him, telling him he wasn't getting up from his chair, *young man*, until he finished at least *one slice* of his favorite pepperoni, meatball and sausage pizza from his favorite Italian restaurant.

The fact is I was worried. I'd have handed him a twenty, gladly, just to see some of that stringy mozzarella hanging off his chin. But I didn't tell him that. Instead I stood there pointing a finger at him and yelling until he started to cry—and then, second-generation depression-brat that I am, I

22

ordered him to bed. Which is exactly what my parents would have done.

Scratch a son, you always get his Dad.

But by Sunday you could see his ribs through his tee-shirt. We kept him out of school Monday and I stayed home from work so we could both be there for our appointment with Doctor Weller. Weller was one of the last of those wonderful old-fashioned GP's, the kind you just about never see anymore. Over seventy years old, he would still stop by your house after office hours if the need arose. In Rye that was as unheard-of as an honest mechanic. Weller believed in homecare, not hospitals. He'd fallen asleep on my sofa one night after checking in on Jenny's bronchitis and slept for two hours straight over an untouched cup of coffee while we tiptoed around him and listened to him snore.

We sat in his office Monday morning answering questions while he checked Danny's eyes, ears, nose and throat, tapped his knees, his back and chest, checked his breathing, took a vial of blood and sent him into the bathroom for a urine sample.

"He looks perfectly fine to me. He's lost five pounds since the last time he was in for a checkup but beyond that I can't see anything wrong with him. Of course we'll have to wait for the blood work. You say he's eaten *nothing?*"

"Absolutely nothing," Susan said.

He sighed. "Wait outside," he said. "Let me talk with him."

In the waiting room Susan picked up a magazine, looked at the cover and returned it to the pile. "*Why?*" she whispered.

An old man with a walker glanced over at us and then looked away. A mother across from us watched her daughter coloring in a Garfield book.

"I don't know," I said. "I wish I did."

I was aware sitting there of an odd detachment, as

23

though this were happening to the rest of them—to them, not me—not *us*.

I have always felt a fundamental core of loneliness in me. Perhaps it comes from being an only child. Perhaps it's my grandfather's sullen thick German blood. I have been alone with my wife and alone with my children, untouchable, unreachable, and I suspect that most of the time they haven't known. It runs deep, this aloneness. I have accommodated it. It informs all my relationships and all my expectations. It makes me almost impossible to surprise by life's grimmer turns of fate.

I was very aware of it now.

Dr. Weller was smiling when he led Danny through the waiting room and asked him to have a seat for a moment while he motioned us inside. But the smile was for Danny. There was nothing real inside it.

We sat down.

"The most extraordinary thing." The doctor shook his head. "I told him he had to eat. He asked me why. I said, Danny, people die every day of starvation. All over the world. If you don't eat, you'll die—it's that simple. Your son looked me straight in the eye and said, '*so?*' "

"Jesus," Susan said.

"He wasn't being flip, believe me—he was asking me a serious question. I said, well, you want to live, don't you? He said, '*should I?*' Believe me, you could have knocked me right off this chair. '*Should* I!' I said of course you should! *Everybody* wants to live.

" '*Why?*' he said.

"My God. I told him that life was beautiful, that life was sacred, that life was *fun!* Wasn't Christmas just around the corner? What about holidays and birthdays and summer vacations? I told him that it was everybody's duty to try to live life to the absolute fullest, to do everything you could in order to be as strong and healthy and happy as humanly possible. And he listened to me. He listened to me and I knew he understood me. He didn't seem the slightest bit

24

worried about any of what I was saying or the slightest bit concerned or unhappy. And when I was done, all he said was, yes—yes, but *I'm not hungry.*"

The doctor looked amazed, confounded.

"I really don't know what to tell you." He picked up a pad. "I'm writing down the name and phone number of a psychotherapist. Not a psychiatrist, mind—this fellow isn't going to push any pills at Danny. A therapist. The only thing I can come up with pending some—to my way of thinking, practically unimaginable—problem with his bloodwork is that Danny has some very serious emotional problems that need exploring and need exploring immediately. This man Field is the best I know. And he's very good with children. Tell him I said to fit you in right away, today if at all possible. We go back a long time, he and I—he'll do as I ask. And I think he'll be able to help Danny."

"Help him do what, doctor?" Susan said. I could sense her losing it. "Help him do what?" she said. "*Find a reason for living?*"

Her voice broke on the last word and suddenly she was sobbing into her hands and I reached over and tried to contact that part of me which might be able to contact her and found it not entirely mute inside me, and held her.

In the night I heard them talking. Danny and the two girls.

It was late and we were getting ready for bed and Susan was in the bathroom brushing her teeth. I stepped out into the hall to go downstairs for one last cigarette from my pack in the kitchen and that was when I heard them whispering. The twins had their room and Danny had his. The whispering was coming from their room.

It was against the rules but the rules were rapidly going to hell these days anyway. Homework was being ignored. Breakfast was coffee and packaged donuts. For Danny, of course, not even that much. Bedtime arrived when we felt exhausted.

Dr. Field had told us that that was all right for a while.

That we should avoid all areas of tension or confrontation within the family for at least the next week or so.

I was *not* to yell at Danny for not eating.

Field had spoken first to him for half an hour in his office and then, for another twenty minutes, to Susan and I. I found him personable and soft-spoken. As yet he had no idea what Danny's problem could be. The gist of what he was able to tell us was that he would need to see Danny every day until he started eating again and probably once or twice a week thereafter.

If he did start eating.

Anyhow, I'd decided to ignore the whispering. I figured if I'd stuck to my guns about quitting the Goddamn cigarettes I'd never have heard it in the first place. But then something Jenny said sailed through the half-open door loud and clear and stopped me.

"I still don't get it," she said. "What's it got to do with that *box*?"

I didn't catch his answer. I walked to the door. A floorboard squeaked. The whispering stopped.

I opened it. They were huddled together on the bed.

"What's what got to do with *what* box?" I said.

They looked at me. My children I thought, had grown up amazingly free of guilty conscience. Rules or no rules. In that they were not like me. There were times I wondered if they were actually my children at all.

"Nothing," Danny said.

"Nothing," said Clarissa and Jenny.

"Come on," I said. "Give. What were you guys just talking about?"

"Just stuff," said Danny.

"*Secret* stuff?" I was kidding, making it sound like it was no big deal.

He shrugged. "Just, you know, stuff."

"Stuff that maybe has to do with why you're not eating? That kind of stuff?"

"*Daaaad.*"

I knew my son. He was easily as stubborn as I was. It didn't take a genius to know when you were not going to get anything further out of him and this was one of those times. "Okay," I said, "back to bed."

He walked past me. I glanced into the bedroom and saw the two girls sitting motionless, staring at me.

"What," I said.

"Nothing," said Clarissa.

"G'night, Daddy," said Jenny.

I said goodnight and went downstairs for my cigarettes. I smoked three of them. I wondered what this whole box business was.

The following morning my girls were not eating.

Things occurred rapidly then. By evening it became apparent that they were taking the same route Danny had taken. They were happy. They were content. And they could not be budged. To me, *we're not hungry* had suddenly become the scariest three words in the English language.

A variation became just as scary when, two nights later, sitting over a steaming baked lasagna she'd worked on all day long, Susan asked me how in the world I expected her to eat while all her children were starving.

And then ate nothing further.

I started getting takeout for one.

McDonald's. Slices of pizza. Buffalo wings from the deli.

By Christmas Day, Danny could not get out of bed unassisted.

The twins were looking gaunt—so was my wife.

There was no Christmas dinner. There wasn't any point to it.

I ate cold fried rice and threw a couple of ribs into the microwave and that was that.

Meantime Field was frankly baffled by the entire thing and told me he was thinking of writing a paper—did I mind? I didn't mind. I didn't care one way or another. Dr. Weller, who normally considered hospitals strictly a last

27

resort, wanted to get Danny on an IV as soon as possible. He was ordering more blood tests. We asked if it could wait till after Christmas. He said it could but not a moment longer. We agreed.

Despite the cold fried rice and the insane circumstances Christmas was actually by far the very best day we'd had in a very long time. Seeing us all together, sitting by the fire, opening packages under the tree—it brought back memories. The cozy warmth of earlier days. It was almost, though certainly not quite, normal. For this day alone I could almost begin to forget my worries about them, forget that Danny would be going into the hospital the next morning—with the twins, no doubt, following pretty close behind. For her part Susan seemed to have no worries. It was as though in joining them in their fast she had also somehow partaken of their lack of concern for it. As though the fast were itself a drug.

I remember laughter from that day, plenty of laughter. Nobody's new clothes fit but my own but we tried them on anyway—there were jokes about the Amazing Colossal Woman and the Incredible Shrinking Man. And the toys and games all fit, and the brand-new hand-carved American-primitive angel I'd bought for the tree.

Believe it or not, we were happy.

But that night I lay in bed and thought about Danny in the hospital the next day and then for some reason about the whispered conversation I'd overheard that seemed so long ago and then about the man with the box and the day it had all begun. I felt like a fool, like somebody who was awakened from a long confused and confusing dream.

I suddenly had to know what *Danny* knew.

I got up and went to his room and shook him gently from his sleep.

I asked him if he remembered that day on the train and the man with the box and then looking into the box and he said that yes he did and then I asked him what was in it.

28

"Nothing," he said.

"Really *nothing*? You mean it was actually empty?"

He nodded.

"But didn't he . . . I remember him telling us it was a *present*."

He nodded again. I still didn't get it. It made no sense to me.

"So you mean it was some kind of joke or something? He was playing some kind of joke on somebody?"

"I don't know. It was just . . . the box was empty."

He looked at me as though it was impossible for him to understand why *I* didn't understand. Empty was empty. That was that.

I let him sleep. For his last night, in his own room.

I told you that things happened rapidly after that and they did, although it hardly seemed so at the time. Three weeks later my son smiled at me sweetly and slipped into a coma and died in just under thirty-two hours. It was unusual, I was told, for the IV not to have sustained a boy his age but sometimes it happened. By then the twins had beds two doors down the hall. Clarissa went on February 3rd and Jenny on February 5th.

My wife, Susan, lingered until the 27th.

And through all of this, through all these weeks now, going back and forth to the hospital each day, working when I was and *am* able and graciously being granted time off whenever I can't, riding into the City from Rye and from the City back to Rye again alone on the train, I look for him. I look through every car. I walk back and forth in case he should get on one stop sooner or one stop later. I don't want to miss him. I'm losing weight.

Oh, I'm eating. Not as well as I should be I suppose but I'm eating.

But I need to find him. To know what my son knew and then passed on to the others. I'm sure that the girls knew, that he passed it on to them that night in the bedroom— some terrible knowledge, some awful peace. And I think

29

somehow, perhaps by being so very much closer to all of my children than I was ever capable of being, that Susan knew too. I'm convinced it's so.

I'm convinced that it was my essential loneliness that set me apart and saved me, and now of course which haunts me, makes me wander through dark corridors of commuter trains waiting for a glimpse of him—him and his damnable present, his gift, his box.

I want to know. It's the only way I can get close to them. I want to see. I *have* to see.

I'm *hungry*.

For Neal McPheeters

Mail Order

It arrived in a plain brown bubble-wrap package. No return address. Nice and private.

Whoever invented bubble-wrap, Howard thought, must be worth a fortune.

He made a mental note to check it. Just for amusement's sake. It was far too late for any investing.

The cover art was strictly cheap, a black and white drawing of some girl screaming bloody murder while shadowy male figures loomed around her—one of them raising a badly executed piece of cutlery in what was vaguely supposed to be her direction.

The video's title was the only word on the box, in big block letters across the front.

Offed.

There was nothing on the back at all.

No credits. No copyright.

Nothing.

That was when his hands began to shake—turning over the box, seeing nothing.

31

Because this just might be . . .

. . . *the honest-to-God real thing.*

After all these years.

He slipped the cassette out of the box and into the VCR and hit the power button. Then *Play*. Sat back in his big brown leather custom-made Lazy-Boy in his oak and mahogany study and watched empty black leader tape roll hissing by.

There was an awful lot of leader. Howard didn't mind.

Anticipation was half the fun of it.

He'd waited six and a half weeks since sending his check to the Los Angeles address listed in *Video Nasties*.

And maybe half his life for this tape.

If it was what it purported to be.

He'd been buying, collecting since college—and that was ten years ago now—starting with the classics like *Blood Feast, Last House on the Left, Mark of the Devil*, and good old *Chainsaw*, then graduating to lesser-known back-shelf items like *Make Them Die Slowly* and *Faces of Death*, both of which included real life footage of maiming, torture, and killing by the way, though mostly what were killed were only animals. And finally, to the truly obscure stuff you could only find in fanzines like *The Film Threat Video Guide* and *Video Nasties*—he subscribed to both. Movies with titles like *Gorgasm, Twisted Tissue* and—his favorite—*Shut Up and Suffer*.

By now he had a closetful. Literally. Right over here behind him.

It was one of the benefits of investing for a living. You had the cash and the modem hooked up to Wall Street. You just stayed here in your suite and used the phone. You had privacy and no secretarial snooping. You remained in the shadows. And in the shadows was right where he liked it. Investing through an investor who invested through investors sometimes. As though he didn't exist at all in a way—unless he wanted to.

And made money like there was no tomorrow.

The paper-trail always led here, no matter how he did it. With checks attached. And he was able to retain his treasured privacy. Which, he reflected, was probably linked to this hobby of his somehow. Way back when.

But he certainly wasn't ashamed of it.

He liked gore. He liked to hear the screams.

So what.

He was . . . different.

So what.

Outside the New York traffic snarled, bleating up at him through the light spring rain.

The TV screen flickered.

The word *Offed* appeared and disappeared again.

There were no titles.

He was aware of the sweat beading on his upper lip, of the tremor purring through his body. It was always the same.

He leaned forward.

Surprisingly, the print was wonderful.

35mm, he thought. Film originally. Not video. And no grain. Good and clear.

And they got down to it too. No preliminaries. Just a medium shot of a motel room, Anywhere USA but not too terribly shabby, bed and mirrored bureau and a bathroom off left—and a girl being led through a door, her back to the Tricky Dick Nixon masks, teeshirts and jeans, one massive belly outdoing the next for gutspill.

The girl looked stoned, drugged-sort-of drifting over to the bed, head lolling, with one man on each arm practically holding her upright while the third disappeared out of frame, presumably to check the camera.

She was blonde and slim, dressed conservatively, wearing a navy blue skirt and a trim white blouse, looking like a stewardess or something, with good hips and very good legs—and for now that was all he could see. Her back was still to him.

33

He was already wishing for a close-up.

Howard didn't know why but he had the feeling the girl was going to be a looker.

They led her to the far side of the bed and sat her down. She slumped to the pillow immediately, buried her head in it while one of the bruisers reached around in front of her and unbuttoned her blouse, laughing—the soundtrack muddy, garbled, not nearly as good as the picture—saying something to his buddy while he tugged the blouse out of her skirtwaist and then lifted it off first one arm and then the other.

She wore a sheer white silk bra and her breasts were modest and pointed. Just the way he liked them.

Tricky Dick One turned her over on her belly so Dickie Two could get at the zipper in the back of her skirt. The girl was wearing heels. He took them off slowly, one by one, and then unzipped the skirt, lifted her a little from the waist and pulled it off her. He patted her behind and laughed. Then drew her slip down over her legs.

Her panties were cut high, to the hip.

For the first time the girl resisted slightly, waving at him as though shooing away an annoying pet, a cat or a dog bothering her on the bed.

"Nooo," she mumbled.

"Yeees," he laughed.

And turned her over. As he did, her face came fully into frame for the very first time.

And Howard froze.

He knew her!

He was ninety-nine percent sure he did! It had been just a glimpse God knows, she was turned away again, but now that he looked at her even the body looked familiar. The legs, the breasts, the willowy arms, the short blond hair.

It had been a hell of a long time and he couldn't even remember her first name at first, Ella or Etta—no, Greta— of course! He'd dated her back in college for a few months and finally dumped her after all kinds of messy shit be-

tween them and he remembered that at the time she had
wanted to be . . .

(. . . my God . . .)

. . . she'd wanted to be . . .

. . . an actress.

Jesus! My God, he remembered her now. Remembered
her perfectly. They'd seen a revival of *Night of the Living
Dead* together. Greta liked this stuff too. It was one thing
they had in common. Spent God knows how many nights
curled up on his Boston sofa watching exactly this sort of
slasher, body-count stuff—simulated, of course.

And now they were . . .

Jesus Christ!

And now they were going to do her!

Right in front of him!

Or were they?

He supposed it depended entirely on whether the film
actually delivered what the ad had promised him.

Bored with the same-old-same-old?
Care to experience the real thing?
Try our video! We guarantee—
OFFED delivers! You'll never
need another violence fix again
in your life, Bunky. We swear it!
On our mothers' graves!
$39.95

What if it *did*?

He pushed *rewind*. Reran the scene. Reran it again. The
girl's head, turning.

It sure as hell looked like Greta.

He suddenly, desperately, needed a drink.

He pushed pause. The image froze and flickered, shot
with horizontal lines.

He walked to the bar and poured himself a scotch.
Downed it and poured himself another.

He thought about her.

She'd liked her sex hard, no doubt about that. Though Jesus, never this hard. He used to kid her that she wore bite-marks the way some women wore jewelry.

And she was kinky. He'd even taped a few things on his own now-primitive camcorder with her, nothing too heavy, and she'd stolen the tapes eventually.

Too bad.

The woman had been damned attractive and an absolute slugger in bed but there was an edge to her he'd never really cared for. Something rough-cut and slightly lower-class in the Jersey accent, in her off-the-rack taste in clothing.

He doubted she'd ever make it in the movies.

And he knew from day one that it wasn't going to last between them.

Of course he hadn't told her that. Not with her crawling all over his dick the way she was, willing to try anything for him—including whips and chains and clips and knives and leather, the whole magilla. No way was he going to tell her that until he had to.

Until something more interesting came along.

And then one day it had come along.

Funny. He couldn't remember her name either.

In had been ugly, though, he remembered that. The end of the thing with Greta. She'd screamed and whined and pleaded. Showed up drunk a couple of times, pounding on his door. Begging.

But the cancer was already finishing his father by then and he knew it was impossible, that he was going to have a lot of money soon and he knew she wasn't up to it. Not with that accent, those tastes.

So it was bye-bye Greta.

Maybe for real now.

Jesus.

He finished the scotch, poured himself another glass just for sipping purposes and returned to his chair.

His nerves were steadier. The scotch expanding inside

him. He reached for the remote and pressed *play*.

The film whirred into motion.

And the knives were out.

Knife, actually. One guy with a long, serrated kitchen knife and the other pulling a pair of metal garden clippers out of his back pocket, the kind you used to trim back branches, holding them up for the camera.

Which now lurched forward a pace or two. Evidently there was no zoom lens and Tricky Dick Three was carrying it nearer to the bed on its tripod.

It was still no closeup, but better.

The woman who still looked ninety-nine percent like Greta moaned but did nothing to resist as the guy with the knife snipped away the shoulder-straps to her bra and then sawed through the center. Her breasts shuddered free. The nipples were pale pink, large, blending away into the paler breast flesh. Just like Greta's.

The man cut through the waistband of her panties and pulled them out from under her.

Like Greta, a real blonde.

Howard gulped his scotch. The goddamn movie just wasn't made for sipping.

The whole idea that this was Greta he was watching— that it even could be Greta—scared the bloody shit out of him. There was something about it so fucking ironic and infinitely more perverse than he'd ever dreamed—maybe even more than he'd ever wanted to dream—that you had to wonder. All these gruesome images. All these years collecting this stuff. All these years searching, looking for . . . what?

Death, obviously.

It had to be. The experience of violent death in which he was both observer and yes, participant. Participant in that he'd bought and paid for this particular tape, he'd sort of even financed the thing in a way. Allowed it to be. He and others like him.

Okay, he'd done it a thousand times.

But now it was someone he knew, someone he'd screwed every which way to Sunday who was going to get seriously hurt here, and you had to wonder.

It was just possible he'd bitten off more than he could chew.

He was about to find out. In spades.

Because Dickie Number Three was lurching forward with the camera again, coming closer, as Dickie Number Two put the clippers back in the pocket of his greasy jeans and grabbed her by both her arms—unfortunately standing in front of her, the asshole—pulled them up over her head and held the wrists pinned to the bed.

Her struggles were feeble, the drug still working.

Until Dickie Number One leaned over with the sharp serrated knife and carved an X on her left breast, the center of the X the center of her nipple, blood pooling up and oozing down her side as she screamed and struggled in earnest, adrenalin kicking in and beating hell out of the sedative so that Dickie Three had come out from behind the camera to grab her legs and hold them while Dickie One carved the right side of her the same as he'd done the left.

And then it was all three of them.

Dickie Two working on her fingers and toes with the clippers, snipping at the joints, joints popping off all over the bed, Dickie One finding imaginative gourmet ways to carve living flesh with a serrated knife and Dickie Three generally relegated to holding down whatever part of her they were busy on at the moment.

While Howard stared open-mouthed and trembling. Twitching. Scotch forgotten. Bolted to his chair.

For twenty-five minutes of this.

Until the coup de grace.

At which point he stood up.

Shouting. The scotch dribbling down to the wall-to-wall carpet.

"Fuck! You motherfucking cocksucking *assholes!*"

*   *   *

They'd decided to shoot the end of it right up close.

Finally, thought Howard, a close-up.

He giggled. Excitement and terror and scotch all kicking in at once. An extremist cocktail.

Oh, my God, Greta, I'm going to watch you die.

On the screen Dickie Three ran gut-bobbing back to the camera and hauled it forward until it stood just three feet from the now-blurry blood-drenched sheets and the glistening red body on the bed that still breathed in and out and tried to move, just barely.

He focused the camera.

And Howard realized two things simultaneously.

One, it was not Greta.

And two, it was not murder.

And he could have killed the whole bunch of them right then and there for a moment, tracked them down and hacked them to fucking bits, for putting him through this.

Not Greta. And not death.

Oh, the girl was a look-alike all right, very similar, but they had left her face pretty much alone all this time except for slashes across the cheeks and shit, the nose was wrong, the eyes were slightly wrong, the cheekbones a bit too prominent—and now that he thought about it, now that the spell was broken, he realized he'd been stupid ever to have thought it could be Greta in the first place, because Greta was the same age as he was or maybe slightly less and this girl was hardly out of her twenties, the age she was then, the age she remained in his imagination.

He felt like a total fucking idiot.

Damned if he didn't know a latex appliance when he saw one.

They were good. Very good. Worthy of Tom Savini. Probably expensive too. Maybe even state of the art. But a motionless closeup camera is a goddamn merciless thing and you could see where the living flesh stopped and FX began as clearly as though they'd signposted them.

So that when the knife slit her open and the hand slipped

39

into what was supposed to be Greta's chest and pulled out what was supposed to be Greta's beating heart but was not Greta's heart nor anybody's nor even Greta, Howard was already on his feet.

Cursing. Mad. Dispirited and disappointed as hell.

And ripped off again.

A week later he thought, well, it was still one hell of a movie, marked it, and added it to his collection.

A month later he saw her.

Really saw her.

She was walking down Central Park South half a block from his apartment just as he was leaving and she looked right at him without the slightest sign of recognition and he damn near walked into a uniformed doorman hailing a taxi—because the Greta he remembered, the almost-Greta in the film, had been an attractive woman, sure, but this Greta, this older, graceful Greta of the perfect legs and silk Armani jacket was absolutely stunning.

What in the hell had happened to her?

He could barely get her name out.

"Greta?"

"My God. Howard."

And her smile was all he needed to ask her out to dinner.

Miraculously, she accepted.

Over duck with truffle sauce at Cafe Luxemborg on the Upper West Side he told her nothing about the very strange movie experience he had recently had and everything about investing—the kick of winning big when his choices were successful, playing down his utter fury at the occasional inevitable defeat. He told her stories. About riding high on Apple and Nintendo and dumping Exxon at exactly the right moment.

And what was she doing?

Well, films had not worked out for her. He'd guessed as

much, naturally. She'd hung around L.A. for a couple of years and then moved into real estate. She had a few other interests, she said, on the side. And she was doing pretty well from the look of it.

And no, she wasn't married.

And no, she wasn't engaged.

There wasn't even a boyfriend. At least none that she was telling him about.

And he couldn't help but wonder if she still got into the same kind of rough stuff in the bedroom as she did in the old days. The thought of it made his mouth water a whole lot more than the duck did, and the duck was the best there was.

And it looked like maybe he was going to find out.

He could tell she still found him attractive. Her body language, the way she looked at him and listened, everything told him she did.

Well, he was still attractive. Why not?

And she . . . utterly beautiful. Success, he supposed, had made her beautiful. The rough city edge to the voice was completely gone. What was left was a deep, resonant purr that made him think of wild warm nights on Caribbean shores, of jungle terraces, of heat and sweat and strange, exotic passions.

In the limo they drove south from the restaurant toward her midtown hotel. The theatres all along Broadway and Eighth Avenue were letting out and traffic was heavy. They talked over splits of champagne. Of old mutual acquaintances barely recalled. Halfway there and stalled in traffic she leaned over and brushed his lips with hers. She smelled lightly of Aliage or something similiar. Her lips were soft, more generous than he remembered.

"You'll come up?"

"Of course. Absolutely."

He was impressed. The hotel was one of the best in town and her room was nothing less than the penthouse.

41

She opened the door and they stepped inside into darkness and she turned to face him, came into his arms, and her mouth was hot and sweet, broke free and locked the door behind him and turned on the lights, the huge bright living room springing into focus, took off her jacket and stood there in front of him smiling, and he thought how strange it was, that he should be here about to make love to a woman who only a month ago he'd thought was going to die—and die horribly—all across his video screen.

Life was very odd.

"I'm glad you're here," she said, stepping toward him again.

"Believe me. So am I."

"It took a while, you know."

He was about to ask her *what did* when they stepped out of the bedroom, out of the darkness there.

Three heavy men in jeans and teeshirts. Beer guts hard, straining their belts.

Even a month later and without the masks they were all too familiar.

And a whole lot uglier than he imagined.

One moved behind him to the door. The others flanked her.

"I told you I had a few sidelines," she said. "Other interests. And I definitely recalled your other interests. I remembered them vividly in fact. I knew you'd be answering the ad sooner or later. Being you, how could you resist it?"

She laughed. "You've become a very private person over the years, you know that, Howard? But then, the rich are always insulated—protected—aren't they? I ought to know. It took me ten years to become . . . protected enough for this. An address was all I needed for you, but no one had one anymore. Who'd have thought you'd be here in New York playing the stock market? You could barely count your change when I knew you."

She sighed and caressed his cheek. Her hand was warm.

*   *   *

42

"In the long run this was really much cheaper than hiring a private detective. And a lot more fun, too. We just ran the ad and waited. We even made a little money. Didn't we, gentlemen."

They smiled. It was not a nice thing to see.

The door to the bedroom opened. The girl who stood there in her white silk camisole was familiar too. The last time he'd seen her she was covered with blood. Now, of course, she was smiling.

"My sister. Doreen, meet Howard. Did you notice the family resemblance, Howard? Didn't you find it striking?"

"What do you . . . ?"

"What do I want? I want to make a movie, of course. Just like we did in the old days. You see I remember how you treated me too. Come here."

She stepped past her sister into the bedroom. The two men followed her. The third prodded Howard in the back with a thick horny knuckle. He had no choice but to follow.

She turned on the lights. They were klieg lights. So that suddenly he was in the spotlight.

A 35mm camera stood on a tripod in the corner of the room.

The king-size bed was covered in plastic.

Thick plastic.

He knew when the guy behind him pushed him onto it.

He tried to scream but one of them stuffed a dirty white rag into his mouth and tied it off with a white silk scarf while the two other men grabbed his wrists and hitched them to the bedposts, and then to his feet, not even bothering to take off his wingtips first, working very efficiently as though they did this all the time and he looked up and saw Greta's sister, the image of her younger self holding up two four-inch stainless-steel fishhooks for him to see, putting them down on the night table and picking up a bone handled razor, showing him that, and then Greta at the beautiful antique bureau touching up her lipstick in the mirror, stripping slowly down to her filmy black bra and

43

panties cut high on the hip just the way he liked them, putting on the black half-mask, the same as her sister was wearing now and turning, the scalpel gleaming in her hand.

"What do you think?" she said. "Can we go ninety minutes?"

The guy behind the camera nodded.

"Sure. If you're careful."

Greta smiled. The generous lips smiled down at him. While Howard thrashed uselessly on the bed.

"You see, Howard. The real thing does exist. Only you're not going to get it mail-order."

The camera whirred.

The clapboard clapped.

Greta walked into the frame.

"Action," she said.

Luck

The night was moonless and quiet save for the crackling of the fire and the liquid tiltback of the Tangleleg whiskey which they passed between them and Faro Bill Brody drawing hard on his Bull Durham and the moans and heavy breathing from Chunk Herbert and the snort and paw of horses and the voices of the men. Their talk had turned to luck, good and bad. The men were of the opinion that theirs had taken a far turn for the worse this day for who could have guessed at Turner's Crossing that the stage would be filled with lawmen and citizens with guns drawn and ready and a posse just out of sight behind them. They had robbed the same stage at the same place at the same time of day three weeks running and never known a problem.

Now Chunk Herbert lay propped against a juniper tree with a chunk of skull missing big as a silver dollar and his brains held in place by the dusty left arm of Canary Joe Hallihan's shirt. Canary Joe himself had gone un-shot. So had Faro Bill Brody to Joe's way of thinking though Faro

Bill kept complaining about the two ragged holes in the right-side brim of his hat—but then what could you expect from a man who'd taken his name from a damnfool frenchie card game dealt by box-springs instead of a righteous human being? Kid Earp had taken a ball to the calf and likely would be limping awhile.

"You still got to figure we're lucky compared to some," Joe said. "Chunk excepted, 'corse.

"I heard of a lot worse luck."

"Ain't that the truth," said The Kid. The Kid was not a kid and no one could remember when he ever had been and no relation to the Earp Brothers either though he liked to affect some mystery about that.

Never you mind who my relations been.

"You remember Thimblerig Jack? Best man with a pea and walnuts I ever seen. You spend your whole day, you ain't gonna find that pea under them three walnuts 'less Jack wants you to. Hands faster'n a rattler hits you. And charm? Man could cheat you out of your entire stake and damn if you ain't thankin' him for havin' a fine old time by the finish of it. Then 'long come that Indian."

"What Indian?" said Faro Bill.

"Big Ute halfbreed name of Jim Murphy. Brings his squaw into town one morning and Jack's got his game all set up on a barrellhead outside Knott's dry goods store and Jack stops her, puts a hand to the squaw's shoulder, he wants to show her a game or two. And this Indian's pretty fast himself. 'Fore you know it he's grabbed Jack's hand and slammed it down on the barrellhead and the Bowie's out and Big Jim Murphy's choppin' fingers."

The others considered.

"That's not luck," said Faro Bill. "He should've known."

"How? Mostly an Indian will knuckle under. He just picked the wrong Indian, that's all. Most Indians are plain sneaky, most are cowards."

They passed the bottle and stared into the fire. Behind them Chunk groaned.

"You say somethin', Chunk?" said the Kid.

"Don't be foolish," said Canary Joe.

"I thought he said somethin'."

"So did I," said Faro Bill. "Sounded like '*Lily*' or '*Liddy*.' "

"Weren't nothin'," said Canary Joe.

"Anyhow, I've heard of worse luck," said Faro Bill. "Heard about it years ago from a damned old Mountain Man name of Thomas Curry."

"You knew a Mountain Man, Bill?" said The Kid.

"Sure did. Met him at the Bucket of Blood Saloon over in Johnston City. Liked to gamble and won more often as not. Some strange breed, those old timers were. Hell, you could barely understand him for the listening. He'd be sitting behind a pair of aces and say something like, '*well, hos! I'll dock off buffler, but then if thar's any meat that runs that can take the shine outen dog, you can slide.*' "

"What's that mean, Bill?" said the Kid.

" '*Well, m'friend, I'll except buffalo, but then if there's any meat afoot better than dog, you're crazy.*' " Some old gent, he was. But did you ever hear about the 'Lost Dutch' Meyers Mine, Kid? Dutch was a prospector out Montana way, struck gold somewhere along the Big Horn with a couple of buddies and erected themselves a cabin so's they could work the river. One morning Sioux attacked and when the smoke cleared Dutch was the only man of three left alive. Fled south to save his sorry scalp. Hit town and sold some pretty fine nuggets, spread word of his find. And that was most unwise, 'cause one of the boys he told was a fella name Bob Heck who backshot Dutch dead and then went out to do a little prospecting on his own. Never did find gold though, since by then the Sioux had burnt the goddamn cabin to the ground so there was not a thing left to mark the spot. Bob Heck got the noose and nobody got the gold. Now there was a pair of damned unlucky fellas."

"How'd they know Sioux burnt it?"

"S'cuse me?"

"If nobody found the cabin, how'd this Thomas Curry know it was Sioux what burned it down?"

Faro Bill shrugged. "Mountain Men just know things, I reckon."

"I can go you one better on bad luck," said Canary Joe. "Only that you won't believe me."

"Give it up anyhow," said the Kid. "We got time."

"We ought to build this fire," said Canary Joe. "Gettin' kinda low and Chunk there needs his heat."

"What Chunk needs is a damn priest," said Faro Bill.

Canary Joe ignored him and rose stiffly onto legs he reflected were probably too old for owlhootery anymore and stepped out into the rich dark behind the four tethered horses to gather what scrub and dry broken timber he could find. The others stared whiskey-dazed into the fire. The Kid took a pull and handed the bottle to Faro Bill who drank and handed it back again. The Kid kicked a twig into the flames and watched it burst and crackle.

"How long you figure he's got?" said the Kid.

"Chunk? How long's it take the soul to flee. God damned if I know."

"You think he can hear us?"

"Don't know."

"Spooks me to think that maybe ol' Chunk can hear us talking 'bout his likely demise."

"Don't talk about it, then."

"All right. I won't."

They passed the bottle and moments passed silent and sullen as kicked dogs until Canary Joe returned to the fire with some old sunbleached logs pale as bones under his arm and dragging with his other hand a tangled pile of scrub across the dry hard-packed earth. He dropped the scrub and then the logs which clattered like tenpins. Joe turned to Chunk behind him.

"You say somethin', Chunk?"

"Now *you're* hearin' him," said the Kid. "This time I ain't heard a thing."

"Thought I did, yeah."

"And you call me foolish."

"You are foolish. Most foolish man I ever met."

"Who was it planned this damn robbery? Who was it got us all shot up? I don't recall doin' it nor Faro Bill nor Chunk neither."

"Gentlemen," said Faro Bill, "we can resolve this. Heads Chunk spoke or tails he didn't." He produced an old smooth featureless silver dollar.

"Faro Bill," said Joe, "I take it back and I want to apologize to the Kid here. *You* are the most foolish man I ever met bar none. You want to gamble on the way the wind blows."

"Done that too."

"I don't doubt ya."

He cracked some scrub and fed it to the flames, knelt and cracked some more.

"You want to know what I know about luck? *Real* bad luck?"

"Sure." Faro Bill passed him the bottle. He drank it down to near-empty, settled down crosslegged and passed it to the Kid.

"Happened to me years ago when I was just a boy, I'd just come west. I was sittin' in Tuttle's Saloon in Newton, Kansas one night and of course we had us a game on. I didn't rightly know the players. I was new to town and lookin' for cattlework though not too hard as yet, arrived as I was just the day before. But these boys were a good enough bunch, I could tell that. Four of us. Lotta laughin'. Nothin' serious. We're drinkin' Snakehead Whiskey, I remember. You ever had a taste?"

"Not that I recall," said Faro Bill.

"Six rattlesnake-heads to the barrell. Tastes like the Devil stirred it with his own boot. Anyhow we're playin' and I'm losin' when in walks this mean-looking dirty little fella, his shirt all stained with tobacco juice, Colt on his hip, hat looks like it's been chewed by bears. Walks over to the bar which I'm facin' thank the lord and orders a drink and drinks it and then another and then turns and eyes the room.

"Other fellas I'm playing with don't appear to notice this boy at all, they're busy with the cards. Only me and that's just 'cause I'm facing him. So that when he orders and downs that third one I'm the only one sees what he's gonna do, I can see it plain in his eyes way before he draws and takes his stance and by the time he starts firing at our table I'm under it, trying to get my own gun off my hip but I'm just a kid myself, I ain't no pistolero, and by the time I've got it out he's shot two of the players in that game and the third, his chair's gone over with him in it and he's scramblin' across the floor toward the door.

"Fella looks at me and I know my day's arrived. Not even time to push over the table for cover and he's ready to fire and I'm still fumblin' around down there and the only thing that saved my ass that day was the bartender and the shotgun behind the bar, I'm tellin' you. Blew that little fella halfway across the room. I had pieces of that kid in my hair, boys. And I can smell the stink of him to this day."

He piled three logs on the fire. They immediately began to smoke.

"Mise'ble excuse for hardwood," he said.

"I don't follow you," said Bill. "What's that got to do with luck?"

"Gettin' to that. When things was quiet again we walked over and had a look at him, those of us who *could* walk. He'd shot two of the boys at my table dead, we never did know why. Anyhow the barkeep who's name was Brocius turned this fella over and you could have seen daylight through the hole in his chest and somebody said, that's Little Dick West, and somebody else said it couldn't be, Little Dick West was shot dead in Witchita more'n a year ago. But the first fella, he insisted, said he knew Little Dick by sight, said that boy was bad luck wherever he went and that he'd personally managed to steer clear of him plenty of times, in Abilene, in Dodge, in Tombstone. He'd seen him shoot a man like a yella dog on the streets of Tombstone.

"The second gent, he insisted too. Little Dick West was shot over a year ago in a Witchita whorehouse, he said. He knew it for a fact and there were other boys in the saloon who said they'd heard the same now that you mention it. Little Dick took two in the chest in Witchita. One even knew the name of the fella who shot him, McLoughlin I think it was, a farmer. Whose house burned down 'bout a month later. With McLoughlin and his wife and kids in it.

"Never could resolve that argument at the time. But it was Brocius the barkeep who killed him so that it was Brocius along with the sheriff who dragged him out to the street to wait on the mortician. Dead man's heavier than you'd think and Brocius had some weight on him and by the time he's through he's puffin'. Now, Tuttles' Saloon has three stairs from the porch to the street, just three. And Brocius is on the second stair when his leg slips out from under him and then next thing you know he's lying across them stairs with his feet pointin' east and his head turned 'round on his neck in a westerly direction."

"Dead?" said the Kid.

"Dead," said Joe.

"That's pretty bad luck, all right," said Faro Bill.

"I ain't finished yet. Couple years later I'm riding into Abilene one evenin'. Naturally I've forgot all about what happened at Tuttles' Saloon by then and I've had a few pulls on the Tangleleg along the trail from the Circle P to town so I'm not payin' much attention and it's only when I'm hitching up to the rail that I notice ain't nobody on the street but me and two other fellas squared off maybe twenty yards away. And before I can even duck for cover they're drawn and firing 'till both their guns are empty and I can smell gunsmoke all the hell over where I am and there ain't but one man standing.

"Townsfolk start appearin' like rats out of a burnin' barn,

crowding 'round this big heavy fella standing in the street reloading his pistol calm as you please, one hellova target and not a scratch on him, and this little fella bleeding into the dust, dead as dead can be. They go over and somebody says, I'll be goddamned! that's Little Dick West! and somebody else says, nah, they buried that backshootin' backstabbin' sonovabitch Little Dick West over in Witchita some few years back and soon there's an argument goin' on that sounds awful familiar to me. So I walk over for a look. You say somethin', Chunk?"

"That time I heard it too," said Faro Bill.

"Me too," said the Kid. "Coulda been one of the horses snortin', though."

"Ain't the horses you fool," said Canary Joe. "Sounded like 'I-ill'."

"He sure as hell is that," said the Kid.

"Go on with the story," said Faro Bill.

"Let's have some more of that Tangleleg, Kid."

"Hell, it's all gone, Joe."

"You got another bottle in your saddlebag, Kid. I saw you put it there."

"Dammit, Joe. I was savin' that for trail-whiskey."

"Won't be no trail for you, you don't find me that bottle."

The Kid stared hard across the fire at him a moment as though considering him serious or not serious and then rose heavily and unsteadily to his feet and disappeared into the dark and they could hear the horses' hooves scuff and paw the ground at this disturbance to their slumber. Canary Joe piled scrub and the last three logs on the fire and waved away the billowed smoke. Faro Bill Brody rolled and lit his Durham. When the Kid returned he had the bottle open and drank once long and defiantly before sitting down again. He passed the bottle to Joe and settled in.

"So as I was sayin', I go for a look."

"Was it Little Dick?" asked the Kid.

"Hard for me to say at the time, Kid. Though later I did develop an opinion. Tobacco stains on his shirt were right.

Chewed-up-lookin' hat was right. 'Bout the right height and weight. Problem was there was a ball in his right eye and another in his cheek some few inches down that played all hell with his good looks. He was dirty, though, even before he hit the street. That you could tell.

"Anyhow, the crowd's still standin' there arguin' 'bout is he or isn't he but me, I need a drink. Wouldn't you fellas? I maybe seen Little Dick West shot dead in Newton, Kansas and now I'm maybe seeing him shot all over again. Kind of thing unnerves a man. So I head for the saloon. I'm just stepping through the doors when I hear another shot and turn and look and there's the crowd movin' away in little waves like when you toss a pebble into a gone-still pond and at the center of this partic'lar pond's the shooter, the big fella, and he's on his knees. And then I watch him fall and then he's squirmin' face down in the dirt."

He took another pull from the bottle and passed it to Faro Bill.

"What happened?" said the Kid.

"Shot his goddamn balls off," said Canary Joe. "Holstering up his Remington Model Three. Don't know how in hell he done it but he managed. Few hours later, word in the saloon was he'd died from loss of blood."

"Hot damn," said the Kid. "That's some yarn all right. You want to pass me that bottle, Bill?"

"Ain't over yet," said Joe. "Not quite. Six months, maybe seven months later I'm in Witchita, on my way to nowhere in partic'lar, just driftin' through. There's a noose back in Montana with my name on it but I ain't worried. I'm in Rowdy Joe Lowe's dance hall, drinkin' and eyein' the ladies, thinking about a little recreational expenditure that night if y'know what I mean. Now, 'member I said Little Dick West was suppos'd to've been shot dead in Witchita?"

"The first time," said the Kid.

"That we know of," said Faro Bill.

"Shot by a farmer whose place burned 'bout a month

later, with him in it. See where I'm goin' on this?" said Canary Joe.

"I think so," said Faro Bill. "You're going to tell us you're in there eyeing the ladies when in walks . . ."

"When in walks Little Dick West. That's right. Stands directly beside me at the bar and orders whiskey, nice as you please. And this time I'm sure. I'm damn sure. There ain't no ball in his cheek or his eyeball this time. He's so close I can smell him and he don't smell good. It's the same damn hat and the same damn tobacco juice all over his shirt and the same damn Colt he pulled in Newton.

"I guess the folks in Witchita got pretty short memories as these things go because nobody even bats an eye seein' him in there. The barkeep serves him, the drinkers keep drinking—hell, a couple of the ladies even give him a look by way of *well, maybe*. But me, I've seen him a bit more recently so to speak and I guess my memory's a little bit better so I pay up for that last one and get the hell out of there fast as I can, because I know for plain honest fact that Little Dick West is the unluckiest man who ever walked the Lord's green earth and that's a certainty."

A wind had come up from the west. The night was colder now those last few hours before dawn and the men drank silently a pull apiece and warmed their hands by the fire and the Kid shook his head thinking about luck and Little Dick West while Faro Bill rolled yet another Durham and lit it with a twig aflame. The horses snorted, chilled in sleep.

"We better get us some rest, boys," said Canary Joe. "Long way to ride yet tomorrow. I'll gather us up some more of that mise'ble firewood I guess, get us through to morning."

He rose to his feet and stepped slowly into the waiting dark.

"*You watch out for Little Dick West, now,*" said Faro Bill laughing and it was then that they heard the echo of his words from the mouth of Chunk Herbert dying against the juniper tree, clear this time and no mistaking them, not *I-ill* or *Lily* but *Li'l Dick West, I shot Li'l Dick West in Dodge City, Kansas* and the fusillade seemed to come from everywhere at once and ended Chunk's luck and their own along with it for good and ever.

The Haunt

I found the place just off East Sunset, only three blocks from the sea, and I got it for a song.

Lauderdale had been hit by a big one again the year before and on the first floor the water damage was extensive. It was no real problem though. I had money. We crewed the place through spring and summer and by start-of-season it was looking fine. I called it the Blue Parrot, after Sam.

And Sam was the main attraction for a while. Drinks are drinks when you come right down to it, even though Shiela and Cindy had instructions to pour stiff ones, to leave the shotglasses under the bar for the time being and buy back for the regulars. As for the girls, you'd be hard pressed to find a waitress or barmaid anywhere near Sunset who wasn't halfway gorgeous. So that left Sam our novelty.

As novelties go I've seen worse. He's an attention-getter for one thing, blue as the Caribbean with a bib of pure white across his chest. And he's big around as the thighs on Schwarzenegger.

We hung a high perch for him to the far left of the bar and if you were sitting over there you could toss him a salted peanut and watch him pluck it out of the air, toss it back like a shot of Cuervo and turn to you with that myopic-looking one-eyed stare and croak, *"thanks, big boy, think can you afford another?"* People swore he sounded like Bacall, though actually he'd learned that line from a hooker who used to come into my first place in Miami. If you threw too wide or low you got the same baleful stare only longer, and then after a while the bone-yellow beak would open. *"God damn drunks!"*

He was ten years old and had plenty of lines by then, so he was good at the bar. But naturally I had ambitions for the place. As Florida goes Lauderdale's a pretty wide-open town. The college kids do that and the gays. So a year later we went topless. We left Sam where he was and put a raised stage on the other side of the bar. The upstairs room was all tables but you could stand at the brass railing and look down at the dancers and at the same time cruise the bar.

We did it right, too. Most of the girls were college girls so the turnover was high but that also meant you had dancers who were young and pretty and wholesome-looking, not beat-up hooker-types. There were a handful of local girls but I stayed away from them in general. Down here you never knew when somebody's drunken boyfriend from Fort Meyers or Punta Gorda was going to come barreling across Alligator Alley with a shotgun in back of his pickup, bent on saving darlin' Maisie from a life of squalor. They brought in a nice crowd, mixed, men and women and mostly young.

We did real well with the wet teeshirt contests and the Best Buns contests and by the time we were open two years to the day I could count on packed houses three nights a week and no real slack time at all. We held our own off season, too, while other places closed down altogether.

Sam got fat. I fell in love with the new bartender.

Bernie was her name and she was older than most,

thirty-four, and she'd been married once the same way I'd been married, which was badly. For me home was a block away, right on Sunrise. Home for her was all the way across town. In no time at all my dresser drawers were full of skimpy teeshirts, shorts and panties, and her sister from Wisconsin was living at the place across town. I never regretted it.

We came up with another attraction that year. Her name was Mary.

Had it not been for Bernie I probably wouldn't have hired her. It would have been too much temptation put in my way. You get used to topless dancers. But nobody got used to Mary.

"Bwwaaak! Major babe alert!" was the first thing out of Sam's mouth when he spotted her. He was only stating the obvious. But there was plenty more than that. The only way I can say it right now is that Mary was *intimidating* to look at—that beautiful. Why in the world she wanted to dance topless for the Blue Parrot I never did figure. She was a pre-med student. Yet she could have been anything—model, movie actress, even, from what I could see, a legitimate dancer. Up on the stage her moves were terrific, if you ever got by that strong perfect body long enough see the moves.

And that glance.

It was amazing how she could rivet an audience with that glance. Her eyes were a pale, pale blue. Incredibly bold. Onstage they seemed to flicker everywhere at once, sweeping the entire ground floor and half the guys in the balcony. I never in my life saw so many men trying to make eye-contact with a woman. And a half-naked woman at that. It was uncanny. From the first night she danced she got the feature spot, and I never heard a single complaint from any of the other girls, all of whom had been there longer than she had. You knew she deserved it.

She had no boyfriends. She told me once that she'd never met a man as tough as she was and I believed her. The only one she flirted with was Sam, who'd wink at her. And I swear that now and then I'd catching him leering.

It was Mary who got the bright idea about the body painting. Like I say, she was a bold one. Here she was, brand new, with the best spot in the show, and she's rocking the boat, trying to change things instead of just leaving well enough alone. If the idea had flopped it wouldn't have helped her much with me. But of course she knew all along it wouldn't flop. After all—they were going to paint *her* body.

The way it worked was that every night the customer got a raffle ticked with his first drink, right off the bat. At midnight I'd step up on the stage with all the tickets in a grey fedora hat and Sam perched on my arm. I'd stir the tickets around and then Sam would dip down and pull us out a winner. One of the girls would bring paintpots and brushes from off stage. Mary would come out and dance, and at the end of the dance she'd strike a pose, freeze, and I'd read the number on the ticket.

I'd hand the winner a pair of scissors so he could snip off her panties—that always got a rise from the crowd—and then the guy would start painting. When we figured he'd been at it long enough we'd black-light the place and bring up the music, and when Mary started dancing again it was wild. The paint was irridescent and the dark was how we got around the laws about booze and dancing and total nudity. It brought the house down every night. The paint was water base so half an hour later she'd be washed off and back again, an encore for a star.

Oh, we were rolling. Friday and Saturday nights we'd turn them away. Before it was a bar the Parrot was a bookshop, used and antique books, and before that an artist's studio. So we only had space for about a hundred-fifty. But a hundred-fifty people all drinking all night is some pretty tidy cash, believe me. We were doing fine.

Then one night we were closing and I saw Bernie feeding Mary double scotches at the bar while the waitresses stacked the chairs. Mary didn't drink much normally so I wondered what was up. I walked over and ordered one myself. I could smell that perfume she always wore, *Possession* it was called, wafting through me like a subtle hunger.

After a while she said, "it's weird, Stu. Tonight during the show? I felt *watched*."

Well, you had to laugh.

The way she looked stopped us though.

"Hey you two, I'm serious. I don't mean the way the guys normally look at you. Shit, I'm used to that. This was. . . . this was something else."

I felt myself freeze inside for a moment. "You mean we got some creep out there? Like that?"

"I don't know. Maybe. Whatever it was, I don't need it."

I watched her gulp the scotch.

There wasn't much to say after that. I promised her I'd keep an eye on the crowd for her, see if I could spot anybody strange out there, and if I did I'd bounce him. I'd see this kind of thing before. Usually these guys are harmless, but you never knew. My promise seemed to help. She finished her double and went home and I just sat a while, aware of the lingering smell of *Possession* and thanking my lucky stars that I had Bernie there with me to remind me that I was much too old to try to comfort her further.

And the next few nights I did look, but there was nothing. Though Mary was saying it was happening *every* night to her now. She would get this feeling. I began to wonder about her. You could see she was troubled. You could see it in her eyes when she performed. They weren't the same—you didn't see the boldness there. She could still hold a crowd absolutely breathless but she wasn't doing it with her eyes anymore, she was doing it with her will and with her body, and you missed something.

Then I started noticing things.

Little things at first. There was a light in the girls' dressing room that didn't seem to want to go off. I'd turn it off at closing and come in next morning and it would be on again.

Now and then on alternate Friday and Saturday nights we'd bring in a live band, local boys, and they were always complaining that somebody was moving their instruments around in the storage room. Now, nobody had a key to that room except Bernie and I, and we sure as hell weren't doing it. We lost that band in a couple of months. I couldn't blame them. Those instruments were costly and all they ever got out of me by way of explanation was a puzzled shrug.

Then the chef started complaining about dishes rattling in the kitchen.

When Bernie and I would open up the place we'd find that somebody had moved the tables and chairs around.

We went through all the possibilities and then some. The dressing-room light was faulty wiring. Kids breaking into the storage room were messing with the instruments and moving the chairs and tables at night. The foundation was settling, rattling the dishes. Of course nothing fit with any-thing else. It was bullshit and we knew it.

We had ghosts. The Parrot was haunted.

I was already half convinced of that when somebody who wasn't there started saying things to Paula.

Paula was one of our dancers, a perky little blonde with a sensational bottom and a gap between her two front teeth like Lauren Hutton's. She was sort of shy, an English lit major if I remember correctly, and the only girl in the club who insisted on wearing pasties. I used to fight with her about the pasties—it was 1996 after all—but the few times I got her to try it without them she couldn't dance worth a damn, so finally I let her keep them. Strange what will give somebody confidence. With the pasties on she was the second best dancer we had. Not in Mary's class but good.

She came off stage one night and trotted over to me and said, "what is this? You teaching Sam ventriloquism or something?"

She was angry, but sort of pale-looking too, as though she'd eaten something that didn't quite agree. I asked her what she was talking about and she said that while she was up there somebody had been speaking to her all the while. And it was like he was standing right there with her or how else could she hear him over the music? So she thought maybe Sam had gotten into the rafters above her, into the lighting.

Sam, of course, was on his perch where he always was. He never flew around. Sam was lazy as hell. I told her that.

"Well, then you're damn well haunted, Stu," she said. "And I'd like to know exactly what you're going to do about it."

I asked her what it was she'd heard.

"The guy was giving me compliments."

"Compliments?"

"Yeah. Likes my breasts. Likes my thighs. He particularly likes my 'derriere'."

"He called it that? Your derriere?"

"Yes."

"Jesus."

"What I want to know is what you intend to do about it."

I thought about it for a while. Hell, there was only one thing I could *think* of doing. "Hold a seance, I guess."

It seemed logical, really. Find out what the guy was up to, what he wanted. See if I could get him to disappear— over to the Seahorse a few blocks away would be nice. No trouble finding a medium. Lauderdale was crawling with them. In every tourist town you get your share of psychics, faith-healers, mediums, whatever. I just needed somebody who knew the appropriate words.

As it turned out Mary knew the words.

"Sure, Stu," she said. "I used to listen to my Aunt Lilian back in Indiana. She was forever trying to summon her brother, Uncle Joe, 'who died of drink' as they say back there. And she'd summon him all right, but I guess he was

62

still boozing on the other side because everything he said came out garbled. But I remember the whole routine."

"Want to try?"

"Sure. Why not? Sooner the better. He talks to her, he watches me. Let's get the bastard. Tomorrow night, after closing."

She scribbled out a shopping list for me. In the morning I went out and purchased everything, white tablecloth, white candles, ceramic candleholders, and a Ouija board. At dinnertime the chef told me that somebody had stuffed one of his chickens with mocha ice cream and wild rice. It wasn't an easy thing, getting him to relax.

That night unseen fingers plucked ever-so-lightly at Paula's pasties.

Things were getting out of hand.

By three o'clock our last customer was gone and we assembled on the stage. I'd set up a table and four chairs, covered the table with the white tablecloth, put the candles in their holders and opened up the Ouija board. Mary and Paula changed into street clothes and then the three of us waited for Bernie to finish cashing out the register. Then we all sat down and I turned off the lights and lit the candles. We closed our eyes and held hands.

I don't remember all of what Mary said that night but it was something about how here we were, four friends, ready to invoke whatever spirit lingered here, how we came in peace and friendship and hoped he'd communicate with us either directly or through the board. She was very polite.

I remember her hand in mine was warm and soft while Bernie's was cooler, rougher, yet somehow far more comforting. I remember smelling *Possession* again, a heady incense. For a while there was just dark and silence. We waited.

"Open your eyes," she said. "We'll try the board. Place your fingertips on the planchette very lightly."

If you've never used a board a planchette is a clear plastic triangular kind of affair with a pin set into it and it's supposed to move around to the letters on the board, the pin spelling out the message. Bernie, Paula and I did as she said and the planchette was a dead slab of nothing. Then Mary put her fingers to it. And the damn thing went careening around the board so fast we could barely keep up with the spelling.

"You're pushing it!" Paula said but I could tell she wasn't. All of us could. There was a sudden sensation in the room that was electric and practically exausting. Mary didn't even bother to deny it. She was too busy watching the swooping, whirling plastic.

About five minutes later we had our message. Bernie wrote it down. I have it in a drawer to this day.

HELLO MY NAME IS FRANK W AND YOU OFFEND ME I DO NOT LIKE OR APPRECIATE RATHER YOUR LIQUOR AND YOUR NAKED DEGRADED WOMEN OR YOUR NOISY DRUNKEN CROWDS AND ESPE-CIALLY THE PAINTING ESPECIALLY THAT IT IS STUPID IT IS DISGRACEFUL AND I HAVE CERTAIN SENSIBILITIES WILL YOU PLEASE DESIST AT ONCE INCIDENTALLY WHAT IS THAT REVOLTING MU-SIC

"Rock'n roll," said Mary.

OH said the board. And then for a while we got nothing.

We asked questions, who he was and why he was here, and got only stubborn silent inactivity for our trouble until finally he said **THIS IS MY HOME I HAVE ALWAYS LIVED HERE IVE BEEN HERE FOREVER THE LIGHT IS GOOD AND BY THE WAY WHAT IS THAT PER-FUME YOURE WEARING**

"*Possession,*" said Mary.

OH said the board. **ITS VERY NICE**

"One of us naked degraded woman he likes, anyway," said Paula.

And that was that.

We sat over drinks and stewed. Bernie kept setting them up for us. Mary would toss Sam a peanut now and then.

We talked well into morning and by the time we were through, Sam, who is pretty good with short-term memory, was re-asking all the questions for us. *"What are we supposed to do? How are we gonna get rid of the sonovabitch? Who is this guy? Anybody got any ideas?"*

"Shut up, Sam," said Bernie.

Suddenly I got it. "The hall of records!" I said.

"Sure," said Mary. "We can find out who he is, anyway."

I didn't get much sleep. By noon Bernie and I were over at the hall of records and it took us till 2:30 to find him. We started too far back, taking him at his word the he'd lived there a long time. But he hadn't. He was the artist, Frank W. Morgan. He'd owned the place for fifteen years just prior to its conversion into a bookshop back in the 1920s. I should have figured it from what he said—**THE LIGHT IS GOOD HERE**. A painter. Of course.

We went from there to the library and looked up reprints of his stuff. I couldn't see why he objected to the body painting. Half his work consisted of nudes. He painted them in mythical, quasi-metaphysical settings, sort of similar to the pre-Raphaelites, that kind of thing, with titles like *Dido and Anaeus, The Lamia, Circe*, and *Penelope at the Spinning Wheel*. All a bit melodramatic for my tastes, a bit precious, but not half bad either. What we had here was the ghost of a pretty eminent man. He had died of heart failure in 1928, a bachelor, at age thirty-seven.

We told Paula and Mary what we had and they couldn't wait to get back to the Ouija board.

The body painting stayed, of course. It was not the business of some cranky ghost to tell me how to make a living. Besides, it was easier on all of us now. Knowing who he was made him much less disturbing. Mary's performance that night was halfway back to normal.

After closing we got him talking again.

We told him what we knew about him. **OH REALLY** he said. We asked him where in the place he'd died. We were curious. **NONE OF YOUR DAMN BUSINESS** he said. We asked him if he liked the girls. We got no answer to that one. We asked him why he painted mythical instead of modern scenes and he said **THE TWENTIES WERE TOO GAUDY FOR ME AND I FORGOT TO ASK WHAT ARE THOSE RIDICULOUS THINGS YOU WEAR ON YOUR NIPPLES**. Paula blushed and told him they were pasties. Finally Mary got what later amounted to an inspiration and asked him if he'd always come when we called him like this. **YES** he said.

She asked him why.

BECAUSE I DAMN WELL HAVE TO he said and suddenly the table began to shake like we had our own private earthquake in the place. You could feel his rage pouring up through the floorboards. Bernie went white as a sheet. It was scary.

And just before it stopped I heard Sam squawking behind me from his perch, his voice high-pitched and shrill. I had never heard Sam scared of anything before and I almost stopped it all right then and there—and of course I know now I should have. But Mary had planted something in my mind. I'm an entrepreneur. I can't help it. It comes with years of practice and gets in the blood and stays there.

He said he had to come when we called him. And he *shook tables*.

The following night he pulled the tablecloth out from under the candlesticks. It shot maybe three feet into the air and then came drifting down behind me. The night after that he floated the table two feet off the floor. On the third night he mashed the planchette on the Ouija board into a flat clear plastic plate.

And the point is, we *asked* him to do these things.

Mary did, actually. He always seemed to respond to Mary while with the rest of us it was iffy. But I figured I could use that too.

"Suppose we do a seance," I said to her, "*before* the end of the show?"

"Huh?"

"We fit him into it."

"You're crazy, Stu."

"Why not? We try it once. If nothing happens, no big loss. If it works, we'll advertise the hell out of him."

We were sitting at the bar and the dinner crowd was slowly arriving. Whatever the cook was doing in the kitchen he was doing right, and it was making me hungry. Mary's scent was working on me in a different way. At the moment I felt lean and smart and avaricious. I smiled at her and she looked at me for a while and then smiled back. And there was that look in her eyes again, that sense of hey, what the hell.

"I don't know, Stu," she said. But she was being coy now. "Suppose you just tell me what you've got in mind."

We set it up.

We gave him the spot right after Paula's, right before the body-painting number. That way if he flopped we'd still have our topper. We dimmed the lights and had a couple of the waitresses carry on the table with the cloth and candles, the Ouija board and the mashed planchette, and meantime I went into a little act of my own, trying to spook the crowd.

I told them all about Frank W. Morgan, all this stuff about him being a painter and dead since 1928 and you should have heard them hoot and holler. They thought we were pulling one, naturally. But I got to them eventually. I made up this story about how he'd been murdered by a former lover, a jealous model. I made it all grim and gothic and by the end of it I had them interested. The place was quiet for once. So quiet that when somebody dropped a soup ladle in the kitchen you could feel half of them jump.

Bernie and Paula and Mary came on dressed in white robes and took their places at the table and I did likewise, lighting the candles while the dimmers faded to black.

And I could feel him there. Even before we called him.

67

Something cold and tough right beside me. And I had the horrible feeling he was smirking.

We got our response from the crowd right off, all the *ooohs* and *ahhhs*, just as soon as the table started to rise, and then again when the candles switched places and when the tablecloth started flapping, and again when the Ouija board just folded up and flew across the room, slamming against the bar. That shut them up entirely. I think they were truly scared by then, scared mostly for Mary, who was doing all the talking, but maybe for themselves too because the feeling in the room had grown so thick and strange and Sam's cawing was so unearthly, starting off like a low groan and going louder and shriller until finally—according to plan, mind you—Mary stood up and told the ghost of Frank W. Morgan to take her robe off and to *do it now* and he did, and of course she was naked underneath. And by then it was a screeching sound Sam was making, a high shrill bird-sound of stark terror.

"Paint me," she said.

I had no idea it was coming. I honestly didn't.

We all knew how he felt about the body painting, and I'd have told her not to if she'd given me any warning. Some people don't believe me but it's the truth. But it was just like her to pull out the stops like that, to make it all theatrical and exciting. It was that boldness again, that daring. The paint cans and brushes were right behind her, in the wings, stage right, waiting, and she knew it.

"Paint me!"

She stood in candlelight, head high, smiling, the scent of *Possession* pouring off her in waves of heat and there wasn't a soul among us who so much as shifted where he sat or stood, just Sam and that ungodly screeching noise, and then it was as if some huge hand just lifted her, six feet up, and I suddenly remembered what she'd said to me, that she'd never met a man as tough as she was and remembered what I'd felt from him just minutes before when we first sat down, because she hung in the air a moment, mouth open in surprise, and all she said was *ooops*. I swear it. *Ooops*. Like she hadn't counted on this at all and then he tossed her. Stage right, into the wings.

We heard a crash and Sam went suddenly silent.

Then all we heard was paint dripping.

It was merciful, I'll give him that much. The angle of the head against the wall told you that. She hadn't suffered.

And he'd painted her, all right.

If we'd thought that was going to be the culmination of it, going to be end of something, it wasn't. The Parrot did not stop being haunted. Far from it.

The cook still has to search around for his colander or his spatulas from time to time and has to watch his stuffings for unlikely substances and Bernie finds scotch bottles hidden in the damnedest places, and we still have to arrange the tables nearly every morning when we open up. We've thrown out the Ouija board, of course. We lay off the hard loud rock 'n roll now and play country music instead, which he seems to like a whole lot better. And nobody paints naked girls anymore in deference to Mary.

I keep smelling *Possession* in every corner of the club.

It's the damnedest thing.

I will allow the man has taste.

Sam has taken to winking into nothingness now, and leering into shadows.

Megan's Law

Well, what the hell would *you* do?

A cop walks up to your door, knocks. You look out the window and see his squad car parked in front of your house. You open the door and this kid half your age with a gun and cuffs and bullet pouches on his belt and a pad, pencil and some flyers in his hand says *'scuse me, sir, good morning, Mr. Albert Walker?* and you say *yes, what can I do for you, Officer?* and he introduces himself and proceeds to inform you on this fine sunny summer nine-thirty Saturday morning smelling of fresh cut grass and dew that there's a goddamn *rapist* moved in two doors up, a fucking *child molester* by the name of Philip Knott, a tier-three high-risk sex criminal and he's informing you by order of the county prosecutor's office.

He tells you that he understands you have a twelve-year-old, *Michelle, is that correct?* and you say that's correct. He asks you to take precautions. He's consulting his notepad to make sure he gets this right. He says *we're asking parents in the neighborhood to reinforce general instructions about stay-*

70

*ing away from strangers and to treat Mr. Knott in particular
as a stranger, to tell their children and their children's care-
takers to make certain you know where they are at all times.
We're asking them to tell their children where Mr. Knott lives
and what he looks like.* And here he hands you a flyer.

You're looking at a mug-shot. Front-view and profile.

Taken six years ago, says the cop.

From the front he isn't bad-looking. Late twenties, dark
hair. High cheekbones, strong jaw, a cleft in the chin and
a wide, sensuous mouth. The eyes look haunted though.
Scary eyes. Dark circles beneath them as though the guy
hasn't been sleeping well or maybe drinks too much. And
then in the side-shot there's the long weird Bob Hope nose
and that spoils everything. The guy's not good-looking at
all. From the side the smudges under the eyes look even
darker.

He goes on to say that should my daughter be approached by Mr. Knott for any reason whatsoever I should
report this to the police as I would any other case of suspected criminal activity. Then he tells me what I *can't* do.
First, I can't convey any of this information to anybody else
in the community. That's the job of the prosecutor's office
and local law enforcement. I'm not even supposed to *discuss*
it. *And any actions taken against Mr. Knott,* he says, *including
vandalism of property, verbal or written threats of harm and/
or physical violence against Mr. Knott personally or against his
family or employer will result in arrest and prosecution. I understand that, don't I?* He's warning me against vigilantism.
I hear him loud and clear but I have some questions of my
own now.

"Hold on. We're talking about the new guy in the Hadley
place, right?"

"That's right."

"He moved in a week ago. And you're only now getting
around to telling me?"

"I understand your concern over the delay, sir. I can only
say that these things move slowly sometimes. Paperwork,

71

bureaucracy, all that kind of thing. But I'd guess he'd be pretty busy with the move anyway, wouldn't you?"

"And there's nothing we can do about this?"

"You can take precautions, sir."

"I mean about getting him out of here."

He shrugs. "Man's got to live somewhere, doesn't he. He's done his time. He's got to see his probation officer every week and verify his address with the prosecutor's office every ninety days. Other than that he's free to go wherever he wants, just like anybody else."

"Just like anybody else."

"Sorry. That's the way it is."

The kid *does* look sorry. I give him that.

I look at the mug shots again. Beneath the photos are the guy's name, description, address, the make of his car—*white Ford Escort*—his plate number, his place of employment—*Gene's Garage*, I know it well—and a description of his offense. *Aggravated sexual assault.*

"You mind telling me what he did?"

"Afraid I can't do that, sir. I'd be violating his civil rights."

"But you know, don't you."

"Yes."

"And it was pretty bad, wasn't it."

The kid just looks at me. The answer's in the look.

"This really stinks."

"I can't argue with that, sir. Have a talk with your daughter. Most of these guys, they don't want to mess around in their own neighborhood anyway. They go elsewhere. Just tell her to be careful and I'm sure things will be fine."

He tells me to have a good day and walks down the steps to the sidewalk and over to Fred Grummon's place next door. I wonder how Fred and Susan are going to take this. Their daughter Linda's eighteen but Fred Junior's only ten. Knott lives in the house right beside them, third one up on our little dead-end street. He knocks at the door. I don't want to watch this. I go inside.

*   *   *

72

It isn't fair. I'm worried damn near all the time now.

In some ways it's worse than fucking Rahway. In Rahway I had Jumma to protect me and even if the price for that was so fucking high I'm lucky I can walk straight, here I got nobody. Nobody I can trust to watch my back. The guys at the garage, I trust the owner but not the rest of those dumb white-trash assholes. They know I'm a damn good mechanic but they'd just as soon kick my ass as look at me.

It's all too new. Maybe that's it. Only one goddamn week in this town. I can't even look at my neighbors.

This Megan's Law thing. It fucks you up! Out in California they firebombed this guy's car, torched the poor bastard, burnt him to death. In Connecticut they got this other guy, about twenty-five of them, beat the shit out of him, somebody they thought did stuff but it was a case of mistaken identity, they fucked up, they got the wrong guy. It'd be funny if it wasn't so fucking scary. What people are capable of.

It's not fair.

Shit, I did my time. Six years. I paid my debt to society.

My slate's clean.

Will it stay clean?

I guess we'll have to wait and see.

So what the hell would you do?

I talked to her, all right. I talked to Michelle that very morning. Showed her the flyer and told her about the guy and I could tell she was scared and I hate that, I hate when Michelle's scared like she was of her crazy rumdumb miserable excuse for a mother but in this case I *had* to scare her, scaring her was my job and I could tell it took. You see this guy, I told her, he says *word one* to you, you tell me and I call the cops. You don't talk to him, you don't go near him. He comes around school and you see him you tell your teacher. Then you call me at the office. Okay?

Okay, Dad.

I love this little girl. She had a terrible, awful time with her mother. I guess Judy was a little nuts when I met her at school thirteen years ago but she wasn't drinking then, she was studying economics and she was bright and pretty with the same fine delicate blond hair and bright blue eyes she gave our daughter and she was a total banshee in bed, she was wild. I married that wildness and our daughter tamed it. Or maybe it's more precise to say that what tamed it was having to take care of her. Having to love her. I don't know.

By the time Michelle was seven I was coming home from the brokerage firm every night to find Judy smashed on vodka. Passed out in the living room if we were lucky or screaming at Michelle if we weren't. By the time my girl was ten she was dead, lying on the floor, her damn fool neck broken against the rim of the kitchen sink. Michelle was the one who found her. I remember her schoolbooks, notebooks and papers scattered across the floor in the hallway. Horror's fallout. The debris of disaster.

For all this time I've been her only protector.

First against my wife, then against the rest of the world.

I wasn't about to stop now.

I got Michelle a sitter that night and went over to Turner's Pub on Myrtle Avenue. If anybody in town had the straight dope on Philip Knott it would be Tommy. *Everybody* talked to Tommy. City councilmen, cops, lawyers, dentists, gynecologists. You almost couldn't *not* talk to him. A more affable Irishman never lived in my opinion. And Tommy took care of you, poured stiff and solid when you were sober and cut you off dry and arranged for a ride home if the time came that you were not.

"Yeah, I heard," Tommy said. "It's a bitch, ain't it."

"You know exactly what he did, Tom?"

He gave me a look. Ice-blue eyes under ginger eyebrows.

"You don't want to hear about it, Al. Honestly."

"Oh yes I do. Jesus, Tommy, wouldn't you?"

He sighed and leaned on the bar.

"All right. Lerner was in a couple days ago after his shift. Said it happened in Livingston back in Autumn of '92.

Little girl ten years old's riding her girlfriend's spare bike home from school, her own bike's busted. She's pedalling hard, going slow up a hill. Knott stops her on the sidewalk easy as pie, puts his hands on the handlebars, tells her he needs to use her bike a minute, he'll bring it right back. She says it's not mine, it's my friend's. Knott punches her in the face, knocks her off the bike and then drags her and the bike into a culvert. Leaves the bike and takes the girl off into the woods. There's nobody around. You sure you want to hear the rest of this, Al? It gets rough."

"I'm sure."

He leaned in closer.

"The bastard strips her and rapes her, stuffs dead leaves into her mouth so she won't scream, does her with a god-damn broken stick for godsake. When he's done he leaves her unconcious and walks back to the culvert, gets the bike and rides off with it nice as you please."

"Christ. How'd they get him?"

"Had a prior for wagging his dick in a playground. And his prints were all over the bike. The stupid sonovabitch, he just left it there on the sidewalk about half a dozen blocks away. Plus the bite marks."

"*Bite* marks?"

He nodded. "All over the poor thing. Matched 'em to Knott's teeth. Lerner figures the girl's lucky she survived. That kind of luck, personally, I'm not so sure of."

"You talk to anybody else about this, Tommy?"

He poured me another scotch.

"Your neighbor across the street. Norm Green. You might want to have a word with him. I would."

The cop had said I wasn't supposed to discuss the matter with my fellow citizens.

This citizen figured, fuck that.

Doc Stringer says I can control this thing if I want to. Stay on the meds, stay with the meditation program and no drinking. I kinda hope he's right. One more screwup like last time and I'll

*have some nigger pole up my ass for the rest of my natural life.
Or unless I get so old nobody wants to bother anymore.*

*It's a bitch, though. You do it the first time, you just naturally
want more. And me, I've done it four times. Though obviously
not in a real long while.*

*My favorite was the second one, the redhead. A real redhead
too. Eighteen, nineteen maybe. I never did find out how old she
was because that one never made the papers. I looked for it,
God knows. But I guess she didn't tell.*

Tough little bitch.

*I wonder how she explained the missing nipple to her boy-
friend or her parents or whoever.*

I hate my job.

I hate this stupid goddamn little town.

*I want to fuck something silly. I want to fuck something till
it screams.*

I couldn't believe it. I talked to Norm Green and he
wouldn't do a thing. Nothing. Not so much as a get-out-
of-town call from a pay phone. He said he was just going
to go with the program, however much he damn well hated
it. And Norm and Beverly have a daughter, Clara, who's
exactly my daughter's age. If she didn't go to St. Philo-
mena's Catholic school she'd be in the same classes as
Michelle. I talked to Fred and Susan Grummon too and
though Susan was obviously terrified Fred said the same
thing as Norm, basically. *The guy will either fuck up or he
won't. If he does they'll put him away again. If he doesn't, no
problem. We talked to our kids and the kids know all about
him. They'll be careful.*

Bullshit. A guy like that is a running sore.

What you did with a running sore was stop it.

I couldn't sleep that night. Every time I closed my eyes
I kept seeing this guy leaning on my daughter's bicycle.
Punching her out. Dragging her into the woods. Tearing
off her blouse, her jeans. And worse.

Michelle doesn't even *ride* a bicycle anymore.

76

I got up feeling groggy but angry too. This guy was not going to fuck with us. No way. Not if I could help it.

Well, what would you do?

All day Sunday I kept looking out the window, watching for a glimpse of a white Ford Escort. Looking for the guy strolling down the sidewalk. I kept staring at the mug shots. The face looked really sinister to me now. The temptation to just walk up the street and knock on the door and beat the living shit out of him when he opened it was strong as the winter wind around here but I resisted. I resisted calling him too. His number was probably unlisted anyhow. When Michelle and some girlfriends went to an afternoon matinee at the Colony I resisted following them.

I was suddenly all will. All purpose and design.

I'm not due at the office these days until ten but Monday I got up early and planted myself on the front porch with a glass of orange juice, some toast and a cup of coffee and watched the street. I figured Knott would probably have to be at the garage by nine and I was right. At quarter to nine I saw his car pull out of the driveway and roll on down the street. I took my breakfast back inside. Michelle was still asleep.

I went out again and walked up to the old Hadley place which was now the Knott place and paused just long enough to reassure myself that what I remembered about the house was right. No matter where you parked in the driveway you had to cross at least a dozen or so feet of lawn along a fieldstone pathway once you came off the front porch steps and the same would be true if you used the back steps and had parked your car in back. Either way was doable.

I went home and showered and shaved and went to work.

Tuesday I got up earlier. This time I skipped breakfast and showered and shaved and brushed my teeth right away and except for my tie and sport jacket, dressed for work. Two years ago a group of us at the office had attended a management seminar at Stowe, Vermont and I still had the ski mask in my drawer so I took that and a pair of leather gloves and my tie and jacket with me and drove to the mall.

I worked my way through college. Every kid in my family did. My brother. My cousins. I worked for my uncle as a repo man. It's no big thing to jimmy a door and hotwire a car once you know how. Back then I got so I could do it in thirty seconds flat. I was a little rusty. It took me forty-five.

The vehicle was a Jeep Wagoneer. I figured four-wheel drive might be handy. It was eight thirty-nine exactly when I pulled up to the curb of the Lindsay place across the street from Knott and a little way down. I left the Wagoneer in gear with my foot on the brake and put on the ski mask rolled up like a hat, ready to pull down. I wasn't worried about being seen parked there. The Lindsays had a summer home in the lakes district up in Sparta. They'd be there until September. It occured to me that for the Lindsays none of this would have happened at all. It'd have no reality whatsoever for them. *If a tree falls in the forest . . .*

At eight forty-two he walked down the steps in front.

I lifted my foot off the brake. I pulled down the mask. I hit the gas and headed for the lawn.

I want to fuck something till it screams but I won't. Not in the immediate future anyway. That I'm pretty sure of. I think I maybe can actually do this thing. Maybe. Maybe it's the meds or maybe it's just being free now not in Rahway anymore and not obsessing all the time as Doc Stringer would say but it's kinda easier now, the urge is less than it was in the joint and a whole lot less than it was before the joint. Yesterday at work I didn't think about doing it once. Not once all fucking day long. First time. I didn't particularly think about being scared either of the other guys. For me that's fucking amazing. I don't know what's changed but something.

I mean, you never know about me.

I'm a major screw-up.
But maybe.

I hit him the first time and he didn't even seem to hear me,
I caught him at the right hip and he went down into the
bushes and I just kept coming never mind the bushes, the
front tires rolling over his legs and I could feel the bump
and hear him scream but what I really needed to do was
get at the chest or the head so I backed up and turned the
wheel a little and put it back into drive and then rode over
him again and this time I heard a kind of *pop* and no scream
at all and when I backed up I saw that my left front tire
had rolled over his neck, that the Wagoneer's weight had
pretty much disconnected his head from his body and had
flattened his neck like roadkill which in fact was exactly
what the little fucker was now.

I backed up onto the street and saw Susan Grummon in
her slip standing at the door to her house looking toward
Knott's and then looking at me and registering the ski mask
and then stepping back inside and slamming the door behind her. Of course she'd call the cops. No problem.

I drove carefully back to the Mall and parked the Wagoneer exactly where I'd found it. I got into my own car
and drove around back to the WalMart Dumpster and
tossed the gloves and ski mask. I drove to the office, put
on the tie and jacket and adjusted the tie in my rear-view
mirror and had a busy and productive day at work.

That night when I came home Michelle told me that the
police had been here and talked to her. That they were
questioning everyone on the street. I figured that was only
natural. As his neighbors we were the likely suspects after
all. They told her to have me call when I got home from
work so I did. We set up an interview for tomorrow morning. Nine o'clock sharp.

I have no problem with that at all. I probably won't even
be late for work, they said.

Michelle, though. Michelle was pretty shook up over the

whole thing. You couldn't blame her. The murder. The police and all.

So I did what I usually do.

I took her to bed.

I comforted her.

What would you do?

If Memory Serves

Patricia sat relaxed in the armchair across the room.

The metronome on the table in front of her had done its work in record time.

"I'd like to speak with Leslie," Hooker said.

The woman looked at him, sighed, and shook her head.

"God! *Leslie* again. I don't get it. What the hell's wrong with speaking to *me* once in a while?"

Hooker shrugged. "You lie. You evade. You try to confuse things. If you didn't lie so much, Susan, maybe I'd want to talk to you more often. Nothing personal."

She pouted, leaned back in the chair and folded her arms across her breasts.

"I'm only trying to cover my butt, y'know," she said.

"I know. And I understand. It just doesn't help matters much at this juncture. Let me talk to Leslie, okay?"

The eyelids fluttered. The woman threw back her head and howled. Then gave him a meek bright sidelong glance and began to whimper.

"*Leslie.* Not Katie."

Katie was a dog.

Only the second such dog ever recorded in the history of MPD—Multiple Personality Disorder. Hooker had written about her extensively in the article he'd done for the *Journal of Psychiatric Medicine*. Speculation mostly and observation of the physical aspects. Crawling, snuffling, howls. Katie's connection to the other personalities had seemed vague at the time. Now, knowing what he did, it was clearer.

"Hi, Doctor Hooker."

"Hi, Leslie."

"I guess you want to talk some more."

"That's right."

"I'm not supposed to."

"Why?"

"Patricia doesn't want me to."

"I think she *does* want you to, Leslie."

"She's scared."

"Scared of what?"

She shifted uncomfortably in the seat, a typical teenage girl wrestling with a problem. Like all the personalities who had emerged so far other than the dog Katie and Lynette, who was only five years old, Leslie had come into the world at sixteen and sixteen she remained.

"They said they'd hurt her, remember? If she talked. They said they'd *kill* her."

"I remember."

"So?"

"So that was quite a long time ago, wasn't it."

Twenty-two years to be exact. The woman sitting in front of him was thirty-eight and the mother of two, both girls, ages eight and ten. Until her divorce a year and a half ago she had been a successful editor for a large paperback book company and then a chronic alcoholic who finally had sought therapy when she found herself having beaten her oldest child with a soup ladle across the face and head without remembering having done so. Four months into

82

treatment the first personality—little Lynette—had emerged.

"I don't know about this, doctor."

"You've done fine so far, Leslie. Why stop now?"

"I don't *want* to stop."

"Then don't. Believe me, it's going to help Patricia enormously in the long run. Enormously."

She thought for a moment and then sighed.

"Okay. I guess I owe her that."

He allowed himself to relax. It was a crucial point. Had she balked here it might have been weeks before she allowed herself to address all this again. It had happened before.

And today, finally, he had Patricia's permission to record their sessions.

"You were talking last time about how they—the Gannets—'passed her around' I think you said."

'Uh-huh."

"And you were talking sexually passed around, correct?"

"Yes."

"Can you tell me *who* her mom and Dad were giving her to?"

"Lots of people. That whole group they had there. Mr. and Mrs. Dennison, Judge Blackburn, Mr. and Mrs. Siddons, Mr. Hayes, Doctor Scott and Mrs. Scott, Mr. Seymour, Miss Naylor."

"The schoolteacher."

"Right. And Mr. Harley. There were others. But those were the main ones."

"Her mom and Dad, did these people pay them for this?"

"No. They just allowed it. It was just okay by them."

"And this was when Patricia was how old?"

"Three. Maybe four."

He suspected it was five. Lynette's age.

The age she'd begun hiding.

"So then what would these people do to her again?"

This was all familiar territory but he needed it for the tape.

"Well, she would be naked pretty much always and they would put their fingers in her, in her bum, in her vagina, and some of the men would put their penises in and sometimes make her put their penises in her mouth, and they would spank her real hard and Doctor Scott, he liked to put these long needles in her . . ."

"Acupuncture needles?"

"I don't know. Just big long needles."

"Go on."

"He'd put them in her, stick them everywhere. And Mrs. Scott always wanted her to lick her vagina."

It was a hallmark of Leslie's personality that none of this seemed to embarrass her in the slightest. She treated this catalogue of childhood horrors with a detachment that was almost clinical. Admirable, he thought, were it not so sad and frightening.

"Mrs. Siddons liked to twist her nipples until she cried. And Miss Naylor always wanted to have her breasts sucked like Patricia was a little baby and she was her mommy. Mr. Hayes would put her in the tub and pee on her and one time he shit on her too. On her belly. Sort of stood over her and bent his legs a little."

"And there were other kids involved, right?"

She nodded. "Danny Scott, Ritchie Siddons, and the Dennison twins."

"Did Patricia ever try to resist at all? Ever try to run away?"

"A couple times she tried. But she was too little to go anywhere. The Gannets beat her bad for it. So she didn't try anymore."

She stopped. Tears were rolling down her cheeks in a sudden stream.

"Leslie?"

Her chin trembled and the large brown eyes were doe's eyes, liquid, innocent.

"Lynette? Is that you?"

"They *hurt* me! Mommy and Daddy . . ."

"I know. It's all right, Lynette. Mommy and Daddy won't hurt you any more. I promise. I swear."

That was true enough. Mommy and Daddy were dead in a car accident nearly ten years before. He was drunk. The telephone pole unforgiving. As far as Hooker was concerned, good riddance.

"They *hurt* me!"

"I know they did, Lynette. But that's all over now. Mommy and Daddy can never hurt you again. You understand?"

She sniffled. The tears abated.

"Are you okay now?"

She hesitated, then nodded.

"Good. If it's all right then, can you let me talk to Leslie again?"

"Oh for chrissakes, *fuck* Leslie!"

The voice was deep and husky.

Sadie.

Only the third time she'd appeared.

The first two times were trouble. He could see this was not going to be an exception. She was up and out of her chair and striding over.

"You want to talk sex, honey? You feel like a turn-on? Is that it? Then you better talk to *me.*"

He was halfway up out of his own chair when she reached down and pushed him back again.

Then lifted her skirt and straddled him.

"Sadie . . ."

"I know. We been through this before. 'It's inappropriate for a patient and therapist' blah blah blah. Loosen up, will ya?" She shrugged off her jacket.

"Get off me, Sadie."

"Loosen up. You know you want little Sadie."

"What I *want* is to talk to . . ."

85

"Yeah, Leslie. I know. But will Leslie do this for you, Doc?"

She pulled the sweater off over her head. Underneath it her breasts were naked. They were lovely breasts, full and firm for her age and the fact that she'd born two children—and judging by the size and shape of the nipples, breast-fed at least one of them.

Lovely but for the scars.

Small puckered burn-scars. Over a dozen on the breasts alone. Many more on her stomach, neck and shoulders.

He could still make out the swastika carved just above her navel.

He had never seen the evidence first-hand before.

"You want to talk about those, Sadie?"

She laughed. "Talk about what? *My tits?*"

"Those burns. The swastika."

She pushed off him angrily and scooped up the sweater and walked to the window. Slipped the sweater on. Walked back to her chair and dug in her purse for a pack of Winston Lights.

Sadie smoked. The others didn't.

"I don't allow cigarettes. You know that, Sadie."

She gave him a look, disgusted, and tossed the pack back into her purse. Sadie would rebel but only so far. Then like all the others she was forced to obey.

"*Oh, fuck you*, Doc. *Talk* to your precious Leslie. Have a wonderful time. You *asshole*."

She dropped into the chair and looked at him. The eyes softened. Her face went slowly neutral.

Leslie again.

Now if he could just keep her here for the duration.

The session was running long. He could see that already. The clock on the wall above and behind her read two-fifty. But this was all much too productive to quit in ten minutes. He had a first-time patient who was probably already outside there in the waiting room—his three o'clock appointment. It wasn't the best way to start a doctor-patient

86

relationship but the man would have to hold on awhile.

It wasn't just Patricia who had something on the line here.

This case was going to make his reputation, no doubt about it. The first article, published six months ago, had gone a long way toward doing that already. AP had picked up on it. My God, *The New York Times*. For Warhol's classic fifteen minutes he and his unnamed patient were famous.

Soon they'd be more so. His first paper was only the beginning.

"Leslie."

"Hi. Hello again."

"We were talking about all the sexual things they did to Patricia. But there were other things too, weren't there."

She nodded.

"Would you mind going over them for me again?"

"There were all the witchy things," she said.

"Like what?"

"They taught her all these chants and stuff, and they would all dress in black and sometimes they'd visit graveyards at night and sometimes dig up bodies and do stuff with the bones and the dead guy's clothes, make up devil potions for the Feast of the Beast or Candlemas and calling up spirits and . . ."

"What do you mean, 'devil potions'?"

"Pee. And wine. And blood."

"Whose blood?"

"Theirs. Anybody's."

"Go on."

"Well, most of the time though, they were in the basement of the Gannets' house. They had a really big basement there. And everybody would be naked. And everybody would have to kiss Mr. Gannet's penis before things started, like all in a line, and then there'd be chanting and people would eat and drink a lot and then they'd bring in the sacrifice."

"What was the sacrifice?"

"Chickens. Cats. Mostly it was dogs."

Dogs like Katie.

It was amazing and highly unusual. Patricia had created this personality in total identification with the dead or soon-to-be dead.

The dead *taken inside* her, made one with her.

A remarkable exercise in compassion.

"And then there was that one time," she said. "You know. Her initiation."

The voice was small and not nearly so matter-of-fact as before. Unsure. Almost frightened.

He knew that tone.

Because it was at this point that Leslie's information had almost always stopped in the past, here or only slightly further. Something about the initiation had been highly traumatic. Hooker knew from sessions past that Patricia had been sixteen years old at the time, the age at which most of the personalities erupted out of her all at once, guardians at the gate of her sanity. He knew that the initiation had occured in her parents' basement. And that was about all he knew.

He looked at the clock. Three o'clock exactly.

To hell with the time. He needed to try.

"Leslie, in the past you haven't wanted to tell me about this, I know. And I understand that it's difficult for you. But this time's going to be different. I'll tell you how and why it's different. You see the tape recorder on the desk there beside you?"

She looked and nodded.

"What's different is that this time I'm *taping* this. And next session I'll play the tape back for Patricia. When I do, Patricia will know and understand what they did to her. She'll understand why she's this way, why *all* of you are this way. And can you guess what happens then?"

She shook her head.

"The pain *stops*. A little more time, a little more therapy, and it stops."

He looked at her, gave it a moment. He thought, *trust me*.

"Tell me about it, Leslie," he said.

For a moment he thought it wouldn't happen. Then she leaned back in the chair and closed her eyes and when she opened them again she was remembering.

"There was a boy," she said. "I don't know where he came from. Not one of the usual boys, I mean. Not one of theirs. Spanish, I think, Cuban or Mexican, about Patricia's age. Patricia had had a lot of some kind of drugs and so had the boy and they both were naked and they put her down on the table, the altar, with the boy standing over her, everybody chanting while he put his penis in and started doing it. He was doing it a long while and it was hurting. And then Mr. Gannet reached over with this knife he had, this sacrifical knife which was very, very sharp, and he cut the boy . . . you know the place, right between the . . . the balls and the asshole? that skin there?"

Hooker nodded.

"And there was blood running out of him, all this blood, running down his legs and dripping off the altar but I guess because of the drugs or because it was doing it, I don't know, he didn't know it at first, he just kept doing it to her but Patricia knew, she could feel it pooling up under her real warm and wet and finally the boy got it too, he started screaming and went to pull out of her but by then Mr. Gannet was around the side of him and cut him across his throat with the knife and Patricia was screaming and the boy was coughing blood, it was all over the place, all over her, *she tasted it*, and all the others were around them catching the blood with bowls, drinking the blood from his neck and from between his legs and she could smell his shit and they were catching that in bowls too and smearing it across their faces, across their mouths, and instead of coming inside her he just released it, you know? He pissed inside her.

"Well, then the boy fell on top of her, he was dead, and

Mr. Gannet handed Patricia the knife and told her to stab him in the name of Lord Satan and she was so scared and so *mad* at the boy—it was weird—so really completely furious at him, that she did. Stabbed him over and over over."

She stopped, puzzled.

"I wonder why she was so *angry* at him? And not at them."

He let her consider it a moment. There wasn't time to get into it now though he knew perfectly well where the anger of one victim toward another usually came from. Another session.

"What happened then?"

She shrugged. "They ate the boy's heart. They smeared her with his blood. Then they did it to her one at a time. Then they let her go upstairs to shower and then they let her sleep."

Ten minutes after three. They'd got through it. It was over.

He felt shaken. Elated too. He couldn't believe what he had here.

"I'm going to count to five, Leslie," he said. "When I get to five I'll be speaking to Patricia again and she'll be awake, rested, relaxed and comfortable and she'll remember none of this. You did very well. Thank you."

"Doctor?"

"Yes?"

"Patricia's scared again."

"She needn't be."

"She knows I told. That I told you *everything*."

"Patricia's going to be fine, believe me. I'm going to count to five now, all right? Close your eyes."

He counted.

Patricia opened her eyes and smiled.

"Well, how'd we do?" she said.

"You did beautifully." He returned her smile. "I want to go over this with you as soon as possible. But I've got another patient outside right now."

He consulted his book.

"How is three o'clock Wednesday—day after tomorrow?"

"Fine."

"We've made a breakthrough here, Patricia. You should know that."

"Really? Then can't you . . . ?"

"No. I'm afraid not. Not right now. This is going to take some time. I'm scheduling you for two hours again Wednesday, all right?"

"All right."

He handed her up the jacket on the floor in front of him. She didn't even ask how it got there. She was practically an old pro at this by now. She gathered up her coat and purse and stood to leave. Hesitated and then turned back to him.

"Should I be worried?" she said.

"Worried about what?"

"I don't know. Just . . . worried."

"No. Not at all. We're already through the worst of it. There are some very difficult issues to face, I won't deny that for a moment, but now at least we know what we're dealing with. We know *for sure*. It's going to take some time. But you're going to have a *life*, Patricia. A full, integrated life. Without hiding. *Without fear*."

She smiled. "I'll see you Wednesday, then, Doctor. And I guess . . . well, I guess we'll just see."

She stepped through the door to the waiting room and closed it gently behind her. He walked to the table beside her empty chair and turned off the recorder. Pushed the rewind button and heard the sibilant hiss of tape which was her voice and his so that he knew it hadn't failed him and then heard it click back into the start position. He unplugged the recorder, walked to his desk, opened the top drawer and slipped it away.

In the waiting room outside he heard a chair thump against the wall. His three o'clock was probably impatient as hell right now, would probably need some soothing of feathers. That was all right. At the moment he felt up to anything. He walked across the room and opened the door.

The man crouched over her, a big man all in black—jacket, shoes, trousers—crouched over her so that Hooker could see her lifeless eyes and open mouth and the back of his head moving side to side just below her chin. There was blood all over the walls and the landscape paintings hung there to set his patients at ease, blood still pulsing up from out of her neck over and around both sides of the man's head, drenching his long black greasy hair and he looked up at Hooker and grinned, his face a thin bright mask of red, teeth dripping paler blood, thinned with saliva. Hooker saw the knife in his left hand and the blood-stained silver pentagram around his neck.

"Session's over," hissed the man. "*Patient's cured.*"

He stepped back through the doorway to his office as though somebody had shoved him. Tried to slam the door. The bloody left hand shot out against it with a crack and thrust him back into the room.

The man stood on the threshold.

For a moment as he approached him Hooker thought of all the people, all the *structure*, all the wealth of invention and will to survive that had just died out there in the waiting room and the only solace was that the tape would outlive them, the man would not know about the tape, his work would go on in a way, and in a way so would she go on, despite and not because of his ambitions for them both though it was not enough, not nearly enough for either of them or for her children. He thought *publish or perish or both* because of course that was what had done it to them and then heard the whimper of a dog which was his whimper as the knife came down and down.

92

Father and Son

The old man feels a cool flutter like the rush of air off tiny wings against his forearm and stirs in bed. He's almost awake on this warm summer night but not quite. The gin takes hold again and drags him back to sleep.

The second time he feels it across his cheek and now he's startled full awake, aware that this is *not right* somehow. Somehow a bird or a bat got into his bedroom and his heart is pounding which it shouldn't be, not after two bypasses, the latest being just two weeks past.

He reaches across the yellowed sheets for the table-lamp and fumbles for the switch. The room snaps into focus. His eyes are still fine even though the rest of him's shot to hell. He looks around and there's no bird nor any bat either. He doesn't know about birds necessarily but bats will go to ground in bright light, find someplace in the shadows to wait it out, like under the bed or in some dark corner so he gets up, woozy from sleep and booze but easier in the heart and searches behind the night-table and bending slowly and carefully under the dresser and as best his skinny legs can manage checks beneath the bed.

Nothing. The bedroom door is closed. Windows too. He's heard that even a warm breeze can kill a man his age if he lies in it long enough so he keeps them that way permanently. Which means there's no way into the room and no way out.

Now ain't that a hell of a thing he thinks. I felt something.

I know goddamn well I did.

And now he's got to piss like a racehorse.

Old prick would have woke me up anyhow he thinks, sooner or later.

He opens the door and shuffles out into the hall, passes his son Joey's room and peers in. Joey's not there. The bed's a mess but then it always is. Probably passed out in front of the TV again he thinks and realizes then that he can hear it dimly, canned laughter, some stupid sitcom, so he bypasses the bathroom for the moment and goes to the living room and there he is in the overstuffed chair. He's snoring, a two-hundred-eighty pound rumble that's nearly as loud as the laughter. There's a bottle of that cheap bourbon he drinks between his legs so that it looks like he's been jerking off on a whiskey bottle and fell asleep halfway through it.

The old man can remember real erections.

He can remember when neither of them were drunks.

It's over fifteen years now since the bright winter morning his wife Ella and Joey's wife Susan went out grocery shopping and then through the windshield of his pickup together—or in Susan's case, only halfway through. He'd been seventy by then and said to hell with it. Joey'd been only fifty-two and weighed in at a trim one-hundred-eighty pounds. Good-looking boy. But Joey'd said to hell with it too.

The old man's bladder's killing him.

He turns and once inside the bathroom closes and locks the door because Joey has been known to blunder in un-

94

announced, they both have, and sits his tired bones down on the toilet. For all the pressure up there you'd think it would come flooding out of him but it doesn't, it takes a whole painful minute or more and once it's started he finds himself gasping, that's how good it feels.

He surveys the bathroom. It's filthy, it's desperate for a cleaning. There's something growing on the shower curtain and it seems to have spread to the tub. Whisps and balls of hair all over the tiled floor, Joey's hair mostly since his own is mostly gone. Even the soap is disgusting. They ought to hire somebody he thinks. He's too weak to clean it and Joey's too goddamn lazy.

He thinks about those wings. That breeze against his cheek.

The strangest goddamn thing.

He's almost finished, it's just dribbling out of him when he hears a crash, glass hitting the floor and breaking and skiddering across hardwood and then he hears a thud. He knows what it is, it can only be one thing. It can only be Joey. Suddenly his heart's pounding again.

"Joey! You okay, son?"

Once his voice had a bellow to it. Now it's all phlegm and gristle.

He flushes the toilet and uses the edge of the sink to help him stand and goes to the door and throws its lock. Pushes it.

The door budges half an inch and stops.

"Joey?"

Through the crack he can see him there lying belly-up on the floor. The bottom of the door in fact is pressing on what for Joey passes for a ribcage. He pushes the door again with the same results. He tries again, really getting his shoulder into it this time, his feet braced against the stained base of the toilet. He pushes with all his might, all eighty-five pounds of him, until he can't push any more.

No go.

He curses the sad silly sonovabitch who made a bathroom door open outward rather than in.

He looks around for something to wedge into the crack. Maybe he can pry the door open. No plunger beneath the sink, Joey's left it in the damn kitchen again. The toilet seat is thicker than the crack and he's got no screwdriver to remove it anyway.

There's no point yelling for help. The bathroom faces the overgrown back yard and the Mackenzies next door are his own driveway and their driveway away and they never come by. Never go near his place. It's arguable if they'd help even if they *did* hear him, the Scots bastards.

No getting through that tiny window either.

He can't count on anybody coming to his rescue. The liquor delivery was yesterday and the soda and junkfood and TV dinners today and neither is due again for another week. His friends are all dead and Joey's had nobody since Susan died and the garage closed down and he started to seriously drink.

It looks like he's going to have to stick around in here awhile. Till Joey comes to.

And then a sickening thought occurs to him. He has to sit back down on the toilet it's so bad. A thought so perfectly formed and awful it makes him dizzy.

Joey's own triple-bypass was a little over year ago. The doctors said the same thing they'd said to him.

Quit drinking.

They hadn't. Neither of them.

So that there's every goddamn chance in the world Joey might never come to. That Joey's gone for good.

It's a bathroom so water's no problem. Booze is though. When the shakes start hitting him he drinks the rubbing alcohol and the aftershave and then Joey's old dusty bottle of cologne. That staves them off for a while but then they're at him again and so is the craving. He can't do much but curse and scream and roll around on the floor holding his knees and jerking, spasming for God knows how long and by the time it's over he's pissed and shit his pyjamas and there are bruises all over him where he's slammed into the toilet or the tub or the pipes.

It's a bathroom so water's no problem. Food is though. He has no sense of time in here not going through what he's going through but he's guessing it's been a few days at least when the hunger finally gets to him so that it's like a mad dog tearing at his stomach and even with Joey's stink drifting in from the hallway he has to eat. He eats a half-full tube of toothpaste and then a full one, chases it with water. He tries a bar of soap but throws it right back up again. He shreds the toilet paper and swallows that. Anything to fill his stomach. The bottle of aspirin is tempting but he knows it's going to kill him if he does so he flushes them down the toilet against the moment they might become inevitable.

He's so weak he can barely sit up straight. He can barely shred the toilet paper and chew and swallow.

He's in and out of focus all the time now, like even his eyes are betraying him. But it's not his eyes, it's the rest of him. He sleeps and doesn't sleep and one is pretty much the same as the other. There's nothing to do but sit or lie there thinking about the past and Ella and the place they used to have down by the river and his dead brother Henry and his dead sister Laurie and his parents both long dead but the one thing he thinks about most is how his son has killed him and when he thinks about that he often as not starts to cry thin miserable old-man's tears because he maybe could have helped him had he not been so goddamn drunk himself, a disgusting excuse for a father and then he thinks about the wings.

He *feels* the wings.

Actually *feels* them now, the tiny brush of air against his cheek. Just like before.

And just like before they wake him up again. He's been sleeping. He's startled.

He hears voices outside, people entering the house, people *having entered* the goddamn house and they're moving down the hallway toward Joey's bloated fly-blown body on the floor and he pulls himself up to tell them he's in here dammit he's not dead yet and the wings rush away with his heart.

Thanks to Dale Meyers Cooper.

The Business

The cockroach was not too big but it was coming right at him, moving in that drunken way they have, a little to the left, a little to the right, appropriate in this place, moving past Mama's beer spill on a trajectory that would take it directly yet indirectly to his Scotch.

"Hey, Billy," he said to the barman. "pass me another napkin, will ya?"

Billy didn't like him. Howard knew that. He couldn't have cared less. He got service because he left a decent tip, and that was that. Billy handed him the cocktail napkin.

Howard squished the bug. If you had a potato chip stuffed with onion dip, that was what it felt like.

Mama didn't notice. First, she was busy talking to his brother Norman and his bimbo soon-to-be-wife girlfriend Sonya, and second, Mama was going blind as a stump, bless her.

He balled up the napkin and set it on the lip of the bar for Billy to throw away, one less bug in the Apple, and sipped his Scotch and listened.

They were talking about the building over on 71st between Columbus and Central Park West. There was a major problem with the plumbing there. One of the tenants had been watching television two nights ago when the wall behind the television started to balloon out at him like some huge sudden off-white zit, and then it started to trickle. It had been necessary for Gonzales to turn off all the water in the building while they knocked in the bedroom wall and then the bathroom wall behind it in order to get at the pipes. All this at eight o'clock at night no less. People wanting to cook, wanting to shower, wanting to do the dishes. Tenants were screaming.

They'd have screamed a lot louder if they'd gotten a look at the poor guy's pipes.

And at their own.

So now his mother and Norman were talking plumbing contractors, and, personally speaking, Howard was bored to tears. Because the decision on who to hire, finally, was not going to be Norman's in any case. Not this time. Not anymore. There was no point discussing it.

Sorry, big brother.

Sure I am.

"Hey, Mama," he said. "Enough with the business. It's Mother's Day. It's a party. We came here to enjoy ourselves, right?"

She turned to him and smiled and patted his hand. He thought Mama had a real nice smile.

When her teeth were in.

"You're right, sonny," she said.

He hated it when she called him sonny, but she did it all the time. It was ridiculous. He was pushing fifty for God's sake, practically bald, he had problems with his cholesterol and his blood pressure. He had weathered two divorces. And now the big guy down at the end of the bar, the Texan or Southerner or whatever the hell he was who always wore the same baseball cap and fishing vest like he was about to go pull some pike out of the Raritan or some damn place was looking at him and snickering. Because Mama had called him sonny. He hated *sonny*.

But it was Mama.

And you had to love Mama.

It was impossible, in fact, for him to even stay mad at her very long. Even when she was treating him like some idiot who would never have half a head for business while his brother Norman got treated almost like the second coming of Nate, their father—with that much respect. It happened sometimes.

Even then he couldn't stay mad at her. Because, unlike Norman, and unlike their dear dead pain-in-the-butt father, Mama always encouraged him in what he *did* do.

Which, granted, wasn't much.

What Howard did was he invested in shows. Off-Broadway shows mostly, especially the cabaret type that were big these days in the supper clubs. Like *Forbidden Broadway* and *Forever Plaid*, though he didn't have a piece of either of these—God knows he wished he had. No, the shows he backed had names like *Spike's Stiletto-Heel Review* and *Recession Drag*. Some made money and some didn't. *Most* didn't. But they kept him busy. And Mama had encouraged him.

So you had to love Mama.

His brother Norman was a whole other matter.

Look at him, he thought. The cheapskate. Standing at the bar drinking well-whiskey in the cheapest joint on Columbus Avenue.

The guy was worth over thirty million dollars.

He'd checked.

"We haven't even ordered yet," said Mama. "Come on. Let's order."

The bartender handed them each a menu.

Silence as they studied the cuisine. Buffalo wings and onion rings and fries. Chicken fingers. Burgers and clubs and reubens. Oh yeah. And the Mother's Day Special Brunch Menu at eight ninety-five, all the Freixinet you could guzzle straight up or mimosa included.

Damn cheapskate.

It was Mother's Day for God's sake!

And Mr. Big Spender says last night at dinner that he's taking them all out for brunch, his treat, how about that! And Mama's delighted of course—and then they wind up here.

Mama didn't seem to mind.

She seemed quite happy in fact.

He minded.

He'd been minding for a long time, and now, finally, he was doing something about it. The wheels were in motion. He'd greased the skids.

Norman was going to fall.

Outside the big plate-glass window the girl of his dreams cruised by on rollerskates, a moment's suggestion of what for Howard was the promise of eternal grace, and was gone.

You could keep your Sonyas, your blond big-breasted short-waisted Little-Annie-Fannies of this world—Howard's tastes were more refined. His notion of a thing of true beauty was five feet, ten inches tall or taller—though he himself was only five-six—long in the leg and in the neck, delicate of wrist and hand, small-breasted, slim-hipped, and young. Especially young. Your basic fashion-model infanta.

And he would have her. He'd have her soon.

He got flushed just thinking about it.

Nobody noticed.

He glanced at Sonya. Her eyes all squinty, puzzling over the one-page menu.

Sonya was pushing thirty. And not his type. Still it galled him that Norman was older and fatter and even more bald than he was and yet he had this younger woman, this *considerably* younger woman, this slightly aging bunny in fact—who was willing to marry him. While Howard remained womanless.

Except, of course, for Mama.

102

It was all about money. He knew that. Norman had the woman because Norman had the money, the buildings and the business all controlled by him, his father's will had set it up that way—with Howard granted a certain amplitude of hard cash but no sure way of turning it into more. While Norman had ten brownstones and four high-rise apartments up his sleeve at all times.

No fair.

"I'll have the Special," said Mama. "Two eggs over easy, the bacon, the toast, and the home fries. Oh, and a mimosa, please."

Billy scribbled it down.

"The Special," said Sonya. "Western omelette, ham, toast, fries, and a glass of just the regular . . . you know . . . the champagne. I mean, no OJ. You know?"

"Make mine the same," said Norman. He hugged her, smiling. She wrapped her tanned, firm naked arm around his waist, hugged him back, and giggled.

They were bonding over a western omelette.

My God.

"Steak and eggs," he said. Billy looked at him. "I know it's not on the menu. But you must have some kind of steak back there. Tell the cook to broil it medium and give me two eggs over easy and some fries. Green salad on the side. With Roquefort dressing. And forget the champagne. Just keep the Dewar's coming."

Mama elbowed him lightly in the ribs, smiling at him conspiratorially. "Spendthrift," she said.

"Only when it's on Norman's tab."

She laughed and leaned over and kissed his cheek. "He is a little tight, isn't he, sonny," she said. She sighed. "But that's all to the good now, isn't it."

He presumed she meant *now that he was marrying Sonya.* Though it was hard to see how even a shop-till-you-drop clothes-horse like Sonya was going to break Norman. If she got the opportunity.

Which she wasn't.

It had actually been very easy to arrange. Even easier to conceive. As a matter of fact it had come to mind right away when Norman announced last month that he and Sonya were going on vacation together, a sort of pre-honeymoon honeymoon. To Mexico.

Mexico, he'd thought immediately. *Where life is cheap.*

Wasn't that an ad for some movie or something?

They'd be gone a week, said Norman. Or longer.

Howard was already focusing on the *or longer* part.

There was a tenant in their 45th Street building in Hell's Kitchen. His name was Castanza. By trade a painter and a carpenter. *Supposedly.* He and Mama and Norman had talked about Castanza many times because on two occasions now, police had been over to the office to question Norman about the man's activities. Had they had any complaints about him? Was he paid up on his rent? What did they know about how he made a living? Had they noticed any significant spending? On the apartment perhaps?

When pressed, one of the investigators suggested—only suggested, mind you, and completely off the record—that they would probably do well to be careful in their dealings with Castanza, that any irregularities in his behavior toward them or any of their tenants should probably be reported immediately to the authorities, that he had been linked—not conclusively linked, but *linked*—to a number of disappearances in various places throughout the city. He and the battered old Ford truck he drove, which the meter maids kept ticketing constantly outside the building.

They'd noticed nothing and heard nothing but the suggestion stuck, distressing and sort of thrilling.

Castanza was possibly dangerous.

Possibly even a killer.

Castanza was from Mexico City.

A wholly conscienceless killer, Howard found, who worked for hire and actually worked pretty modestly. He was already down there. Waiting for Norman's flight, the red-eye out of Kennedy this evening.

104

So that what Norman and Sonya would find down there was not the Mexico City of green expansive parks, monuments and plazas, of cappuccino in chic cafés and romantic moonlight strolls. What they would find down there was death.

He did not know where or how. He did not care to know. That was up to Castanza. The man had assured him that in Mexico it would not be difficult to make it appear drug related or perhaps *brujo* related—a touch of Santeria. Did he have a preference?

He did not.

The man knew Norman well and had no love for his landlord. Maybe that was why Howard was getting the price he was getting. Sonya he didn't know at all—but Sonya was just window dressing anyway, she was *nada*, just some woman who'd be traveling with Norman.

By next week, the business would belong to him.

A begrudging provision of Nate's will.

Nate would be turning over in his grave right about now. Mentally, Howard gave him the finger. The men in his family had always been prize bastards, and his Dad was no exception.

Howard was looking at his brother for the very last time.

As far as he was concerned it was *about* time.

It would all be him and Mama now.

That was fine.

He thought all this as the food arrived and they ate—you might even say he savored it.

It was sure much easier to chew than the steak.

"I'd like to propose a toast," said Norman. His fork clattered noisily to his empty plate. *First one started, first one finished. Every time.* "You need champagne for this, little brother. Come on. Billy? Set my brother up, will you?"

"I don't drink champagne," said Howard. "Especially that stuff. You know that."

"One glass won't kill you. I want to make a proper toast here, all right? Gimme a break."

Norman was smiling, his lips still greasy from the eggs and fries, and flecked with crumbs of toast. It was amazing to Howard that his mother had given birth to something so repulsive.

He guessed he might as well go along with it, though.. It was a holiday, right?

"Okay," he said. "One glass. You got anything better than that?" he asked the barman.

Billy shrugged. "I can give you a split of Korbel *Brut*."

"Jesus. Yeah, okay."

The bartender popped open the bottle and poured, then freshened Mama's, Norman's, and Sonya's glasses with the Freixinet. Howard gulped the dregs of his Scotch, and they raised their glasses.

"To my brother," Norman said.

"Huh?"

"To you."

"It's Mother's Day. What's to toast me for?"

And then all three of them were smiling, looking at him.

Oh, cute, he thought. I got some kind of conspiracy going here.

"It's a surprise," said Norman. "Believe me, you're going to like it. Drink up. Cheers, everybody."

They drank.

Howard could already imagine the Korbel headache.

"Here's the story, little brother," Norman said. "You know that me and Sonya are getting married next month, right? Right. Okay, so the two of us have been talking, and then we talked it over with Mama, and . . . well, the point is I'm not getting any younger, you know? Not that I'm all that much older than you are but the point is I'm not getting any younger, right? and Sonya and me, we're sick of the city. Crowds, hassles, dirt. Remember we were in Barbados last year? We keep thinking Barbados, Sonya and me. Now I know you've always wanted to run the business but Dad's will being Dad's will, it was always me who ran the business. But I tell you, I got plenty of money, I got

106

plenty of investments, hell I'll be dead before I spend it all! So guess what, I'm giving it to you."

"Giving me . . . ?"

"The business, you shmuck!" he laughed. "I'm giving you the business!"

"Isn't that *wonderful*, sonny!" said Mama. She leaned over and kissed him. Norman held out his hand.

"Congratulations, little brother."

Howard shook his brother's hand. His dead brother's hand.

He considered his options.

There weren't many.

There was no way to call off Castanza. He didn't even know where or how to reach the man. Norman's tickets were already paid for and short of Mama having a stroke or a heart attack right there at the bar, nothing anybody said or did—especially anything *he* said or did—was going to keep him and Sonya from climbing on that plane in four hours. Unless, of course, Howard were to admit to what he'd done.

If he admitted to what he'd done, he certainly wouldn't be getting the business. In fact, Norman was perfectly capable of having his ass thrown in jail. He wouldn't have blamed him.

His options were . . . limited.

Sorry, Norm, he thought. Who'd have guessed you'd turn soft over a blonde after all these years of hardball.

"I don't know what to say," he said. "I'm . . . I guess I'm overwhelmed, Norman. I can't believe it."

"Believe it, little brother. The transfer papers'll be on your desk in the morning. You're somebody's landlord now, buddy. Enjoy yourself."

Sonya came over and kissed his cheek.

She smelled of Tigress and fried eggs.

Mama gave him a hug.

"You'll do a wonderful job. I know you will, sonny."

"Thanks, Ma."

Over her shoulder he saw Norman check his Rolex.

"We better get going now, Mama," he said. "We got to get you packed up."

"Huh?"

Norman sighed. "Right, we forgot to tell you. Sonya's mom and Dad are coming in tomorrow, her mother's sister's in St. Luke's. What is it, Sonya, colonostomy?"

"*Colostomy.*"

"Colostomy. So anyway, Sonya can't go. So I invited Mama."

"You invited Mama? To Mexico?"

Norman laughed. "Sure, to Mexico. Where am I going, Hoboken? Mama's never seen it and I figured what the hell, it's either that or eat the tickets and why not."

"You'll have a *great* time," said Sonya.

"I'm sure we will," said Mama, smiling. "I haven't been anywhere with one of my boys in twenty years. Of course we will!"

Castanza doesn't know her, thought Howard. Not even a description. Castanza said the woman was *nada*. Just somebody traveling with Norman. Window-dressing.

My God, *Mama!*

Mama who had supported him, raised him, encouraged him. Who had, by marrying Nate forty-two years ago in the first place, then bearing two children in the second place, handed him his goddamn life!

He considered his options.

They were very much the same options he had considered when it was only Norman and Sonya he was worrying about. So it didn't take him long, just a moment or so while he pushed aside the half-empty champagne glass and signaled to Billy for another Dewar's rocks, one that he supposed would be the first of many—though it was still four hours to flight time, and he knew he'd have to be careful on the drinking.

He knew he shouldn't be too drunk when they boarded.

Norman wouldn't care.

But Mama would worry.

Mother and Daughter

When my father left, my mother covered all the mirrors.

My father was a jazz pianist and a good one. Maybe too good.

"He hears too much," my mother said to us once. "It's driving him crazy."

She would have been the one to know.

But it was true. My father heard *everything*. Taking in a conversation halfway across a crowded restaurant was nothing for him. Riding down the highway he could hear the wind in the trees over the grumbling of his car and my mother's backseat driving. Most people sleep through a night's gentle rain. My father couldn't. He had perfect pitch and could reproduce a seagull's call or a blackbird's on the piano, a *percussive* instrument no less, so well that my sister and I knew exactly which was which. He could play the theme from *Picnic* on one hand and the theme from *Gone with the Wind* on the other simultaneously.

His gift was his curse.

There was no way he could stand the City. Not just New

York City but *any* city—which played hell with his career as a musician and limited him mostly to the small clubs nearby around the Jersey shore. In tourist season even lazy old Cape May would make him surly. His cure for surliness was a scotch bottle. My father was functionally drunk from June to September and throughout every major holiday season. We took it for granted that he would be.

What we didn't expect was for him to leave us.

One cold clear night in February while all of us were sleeping he got up and drove away.

My mother covered the mirrors.

I was only eleven at the time but my sister Louise was sixteen. What for me was just a dumb, weird adult inconvenience to her was a disaster.

"Are you *crazy?*" she said to my mother.

She was—beginning to go there at least. I know that now. But our household had never been Leave it to Beaver *anyway. The mirrors were just more of the same as far as I could see.*

"Why are you doing this to me?"

She wasn't. She was doing it for herself. My mother was as vain about her looks as my father had been proud of them and in covering the mirrors she was saving those eyes, that skin, that wild shock of hair toward the day he returned. So she wouldn't see the time passing, reflected in her face.

She knew he'd return. Against all hope we heard it from her again and again. While it was probably her bickering and constant chattering that finally drove him away.

"How am I supposed to have any friends over?"

She couldn't. It was too embarassing.

"*Everybody* has friends over. You know what this is doing to my life?"

She meant her social life. What it was doing was ruining it. But that was partly her own fault.

My sister felt ashamed.

It also nearly destroyed the family business. We'd been running a modest little bed and breakfast out of the six-bedroom Victorian gingerbread my mother had inherited from her sister and it was pretty near impossible to explain mirrors shrouded in Laura Ashley prints to paying guests. My mother didn't even try. Instead she adapted—replaced the large oval dining-room mirror with a Neal McPheeters seascape and opened the room up for a limited-menu breakfast and dinner. My mother was a good cook if slightly prone to thick floury sauces and people seemed to like the intimacy of a restaurant which could seat no more than sixteen at a time.

We survived. I survived handily. My sister Louise a lot less so.

She was ashamed. She was guilty because *she was ashamed. It lasted the rest of her life.*

For my mother it took a few years before the bitter truth set in. Despite the hopeful litany—*when your father gets this out of his system*—she eventually must have realized he wasn't coming back. Their wedding photo stayed on the mantle above the fireplace in our living room but gradually lost its power to draw her glance. I got to wondering why she didn't cover that too. We got Christmas cards and birthday cards from Oregon, Colorado, Vermont and Maine signed in my father's small neat hand. There was never a return address. My mother got the occasional crisp one-hundred-dollar bill. There was never a note.

Then he missed my sister's twenty-first birthday and a few months later, my sixteenth. The hundred-dollar bills stopped coming.

Louise and I assumed he was dead.

My mother never talked about it.

Louise and I did, plenty of times. There was a place we used to like to go down by the Point off St. Mary's By the Sea, a nun's retreat. We hardly ever saw any nuns, just fishermen. We'd take the old boardwalk path over the dunes down to a long breakwater jetty built of huge flat slabs of granite set with pilings and cemented together by

111

pebbled concrete. Over years of tidal pull and pounding surf the concrete had disintegrated into white glinting chunks which deposited themselves into the fissures between the rocks after about thirty yards out or so. The jetty continued on for another sixty, black and jagged and slippery green with lichen.

On the one side of the jetty was the wild Atlantic, on the other the calm beginnings of the Delaware Bay.

It was a place of contrasts, a good place to sit and think.

I remember lying on the sand on the Atlantic side one warm September afternoon and asking my sister why she didn't just leave. Why she wasn't going off to college like the other kids. Hell, she had the grades.

"She needs me here," she said. "How's she going to run the restaurant?"

"She yells at you."

"Everybody yells sometimes."

"Dad didn't."

"No. Dad just ran away. I'd rather get yelled at, wouldn't you?"

"You figure he's dead?"

"I don't know."

I remember I had on the bright orange bathing trunks I used to favor and that Louise, in her flowered modest two-piece, had a little bit more belly than she might have liked.

"I figure he's dead," I said. "It used to be sometimes, every once in a while, it'd be like I could feel him, y'know? Just sort of like know he was around somewhere. Not nearby or anything but around. I haven't felt that for a long time now. You think that's wierd?"

"No."

"You think we'll ever know what happened?"

"No. Not if we don't by now."

"I think you should leave. I think you should go away to school. She can get somebody else to work the restaurant."

And another time much later, in full summer. Louise

and I standing on the rocks watching the sand-fleas swarm through the bright wet lichen at low tide.

"I should have gone," she said. "She hardly speaks to me. Either that or she's going on and on about something and half the time I don't know what the hell she's talking about. I should have gone, dammit. Now I never will."

"Sure you will. You can do it anytime."

I was leaving in the fall—flying off to college. I wasn't planning on returning anytime soon thereafter, either.

"It'd be like running away," she said. "It would be just like Dad."

"No it wouldn't."

"How can I leave her here all by herself, Steven? You know she forgot to turn off one of the back burners last night? If I hadn't caught it, the whole damn house could have gone up."

"Jesus."

"I wasn't going to tell you."

"Why not?"

She shrugged. "You're leaving."

I flew to Boston. My sister drove me to Newark Airport and waited for me to board. Waving to me from the gate I saw a plain but not unattractive young woman dressed in jeans and workshirt who, in all her twenty-three years, had had only three boyfriends, each of them very briefly. I couldn't even be sure she wasn't still a virgin.

On the plane I thought about my mother.

By then the lines around her mouth were already deeply set beneath the hollows of her cheeks. She'd begun to stoop slightly. Her hair had begun to dull and thin. Her eyes appeared to have somehow settled more deeply into their sockets like sinking stones. It was as though her entire body were slowly turning in on itself—as though my father were still alive inside her however he might or might not be in the physical world and consuming her from within.

She was growing old before my sister's eyes and mine if not her own.

The mirrors were still covered.

The men in our family leave, I thought. The women stay.

My mother's osteoporosis set in my senior year.

I was twenty-two. Louise was twenty-seven and called me a few weeks before Thanksgiving to say that my mother had bumped her hip against the kitchen table. She'd fractured the hip and fallen. In falling she'd managed to fracture her wrist in two places. The hip was the main problem. It would keep her in the hospital for a week or so at the very least. I asked Louise if she wanted me to come home and help her out for a while.

"I can handle it," she said.

"You sure?"

"I'm sure."

I took her at her word. There was a girl in Cambridge with soft red hair and a washboard belly who was screwing the daylights out of me. I called my mother twice in the hospital. She sounded depressed but otherwise surprisingly okay. Her talk was all doctors and bowel movements and bad food. Typical hospital-patient-talk, not mindless chatter. Then Louise phoned me to tell me she was home. She said she was sleeping and I said not to wake her.

I went to Cambridge for my own type of thanksgiving and home only for Christmas. Louise met me at the airport. I was shocked at how thin she'd gotten since just that summer. Her hipbones showed through her jeans. Her breasts had practically disappeared. When I told her she could stand to gain a few pounds she laughed.

"I know, I know," she said. "*Mom's taking me with her, right?*"

When we got home I saw what she meant. The house was as neat and clean as always but it was none of my mother's doing. My mother was confined to her bed. Only a week before she'd stepped *out* of bed and her left foot hit

114

the floor the wrong way and now she'd broken a toe. They hadn't told me.

There was a throw-rug by the bed now. Too little too late.

My mother's flesh sagged off her brittle bones. When I hugged her it was like hugging a human-sized sparrow.

She was turning sixty-five in January. She looked to me more like eighty.

I figured with her in bed that except for in her own room we could at least unshroud the mirrors.

Louise shook her head. "I don't think so. I'm not all that big on looking at myself these days either. Leave them."

My mother was in and out of sleep a lot. That was the medication for the pain. Awake she was usually lucid and kept wanting to set her affairs in order, to tell us for the umpteenth time where her will was or her insurance papers or the deed for the house. As though she was planning on dying the next day. She seemed to think she was still back at the hospital now and then. Bitching about the doctors or the nurses or the food. Or else she'd be half-asleep, and that was when she'd really start talking ragtime.

"You got your dollar? Good boy. Go on down to Murphy's and get us a bucket of beer, okay? And make sure get change. Can't trust that Murphy. You got your dollar bill? Okay . . . good boy . . ."

On *that* one Louise and I finally determined that what she was doing was talking to her dead brother Lloyd—but *in the voice of her own mother*. It had to be. She was back in Newark, somewhere in the late 1930s.

Her brother Lloyd was killed in Bataan during World War II.

Christmas for my sister and me was cleaning bedpans and checking her for bedsores and doing loads of dirty laundry and turning her and and wiping her chin. That and the restaurant. We closed it down Christmas Eve and Christmas Day and then realized we had nothing much to do. We hadn't bothered with a tree or decorations and the exchange of presents Christmas morning took maybe all of ten minutes. For her, a silver bracelet I'd picked out in an antique store in Cambridge. Though I couldn't have known it at the time, not a good selection. The bracelet made her wrist look even thinner than it was. For me—the lit major—a handsome boxed collection of the tragedies of Sophocles, Euripides and Aeschylus. We sat around the television. I glanced through the books.

"We could go to the Point," she said.

"Pretty damn cold for the Point. And then what about her?"

"She'd be okay for a while."

I thought about it.

"Nah. Forget it. Never mind. It was only a thought."

Osteoporosis is pain, and pain strains the heart.

Against all expectations my mother lasted till April of the following year. I'd visited as often as my teaching schedule would permit and had watched my sister deteriorate by degrees almost as my mother had before her, but without the added problem—or excuse—of physical disease. I could only hope that now that this was finally over Louise could bounce back to something approaching a normal life. She'd never had one.

At the funeral service she was all skin and bones draped loosely in black. I'd only just flown in. My flight out of Logan was delayed and I'd barely made it.

"She wanted to be cremated," she told me.

"She did? Since when?"

We'd greeted our fellow mourners. There were a surprising number though I actually knew hardly any of them. Some went back all the way to my father's day as a musician. Louise and I were seated in the front row with the low hum of organ-music in our ears and the closed pine casket to our right. We were waiting for the minister to begin.

"It surprised me too. She said a funny thing, Steven.

116

Funny for her, anyway. She said she wanted to get the hell out of here, finally."

"*Let us pray*," said the minister.

We bowed our heads.

"I didn't blame her," she whispered. "So do I."

And that was my wish for my sister. That was what I was praying for at the funeral home that morning. Not for my mother's dear departed soul.

But that my sister was finally out from under her for good.

The day she was cremated we took the ashes directly to the Point.

Louise's idea.

"She wanted to get away from here," she said. "Wind and water. I can't think of a better way, can you?"

The sky was the kind of flat slate grey you get with an oncoming storm. I'd have been happy to put this off for another time—it looked like we were going to get rained on any moment. But Louise was having none of that. She got out of the car with the small white heavy cardboard box in her hands and headed up the boardwalk to the dunes. By the time I passed the Sisters of St. Joseph sign at their base she was halfway to the top.

I caught up to her about twenty yards down the jetty, just where the concrete starts to crack and fissure. To our right the Bay rippled gently under a steady southwesterly wind. On the ocean side the whitecaps slapped and then hissed across the flat black rocks. I caught her arm. I had to yell for her to hear me.

"That's far enough!" I said.

"What?"

"I said let's do it! This is fine."

"Just a little more. Let's do it right. We owe it to her, Steven!"

"We don't owe her *anything* for God's sake. She's *gone*."

I wanted to say *you* don't owe her anything but I didn't. "Just a little more."

She stepped out ahead of me. I was right behind but made no further attempt to stop her. The rocks were wet with spray and beginning to get slippery where there wasn't much of the concrete so you had to watch your footing. And then there was no concrete at all. Walking became treacherous.

We were about halfway down the jetty, out forty-five yards or so. The air was thick and cold with spray.

"Louise!" I thought, *Jesus, sis, enough's enough.*

She stopped which was a big relief to me and turned and smiled and then squatted and started pulling open the cardboard box to get at the thick plastic bag inside which contained the powder-and-bone remains of my mother and I stepped forward and suddenly saw it building off to her left and started to yell, to scream at her but there wasn't even enough time for that, she had the bag out of the box and that was when the rogue wave hit her like a huge grey-and-white cat's-paw and lifted her off the rocks and down to the sea. I slipped and ran my way to where she'd been but as the foam receded bubbling off the rocks all I could see below me were two pale slim hands reaching up empty, clawing through the unsustaining water and then pulled down and under into darkness.

I saw a black form that I knew was my sister race away from me down the breakwater and strike the rocks and then a second time toward the very end of the jetty and once, just once, the sealed plastic envelope riding high atop the waves, a chalky message in a plastic bottle. Then another wave broke hard right in front of me and the rain began and I backed away.

I backed away from all of it.

I turned and walked toward the dunes and toward the telephones at a retreat for an order of nuns.

*　　*　　*

When the police were through and the report was duly filed I drove myself home declining their kind offer and drank the way my father had, scotch neat in a tumbler, and wept for us all and then in the small hours of the morning I got up and uncovered all the mirrors.

When the Penny Drops

for Mort Levin

Bear with me.

I have a story to tell but first, bear with me. It'll take just a moment.

Here's the thesis.

It's from the mysterious that we make the leap to godly grace or evil.

And only from there.

A little knowlege, which is all we'll ever have, is a dangerous thing.

My wife and I were having dinner with friends one evening some years ago at an outdoor cafe on Columbus Avenue and as sometimes happens even when you don't particularly want it to happen the conversation got around to religion, organized and otherwise—and I recalled the story about the Eskimo and the Missionary. The Eskimo asks the Missionary, *if I knew nothing at all about this God of yours and nothing about sin, would I go to hell?* and the Missionary says no, of course not.

Then why on earth, asks the Eskimo, did you tell me?

My wife laughed. My friends, both of whom would go on to be critics for the *New York Times Book Review*, smiled thinly.

But the point of the story I think is not that innocence is grace or even good. The Eskimo is not the Noble Savage. It is that knowlege is never complete, it brings with it a core of mystery, of the seemingly impenetrable—and with that a dangerous complexity of light and dark, brightness and shadow which must be penetrated at least to some degree even to make out everyday objects against the looming sky or teeming earth and, lest we stumble, begin to see.

But there I go, talking like a cameraman again. Sorry.

At the time of our conversation on Columbus Avenue I'd been working for ABC News for roughly five years. I'd photographed the Super Bowl and the Rangers, crime scenes and celebrity galas, floods in Iowa and fires in California, mayoral and presidential campaigns and other natural disasters. I liked the work almost as much as I'd loved my Brownie box camera as a boy, roaming the deep Maine woods. I liked the business of watching, the keen eye, the quick fine moment of reaction when the picture either works or doesn't, I liked the frame of things and the roiling images.

My wife Laura was a journalist for the airline industry. This meant that we were hardly ever home at the same time. The two of us were always flying off somewhere, Laura to cover a convention or a scandal or a merger, myself to God knows where and to God knows what purpose, at the service of some breaking story. It was the major reason we had no children. I think it was also the major reason we were so happy, at least initially. As newlyweds we had no time to doubt one another or question each other's decisions, to deal with the small personal peeves

121

and grievances that can separate two people starting off together. Time was flowing fast and our business was mostly to hang on—and to hang onto one another in the process.

And over time it deepened. There's a sheer simple joy in cooperating with another living soul under difficult circumstances that's highly underrated. For two people who are mostly apart and provided that there's love to begin with, every meeting is glue. It is a soft glue which allows for great elastic pullings apart, thin fibrous stretchings over cities and continents, space and time. But each strand is of exactly the same composition. It *wants* to come together. Its chemical goal is to return to the unity from which it sprang in the first place. And it does.

It did for us.

But in the summer of 1969 we'd been married over a year and we'd yet to have a honeymoon of any real duration. We'd snatch a long summer weekend at Sag Harbor between assignments and say, okay, this is our honeymoon or else schedule a couple of days to rent a car and drive upstate for Thanksgiving turkey dinner at some country inn and that was our honeymoon too. Our honeymoons were like bright Fall leaves in a swirling wind, hard to catch but lovely when you did.

It was August and so hot in Manhattan that most of the cabbies smelled like old salami sandwiches left out to bake in the sun. I'd just finished covering Woodstock, four hundred thousand kids intent on grabbing peace and love and drugs and music with both hands, a three-day sweet-minded nightmare of traffic, rain, mud and awful sanitation. The week before I'd been in Los Angeles covering the Tate murders. I was burnt out and exhausted. I begged a break in the great unending chain of stories and miraculously I got one—five days off. Nine when you counted the weekends.

And where was Laura? Laura was in Athens, working on

122

an article about Olympic Airlines. It turned out she was nearly finished. I hopped a plane.

We didn't stay there. Only the most weak-kneed tourists do. Athens was bombed heavily during the Second World War and then jerrybuilt thereafter. Other than Plaka—the Old Town near the Parthenon—and Lycabettus Hill across the valley, Athens is not a fine city. It's grey and homely to the eye. We spent one night with me recuperating from the flight and the first thing next morning, headed by cab for the port of Pireaus and then by ferry to Mykonos in the Cyclades.

In August inland Mykonos is sere as a desert. You half expect to see a barefoot prophet, staff in hand, walk over the next rise. You're lucky to see a green thing anywhere unless it's a tourist's crumpled pack of Salems. On the shore, though, there's always a breeze and you can be comfortable sitting in ninety degree weather all day long. Laura and I stayed by the shore, in a small eight-room hotel which overlooked the harbor.

We had a wonderful time. We spent days basking under clear skies and swimming the turquoise sea at a nude beach which could only be reached by ferry, Laura careful of the pale tender breastflesh which prior to then had never seen the sun. We spent warm breezy evenings sitting in the outdoor tavernas over wine and *mezes*, seaweed-green *dolmadakia*, grilled shrimp and calamari, fish-roe *taramasalata* and spicy *keftedes*. Nights we went back to each other's bodies laughing like street kids with a secret. Or like swimmers adrift in the Aegean, buoyed by ageless waters.

We met French tourists and English tourists and Dutch tourists and many of the locals—those who still retained the fortitude and amiability to deal with all these outsiders three months into the season. We struggled with language. There was a lot of laughing and dancing in the clubs and a lot of drinking and no headaches in the morning whatsoever for either of us.

The night before we were set to leave we had dinner at

the Sunset Bar on the side of the island opposite the harbor and watched a magnificent red ball descend into slowly darkening waters, bluegreen to purple to black. We waved to an Australian couple we knew sitting at a nearby table but didn't invite them over. We were saying goodbye to the island. The honeymoon—our first real honeymoon—was almost over. We took our time over wine and dinner and creme caramel afterwards and rich dark coffee. We took a couple glasses of Metaxa brandy after that.

I paid the bill and we got up and hand in hand roamed the island in the style to which we'd become accustomed, getting ourselves purposely, happily lost in the narrow whitewashed streets which wound uphill and down and then up again past windmills stark against the seascape and shops and small whitewashed houses with blue milkpaint shutters. Every now and then we could hear music from the clubs spill through the warm windless night, distant echos of Dionysus. Finally our hotel was near. We decided on one last brandy at a harborside taverna.

We sat at an outdoor table. And that was when I realized my pocket was empty.

That my wallet was missing.

To retrace our steps was impossible. Too much meandering down too many streets in a town designed specifically as a labyrinth to foil ancient pirates. There was only one hope of finding the damn thing and that was that I'd dropped it back at the restaurant after paying our bill. We searched the ground anyway. And now there was nothing happy about getting lost along the way. We made wrong turns, bad decisions, we had to retrace our steps. I began to feel the way those pirates must have felt, frustrated and bewildered and angry. *Those goddamn Mykonians!* Couldn't they draw a single straight line to *anywhere*?

Finally we found our way to the restaurant and hailed our waiter. He was grinning, happy to see us again. He had just enough English to understand what we were saying. His grin vanished into a grimace like a sudden squall at sea. He was instantly all business, a tall thin aproned squall himself, peering under tables, collaring every waiter, every busboy, going from table to table asking the patrons and into the kitchen to question the cooks. It took maybe all of ten minutes, that's how fast he was and when he returned to us he looked so dejected you'd have thought it was *his* wallet, not mine. Or that it was some close relative I'd lost and not a wallet at all.

We thanked him and started home. He'd refused Laura's offer of a tip. We didn't push it. He was a good man and he had pride.

I tried not to be sullen.

Losing the wallet was a major annoyance, especially in a foreign country but that was *all* it was—that was what I kept telling myself. Don't spoil five terrific days over one curdled night. I still had my passport and Laura had plenty of cash. No problem. But it hung there in the air ahead of us with each step we took, something dark and empty-feeling pressing my head down to scan and search the street in front of me.

We climbed the steps to the hotel. In the lobby Theodoro, the night man, was grinning at us from behind the desk and I remember having the small-minded thought that inappropriate grinning was perhaps a Greek trait.

"*Paracalo*," he said. *Please*. He held up his hand like a traffic cop.

He reached into the desk drawer and pulled out my wallet.

"A gentleman returns this to you," he said.

He handed it to me. License, credit cards, drachmas, U.S. money. Not a thing was missing.

I was used to New York. I was used to London or Rome or Paris. Amazing.

Of course, I thought. The address was printed on the hotel's card and the card was in the wallet. Still amazing.

"Who was he? Did he leave a name?"

I figured he deserved a reward.

125

He shook his head. "I do not know him. He ask me for an envelope and piece of paper. For you."

He handed me the envelope and I opened it. In a neat blue felt-tip scrawl the man had written *Do the same for someone else someday*.

That was all.

I remember that I did feel touched. It was such a generous thing to do, such a delightful thing to say to me. But I did not immediately feel touched by mystery.

It brushed by me all the same.

I have almost nothing left of my father. My mother and he divorced bitterly when I was only sixteen. He moved from our home in New Jersey to Florida and took up with a woman he met on the plane en route to Fort Meyers. I never visited. One night about eighteen months later he was coming home drunk from a party and wrapped his car around a tree. He lingered a few days, she died instantly. I didn't go to his funeral either though I regret that now. But at the time I was still too angry.

I have a few old photos, those few my mother didn't burn after he left and I have his ring. He left it on my night table the day he moved his things. The ring is gold with a large ruby inset, squarish and heavy. For a long time I wouldn't wear it, not even after he died. It sat in my drawer straight through college and for years thereafter. I don't know exactly what made me change my mind about the ring except that I've heard it said that we never renounce the ones we love, we replace them. And perhaps by then I'd replaced my hurt angry love for my father with a far gentler love for Laura.

But once I began I wore it every day. I took it off only to go to bed at night and to wash my hands. Putting the ring on again every morning was as much unconscious ritual as shaving or brushing my teeth.

One night in October of 1989 I was in a bar in Greenwich Village called the Lion's Head drinking with some

126

friends. I wasn't known there, my friends were. It was their local bar. Laura was out of town again. I was restless.

At some point I got up and went to the john to relieve my bladder and afterwards I washed my hands and then I continued drinking. When it became clear that one more Dewar's rocks was going to send me well over the top I quit and paid the tab and said goodnight and hailed a cab uptown. It was almost midnight.

The cab was at 10th Avenue and 57th Street before I missed the ring.

I knew what I'd done right away. I'd left it on the sink when I washed my hands.

I felt a kind of panic. Cabbies as a rule are not terribly flexible and this one must have thought I was crazy. I told him to turn around *now* and head back to the Lion's Head as fast as he could and that if he got there in less than twenty minutes he'd get twenty dollars tip. We were there in twenty-five. I gave him the twenty anyhow.

My friends were gone. In the bathroom the ring was gone too. I went to the bartender. He smiled and put my ring on the bar and turned a cocktail napkin face-up in front of me. At first I thought he was going to pour me a drink. And then I read the napkin.

Do the same for someone else someday, it read.

The hand was barely legible. The bartender didn't know the guy, said he'd never seen him before. Said he had a few beers and left. Good tipper. Average height, average build. Joe Average.

I remembered Mykonos. I entered mystery.

Mystery seethes with promise and promiscuity. Most of the creatures of the earth are born in huge numbers, an almost unimaginable promise of life each Spring, the vast majority of them only in order to die ugly and die young before they are fully formed. Billions upon billions of insect larva—maggot, grub, caterpillar, lacewing, mosquito. Their entire business is in the jaws, in the eating. That and the business of transformation. Killing cabbage leaf and cotton leaf, oak and elm, only to be hunted down by other larger creatures who've developed a taste for them as specifically as theirs for cabbage—or to be eaten alive from within by the swarming hatchlings of some parasite. A specific taste of the parasite's too. And again like the larva, also measured in the billions born and billions dying, because these same parasites are themselves very tasty to other critters. Promise and promiscuity. That's the business of living and the entire mystery is why. To what end? To perpetuate exactly what?

That and transformation. Take a stumpy furry crawling earth-bound body and turn it light as a feather, give it delicate lacy wings. Turn rending jaws to sipping proboscis.

The word *larva* means *ghost* or *mask*.

I was, I suppose, in my larval stage.

I'm past it now.

I know what I fed upon, my own personal version of the cabbage leaf. I fed upon my work, on the world I saw through the viewfinder. A limited world and in no sense a true world but my own, one I was capable of and even adept at seeing.

That and Laura.

That very first night many years ago we met awkwardly, Laura and I, over dinner with mutual friends at their East Side apartment. Neither of us knew the other was supposed to be there. It was an ambush for us both and it didn't work out one bit. My excuse leaving was *her* leaving. I was going to be a gentleman and see her to a cab and anyway, I had to work next morning. Good night, folks. And don't try this again.

Then on the street a strange thing happened. We started talking about how awful and awkward it was up there and we both started laughing—genuinely laughing for the first time that night. We made fun of our friends all the way to the corner. When the cab pulled up on an impulse I asked her if she had a good memory for numbers and she said yes, as a matter of fact she did. I rattled off my telephone number and she smiled and nodded and the cab pulled away.

It was a month before she called me. I'd almost forgotten all about her. Wasn't even certain I'd recognize her. But when she stepped into the bar and we started talking it didn't take more than an hour before I knew I'd never forget her. Not this woman. This one was a keeper. Funny and smart and once you started really looking, lovely. And we couldn't stop talking and after a while we couldn't stop touching each other either—it was like kind of horizontal gravity. Hand upon hand, hand reaching up to touch arm or shoulder and finally in the wee dazed hours of the morning in this Midtown upscale bar new to both of us and almost empty, almost closing and in full view of the bartender, hand to cheek and lips to lips, yes, Laura and I necking in front of strangers, necking gently like a pair of teenagers, like people we might view with amusement or disapproval had it not been us doing the kissing. Intoxicated and not with drink. And that was the way it stayed.

It stayed that way until last year.

It was July and hot and we were both in the city for a change.

Laura was going to make dinner, a light salad, some bread and cheese. She'd gone into the liquor store to pick out a bottle of wine. I was across the street at the Pathmark buying cigarettes. Trying to quit hadn't taken again.

Despite its reputation Manhattan isn't all that dangerous, especially not around Lincoln Center. I'm told we have the safest precinct in the City. But safety's a relative matter. Tell the one doomed goose in thirty who flies off the lake with the rest and gets blown out of the sky by some hunter that basically, he's been safe.

The gunman must have thought the store was empty. Laura was squatting in the aisle reading wine labels when he walked in and demanded money from the kid at the counter. Then she must have stood and startled him. The weapon was a thirty-eight and the range was close, no more than a dozen feet and he shot her three times, in the face, hip and chest and then ran away in panic. She would have survived the first two bullets. But the third found her heart exactly.

I heard nothing. No shots. I saw no one running away. What I did see was a group of five or six people peering in through the doorway to the liquor store. No police yet, no sirens. But it didn't *look* right. And Laura was inside. I crossed the street feeling like I was slogging through mud, my head suddenly pounding. For the first time in years I could feel my heartbeat. I elbowed through the crowd and into the store.

I won't describe this in any detail. I refuse to. There are some things not worth telling. My wife, my lover, my twenty-eight-year companion, the woman I slept with and woke with and laughed with and held in my arms was dead on the floor in a pool of blood and wine studded with bright stained shards of glass and that's all you need to know.

But at times like these you notice, you *see* the craziest things and they loom with their own unaccustomed weight. I saw not the racks and rows of bottles but the fluorescent lights overhead, columns bright as suns. I saw the spinning fan above me, like a propeller displaced from its ship and planted in the ceiling. I saw cracks in the walls like the veins in some huge wrist. I turned to look for help from whoever was at the counter but the boy had long since gone looking for a policeman, before I even arrived.

In front of me the cash register was a small grey mountain. It looked impregnable. There was a wicker basket of corkscrews and bottle openers beside it like somebody's jagged metal picnic.

And beside that a small box of pennies.

It was the box that did it, that finally made my legs go, that made the world tilt and fall.

*   *   *

Three's the charm they say.

In my Webster's II Dictionary definition number six for *charm* is *incantation of a magic word or verse.*

I have never believed in magic. Unless magic was the captured image. Life lived over and over again in patterns on a screen.

Or unless magic was Laura.

But the ring had already introduced me to mystery.

Remember my thesis? *It's from the mysterious that we make the leap to godly grace or evil.*

And only from there.

You see these penny boxes all around in New York City. In Love Cosmetics. At Tower Video. You see them everywhere. Usually all they say is *take a penny, leave a penny* but with this one someone had gotten more elaborate.

It said *take one if you need one.*

And do the same for someone else someday.

They never caught the man who killed her. The kid behind the counter's description was impressionistic. Male, mid-to-late twenties, caucasian or light Hispanic, Jets teeshirt and jeans. Medium height, medium weight, medium build.

All those mediums. All those greys.

A thief in shadow. A killer under fluorescent light.

A dangerous complexity of light and dark, brightness and shadow. Promise and promiscuity. That was what killed her. And I ask *to what end? To perpetuate exactly what?*

I sold some stocks. I gave notice at ABC. I was no longer interested in that kind of seeing. I started looking elsewhere.

The world pushes pins on a bulletin board we pass daily and on that board are scraps of paper, messages which have

131

no order or design but of which we must make order and design for better or worse.

If not we go mad.

I did my homework and found the right location for the store, a place down on the Lower East Side in Alphabet City. I closed the sale within a month. The gun permit took longer and I waited for that to come along before the opening. In the meantime I made arrangements with the liquor distributors and did some remodeling. When the permit came through I bought a thirty-eight Smith & Wesson and put it on a shelf behind the register. It's there now.

The store's been robbed four times over the past fourteen months so I got it for a song. I figure it's only a matter of time before somebody tries again. I'm not looking for the guy who shot Laura. I know the odds on that. But somebody. Please god.

Someone else someday.

I've got to give it back.

The wallet. The ring.

The penny.

Rabid Squirrels in Love

From the Journal of Kathleen McGill
Augusta, Maine
June 8th, 10:30 p.m.

He's the cutest man I ever laid eyes on unless you count the movies. That's the first thing.

The second thing is he scares me.

And I want to write this down now because I don't know which I like better to tell the truth, the good looks or the scary part. (Isn't that weird?) Mama gave me this big brown leather notebook about four years ago right after they pulled my skinny butt out of college (and thank God they did!) in hopes that I'd write down my thoughts and feelings about the drugs and Kenneth and of course, about Daddy, for Father Sylvestery or Doctor Todd. But I never did use it then. Now I feel confused, and I want to.

He's got a violent side for starters.

I saw that today.

I'm working as an aide at Augusta Mental Health. I'm a recreational therapist and he's an attendant, usually on the locked ward. I know getting a job in a mental health facility is a little strange for somebody who's had problems of her own. But I suspect he's had them too. I bet a lot us who work here have.

I guess maybe it takes one to know one, right?

It's pretty good though. I work both the locked and unlocked wards, with both men and women, all ages. I take them to the pool for swim therapy, take them out for walks or volleyball, play ping pong or bumper pool with them in the game room. When the weather's nice we go out for picnics or over to the park to feed the ducks. I'm supposed to loosen them up, basically, and encourage them to talk. Which is hard because a lot of them are mostly nonverbal to begin with and all that Haldol, Stelazine and Thorazine doesn't help any. Some of the older ones have even had lobotomies or shock therapy before the courts made them illegal. Talking to them is like talking to to a spruce tree.

I get to wear street clothes, which is nice. It's been hot this summer so most of the time I'm either in short-shorts or bikinis, even around the men, the theory being that if some of them are going to go back into society one day, back on the streets, they're for sure going to see women wearing this stuff, some with bodies a whole lot better than mine, so they might as well see them in here too, in a more controlled environment. Even though a lot of these guys were committed for something involving sex, everything from exposing themselves to little kids to rape.

I'm the youngest person in the facility, male or female.

I've never worried about that until today. Though I've seen some pretty strange stuff, believe me.

There's one man, Mr. Schap, he's about forty, and I guess he was taught that masturbation's bad or something, so he'll go into these sexual seizures that are almost like epileptic seizures and bite out big chunks of his hands so he won't start playing with his penis. You've got to restrain him or it's gruesome.

Then there's Gideon, who's old enough to be my grandfather. He mostly walks around all day in his grey suit singing "Jesse James was a man who roamed through the West" or "let's turn off the lights and go to bed" over and over again in this gravelly sing-song voice, lying down on the floor for a while, mooching a cigarette from somebody now and then, singing and walking some more. But then one day we found him standing naked in the middle of the hall, staring at a ventilator duct. He had this enormous hard-on. All it was was a ventilator duct! You got to wonder.

So strange shit happens. But today Baby Huey stuck his hand up my bikini bottom and I guess that definitely started something.

We call him Baby Huey because he looks like this big giant chicken. He's fat and pointy-faced and sort of lumbers through the halls like that character in the old cartoons. He almost never speaks. And usually he's harmless. But we were down at the pool today, sitting at the edge and just kicking at the water, splashing, Billy Osserman on one side of me and Baby Huey on the other. Billy was talking about old cars (he used to restore them before his breakdown) and it was a little hard to follow because I know nothing at all about cars, so I was paying attention to him, not Huey, until I felt Huey's fingers groping for my pubic hair.

I slapped his hand away and laughed and gave him a look like, what do you think *you're* doing? And he said, I want to fuck you. So I said, well, you can't, keep your hands to yourself. He looked at me real hard and said, *then I want to kill you, bitch*.

Well you can't do that either I said, and got up and walked away. I kind of made a joke of it. But I have to admit, he shook me a little.

Then this evening we were in the dayroom with a bunch of the patients, Baby Huey included, watching *Gilligan's*

Island on television. I was talking to Gloria in the nurse's station, which is this big enclosed cubicle with non-breakable floor-to-ceiling windows on three sides facing a wall in back and two doors you can lock if you need to. You always lock them when you leave because that's where we keep the medications. But other than that, in six whole months we'd never bothered.

Stephen (that's this guy, the attendant I was talking about, the cute one) was out there sweeping the floor when Baby Huey stood up and heaved his metal folding chair directly at my head. Threw it *hard*. It bounced off the window but I damn near had a heart attack anyhow. And then all of a sudden he's running for the door. With me and Gloria inside still too freaked to get our asses in gear to go over and lock it.

Hey! Stephen shouts but Huey doesn't stop, so Stephen reaches out with the broom and whacks him on the side of the head. Huey falls down all right but sort of slides on his big fat belly with the momentum and by the time I get to the door to lock it he's slid halfway through, so now I can't lock it, and he's reaching for my legs, spitting and growling like he really *does* want to kill me. And the next thing I know Stephen's on top of him, with one hand on his forehead pulling his head up and the other on his windpipe, choking him.

Huey goes all red in the face, gasping for air but not getting any and we see him sort of start to go blue so Gloria and I are both shouting at Stephen to stop! stop it! you're killing him!

And then the weirdest thing happened. Scary and sexy, both at the same time.

Stephen looked up at me and grinned and winked and said, "present for you, Kath," gave Huey's throat one more little squeeze like you'd squeeze a lemon and dropped him passed out cold to the floor.

I didn't even know he knew my name.

We talked over coffee after that (I made Gloria promise

136

not to say anything, because you could get fired for using that kind of force on a patient!) and I told Stephen about what happened by the pool. He said a guy like that ought to be castrated, not incarcerated, and I wasn't sure if he was kidding or not even though when he said it he was smiling.

I asked him where he learned to do that thing with the windpipe and he said from his father. I sure didn't want to talk about fathers because I never could do anything right by mine God knows, so I let that matter drop. Then our break was over and we had to go back to work. But just before we did he asked if he could see me sometime.

I said yes. He said when, and we settled on Saturday night.

And now I'm honestly not sure that was smart. He's too damned attractive, you know? Just like Kenneth was, though in fact in the looks department, Stephen has Kenneth beat by a mile. Which probably only makes it worse. Because look what I got living that year with Kenneth. A crystal meth habit that nearly killed me, rotten grades in school and three long years in therapy.

But besides that, there's this violent thing. Kenneth was hardly ever real violent despite the biker stuff, mostly just screwed up. But I watched Stephen with Huey and I know he enjoyed it, what he was doing, choking him. I'm sure he did. I could see it in his eyes, in that big wide sexy grin.

I'm not real religious or anything God knows but I wonder if enjoying himself that way isn't some sort of sin.

I just hope I know what I'm getting myself into.

I should probably call it off.

But probably I won't.

Kathleen read the entry thinking, well, I wanted to remember how I got involved in this. And now I do.

It doesn't help. It was seventeen years ago and it doesn't stop the moaning sounds, the muffled screams. It doesn't mean a thing.

She remembered how he used to let his long hair down out of the ponytail after work hours back then, shaking it free. Weekends he would never shave. He wore sandals and bellbottoms and lovebeads and an ankh around his neck, the Egyptian symbol for life. They read *Siddartha* and Kahlil Gilbran.

Now he was clean-cut. He said that people didn't want some shaggy carpenter in their homes unless it was maybe Jesus Christ, and probably not even him.

But he was so handsome in those days that she sometimes wondered what he saw in her. He could have had anybody. She had never been anything but just short of pretty. Though her figure was good especially her breasts and she had nice soft curly red-brown hair.

She closed the journal and left it lying on the bed and went to the kitchen for a cup of coffee. She poured it and put the mug in the microwave and turned it on. The sounds were louder here. She could hear them over the microwave's hum. He's got to soundproof the place a whole lot better if he's going to keep this up, she thought.

It's driving me crazy.

God. What am I doing here?

She took the coffee out of the microwave and opened the kitchen door that led down to the basement.

The sounds were louder still.

Well, better the kid than me, she thought. At least we got past that part. You want to keep that in mind when you think about complaining, about the noise or about anything having to do with him. Take a look at the drawerful of polaroids if you need to be reminded. It could be you down there again. Doing whatever he wanted you to do, just because you loved him.

Why do you love him, anyway?

She had no answer that immediately came to mind though he could be very attentive and kind sometimes, come home with little gifts for her, a pair of earrings, flowers. But it was more that they were just fated to be together, and that was that. She couldn't imagine life without him. She loved him because she did.

Despite his little habits.

She wondered what was going on. The boy was hardly ever this loud. Not any more. Usually the boy was passive, almost one step up from catatonic, and she knew one when she saw one. She still saw her share of catatonics these days even if he was free of all that now. It had turned out he was handy, could build things. Like Jesus. A carpenter.

He wouldn't mind if she went downstairs for a look. He never did.

With him nothing was private.

She stepped out onto the landing, sipped carefully at the steaming coffee and let it warm her hands as she started down.

It was cool these days for September and even colder in the basement by at least about ten degrees. She felt goose-flesh on her arms and legs and felt her nipples stiffen beneath the loose white extra-large Superbowl teeshirt as she hit the concrete floor. Stephen always seemed to think that her nipples stiffening down here in the basement was some form of erotic anticipation on her part but in reality it was just the cold. Though she would never tell him that. Let him think what he wanted to think.

She saw dust-bunnies amid the paint cans and empty flowerpots beneath the wooden stairwell. She'd have to clean up a bit down here. She smelled bleach and laundry detergent in the humid musty air along with some other smell she couldn't quite place. None were smells she liked. Maybe at some point she'd get the boy to start doing the laundry for her so she wouldn't have to bother. She'd mention it to Stephen.

What was the point of having a slave, for chrissake, if he never did any work?

She opened the door to what Stephen called his Den of Impunity and despite what she'd seen over the past two weeks and despite what she'd been through herself for years and years before that she damn near dropped her coffee.

He had the boy manacled to the X-frame he'd made for him again—naked, gagged and blindfolded. Nothing new there. But Stephen was playing with electricity this time. That *was* new. There was a patch of black electrician's tape over each of the boy's nipples and at each of his inner thighs. The patch on his left thigh seemed to have come undone. She could see wet burst-open blisters there. Wires ran from beneath the tape to the circuit breaker which in turn plugged into the wall socket. She smelled burnt flesh and burnt hair. That was the other stinky stuff along with the bleach and detergent.

He'd been sitting in a director's chair by the wall switch so he could turn it on and off at will but now the chair was pushed back to one side and he stood in front of the boy, pounding at his heart, tearing at the gag, breathing into his parted lips.

"Fuck," he kept saying. "Fuckfuckfuckfuck*fuck*. You're a fucking *kid* for godsakes, you're supposed to be strong. Strong, you get it? You fucking better not die on me!"

She saw he was scared and something inside her was glad he was scared, some voice inside her said it was damn well time. But she was freaking too.

Accessory to murder.

Oh, God, she thought. Don't let him die. Please God please. Don't let us get caught doing this thing. *I* didn't do it. *I* didn't kidnap him. It's not my fault. I didn't do *anything* except just go along with it. I don't want to go to jail, I couldn't *stand* to go to jail. Living this way has been a lot like jail sometimes but I couldn't handle the real thing god, no way.

He was working at the ropes now, had the left arm untied so that the boy's body lolled to the right and he was working to free his left leg. He seemed only now to notice Kath was even in the room.

"Help me get him down! Get your ass *over* here goddammit!" His voice like a smack across the face. She moved.

Her fingers tore at the rope around the boy's wrists but struggle and sweat had tightened them so that she wondered how long he'd been at this, the knots wouldn't give beneath her fingers and she heard herself saying *oh, oh, oh,* as she breathed like she was listening to another person separate from herself while a nail on her index finger cracked and broke and the cool slimy texture of the boy's cheek brushed her own and then she had his wrist free, the chill wet naked flesh and soaked matted shoulder-length hair brushing across her own bare arms, across her face and neck as she slid her arms under and through the boy's armpits first to support him and then to lay him down across the concrete, face turned toward her and bruised mouth open and *so young*, she suddenly thought, not knowing if she meant the boy or herself or what.

She felt for a pulse. Listened for a heartbeat.

Oh god, she thought. *Whatever you want me to do, I swear I'll do it.* Yours forever I swear.

Just get us out of this.

Please. Just this once.

Just this once please please please let me please get lucky.

They walked and walked, eight of them, silent, watching.

The pair of uniformed policemen seemed largely oblivious, talking quietly, now and then making a joke and smiling.

It was cold. Her nose was running. Across from her she could see that Stephen's was too. Her mittens stuck to the wood. She stamped her feet to get the circulation going. Inside the boots her toes felt raw and brittle and achy.

Enough of this, she thought. Enough of this bullshit.

She was betting Stephen felt the same. She hoped so. She watched him move roughly in step with the others. Runny nose or not she thought he was still the most handsome man she'd ever met.

And they all of them must have seen her nearly at once right then because the circle slowed and the signs all went out in her direction, Kath's too, fulfilling her promise, pointed toward this thin small teenage black girl in the ratty Augusta High School jacket walking toward them with her head down and shoulders hunched, walking purposefully toward the door where the two policemen waited, her dark eyes cast down so as not to read the signs which said PRO CHOICE IS NO CHOICE and ABORTION IS LEGALIZED GENOCIDE and HE'S A CHILD, NOT A CHOICE—*that is if she could fucking well read at all*, Kath thought, any better than the dumb cracker in the cellar—and she smiled as Stephen held out the tiny pink plastic twelve-week fetus cupped tenderly in his hand.

Sundays

Someone once said to me that if you want to make God laugh, just tell him your plans. Just tell him who you are.

I lie beside her watching her sleep in the light from the street, watching her face and her breasts rise and fall and think how she and I are not one person but so many, both of us and all of us for that matter each uncertainly housed in a single wrap of flesh, and memory intrudes like thick smoke from a woodfire and surrounds us in our bed.

My father Bradford Collier was a squirrel hunter and a good one. I remember him sitting rocking in the shade of our porch his Sunday afternoons off with his old .22 cradled in his lap and watching the stand of four grouped tall black oak trees far across the field which the squirrels would naturally favor for their rich crop of acorns and we inside would hear the short flat bark of the rifle maybe half a dozen times over an hour and then his boots moving slowly down the wooden steps. There'd be silence and then we'd hear the boots again and Anne and Mary Jo and I would rush out from the kitchen to find him working on the five or six he'd shot, pinching the loose skin of the back to slit with his knife and inserting his fingers to tear and peel it away like a too-tight glove, cutting off head and tail and feet and slicing the belly open to flip out the tiny entrails.

Should he decide a hike was the order of the day there was another stand of six hundred-year-old oaks down by the brook about half a mile away. He'd disappear down there for a while.

They were clean kills nearly every time though like any other hunter he'd had to slit a throat or two. But what my father shot normally didn't suffer much. And my mother's stews were fine.

My father considered squirrels vermin, though. Pests. Even if they did make for good eating. So that it was a surprise to all of us when in the summer of 1957 when I was just turned eleven and my sisters Anne and Mary Jo were twelve and ten my father returned from the stand of oaks with five dead eastern greys in one hand and in the other, one that was very much alive, held by the scruff of the neck and trying hard against all hope to bite him.

"Must've fallen out of a tree," he said. "And fallen long and hard. See? Front paw's broken. Danny, you get on into the kitchen and ask your mother for some string and good thick twine. Girls, get a couple of those popsicles you been suckin' on all summer long out of the freezer. Eat 'em fast or run 'em under the water, I don't care which."

He lay the five dead greys out on the porch and we did as we were told. My mother came out to join us and take hold of the squirrel by the scruff of the neck and the base of the tail while we watched my father cut and loop the twine around his jaws and snout in an expert bowline knot so he could bite no longer and once that was done had her turn him over on his side. He used his hunting knife on the popsicle sticks stained pink and orange and cut a length of string. The squirrel chattered and scrabbled at the wood but could gain no purchase.

144

"Hold him tight now, Marge. This will hurt."

But seeing those two big gloved hands coming toward him much have frightened the squirrel to such degree that he stopped resisting entirely and simply rolled his eyes. Even when my father took his delicate paw and forearm and gave them a sharp jerk apart he just jumped once and then lay still and panting. My father splinted the leg with the popsicle sticks and wrapped it tight with string.

"Take that twine and make me another bowline, Danny. We'll collar him and tie him off to this post here and see what happens. If he doesn't go into shock on us he might be fine in a week or so."

"Shock?"

"From pain. Or what we just did to him. Either one could kill him."

And once we had him sitting up dazed and baffled and leashed to the support stud with his makeshift muzzle removed my father did an astonishing thing. *He took a glove off and ran his hand across the squirrel's back.* Just once. *Bradford Collier* did that. A man who never had use for animals in his life unless they were working animals, a cat who was a good mouser or a guard-dog maybe, and who considered the greys nothing more than fat rats with furry tails. Who happened to taste good and were cheap at twice the price.

"Husk some walnuts, kids. Put 'em nearby and then leave him alone awhile. That's one scared animal."

In time my father actually allowed us to name him. It took some spirited wrangling between the three of us but we did. We named him Charlie after Steinbeck's *Travels with Charlie*. My older sister Anne's idea. I thought it was dumb to name a squirrel after a dog but Mary Jo sided with her and that was that.

Charlie took to the easy life right away. A bowl of water on the porch in front of him and all the acorns and walnuts he could eat. He never again tried to bite. In a couple of weeks my father determined he'd healed and removed the

145

splint and though he ever after favored the leg he got around well enough and was quick enough so that once we let him off his leash you had to be careful opening the screen door or the next thing you knew he'd be inside, barking and chattering at the furniture and climbing it too.

There was nothing he couldn't get into. No cabinet or drawer was safe. But he never made much mess except somehow to *displace* things. A fork in my father's socks-drawer, my old cat's-eye marbles mixed in with the spoons. So after awhile we tolerated him inside and got used to his invasions. My mother bought mason jars to protect the beans, rice and macaroni. My father, who was as good with woodworking as he was with the wrench down at his garage, even went so far as to cut him a small hinged trap at the base of the door to the porch so Charlie could come and go as he pleased.

He never once went back to the stand of oaks across the field. Not that we knew of. In fact we observed that he wasn't much for trees in general anymore. He seemed to prefer to stay in or around the house, under the porch or in the tall fieldgrass and the low scrub beyond. Maybe it was remembering that fall, that height, that sudden break. He'd climb the bookshelves or the bedposts or the banister up to our rooms handily enough—my mother was forever polishing the tiny scratch-marks he left behind with wood-stain. She didn't seem to mind. She said Charlie was just antiquing her furniture. But the trees he mostly left alone.

He climbed us too.

He seemed to know not to go for a bare leg or arm but if you were wearing pants or jeans or especially a jacket—he liked to rummage through deep open pockets—he'd be up and over you and riding your shoulder in a matter of seconds. You could walk around with him that way and he'd just hold on perfectly balanced like some strange furry added appendage.

Only my father wouldn't tolerate it. Like the rest of us he'd feed Charlie a walnut now and then but *that* far he refused to go. He was almost as fast with his hands as Charlie was on his feet and would pluck him off like an annoying bug and drop him soundly to the floor. Charlie was persistant, though. It was almost as though my father were the one he *really wanted* to climb and the rest of us were just amusement. Walking monkey-bars. Finally it got through to him that he just wasn't wanted but I'd still catch him watching my father sometimes, that nervous sidelong glance, chittering, nose twitching, and was never quite sure that someday, sometime, damned if he wasn't going to try again.

My father still continued to hunt. Twice a month, maybe. Across the field or down by the shady brook.

And I sometimes wondered what Charlie thought if he thought anything at all of the scent of squirrel-meat steaming in our stewpot. I look back on it now and how we could actually eat the stuff with him running around underfoot is something I'll never understand. But we did.

As I say, we're not one thing, we're many. We're capable of all kinds of balancing acts in our heads. Until something or someone tips the balance.

The way my wife beside me's tipping it now.

That winter was a cold one in northern Jersey and the snow fell thick into five-and-six-foot drifts against the house and mostly Charlie stayed indoors. He liked the mantle over the fireplace which I always thought unnatural since wild animals are supposed to be afraid of fire or even the scent of fire but for Charlie the hotter the fire in the grate the better. He'd fall asleep up there basking in the updrafts.

Come spring and he was using the trapdoor again and using it a lot, his comings and goings according to some design unknowable to us but clearly urgent to him. He'd either be flying through the trap constantly back and forth or else he'd disappear for hours at a time. We suspected sex of course, though only Anne and Mary Jo and I would talk about it and only in private. Parents weren't comfortable talking with kids about sex back then.

"I wonder how squirrels do it," said Mary Jo.

"With their penises, silly," said Anne. "Just like everybody else."

"Charlie's gettin' some!" I laughed. They ignored me.

"Anybody ever see Charlie's penis?" asked Mary Jo.

"Not me."

"Ugh," said Anne. "Spare me!"

I rarely went along with my father on his Sunday excursions down to the brook and never once in memory shot from the porch at all. At an age when most boys would shoot at most anything that moved with rifle, bow or slingshot I had no taste for bloodsports.

One afternoon in May he asked as he often did though and this time I accepted. I think I was angry with Anne for some reason and felt the need to get out of the house that day. Anne could be bossy or else she and Mary Jo would side together against me in an argument and that could make me furious. Whatever the reason, I went.

My father and I never talked much and didn't that day either. I followed him through the tall fieldgrass into the woods and found his well-beaten trail down to the brook, both our .22s held at port arms. I had no intention of using mine. It was there because my father wanted it to be. I was a miserable shot and my father knew it but it was a formal thing with him. You didn't go hunting unarmed. It simply wasn't done.

His habit was to walk first to the brook and then approach the stand of oaks from there, the fast-running water masking whatever sounds we might make along the dirt embankment. It had rained the day before, the brook swollen with water the color of coffee with a dash of cream. I could never have found the exact spot to cut up to the trees from there amid the tangled foliage had I been alone but my father had no problem and I saw that he'd worn a path of sorts there too barely noticeable amid the scrub. I could see the six tall trees about forty yards away up a gentle slope.

We walked twenty of those yards and stopped at the edge of the clearing and knelt each of us on one knee and my father started firing, small sharp cracks in that wide open space that could have been branches breaking and the first squirrel slammed against the tree-trunk twenty feet up as though a hand had pushed it and then fell and my father worked the bolt and chambered another round and fired as another raced across the high branches of the same tree and tumbled bouncing from limb to limb. By then squirrels were racing barking across the ground and pouring down off the trees but my father took his time and squeezed off two more rounds. I saw one big grey somersault across the ground and another skitter and roll just as it reached the bushes. He missed with the fifth round but the sixth caught another where the bole met the root system of a second tree and flipped it on its back, the .22 round going through the squirrel entirely and chipping at the green wood behind him.

"Five's enough," my father said.

It had taken just moments.

We stood and he took the canvas sack off his belt and we went to harvest them.

"Good shooting."

"Thanks."

"Five out of six and they were really *moving*!"

"They were, weren't they."

I wasn't nearly as excited as I was trying to sound but something told me my father expected it. The greys were still barking angrily at us yards away in the safety of heavy scrub. My father moved slowly and methodically, prodding them with a stick to make sure they were fully dead and wouldn't bite and then picking them up by the scruff of the neck with one gloved hand and shoving them into the sack.

"Uh-oh. Damn."

"What?"

We had four of them in the sack and were walking toward the scrub. My father suddenly picked up his pace considerably, the closest I ever saw him come to running.

"The one I shot at the edge here. I think he's gone."

We got to where the grey ought to have been and wasn't.

"Maybe you missed him."

"I didn't miss him. Look here."

He was looking at a cluster of ferns. I could see blood speckling the leaves, glistening in the sun. Behind them the scrub was all thick briers. The day was hot. Neither of us was wearing much. A short-sleeve shirt for my father, a teeshirt for me.

"We've got to find him. You can't leave an animal like that. Come on. He couldn't have gotten far."

We plunged carefully into the scrub, my father plucking the stems away and holding them back for me with his gloved fingers while I did my best to keep them at a distance with the barrel and stock of my rifle.

The briers were thickest down low so we couldn't try to follow a blood trail. We'd have cut ourselves to shreds trying. We might have had more luck splitting up but he knew I needed him to hold back the briers for me. We searched for well over an hour. By the time my father gave it up my skin felt like it was crawling with small biting insects and my arms and face were streaked with sweat and blood. I washed them in the brook and we headed home.

My mother and sisters had gone to town shopping so the car was gone and the yard was empty. We crossed the field of waving grass in silence. I remember glancing at my father and that his face was grim. He hated losing that squirrel.

I don't know how it was that I should be the one who saw it first because only a year or so later I'd be wearing glasses and my father's vision was 20-20 and we were walking side by side. We were about eight feet from the porch. I remember thinking he *should* have been the one and not me. I don't know why I felt that way but I still do. That somehow it wasn't right.

I think I came close to falling then. I know I staggered, that it felt like somebody had pushed me suddenly hard in the chest and that was what had forced the gasp out of me like a silent call for help, my *body* calling for help where there was none.

"What?" my father said and then looked where I was looking at the blood-trail leading up the three porch steps to the landing, smeared across the landing as with a single long stroke of a half-dry paint-brush all the way to Charlie's trap door, a direct and determined line to that door he'd painted with the very life of him.

I knew what we'd find in there, that it was impossible for him to have come this far bleeding this much and still be alive and when my father flung open the door and we saw him on the rug, lying on his side and shot in the very same shattered shoulder that once had housed a broken leg, I saw that I was right, though we'd missed him by a matter of minutes only. His body was still warm. I touched him and looked into his glazed open eyes and tried hard not to cry. We knelt there.

"He came home looking for us," my father said quietly.

I don't know why I said what I did. It wasn't anger or accusation and it wasn't just sadness either but it came out of me like a fleeing bird and it was true.

"He came home looking for *you*, dad." I said. "Not us. You."

I'll never forget the look on my father's face that day.

I remember it better than the look on any face I've ever seen before or since except maybe this one here on the pillow in front of me, sleeping now but only hours ago curled in on itself and nearly unrecognizable in anger and hurt which is the face I'll remember when she leaves tomorrow, not this familiar face but that one. She told me early on even before we were married that the one thing

151

she couldn't handle was if I were unfaithful because that's what her father was and that was what I was and what I was again and since she knows it now she *will* leave. She's as good as her word.

My father never hunted again. The rifle went into the basement to rust away. Something in him changed after Charlie. He went out with my mother more on Sundays for one thing. We were old enough to fend for ourselves by then. And then later he began to drink more.

And later still, once we were in college, stopped drinking. And when he was old and sick became a bitter man.

We're many things, all of us, blown by so many unexpected winds.

And I have to wonder, who am I now and what will I be tomorrow?

What have I done?

And what will I do with my own Sundays once she's gone?

For Anush and Misty

Twins

For June and me since our earliest rememberings and except for our years in New York City the world's always been a hostile place.

So this is nothing new, really.

We were born fraternal twins at three minutes past midnight and ten past midnight respectively on October 31, 1956 in the first windy minutes of Halloween. Mischief Night as it was called then. While we two were screaming our first tiny outrage at being thrust out of someplace wholly warm and secure—that single place on earth I believe in which there's never any need or any good reason to scream—much older kids were out soaping windows or letting air out of tires or setting fire to brown paper sacks full of dogshit on their neighbors' porches.

There's a Scots belief that when a woman bares a boy-child and girl-child together she'll never have another. Our mother never did.

But that was okay with both our parents. My mother Hanna didn't care much for sex in the first place. She had

us and that was all she wanted. Sex was kids. Period. The
act itself was ugly, slippery and revolting. Hanna's feeling
was that enough was enough. And now that my father Willie had satisfied her in the only way she was capable of
being satisfied he was happy too. He could fuck around all
he wanted on the side. He had a sporting-goods store right
down by the lake. A prime location both for business and
for poaching because there were more and more tourists
coming in every year and all those ladies in sundresses
needed all that good advice on bait and rod and tackle.

I suspect my father died happy.

That summer we were six years old. For some reason
unknown to us Hanna decided to visit my father at the
shop around lunch-time and brought along June and me
and I remember seeing a big ruddy-faced man in a cowboy
hat standing at the counter with Pete Miller the hired help,
the big man sighting down an over-and-under shotgun
while Pete placed upon the counter a yellow box of shells,
Pete looking worried at my mother as we passed through
the store and saying something to her and she just waving
back at him and marching us down the aisle to the back
storage room where my father would be taking his lunch.
Which he sort of was.

She was a long lean brunette with the biggest breasts I've
seen in all the years since and my father Willie had one of
them in his mouth, or a part of one, his face buried in her
flesh and her legs wrapped around his butt which was naked and slamming her back against the wall with the *Play-
boy* calendar hung from it and the drapes pulled to and my
mother and June and I just stopped and stood there looking, June and I thinking it was funny, smiling, because
there was my father naked with this strange naked woman
doing *something* to one another, the two of us starting to
giggle and I don't know what my mother would have done
if she'd had the time but whatever it might have been she
didn't because the big man in the cowboy hat pushed past

154

her striding into the room, little Pete behind him pulling on his arm and the big man just shrugging him off and raising the shotgun and I remember my father turning at the sudden commotion and the scared open-mouthed look the brunette was wearing like she'd seen a view of the world that was intolerable just before the man screamed *son-of-a-BITCH* and fired. One barrel was all it took at that range and both their heads were blood and bone and scrap against the wall.

The man later said that he wished he'd aimed slightly to the left.

She was a whore but he'd known worse.

My mother took over the store and kept it running well enough to put us both through college but she was never the same after that.

Neither were we.

We'd always been special, June and I. Somehow we were aware of that from the beginning. Like old married people we'd finish each other's sentences. Even before we were old enough to fully *form* decent sentences. We'd be out playing in the woods by the lake. *Henry*, she'd say, *I wanna . . .*

. . . go pee, I'd say. Me *first*, I'd say and we would.

There's another belief that twins possess such uncommon bonds of sympathy that each will know immediately when danger or misfortune threatens the other even when separated over long distances. Likewise that any particularly special state of happiness or wellbeing in the one will be reflected in the other. Until college we were separated for hardly moments but both beliefs were certainly true of us as kids. My mother said that as infants we would quit squalling and fall asleep in our cribs at exactly the same moment, then wake together mornings and begin wailing for the breast as though our internal clocks were precisely one. We learned to walk the same day. June's first word was *mama* and mine was *papa* but they came out of our mouths within fifteen minutes of one another one Sunday afternoon while we were playing on the living room floor, my father in front of the TV set and my mother ironing and my mother's somewhat sexist explanation for why the words were not the very *same* word was that it was natural each gender should gravitate toward its own and her reasoning on the order of the words was that like a good boy I was just being polite.

Until the hour my father was shot naked in the back room we had little curiosity about our bodies. We bathed together of course and knew full well we weren't made the same. It wasn't a problem for us. In most other ways we felt *exactly* the same.

We've discussed it over the years.

We've come to the conclusion that it was as though we lived in two worlds at once back then. There was the world of June and Henry along with everybody and everything else. Then there was the world of June and Henry. The first world was by turns fun and new and confusing and it needed to be learned. The second was known from the start.

Before my father died our bodies belonged to the second world. Known and completely accepted. But each of us had seen something else that afternoon beyond the sudden splash of blood and death that lingered. Something *linked* to the dying but not directly of it.

Because when my father was shot he was still inside her.

We saw that clearly as he turned at the noise behind him from where we stood to one side in the doorway. The thick pole of his cock half in and half out of her and how that was possible we had no idea but when he fell our attention was still there, on his cock and not on the gore spewed across the wall and ceiling, on his swollen glistening flesh dwindling and falling to his thigh like a flower parched and dying.

Only then did we even seem to *hear* Hanna screaming beside us or truly see the ruin wreaked upon the bodies or become aware of the big man shouldering Pete aside and heading for the front door.

It was only when the flower died.

And after that, alone in the woods down by the lake or at home in the bath or the bedroom, we were pretty curious indeed.

A few times Hanna caught us. And that was a problem bigger than it might have been because once the fact that my father had gone to his Maker with his pants down got to be common knowledge around town my mother developed a sudden Baptist streak which went not only to churchgoing but to pamphleteering and preaching to anybody who'd bother to listen. It also went to severe punishments for little boys and little girls who *said* they were just playing doctor while the Lord knew and *she* knew that what they were really doing was carnal and sinful and damned.

We were locked in closets—separate ones—for hours at a time. We were spanked, pinched and knuckle-jabbed where it wouldn't show, denied dinner or breakfast or lunch or sometimes all three of them together. There was a braided knotted rope left hanging on the door to the attic at all times to remind us of those other times when she'd used it. We were raved at, sermonized, forced to pray. We *would* be taught a lesson.

We never did learn.

We wanted to see the flower rise. The only problem was the *when* and *how*. We knew it would eventually.

We wanted to see just what would go inside her and how far.

I remember her first orgasm as well as I do my own. I think I might've even shared it in a way. It was the summer of 1967 and we were eleven. The Summer of Flowers was what the hippies were calling it. The day was sunny and we were down by the lake, a fairly secluded spot you could only reach by boat since the woods were still thick for acres behind it. The owner believed in rabbit and deer hunting, not real estate and was considered a goddamn lunatic by most everyone else in town as a result.

We'd go skinny-dipping. Almost always we were the only ones around.

That day as we lay naked in the sun on an old beat-up checkered quilt I had two fingers inside her and she was wet and slippery of her own accord which was new over the past year and fascinating to us and she showed me how to guide the fingers on the outside too, in and out and up with what must for her have been a final understanding, a final access to expertise in her own nature. When she began to shake I withdrew, frightened that I was hurting her but she said *no no no* and pressed my fingers back to her and shut her eyes and worked the fingers as though they were her own.

She arched her back and moaned and I could feel her shudder all the way up my arm and began to shake myself as though some sudden breath of December had moved across the lake.

She fell back laughing, trying to catch her breath and then I was laughing too.

"My god," she said. "What *was* that? I want to *die* like that, Hank! God I do. And Mama thinks there's something *wrong* with this? Hanna's crazy!"

We laughed some more and she reached up to tickle me, she was apt to do that all of a sudden and I squirmed over on top of her and tickled her back and we rolled around that way off the quilt and on again. We lay down exhausted.

"Put your fingers back in me," she said. "Leave your hand there. I want us to fall asleep that way. Okay?"

"Okay."

It was nearly noon and the blue sky unbroken by any cloud anywhere and we slept in no time at all.

We woke to somebody saying *shit*, look *at that*! and laughing and somebody else saying *Jesus, that's Hank and June*! and we saw Danny Beach and Phil Auton heading toward shore in Danny's old rowboat, two kids in our class at school for godsakes, both of them laughing and yelling our names now that we were awake and sitting up staring at them, June with one hand between her legs to that spot mine had just deserted and the forearm of her other arm across the wide pale nipples and her breasts only just beginning to show.

Perverts! Fuckin' queers! they drifted toward us shouting, the last of which of course made no sense at all. I scrambled into my jeans and tossed June hers along with her tee shirt and she stood with her back to them while they yelled *nice ass, Juney! turn around, babe!* and pulled them on. We slipped on our U.S. Keds and I grabbed my shirt and the blanket and we ran off into the woods. It was the only thing we could think to do. Just to get away from them there.

We were shaken. Now everybody'd know. We walked along the deer-paths, June in the lead, going nowhere in particular, just moving deeper into the woods. After a while she turned.

"D'you think they'd sink the rowboat on us?"

"Wouldn't dare," I said.

"Do you think they saw where your hand was?"

"I dunno."

But I did know. I'd seen Danny Beach staring directly at it. Staring between her wide-open legs. And it was as though she read my thoughts again, was completing yet another of my sentences.

"But you're pretty sure they did, huh."

"Yeah. I guess. Pretty sure."

"Okay. Then we're screwed," she said.

We walked a while in silence.

"I don't care," she said finally. "Let them tell their parents. Let them tell the whole goddamn school, the whole goddamn town. What we did was nice. And we're doing it again, aren't we."

She looked back at me for an answer and I had to laugh and shake my head, it was so much June.

"Sure we are," I said.

*   *   *

My own first orgasm was inside her. The following summer.

We were twelve.

Hanna was in church where lately we had refused to go
and we were big enough by then and Hanna sufficiently
small beside us so that rage hell and damnation though she
might she had no choice but to accept our decision. Besides, she now knew what the whole town knew. I suspect
she was secretly glad we stayed away.

We were on my bed. We had made the flower grow.

I slipped into her as easily as a finger into a jar of jam
and just as sweetly and began to spasm within only a few
thrusts, June bucking up to meet me. It seemed I'd never
stop coming—for a terrifying moment I thought I was
hemorrhaging, pumping out blood inside her—these
rythmic pulses so blinding and electric and soon she was
rising from a pool of me.

We lay side by side in each other's arms, not caring a
damn about the glistening sheets beside us. Each of us
smiling, the curtain behind us fluttering in the cut-grass-
smelling summer breeze.

"If Willie'd been that fast," she whispered, "*he might be
alive today.*"

"You *bitch*!" I grabbed her and started to tickle. "You just
goddamn *wait* 'till next time!"

Then we both looked at one another and howled
"WHEN!"

In September of our junior year in high school they tried
to get her.

I was working the counter nights at Silverman's Drugstore and Soda Shop and it was nearly closing time and
June always came by to walk me home. Her habit was to
stop in at 9:45, just enough time to have a chocolate egg
cream with me before I locked up and not enough time so
that it was likely she'd run into classmates.

We had friends among them but not many. Other outcasts like us. We used to call them the Halt, the Lame and the Blind. Actually they were more like the Exceptionally Gifted or Bright, the Ill-Favored and the Meek. But outcasts all the same. June and I were exceptions, being none of these exactly—I having grown up fairly good looking in a dark-eyed, hooded way and June having captured full womanly beauty at the ripe old age of seventeen. We were smart enough but not brilliant. And neither of us was meek.

On this cool September evening she was late. Only five minutes late but that was enough to make me close down early at some vague undeterminate urging and as I turned off the lights and locked the doors my pulse was racing. I could hardly breathe. Our house was just five blocks away, two down Main and three along West Cedar which was one of the perks of working at Silverman's in the first place. You would walk there. But this night I took it at a run and I found them in a little stretch of wooded area a block short of our house. I saw them only as moving shapes in the moonlight through the scrub and birch and bramble but I saw them from the street as though I knew exactly where they'd be.

Danny Beach was one of them and the other three were seniors and we knew them well. She'd not gone easy. When I got close enough I saw that one of the seniors had a long thin bleeding gash along his cheekbone and the other was bleeding from the head from what must have been a rock and that was the one who had his pants down kneeling in front of her while Danny held her arms and the other two her legs. So it was that one I went for, the one with the head-wound, kneeling.

I don't know where the rotten log came from but it was big enough in my hands and I took him exactly where the rock-wound glistened in the moonlight, rotten bark flying and when he went down Danny got scared and let go of her arms which was a mistake so that by the time I cracked the ribs of the biggest of them, the one whose face she'd scratched, the other was off and running and June had Danny in a headlock and was pummelling his face in fury. I let her hit him a while and then said *hey, sis, don't kill him for godsakes*, though it was certainly possible I'd concussed the other guy into oblivion. He sure didn't move.

But my voice seemed to calm her somehow. She let Danny off with a bloody nose and lip and he and the guy with the cracked ribs hobbled off through the woods yelling that that they were going to fuck us up, *you hear that? you fucking perverts are gonna get yours!* but by then the guy on the ground was stirring so just we picked June's panties and purse up off the wet leaves and left him there and walked away. The panties were torn. She stuffed them in her purse.

"They hurt you?"

"Bruises. Bastards."

"You want to tell somebody about this? The police?"

"Jesus, no. That's all we need. I don't think they'll try it again, do you?"

"No. I doubt it"

"Then let's just leave it. Want to have that egg cream now?"

"Good idea."

The night the dead began to rise we'd been living in New York City for eighteen years. Neither of us was particularly well-equipped to deal with Manhattan at first, armed with nothing more than B.A.s in English against an already Masters-in-Finance world. I worked as a reader and then as an agent in a literary agency while June tried her hand at acting under her new name, Celia Night. Over the years she'd done a few print ads, a non-union commercial, a lot of off-off-Broadway, a few seasons of summer stock and a walk-on in *One Life to Live*. Like most actors in New York she got by waiting tables. She kept her eyes open though and she wasn't stupid. When I went out on my own as an agent and started to make some good money we went in with a friend and bought a restaurant, stole an excellent texmex chef from a rival and kept the price down on the tequila. We did fine.

We were happy. We lived together as husband and wife. Boyfriend and girlfriend. Significant Others. Whatever you wanted to call it.

It was Manhattan. There was nobody to question us. Nobody to care.

The highrise on West 68th was built like a bunker against fires, all concrete walls and steel doors. So we were in no real danger at all that night. We just sat in the condo bedroom watching the news coverage on CNN, phoning friends when it was possible to get through to them and twice listening at the door to sounds of mayhem in the hall or else gazing out our sixth-floor window to the dead wandering through the eerie empty streets or being shot down by police. Tiny cracklings far below.

The homeless got the worst of it that night and over the days that followed. Dead or alive they were easy targets, half of them with senses already dulled by drugs or booze or mania and their population plummeted. But Manhattan never shut down the way more rural areas had done. Closed off to bridge-and-tunnel traffic the City's dead proved almost manageable. For how long that would continue we didn't know. But by the time we ran out of food a week later our walk across the street to the Food Emporium was no more eventful than usual, though the shelves looked skeletal. Deliveries were going to be a problem.

Then the city legislature reversed a decades-old policy about the right to bear arms in public and we picked out a brand-new Ladysmith for June and a used Colt Python for me. We practiced at the crowded new firing range a few blocks down on Broadway at what used to be the World Gym.

Don't worry. You'll get better at this, June said.

I never did.

Another week or so passed and I worked at home by computer, e-mail, fax and phone and June left the restaurant to the manager. Business was way off anyway and supplies were hard to come by.

We spent a lot of time in bed.

Then the day before yesterday our Aunt Joan called, Hanna's sister. Our mother had died that morning and risen and died again. Both times shot by a Remington double-barrel shotgun, the first wielded by a dead-panicked thief who hadn't the cash to pay for it but was scared to be without it and the second in the hands of old Pete Miller, who'd moved into the apartment over the store when his wife died God only knows how long ago and who'd heard the blast and perhaps remembering my father got downstairs just in time to see her struggling to rise off the floor, shooting her down his final act as hired help.

Were we coming to the funeral? my Aunt Joan wanted to know.

Neither of us liked the idea at all. Our mother had been religion-crazed for years, grown more and more fervent as she got older. She'd helped us only grudgingly through college. Mostly we'd lived on scholarships. It was possible the only reason she did as much for us as she did was to get us out of town.

We embarrassed her and she embarrassed us.

It wasn't as though we loved her. June and I loved only each other.

"I'll go," I said. "Somebody ought to."

"You don't want to go."

"Neither do you. I'll go."

"Are we going to keep the shop?"

"Hell no. She should have sold it years ago. I bet Pete'll buy it. He hasn't spent his first dime yet."

So this morning I picked up a rental car at Hertz a few blocks away and headed for the Lincoln Tunnel. Traffic was light. At the entrance to the Tunnel a grim-faced balding man with a .38 police special on his hip handed me a pass which I'd have to present on the way back along with the usual toll.

Three hours later I was at the lake.

The turnout this afternoon was small. A handful of fellow-traveller Baptists toting rifles and shotguns. Aunt Joan, unarmed but for the fierce set to her jaw. Me, the pastor and old Pete all wearing sidearms under our jackets. I pled June out to ill-health to those few who bothered asking. The day was mild and the cemetery was old and there was so much recently turned earth it looked like we were holding services in the midst of an ant colony. June had wired flowers and so had the church and so had my Aunt and Pete.

Pete seemed to be taking it the worst.

Hanna had been a difficult woman but probably it was difficult too for Pete to shoot her.

I didn't get to ask him about the store.

I didn't get through the service.

Halfway into the Lord's Prayer I felt a buzzing in my head like a television tuned to nothing but loud static and knew that June was gone.

It was good that as family I was seated on a folding chair because in those first few moments I couldn't have trusted my legs to do anything but buckle. I must have said something because my Aunt gave me a look and a deeper frown than usual but then I saw reflected in her eyes a grave concern and tentatively at first she touched my shoulder and then pulled me over and wrapped her arms around me while I sobbed and stopped the service howling my grief for what reason neither she nor any other could begin to understand.

I drove back knowing exactly where to find her.

Under what circumstance or where it had happened to her I would never discover but once it was over she'd gone home to our apartment, the same sort of instinct that took some of the dead to Times Square or their favorite bar or restaurant or back to their office buildings or shopping malls or homeless haunts beneath the stairs.

So that I found her where I expected her to be, at home in our bed, June naked and waiting for me, her little brother by seven minutes only, the world a hostile place once again for both of us in which there is need and very good reason to scream, the bright eyes empty and the gash in her neck ugly as badly butchered meat but waiting there in our bed for all that, waiting for the flower to rise one final time maybe or waiting for nothing at all but that other part of her which lived.

There's another Scots belief that when one twin dies the other will not as a rule live long, but that if he does somehow survive the vitality and strength of the dead twin passes on to him, even sometimes to the point of giving him strange new healing powers like the power to cure thrush by breathing down the throat of the sufferer. I have no use for healing powers even if that were true. And I don't particularly care to breathe down anyone's throat but June's.

I've closed our bedroom door and propped a chair against the doorknob in order to sit in the living room and write this down. I've half expected pounding, growling, sounds of that raging hunger they all seem to have turned toward me now but there have been no sounds, nothing at all.

She's waiting in our bed. When I last saw her, her hand rested gently between her legs.

I've given a lot of thought to it and there's only one thing I can really think to do. Lie down beside her and let her create in me a wound which is in some way twin to her own and then before I pass into wherever it is they go, turn the Colt on her and then on me. I won't let the two of us

166

be damned even today, when half the world is.

We were born on Mischief Night, June and I. The first windy moments of Halloween.

We've done nothing wrong.

Amid the Walking
Wounded

It was four in the morning, the Hour of the Wolf he later thought, the hour when statistically most people died who were going to die on any given night and he awakened in the condo guestroom thinking that something had shaken him awake, an earthquake, a tremor—though this was Sarasota not California and besides, he'd been awakened by an earthquake many years ago one night in San Diego and this was somehow not quite the same. The glow outside the bedroom window faded even as he woke so that he couldn't be sure it was not in some way related to his sleep. He was aware of a trickling inside his nose, a thin nasal discharge, unusual because he was a smoker and used to denser emissions. He sniffed it up into his throat and thought it tasted wrong.

The guestroom had its own bathroom just around the corner so he put on his glasses and got up and turned on the light and spit the stuff into the sink and saw that it was blood and as he leaned over the sink it began leaking out his nose in a thin unsteady stream like a faucet badly in need of new washers. He pinched his nose and stood straight, tilted back his head and felt it run down the back of his throat, suddenly heavier now so that it almost choked him, the gag reponse kicking in and he thought, now what the hell is *this*? so he leaned forward again and took his hand away from his nose and watched it pouring out of him.

He grabbed a handtowel, pressed it under and over his nose and pinched again. *One seriously major fucking bloody nose*, he thought, unaware as yet that he was not alone, that others in town had awakened bleeding from the nose that night though none of them had been taking aspirin, eight pills a day for over a month's time trying to fight off some stupid tennis elbow without resorting to a painful shot of cortisone directly into the swollen tendon— unaware too that aspirin was not just an anti-inflammatory but a blood-thinner, which was why he was not going to be doing any clotting at the moment.

The towel, pink, was turning red. The pressure wasn't working.

If he put his head up it poured down his throat—he could taste it now, salty, rich and coppery. If he put his head down it poured out his nose. Straight-up, he was an equal-opportunity bleeder, it came out both places.

He couldn't do this alone. He had to wake her. He crossed the hall.

"Ann? Annie?"

There was a streetlight outside her window. Her pale bare back and shoulders told him that she still slept nude.

"Annie. I'm bleeding."

She had always departed sleep like a drunk with one last shot left inside the bottle.

"Whaaaa?"

"Bleeding. *Help*." It was hard to talk with the stuff gliding down his throat and the towel pressed over his face. She

169

rolled over squinting at him, the sheet pulled up to cover her breasts.

"What'd you do to yourself?"

"Nosebleed. Bad." He spoke softly. He didn't want to wake her son David in the next room. There was no point in disturbing the sleep of a fourteen-year-old.

She sat up. "Pinch it."

"I'm pinching it. Won't stop."

He turned and went back to the bathroom so she could get out of bed and put on a robe. He was not allowed to see her naked anymore. He leaned over the sink and took away the towel and watched it slide out of him bright red against the porcelain and swirl down the drain.

"Ice," she said behind him and then saw the extent of what was happening to him and said *Jesus* while he pinched his nose and tilted back his head and swallowed and then she said *ice* again. "I'll get some."

He tried blowing out into his closed nostrils the way you did to pop the pressure in your ears in a descending plane and all he succeeded in doing was to fog up his glasses. Huh? He took them off and looked at them. The lenses were clear. He looked in the mirror. There were beads of red at each of his tear-ducts.

He was bleeding from the eyes.

It was the eyes that were fogged, not his goddamn glasses. She came back with ice wrapped in a dishtowel.

"I'm bleeding from the eyes," he told her. "If it's the ebola virus, just shoot me."

"Eyes and nose are connected." She hadn't grown up a nurse's daughter for nothing. "Here."

He took the icepack and arranged it over his nose, tucked the corners of the dishtowel beneath. Within moments the towel was red. The ice felt good but it wasn't helping either.

"Here."

She'd taken some tissues and wrapped them thick around a pair of Q-tips.

170

"Put these up inside. Then pinch again."

He did as he was told. He liked the way she was rushing to his aid. It was the closest he'd felt to her for quite some time. He managed a goofy smile into her wide dark eyes and worried face. *Ain't this something?* He pinched his nose till it hurt.

The makeshift packs soaked through. He was dripping all over his teeshirt. She handed him some tissues.

"Jesus, Alan. Should I call 911?"

He nodded. "You better."

The ambulance attendants were both half his age, somewhere in their twenties and the one with the short curly hair suggested placing a penny in the center of his mouth between his teeth and upper lip and then pressing down hard on the lip, a remedy that apparently had worked for his grandmother but which did not do a thing for him and left him with the taste of filthy copper in his mouth, a darker version of the taste of blood. Annie asked if she should go with him and he said no, stay with David, get some sleep, I'll call if I need you. She had to write down their number because at the moment he couldn't for the life of him remember.

Inside the ambulance he began to bleed heavily and the attendant sitting inside across from him couldn't seem to find any tissues nor anything for him to bleed into. Eventually he came up with a long plastic bag that looked like a heavier grade of Zip-loc which he had to hold open with one hand while dealing with his leaking nose with the other. A small box of tissues was located and placed in his lap. When one wad of tissues filled with blood he would hurriedly shove it into the bag and pull more from the box, his nose held low into the bag to prevent him from bleeding all over his khaki shorts. The attendant did nothing further to help him after finding him the bag and tissues. This was not the way it happened on *ER* or *Chicago Hope*.

The emergency room was reassuringly clean and, at five

171

in the morning, nearly deserted but for him and a skeleton staff. They did not insist he sign in. Instead a chubby nurse's aide stood in front of him with a clipboard taking down the pertinent information, leaving him to deal with his nose, replacing the half-full Zip-loc bag with a succession of pink plastic kidney-shaped vomit bowls but otherwise treating him as though it were ninety-nine percent certain he had AIDS.

He didn't mind. As long as the pink plastic bowls kept coming and the tissues were handy.

He was beginning to feel light-headed. He supposed it was loss of blood. He couldn't remember Annie's address though he'd written her from his New York apartment countless times in the past four years since she'd moved away and knew her address—quite literally—by heart. He couldn't remember his social security number either. The nurse's aide had to dig into his back pocket to get his wallet. The card was in there along with his insurance card. He couldn't do it for her because his hands, now covered with brown dried blood, were occupied trying to stop fresh red blood from flowing.

The ER doctor was also half his age, oriental, handsome and built like a swimmer with wide shoulders and a narrow waist, like the rest of the staff quite friendly and cheerful at this ungodly hour but unlike them seemingly unafraid to touch him even after, having swallowed so much of his own blood, he vomited much of it back into one of the pink plastic bowls. He asked Alan if he was taking any drugs. And that was when he learned about the blood-thinning properties of aspirin. He thought that at least he was probably not going to have a heart attack. He supposed it was something.

The doctor used a kind of suction device to suck blood from each of his nostrils into a tube trying to clear them but that didn't work which Alan could have told him, there was far too much to replace it with, so he packed him with what he called pledgets, which looked like a pair of tampons mounted on sticks, shoved them high and deep into the nasal cavities and told him to wait and see if they managed to stop the bleeding.

Miraculously, they did.

Half an hour later they released him. He phoned Annie and she drove him back to the condo and he washed his hands and face and changed his clothes and they each went back to bed.

He woke needing to use the toilet and found that both his shit and piss had turned black. A tiny black droplet clung to his penis. He shook it off. He supposed he'd learned something—a vampire's shit and urine would always be black. He wondered if Anne Rice could find a way to make this glamourous.

The second time he woke he was bleeding again. He squeezed at the pledgets as he'd been told to do should this occur but the bleeding wouldn't stop. He roused Ann and this time she insisted on driving him to the hospital herself, handing him her own newly opened box of Puffs to place in his lap. Upstairs David continued to sleep his heavy adolescent sleep. It was just as well. The boy was only fond of blood in horror movies.

The chubby nurse's aide was gone when he arrived but the pink plastic bowls were there and he used them, sat in the same room he'd left only hours before while his doctor, the swimmer, summoned an Ear Nose and Throat man who arrived shortly after he'd sent Annie back home.

By now he felt weak as a newborn colt, rubber-legged and woozy. It seemed he needed to grow a new pair of hands to juggle his kidney-shaped pan, eyeglasses, tissues and tissue boxes, all the while holding his nose and spitting, vomiting, dripping and swallowing blood at intervals.

He felt vaguely ridiculous, amused. A bloody nose for chrissake.

What he felt next was pain that lasted quite a while as

the ENT man—another healthy Florida specimen, a young Irishman who arrived in pleated shorts and polo shirt—withdrew the pledgets and peered into his nose with a long thin tubular lighted microscope, determined that it was only from the right nostril that he was actually bleeding, and then repacked it with so much stuff that by the time it was finished he felt like a small dog had crawled up and died in there.

A half-inch square accordion-type gauze ribbon coated in Vaseline, four feet of it folded back-to-back compacted tight into itself and pushed in deep. In front of that another tampon-like pledget, this one removable by means of a string. In front of that something called a Foley catheter which inflated like a balloon. Another four feet of folded ribbon. Another pledget.

He had no idea there was so much room inside his face. The man was hearty but not gentle.

He was given drugs against the pain and possible infection and put into a wheelchair and wheeled into an elevator and settled into a hospital bed for forty-eight hours' observation. Once again a nurse had to find and read his insurance and social security cards. The drugs had kicked in by then and so had the loss of blood. He didn't even know where his wallet was though he suspected it was in its usual place, his back pocket.

The bed next to him was empty. The ward, quiet.

He slept.

He awoke sneezing, coughing blood, a bright stunning spray across the sheets—*it could not get out his nose so instead it was sliding down his throat again, his very heartbeat betraying him, pulsing thin curtains, washes of blood over his pharynx, larynx, down into his trachea.* He gagged and reached for bowl at the table by the bed and vomited violently, blood and bile, something thick in the back of his throat remaining gagging him, something thick and solid like a heavy ball of mucus making him want to puke again so he reached into his mouth to clear it, reached in with

174

thumb and forefinger and grasped it, slippery and sodden, and pulled.

And at first he couldn't understand what it was but it was long, taut, and would not part company with his throat so he pulled again until it was out of his mouth and he could see the thing, and then he couldn't believe what he'd done, that it was even possible to do this thing but he had it between his fingers, he was staring at it covered with slime and blood, nearly a foot and a half of the accordion ribbon packed inside his nose. He'd sneezed it out or caughed it out through his pharynx and now he was holding it like a tiny extra-long tongue and it continued to gag him so he reached for the call-button and pushed and fought the urge to vomit, waiting.

"What in the world have you done?"

It was the pretty nurse, a strong young blonde with a wedding ring, the one who'd admitted him and got him into bed. She looked as though she didn't know whether to be shocked or angry or amused with him.

"Damned if I know," he said around the ribbon. *Aaand ithh eye-o.*

He vomited again. There was a lot of it this time.

"Uh-oh," she said. "I'm going to call your doctor. He may have to cauterize whatever's bleeding up in there. I'll get some scissors meantime, snip that back for you, okay?"

He nodded and then sat there holding the thing. He shook his head. *A goddamn bloody nose.*

It occured to him much later that an operation followed by a hospital stay under heavy medication combined with heavy loss of blood was a lot like drifting through a thick fetal sea from which you occasionally surfaced to glimpse fuzzy snatches of sky. In his younger days he'd dropped acid while floating in the warm Aegean and there were similarities. He awoke to orderlies serving food and nurses taking his blood pressure and handing him paper cups of

175

medication. None of it grounded him for long. Mostly he slept and dreamed.

He remembered the dreams vividly, huge segments of them crowded spinning inside his head with unaccustomed clarity of detail and feeling—and then he'd seem to blink and they'd be gone, just like that, his mind occupied solely by the business of healing his ruptured body. Adjusting the new packing to relieve the pressure, swallowing the pill, nibbling the food. Then hurrying back to dream.

There was something ultimately lonely, he thought, about the process of healing. Nobody could really help you. All they could do was be reasonably attentive to your needs. He began to look forward to his momentary visits from the pretty blonde nurse because of all the hospital staff she seemed the wittiest and most cheerful and he liked her Southern accent, but ultimately he was completely alone in this. He'd told Annie not to call for a while after her first phone call woke him, he was fine but he was not up to conversation yet. And that felt lonely too.

When the black man with the haunted eyes appeared in the bed beside him by the window he was not really surprised. He assumed a lot went on in his room that he wasn't aware of. He'd looked over at the window to see if it was day or night because as usual he had no idea, no concept of time whatsoever, and there he was lying flat on his back and covered to the chin, hooked up to some sort of monitor and an elaborate IV device of tubes and wires much different from his own, his face thin to emaciation, drawn and grey in the moonlight, eyes open wide and focused in his direction but, Alan thought, not seeing him, or seeing through him—and this he proved with a smile and a nod into the man's wide unblinking gaze.

Possibly some sort of brain damage, he thought, poor guy, knowing somehow that this man's loneliness far exceeded his own, and moments later forgot him and returned to sleep.

*   *   *

176

Imagine the seats on a slowly moving ferris wheel, only the seats are perfectly stable, they don't rock back in forth as the seats on a ferris wheel do, they remain perfectly steady, and then imagine that they are not seats at all but a set of flat gleaming slabs of thick heavy highly polished glass or metal or even wood, dark, so that it is impossible to tell which—and now imagine that there is no wheel—nothing whatever holding them together but the slow steady measured glide itself and that each is the size and shape of a closet door laid flat, and that there are not only one set but countless sets, intricately moving in and out and past each other, almost but never quite touching, so that you can step up or down or to the side on any of them without ever once losing your footing.

It is like dancing. It gets you nowhere. But it's pleasurable.

That was what he dreamed.

He was alone in the dream for quite a while, until Annie appeared, a younger Annie, looking much the same as she did the day he met her sitting across from him on the plane from L.A. with her two-year-old son beside her over a dozen years ago. Her hair was short as it was then as was her skirt and she was stepping toward him in a roundabout way, one step forward and one to the side, drifting over and under him and he wasn't even sure she was aware of his presence, it was as though he were invisible, because she never looked directly at him until she turned and said, *you left us nowhere, you know that?* which was not an accusation but merely a statement of fact and he nodded and began to cry because of course it was true, aside from these infrequent visits and the phone calls and letters he had come unstuck from them somehow, let them fend for themselves alone.

He woke and saw the black man standing in the doorway, peering out into the corridor, turning his head slowly as though searching for someone with those wide empty eyes and he thought for a moment that the man should not be out of bed, not with all those wires and tubes still attached to him reaching all the way across the room past

177

the foot of his own bed but then heard movement to the other side of the darkened room and turned to see the form of a small squat woman who appeared to be adjusting the instruments, doing something to the instruments, a nurse or a nurse's aide he supposed so he guessed it was all right for the man to be there. He looked back at him in the doorway and closed his eyes, trying but failing to find his way back into the dream, wanting to explain to Annie the inexplicable.

It was almost dawn when the arm woke him.

He had all but forgotten about the arm, the inflamed swollen tendon that had started him on aspirin and landed him here in the first place. The drugs had masked that pain too. Now the arm jerked him suddenly concious, jerked hard twice down along his side as though some sort of electric shock had animated it, something beyond his will or perhaps inside his dream, needles of pain from the elbow rising above the constant throbbing wound inside his face.

He guessed more drugs were in order.

He was hurting himself here.

He pressed the call button and waited for the voice on the intercom.

"Yes? What can I do for you?"

"I need a shot or a pill or something."

"Pain?"

"Yes."

"I'll tell your nurse."

They were fast, he gave them that. The pretty blond nurse was beside him almost instantly, or perhaps despite his pain he'd drifted, he didn't know. She offered him a paper cup with two bright blue pills inside.

"You hurt yourself awake, did you?"

"I guess. Yeah, my arm."

"Your arm?"

"Tennis elbow. Didn't even get to play tennis. Did it in a gym over a month ago."

She shook her head, smiling, while he took the pill and a sip of water. "You're not having a real good holiday, are you?"

"Not really, no."

She patted his shoulder. "You'll sleep for a while now."

When she was gone he lay there waiting for the pain to recede, trying to relax so that he could sleep again. He turned and saw the black man staring at him as before, and saw that the man now nestled in a thicket of tubes and wires, connected to each of his arms, running under the bedcovers to his legs, another perhaps a catheter, two more patched to his collarbones, one running to his nose and the thickest of them into his half-open mouth. Behind him lights on a tall wide panel glowed red and blue in the dark.

By morning it was gone. All of it. Alan was lying on his side so that the empty bed and the empty space behind it and the light spilling in from the window were the first things he noticed.

The next thing was the smell of eggs and bacon. He did his best by the food set in front of him though it was tasteless and none too warm and the toast was hard and dry. He drank his juice and tea. When the nurse came in with his pills—a new nurse, middle-aged, black and heavy-waisted, one he'd never seen—he asked her about the man in the bed beside him.

"Nobody beside you," she said.

"What?"

"You been all alone here. I just came on but first thing I did was check the charts. Always do. Procedure. You're lucky it's summer-time, with all the snowbirds gone, or we'd be up to our ears here. You got the place all to yourself."

"That's impossible. I saw this guy three times, twice in the bed and once standing right there in the doorway. He looked terrible. He was hooked up to all kinds of tubes, instruments."

" 'Fraid you were dreaming. You take a little pain-killer, you take a little imagination, mix and stir. Happens all the time."

"I'm an appellate lawyer. I don't *have* an imagination."

She smiled. "You were all alone, sir, all night long. I swear."

Some sort of mix-up with the charts, he thought. The man had been there. He wasn't delusional. He knew the difference between dreams and reality. For now the dreams were the more vivid of the two. It was still one way to tell them apart.

Wait till the shift changes, he thought. Ask the other nurse, the blonde. She'd given him a pill last night. The black man had been there. And he was on her watch.

He dreamed and drifted all day long. Sometime during the afternoon Annie and David came by to visit and he told David about coughing up the accordion ribbon and what he'd learned about the color of a vampire's shit. Teenage kids were into things like that he thought, the grosser the better. That and Annie's cool lips on his forehead were about all he remembered of their visit. He remembered lunch and dinner, though not what he ate. He remembered the doctor coming by and that he no longer wore the shorts and polo shirt as he took his pulse and blood pressure but instead the pro forma white lab coat and trousers. He decided he liked him better the other way.

"Sure," she said. "I remember. You hurt yourself awake."

"You remember the guy in the bed beside me?"

"Who?"

"The black man. I don't know what was wrong with him but he looked pretty bad."

"You know what your doctor's giving you for pain?"

"No."

"It's called hydrocodone, honey. In the dose you're getting, it's as mean as morphine, only it's not addictive. I wouldn't be surprised it you told me you were seeing Elvis in that bed over there, let alone some black fella."

He *hurt himself awake* again that night.

This time he was batting at his aching face—at his nose. He was batting at the culprit, at the source of his misery. As though he wanted to start himself bleeding again.

What was he doing? Why was he doing this?

His dream had been intense and strange. They were alone inside a long grey tube, he and Annie, empty of everything but the two of them and stretching off into some dazzling bright infinity and he was pulling at her clothes, her blouse, her jacket, trying to rouse her and get her to her feet while she crouched in front of him saying nothing, doing nothing, as though his presence beside her meant nothing at all to her one way or another. He felt frightened, adrift, panicked.

He woke in pain batting at his face and reached for the call button to call his nurse for yet another pill but the black man's big hand stopped him, fingers grasping his wrist. The man was standing by his bedside. The fingers were long and smooth and dry, his grip astonishingly firm.

He looked up into the wide brown eyes that did not seem to focus upon him but instead to look beyond him, into vast distances, and saw the wires and tubes trailing off behind him past the other bed where the squat dark form he realized was no nurse nor nurse's aid hovered over the panel of instruments and a voice inside his head said *no, we're not finished yet, my accident became yours and I'm very much sorry for that but it happens sometimes and for now no interruptions please, we need the facilities, deal with your own pain as I am dealing with mine* and he thought, I'm dreaming, this is crazy, this is the drug but the voice inside said *no, not crazy, only alone in this, alone together here in this room and the nurse cannot see, cannot know, the nurse is not in pain as you and I, you'll only disturb her, you can live with that, can't you* and he nodded yes because suddenly he thought that of course he could. *Good,* the voice said, *a short time, stop hurting yourself and instead of her, dream of me, you've been doing that already but she always gets in, doesn't she.* He nodded again and felt the pressure lessen on his wrist. *Stop hurting yourself. She is not the pain nor are you. Rest. Sleep.*

The man sat back on his own bed and rested, adjusted the wires, smoothed them over his chest. The dark female figure resumed her work at the lighted panel. The man's touch was like a drug. Better. The pain was vanishing. He didn't need the call button. Or perhaps he was just living with the pain, he didn't know. One more night, he thought. One more morning, maybe.

Maybe there were things he could do for her and the boy that he hadn't done, things to make it better. But he needed to let go of that now.

He dreamed of a ferris wheel. Only there was no wheel. He dreamed of a thousand wheels intersecting.

He stepped down and up and forward and side to side.

The Great San Diego
Sleazy Bimbo
Massacre

Bernice came in the back way and slammed the screen door in the sick face of the San Diego sun mewling on the porch. Ramona was just sitting down to her third cup of Sanka.

"Jesus," said Ramona. "Kick a fucking hole in it, why don't you."

Ramona was cranky today.

"You want coffee?"

"Gin. Got any gin?"

"You kidding? It's nine in the fucking morning."

"Okay. All right. Coffee."

Ramona still had on her pale blue rayon nightgown. On her feet were a pair of fuzzy pink slippers. A worker ant crawled recklessly up her thigh.

She didn't notice.

Bernice sat down and crossed her legs. Nylon shrieked against nylon.

Ramona's hangover was a living, breathing thing. A white worm eating brainmeat. *Chomp*.

She got up and poured some boiled water from a saucepan into a cracked clay mug and then stirred in the Sanka. From habit she added cream and sugar for Bernice and set it in front of her. Coagulant grains of Sanka swirled in the eddy of the teaspoon. Floodwater and debris.

"That fucking Howard," said Ramona. "Look. Look at this."

She tilted back her head, stared up at the lime-green stucco ceiling. Bernice leaned in to examine her: Just beneath her chin was a small red mark. A hickey

"Oh, it doesn't show, 'Mona. You can hardly see it at all unless you get right up on top of you. Just keep your head down is all."

"Yeah. Keep my head down."

She opened a can of light chunk tuna in oil and dumped it into a bowl.

"Listen," she said. "I'm sick of that sonovabitch. I'll give you a thousand dollars to run him over for me."

Bernice's mouth dropped open, burying the mole in her neck between two folds of creamy flesh. The mole was used to the dark.

"*What?*" she said.

"I mean it. I'll give you a thousand dollars to run the fucker over. Do it tomorrow morning. Just back over him in the car when he walks out the door to go to work and you get the money. Accident. Adjoining driveways. Oops, sorry."

"'Mona! I couldn't do that."

"Could you do it for a thousand five?"

"No! Of course not!"

Ramona smashed the tuna with a fork. Added mayo and powdered mustard and a pinch of dill. Mixed it up and tasted it. She'd forgotten the salt. It needed salt. She added it and tasted it again. She handed Bernice the fork.

"Taste," she said.

In Bernice's opinion it could have used some sour pickle.

Ramona turned to her, suddenly passionate, her eyes hard and narrow.

The ant paused on her thigh, startled.

"I got to have him dead, Bernice. I mean it. The bastard hasn't got a penny. They're taking away my charge cards one by one. Do you have any idea what that does to me, Bernice? I mean, I offer you a thousand and it's more than I can afford. I'm desperate. I can't stand the sight of that sonovabitch anymore."

She pointed to the hickey, strident and complacent beneath her chin.

"I haven't had one of these things since I was sixteen. And I didn't like them then. I want him dead. Those debts are mostly all in his name, not mine. He can't hold a job and he wants to fuck all the time and I'm sick of him. Two thousand. That's the best I can do."

"Jeez, Mona. I couldn't kill somebody."

"Sure you could. I could kill Albert for you, if you asked me to."

"I don't *want* you to kill Albert."

"I know that but I could do it for you if you did. It's just . . . harder when it's your own husband. I dunno. Maybe some kind of . . . affection there for the dumb cocksucker. Really. I need your strength. Don't bleed me, Bernice. Don't gouge me. Take two thousand."

She sat down.

"Gee, 'Mona. I don't know what to say."

"You're my best friend. Kill him for me. Please?"

Bernice had a bite of tuna.

The worker ant entered the dark, liver-scented forest of her pubic hair and trudged forward. Drink and anger had clouded her perceptions. She scratched her thigh where the ant had been five minutes previously.

Bernice sighed. "You sure you ain't got any gin?"

She tried to picture herself as a man killer. All that came to her was an image in platinum wig and black sheath dress, smoke from her .45 mingling with the smoke from her cigarette dangling from her rouged and bee-stung lips.

She'd run a cat over once. A little thump. Howard would be a much bigger thump.

"I can't" she said. "Anyway, if it's got to be done then *you* should do it and don't stop me now Ramona because here's why."

She took a deep breath, aware of her heartbeat. Her nipples tingled against the tired blue terrycloth of her housedress. Nylon hissed as she crossed her legs. These goddamn garters were ruining them.

"You remember a long while ago, I think it was in Michigan, there was this guy who was beating up on his wife all the time? And she set fire to his bed one night while he was sleeping? Used gasoline? Well, you could do that. I mean, not with the gasoline because you don't want to burn the place up or anything, but just say he was beating up on you and so you killed him. The jury let *her* off. There've been others too. I just can't think of 'em. I'd back you up on it, I swear."

She was getting kind of wet down there thinking about it, excited.

"See, you could kill him and try *not* to get caught, but if you *did* get caught, you could say it was justifiable killing. But, if I kill him and I get caught, I'm screwed. See?"

Ramona nibbled the tuna abstractedly. She considered Bernice's point. It was a good point.

Trouble was, she lacked the confidence. You needed confidence to kill a man.

She imagined herself with confidence.

She saw herself lying beside him in bed, sharp scissors in her hand glinting in the light from the streetlamp, smiling as she lifts the sheet off his warm, night-smelling, fat hairy body. Then snipping at the base of his neck, a tiny incision. Delightfully, he doesn't stir. He's snoring. Quickly, easily, she cuts a perfect line from the incision down through his navel to his cock. His intestines pop out

186

like a grey wet slippery messy steaming Jack-in-the-Box. She reaches in under the intestines through the sticky goo, goes up through the ribcage, and draws out his heart. The heart is still beating. Though Howard is no longer snoring. She mashes his heart against the bedroom wall, squooshes it completely.

" 'Mona?" Bernice was saying. " 'Mona? What'ya think?"

"Hmmm?"

She lacked confidence.

The worker ant climbed over labia arid and joyless as the desert.

The tuna was nearly gone.

"I can't do it by myself," she said. "You got to help me."

"Ramona, I *can't* help you. What if they *caught* me? What excuse have I got?"

"We could say I forced you. I was so crazy I threatened your life and Albert's life and you had to go along. You were afraid of me. I'd back you all the way. I'd be as crazy as a fucking loon."

Bernice made a face. "I just don't know, Ramona."

'Mona was on a roll now.

"Listen, Howard's got an insurance policy for thirty thousand. If we make it look like an accident that's double indemnity, that's sixty. Help me do it and I'll give you thirty. That's half. How's that sound?"

"Thirty thousand dollars?"

"Right."

"Gee."

She considered it.

"You only offered me a thousand at first."

Ramona didn't comment.

She could see Bernice's nipples stiffen under the terry housedress. Let her think about it. It took two years for Albert to make that kind of cash. Ramona felt pretty good about things for the first real time that day.

Though Bernice ought to lose some weight in her opinion. Those nipples could stand to ride a little higher.

"Okay," said Bernice. "I'll do it. Only *I'm* not doing this alone, either. No riding over him in the driveway or anything. Whatever we do, we do together. Is that agreed?"

"Agreed."

Now what the fuck was that?

She stood up and brushed hard at her belly. The itching, crawling feeling stopped abruptly.

It took three more hours for the body to be discovered curled in the hollow of her navel.

"Want more Sanka?" she said.

"Fuck Sanka," said Bernice. "Haven't you got any *gin?*"

Ramona sighed and pulled out the bottle.

Two more weeks had elapsed and Howard was still alive.

They sat alone together in a bar. The bar was all pink and red. The lighting was dim. It was like sitting in something's stomach.

Ramona was on her third banana daiquiri. Bernice ordered another pink gin from the barman. She was one ahead, but the liquor made her happy.

"Make it a double," she said.

"Bernice, don't get drunk, for chrissake, will ya?"

"My head is perfectly clear, 'Mona," she said pointedly. "It's not me who keeps coming up with these ideas."

"Don't be a smartass."

"I'm not. I'm not the smartass here."

It was loud enough and testy enough so that the topless dancer behind the bar, an Irish girl with a face as broad and squat as a piano and breasts the color of old tin cans, missed a bump.

The barman put the double pink gin in front of the fat one, wishing these two would stop arguing. It was giving him a headache. Besides, the thinner one wasn't so bad looking. He crossed a pair of treetrunk arms and smiled at her.

Ramona caught the glance. Right here was a side of beef.

"So what *happened?*" asked Bernice.

"He didn't eat it. The fucker."

The two of them were the only customers. The barman and dancer each found them interesting—for different reasons. The barman was trying to discern the elusive outline of Ramona's pale nipples beneath her open cardigan and sheer mauve blouse. The dancer waxed more introspective: *he didn't eat what?* She moved her legs listlessly forward and back and tried to remember not to knit her brow.

"Jeez," said Bernice, "and here I am spending the whole day cutting the sacs off the goddamn bugs and baking the pie. Doesn't he *like* apple pie?"

"Of course he does. He ate the crust. He said it was good, by the way. I guess it's the tarantula he doesn't like."

She gulped the drink.

"It was pretty disgusting to look at, tell you the truth. Poison turned it kind of greenish brown. *I* wouldn't have eaten it. I told him the apples must have gone bad or something."

"He bought that?"

"Of course he bought it. He bought the wax on the front steps, didn't he?"

"He has a wonderful sense of balance, 'Mona."

"And he bought it when I dropped the toaster into the bathtub, didn't he?"

"We should of scraped the insulation better. We'd of had him."

"I know that. The point is Howard's the dumbest jerk walking. That's what got me into this mess, remember?"

"Yeah."

Melancholy set in.

Bernice downed her double and motioned to the barman for another.

They watched him move down the bar. Enormous shoulders on the guy. From the rear you couldn't see his big pot belly and his ass and hips were nice.

"Not bad, huh," said Bernice.

189

"Jesus, no. Big sonovabitch. You might need a shoehorn to get him in, though."

"Yeah. A guy like that could be awful big."

"You never know. I've seen his type with peckers no bigger than a car key." She smiled conspiratorially. "I bet we can find out, though."

She slipped off her sweater and draped it over the barstool. Then took each of her nipples between thumb and forefinger and twisted gently. They gorged and grew.

The barman returned with Bernice's pink gin and noted the improvements. He met her eyes and saw the promise there. Ramona ordered another daiquiri. He swallowed and turned away. And Ramona saw what she wanted to see.

"That's a cattle prod he's got in there," she said—betraying her West Chicago background. "One more drink and I'm gonna want to suck that."

Bernice giggled. "Want company?"

"Hell, no."

The barman returned with her drink. There was an easy familiarity in his manner now. It spoke of long exposure to cheap and beautiful women in every dark corner of the damp, pungent continent of sex. He leaned close over the bar.

"Anything else I can do for you ladies?"

"We gotta talk," said Bernice.

"Later," said Ramona.

The barman felt certain he could afford to be expansive. "Sure," he said and moved away.

"I say we disconnect the brakes on the Mercury," said Bernice.

"I don't know how. Do you?"

"No. But we could climb in under there and disconnect everything we saw and probably something would be the brakes."

"Shit, Bernice. We'd probably make it so the car won't start. How are you gonna kill him that way?"

"Yeah. You're right. Too risky."

"I still like the pancakes, though. You still like the pancakes?"

"The pancakes is good," said Bernice.

She nodded sagely, tapping her fingernails against the bar. The fingernails were maroon because her dress was burgundy and her pumps were cherry. She looked perfectly at home in the gastric decor of the bar.

"You still got the LSD?" she asked.

"All ground up and waiting to go in the batter. Problem is he keeps saying he gets breakfast at the plant so all he wants is coffee. Maybe Saturday, though."

"'Mona, I have to go to my sister-in-law's for dinner on Saturday! I told you that. Look, let's run over everything again and just pick something. I want to get this over with. Right now."

Ramona nodded. Waiting for Saturday was an inconvenience for her as well. Take that barman there. She would have liked to bring him home and give it to him the proper way. With Howard in the picture she'd probably have to settle for a quick one up against the urinals in the men's room. Time was a-wasting.

She caught his eye. She ran her tongue slowly, wetly, over her lips. The barman smiled and winked.

The topless dancer glanced down at her breasts and compared them to Ramona's. Unhappily they came up short. She decided to wear them more defiantly.

"Okay," said Ramona. "There's downers in the Budweiser and the lye in the bean soup. I still think we could put the .45 slugs in the carburator. They'd explode and blow his brains out. We could say it was kids."

"We'd still have to find the carburator."

"Yeah. Now, our best bet would be to figure out some way to get the hypodermic needle fixed and shoot an air bubble into him. But you had to go and drop the goddamn thing."

"I'm sorry, 'Mona. It was just such a *good* idea it made me nervous."

191

"That's all right, Bernice. You have to allow for these things. But we have to count that out for now. And I still think it would be hard to make a stabbing death look like he had an accident."

"I think bullets in the carburator is chancy."

"Maybe. But to be honest, handling lye fucking worries me."

"Me too."

"So given the time factor, I'd say death by beer."

The barman leaned over the bar. "Why don't you just bludgeon the sonovabitch to death?" he asked.

"Oh christ," said Ramona. "Shows how much *you* know. You realize the guy we're talking about is as big as you are? You figure I could bludgeon *you* to death?"

The barman shrugged. "There's two of you. He sleeps, don't he?"

"Yeah, smarty, he sleeps."

"So, you get him some night when he's had a few, you kill him and then toss him over the rocks somewhere and it looks like he got drunk and took a walk where he shouldn't of been walking. What's the big deal?"

Bernice had had about enough of this. It wasn't her tits he had his eye on after all.

"Hey," she said. "Who asked you? You want to hire on to do the work or what?"

"Hell, no."

"Then suppose you just pour me and my friend another and if we want your advice, we'll ask for it. Okay?"

"Easy, Bernice," said Ramona. "The nice man was just about to buy us a round. Weren't you?"

She smiled. He decided he didn't mind the peach lipstick smear along the bottom of her front teeth.

"Well, yeah," he said. "Now that you mention it."

"You're a doll."

She glanced at Bernice. It was obvious her doubles were finally catching up to her. She slumped on the barstool. The mole on her neck had not made an appearance in over

192

twenty minutes now. Her upper lip tended to tuck itself into her lower lip, and then vice versa, like a pair of worms wrestling across her pale rouged face.

"You better lay off the sauce a little," said Ramona.

She hated to see her friend like this. It certainly wasn't doing her figure any good. Now, Ramona could drink all night without even gaining a pound. She was proud of that. Proud of her figure, of her good legs and her dark thick hair. Mother had called these "attributes"—meaning they would help her get a man. Well she had got one all right. And now this pudgy dimpled barfly would help her get rid of him. If she could dry her out sufficiently.

"I'll lay off," said Bernice. She was beginning to slur her words. "You lay off too. So. We gonna beer him to death or what?"

"Huh? Oh. Sure," said Ramona. She'd been eyeing the barman. She was getting a little drinky-drunk herself she suspected.

Above them the dancer frowned and checked her Timex.

"Quarter to three," she said. "Time for me to break."

She started to climb off the bar. The silver high-heel pumps made her awkward. She looked for some help from the barman. But the barman was over with the girls, grinning wolfishly at Ramona. "Fuck it," she muttered. She eased herself down gingerly. As though slipping into Arctic seas.

On her way to the john she skidded to a stop behind them. The fat one seemed to be dozing. The other was staring at the barman through smoky, half closed lids, mumbling rut and endearment.

The dancer leaned in close to her tiny festooned ear.

"Honey, why don't you just climb on over that bar and *have* some," she said. "Then maybe you won't have to kill the other guy, y'know? Just leave a little left for me."

"*Hell* of an idea," said Ramona.

Bernice jerked violently upright.

"Gotta piss," she said. "Where's the toilet?"

But Ramona was already gone, and if the barman heard her he didn't bother to respond. Instead he responded to Ramona, who had his pants and jockey shorts down around his ankles and a slurping mouthful of barkeep.

"Whereza fucking toilet?" said Bernice.

She clambered off the barstool, tripped and fell, and suddenly was sitting again. Only lower. In the peasoup haze of her disorientation she did the only thing left open to her.

She used the floor.

The Budweiser murder did not come off.

Bernice and Ramona dropped ten downers each into his beercan. Ramona delivered it. And Howard drank it while watching *Hollywood's Greatest Boners* that night. But the drug dropped out of solution and sat uselessly at the bottom of the can, thick white sludge.

On Saturday Ramona tried to feed him her LSD pancakes. But Howard wasn't hungry and said that her pancakes were always leadburgers anyway.

On Sunday they dropped two dozen bullets into the carburator of the Mercury. When Howard tried to start it up for his beer-run over the the 7-Eleven the car just burped and died.

By Monday they were frantic.

"It's impossible to kill the sonovabitch," said Ramona. "I've decided that a woman simply can not kill a man. Anything we've heard to the contrary is filthy lies."

"Let's think," said Bernice.

They did.

"There's the lye," said Ramona.

"What good is the lye if the guy won't eat your cooking?"

Ramona sighed. "I guess he's never really liked it much."

"Know what I'm beginning to think, 'Mona? I'm beginning to think that that bartender . . ."

"Stanley."

". . . that Stanley had the right idea. Let's just get something heavy and bash the sonovabitch."

194

Ramona sighed again. It was more like a wheeze. Cigarettes, drinks, and countless sleepless nights all chuckling inside her lungs.

"So we just find something to whack him with, right?"

"It'd have to be disposable. You couldn't just leave it afterwards."

"That leaves out the tire iron. And the golf clubs. I'm damned if I'm buying new golf clubs."

"Has he got a baseball bat?"

"Yeah."

"You like baseball?"

"Hell, no."

"Make it the baseball bat then. Then we just got to find a convenient cliff to dump him over."

Ramona thought a moment. "Okay. But who does the bashing?"

"We both do. We'll flip a coin to see who goes first."

Ramona thought that was fair.

"Want to do it tonight?"

Bernice hesitated.

"Come on, Bernice. I got a date with Stanley tomorrow. I thought this would all be long over by now. Let's do it. What do you say?"

Bernice considered, then giggled.

"Gee. When do you think they'll pay on the policy, 'Mona?"

"Let's flip," said Ramona.

They found a quarter. Bernice won.

Heads.

In the upstairs bedroom the warm wet San Diego darkness clung to the room like used sweatsocks to a filthy pair of feet. On the bed, beneath the totally unnecessary—and now, ironical—comforter, Howard lay asleep, his high bulbous forehead awash with dreams.

In his dream, fueled by Kentucky bourbon, it was al-

195

ready morning. Howard was in the bathroom, breaking into a brand new bottle of Listerine.

The cap wouldn't give. Howard turned the bottle upside down and tapped it twice on the green porcelain sink. That did the trick. He threw back his head and tasted some.

It tasted like Old Grandad.

He gargled, swallowed, and slugged again. Delighted, he finished the bottle. Looked in the cabinet and underneath the sink for another. There was still the problem of his breath.

He unscrewed the cap from a shampoo bottle and tasted it.

Eighty proof.

Amazed and laughing he drained it. Then a bottle of hair tonic. A bottle of aftershave. Ramona's roll-on deodorant.

What a morning.

Ramona and Bernice tiptoed shoeless up the stairs and opened the bedroom door. A shaft of light and a tired current of thick warm air preceeded them into the room. Bernice carried Howard's Louisville Slugger in her right hand, laving its neck with an unaccustomed slick of feminine perspiration.

They waited till their eyes adjusted to the dark and could see something of the green and silver wallpaper.

"I don't know about this," whispered Bernice.

"You better know." Said Ramona.

"I don't feel so good about this, 'Mona. Look how peaceful he looks lying there. Oh! He looks just like a baby."

Howard did look childlike. The illusion was enhanced by the pillow clutched in his hands, one corner of which tilted toward his open mouth—in the murk of his dream, the hydrogen peroxide that was actually whiskey, guzzled in early morning greed.

"Yeah, he's cute all right," said Ramona. "Whack the fucker right now or I swear you'll hear about it later."

She did not exactly know what she meant by that. But

Bernice seemed to know. And suddenly they were in accord, and Howard's doom was writ.

"Sorry, How'," said Bernice.

She stepped toward the bed and raised the Slugger.

"I am too," whispered Ramona. Though a good half of that was drama.

The bat arced down. Bernice's aim was true.

Wood on wood. The second piece, slightly wet.

As for Howard, all he heard was a single slap. All he saw was the red-out of his dream. All he felt was the onset of a killer hangover.

It figured.

The girls came down all bloody and excited.

"We did it," said Bernice.

"We sure did," Ramona said. "Look at my pants. They're sopping."

It was not just blood she was talking about, though there was plenty of that.

It was difficult for her to remember exactly when it had happened.

They had hit him twenty-four times in succession, one after the other. Toward the end they'd become more sporting, bashing him two or three times before surrendering up the bat. Trying swings.

His skull was fractured in sixteen places, his collarbone was shattered and his windpipe. They'd broken his shoulder, vertebra and hip. The blow to the hip had been Bernice's. She'd been trying out her golf grip, skylarking a bit.

Blood and brains splashed across the walls and windows with each successive blow to the head—and it was immediately after delivering one of these that Ramona had her little accident. She's said nothing to Bernice. Just leaned against the door and waited until the flashing stopped.

She wondered if she'd ever need sex again.

The place was a mess. Howard was dead and enough was enough. Ramona called a halt.

She took some cotton from her first-aid kit in the bathroom and stuffed it into his ears, nose and mouth to stop the bleeding. She wrapped his head turban-style in a pink bath towel and then waited to see if his brains would seep through. They did.

She took another towel from the linen closet and wrapped it around the first one.

Meanwhile Bernice dressed him in his favorite black-and-red checked hunting jacket, a pair of old blue jeans, red shirt, and green socks. The cowboy boots were a problem. Ramona had to help her.

They taped his wrists together over his hard beer-glutted stomach so they wouldn't just dangle. Taped his ankles together so they'd be easier to grip when they started lugging. Ramona wound gauze and more tape over the towels. Round and round. Howard looked like a mummy dressed for Opening Day of rabbit season.

They finished their coffee downstairs, took a breather, and then went back for the body. They pushed and pulled. Finally Howard lay face-up on the porch in back of the house, with a trail of blood and brain-matter leading back upstairs to the bedroom as though he'd forgotten something.

"Bring the car around," said Ramona, "while I clean up a little."

"Got enough paper towels?"

"I think. I may have to borrow from you, though."

"That's okay."

By the time Bernice returned the flies were buzzing. Ramona was on the staircase with a roll of paper towels and a box of SOS. Bernice shooed flies as best she could.

It was a mistake. In the warm, gulf-stream turbulence of her flailing arms two of them were propelled upstairs toward Ramona crouched intent upon flecks and smears on her off-white staircase, and then beyond—some primitive homing instinct impelling them toward a candy-store bedroom full of fresh gore, buzzing their rapture into the San Diego night.

In less than an hour the room was filled with flying mosquitoes, houseflies, mites and midges, partying on the remains of Howard.

While Bernice drove twenty-five miles out of town, removed Howard's tape and turbans, dumped him off a cliff significant enough to cause major increased damage to his body and then drove back to town, Ramona struggled with the blood and insects.

While Bernice cleaned the car and porch, Ramona continued same.

Finally Bernice came up with the bug spray and another roll of paper towels. It helped.

By sunup, six hours later, the blood on the windowsills and the shiny silver wallpaper had turned a light, coral pink and they decided to quit. They took out the garbage. Ramona poured them drinks.

They drank 'til about 8:30.

"Think it's safe to call now?" asked Bernice.

"I guess. It's just a missing persons thing. They're not gonna come looking for him just yet. Later on we can buy some paint. Fix things up a little."

"Won't that look suspicious, 'Mona?"

"Nah. We'll get waterbase. It dries faster. Dial 'em. And then I think I'd better call and cancel that date with Stanley. I'm bushed."

Ramona sipped her scotch. Bernice dialed, handed her the receiver and sat down to her gin. Tasted it. Stared at it.

Looking sort of puzzled.

The number rang.

" 'Mona?" said Bernice.

"Shhh. Wait. I've got them."

She finished her drink while Ramona spoke to the sergeant. Got up and filled her own glass and 'Mona's again.

She listened. Except for what was bothering her, things seemed to be going smoothly.

Her husband had been out all night, Ramona said. This was very unusual for him. She was worried, she said, afraid something had happened. No, she hadn't checked with the hospitals yet. She assumed the first thing you did was call the police.

Sure, she'd hold a minute.

"This is easy," she said to Bernice. "Cop's real nice. Real polite."

" 'Mona?" said Bernice. "I've been thinking."

"Wait." The cop was back again.

Ramona gave him her own name and Howard's and then their address and phone number. She could hear him typing in the background. He was slow. Two fingers, probably.

The cop wanted to know what he was wearing.

She made it sound uncertain. Red shirt, jeans, hunting jacket, boots or maybe sneakers. He asked for a general description. She gave it to him.

He put her on hold again.

"Mona, I got to *ask* you something," said Bernice.

"What." Ramona was annoyed with her. It was probably lack of sleep. Made her fucking cranky.

Bernice looked agitated.

" 'Mona, I seem to remember you put cotton or something in his mouth, in his ears and stuff. Did you?"

"Of course I did. He was bleeding like a stuck pig. Didn't you . . . ?"

"I didn't see it! I mean, I didn't want to *look* at him, you know? At his face? I mean, I saw it there when you did it but then I just forgot, I just pulled off the tape and towels and stuff and . . ."

"Jesus Christ, Bernice! It's supposed to be a fucking *accident!*"

"Oh God! Oh God!"

Ramona was thinking. Fast.

"It's all right. It's all right. We'll find him. We'll get to

200

him before the cops do and we'll get the stuff out of him and . . . hello?"

"You talking to me?" asked the cop.

"I . . . uh, no. I've got a friend here. I'm a little shook, you know?"

"Sure." The voice was reassuring. "It's good you got a buddy there. I just thought maybe you was talking to me. It wouldn't matter, of course. Soon as I get off the phone with you, see, I play back the tape, check to see if I missed somethin'."

"Tape?"

"Yeah, we pick up all 911s these days. Routine. Tape hold and all. It's a good thing, really. What if somethin' was to happen to you while I've got you stuck on hold? No good. This way we know."

She shouldn't worry about Howard, he said. Usually they just took a ride, had a few and then came back again. Ramona thanked him. He was really very nice.

She replaced the princess phone. She looked at Bernice, weepy-eyed and sniffing. The red of Bernice's eyes seemed to inflame the soft pale flesh around them, seemed to seep into nose and cheeks. Her friend looked like one of those sad disgusting disposable old men who play Santa Claus in department stores at Christmas time.

Her own face composed itself.

Too bad, she thought, that she still had to depend on her.

Maybe they could find a way around that.

"Just remember," she said. "The fucker beat me."

201

The Holding Cell

Only one of them looked or acted crazy.

Only one of them even looked dangerous.

Two out of six, he thought.

It could be worse.

The door slid shut behind him, clanging into place.

"Cell," muttered the crazy guy, head swaying side to side, his long matted hair swaying too. That was how he knew the guy was crazy—saying "cell" like that and swaying back and forth. "You're in it now."

Well, he knew that too.

The walls of the holding cell were cinderblock, painted white. Before that they had been red. The underpaint showed through like veins in a bloodshot eye.

"You're in it now."

He walked past them and sat on a wooden bench in back, one of only four benches for the seven of them, aware of their eyes on him, on his new silk shirt and two-tone Paul Stuart shoes. *How come they didn't take the laces?* he thought, *along with his belt and tie and blazer.*

You could hang yourself with a pair of laces, right?

Not that he was about to hang himself over a DUI. Even if it was his first. Still, he considered it a strange omission.

Somebody else could hang you.

The others were all wearing jeans and running shoes in various states of repair. Teeshirts. A black kid in a tie-dye muscle-shirt. Even the little thin guy in back with glasses—jeans, a teeshirt and running shoes. Variations on a theme. What had he expected? Imagination? Everybody but the tall, sandy-haired guy sitting in front, across from the enormous sleeping fat kid. The sandy-haired guy was wearing prison orange and a red ID bracelet on his wrist. He looked like a hospital attendant, only nastier.

He did have the Reeboks, though.

He was aware of class distinctions.

The cell smelled of pine disinfectant, human shit and more faintly, urine. A metal-frame toilet sat in the middle of the room—aside from the benches its only item of furniture. Apparently it had been recently used. He hoped he wouldn't need to.

He sat back against the wall, closed his eyes and tried to sleep. The walls were moist, damp, almost sticky. But he knew that sleep was the best thing now. Sleep would see him through.

It was going to be a long night.

His arresting officer, J. Johansson of the SPD, badge number 42789, had explained to him that under Florida State Law DUI carried a minimum of eight hours dry-out before you could even make bail.

It was now, he guessed, about three in the morning. That was only an estimate. They'd taken his watch and he'd seen no clocks around anywhere. Already his sense of time was tenuous. Probably they had planned it that way. But assuming it was three that meant it would be eleven, minimum, before he could get out of there, even if everything was all right with Ann, if she'd found her way home all right and was working on bail.

And that was not wholly certain.

She was new in town for one thing. Brand new job in a brand new state. Didn't even know all the streets yet. And the layout of the town didn't help. From what he could see it was a fucking maze—old bumpy roads intersecting into new stretches of highway, half of them one-way, the other half unmarked. Swamp to the left and swamp to the right.

He bet these roads *ate* out-of-towners.

He wondered where she was. Or if she even *knew* where she was.

It wasn't her fault. He couldn't even blame her for getting them lost and then telling him to turn when it was really too late to turn, so that he had to slam on the brakes and veer from the left lane into the right, which was what had got him noticed by the cruiser in the first place. She was new. He was just a visitor. It was a case of the blind leading the blind, both of them drinking—moderately, he'd thought, and then only wine—from four-thirty that evening to about two in the morning at her office Christmas party.

He'd blown a hefty .165 on the intoxilyzer.

He guessed that, moderately or not, seven to eight hours was a lot of drinking.

Jesus. I hope you made it, Annie. . . .

Because there was also the fact that she'd given the cops one hell of a hard time. It wasn't too difficult to imagine her sitting in county jail herself—women's division. He remembered her leaning out the driver's side window, half-way out the window, looking like she was about to climb out the rest of the way and punch somebody as they told him to recite the alphabet and close his eyes and touch his nose and walk the line heel to toe, heel to toe, frisked him and cuffed him and stuffed him into he squad car. He remembered her screaming, what the *hell* are you *doing* to him? crazy about her for her relentless Irish temper even as he was scared for her when Johansson said to *get back in the car! Right! Now!* hand on his revolver and command-

voice up full throttle, no doubt fully aware that he would not be the first or last cop to be blown away by some irate lady on the occasion of her husband's arrest.

He was worried about her. She was angry. She was easily as high as he was. And as of a few minutes ago, she was not home.

At the station they'd booked him, printed him, taken mug shots, relieved him of his cigarettes and valuables, frisked him a second time, read him his Miranda, had him sign six or seven forms he was much too wired and basically disoriented to even bother reading, questioned him, and then allowed him his phone call.

He left a message on her answering machine. *Help!* probably sounding a lot more cheerful than he felt because by then the headache had kicked in in a big way and he was cold without his blazer, shivering with nerves and the cold damp of the station house, and he had just been booked for committing a crime for the very first time in his forty-five year-old life.

He felt no guilt about it. He had somehow contrived to feel guilt about almost nothing these days.

He could try to phone again later, they said.

Great.

It was something, he guessed, to look forward to.

He gazed around the holding cell. He did not like the look of the crazy guy, who was unfortunately sharing his bench, sprawled across it lying on his back and leaving him only a narrow spot against the wall, staring up wide-eyed at the ceiling, eyes glazed, pupils darting like flies trapped under milky glass. He did not like the way the lips moved soundlessly.

"Whatcha in for?"

It was the guy sitting across from him.

The guy looked middle-aged, maybe fifty-five—and harmless enough. His jeans and Nikes were new and clean and he did not seem to need to glare or mutter.

"DUI."

The guy shook his head knowingly. "Me too," he said. "You want to hear the worst fucking thing though? It was my goddamn *wife* who turned me in. You believe that? I go out for a six-pack, she calls the cops and tells them I'm fucking drunk out there and driving without a license. Tells them right where I'm headed. Do you *believe* that shit?"

He had the attention of everybody in the cell, all except the fat kid up front sleeping off his drunk. Even the crazy guy had turned in his direction. Everybody smiling. Amused.

The guy himself was not amused.

"I get out of here, I'm gonna cut her *tits* off!"

"First time?" It was the sandy-haired guy wearing prison orange. Getting up and walking over, laughing. Then squatting, digging in his shoe and pulling out a cigarette from one side and a book of matches from the other.

He took a glance toward the narrow cell window, cupped the smoke and lit it.

"Nah."

"Guess you should of cut 'em off last time then."

"You're right. I should've. Jesus! I been dying for one of these! What you in for?"

He took a deep drag and passed it to the guy. He spoke with a deep southern accent. "Skipped bail on a second-offense armed robbery. Guess I'll be around awhile. Fuck it."

They smoked in silence, waving the cigarette like kids in a high school boy's room to make it less conspicuous.

The crazy guy got up, walked over and held out his hand. The hand was black with matted filth. "Mind?"

"Fuck it." The con in prison orange handed him the butt. "Finish the damn thing."

The crazy guy took two deep drags. Then the cigarette disappeared into his clenched fist, ember and all. He lay down again. The fist went up to his mouth. He commenced chewing.

They're all crazy, he thought.

206

It occurred to him, not for the first time, that he could have been in bed with Ann by now. Every fine, smooth, fragrant inch of her.

Just sleep, he thought. *Get some sleep. In a while try to make your call again. Meantime, try to pass the night. Sleep. Get yourself lost. Get the hell out of here. . . .*

And miraculously, he did sleep.

Maybe it was the alcohol working or the late hour or the nerves exhausting him or all of these together but he slept, head pressed back against the sticky cinderblock wall.

He slept fitfully. Waking often.

There were snatches of conversation.

"Jesus! What time is it? You'd think they'd give you a fucking *clock* at least!"

". . . ran a warrant for beating up on her."

". . . second offense. Let's see. I think it's a $500 minimum and ninety days. I'm not sure though. . . ."

"Did you *taste* that stuff? What the hell was that stuff?"

"Peanut butter."

"*Peanut* butter? The fuck it was peanut butter!"

From time to time the door would slide open and a guard would call one of them outside. They'd be gone a while and then come back holding a single sheet of paper. He was not even curious as to what was written on the paper. He assumed he'd find out, eventually.

Instead, he was wholly engulfed by a single urgent need to escape the whole damn thing. The only escape available to him was sleep. The crazy guy was snoring. So was the kid with the enormous belly. He envied them the thoroughness of their immersion.

Finally, he heard his name.

He got up and saw that they'd all been sleeping, the sound of his name and the sliding metal door blinking everyone suddenly awake.

The sullen black kid in the tie-dye muscle-shirt was gone. It didn't even occur to him to wonder where or why.

207

The rules here, the everyday reality of the place, were unknown to him.

In the hall a guard handed him two sheets of computer paper mounted on a clipboard and told him to sign the top copy. The other one was his. NOTICE TO APPEAR FOR ARRAIGNMENT the papers said. They noted the charge, the date, his docket number, and the amount of his bond. The bond was all that interested him—$369.00. He felt relieved. It was not going to be a problem. Ann would have that much on hand.

If he could reach her.

"Can I try that call again now?" he asked.

"What call?"

"I couldn't get through before. They said I could try a little later."

The guard looked at him without expression and nodded. He unlocked and opened the holding cell door.

"I'll let you know."

The door slammed shut. He walked back inside. The holding cell was silent. They sprawled across the benches. The belly of the fat kid looked like it was melting all around him under the dirty white teeshirt. The crazy guy was still snoring. Despite the missing black kid there was no more room for him now than before.

He decided to try the cell floor. At least he could lie down.

He curled himself up into a fetal ball, one arm raised to pillow his head. And in moments he was asleep again. A strange half-sleep in which he was partly aware of his surroundings and even of himself thinking, of his mind working, and partly not.

He thought he had never slept like this before in his entire life.

It was as though he was allowing himself to disappear. Hoping to disappear off the face of the earth.

You are very depressed, he thought.

It didn't take a degree in psych to figure what this was.

It was total avoidance, total *immersion* in avoidance—some waking part of him considered this even as he was dozing. He felt thin inside as a piece of paper, weightless, waiting to be lifted out of here. By contrast, his head felt thick and heavy with sleep, as though he'd been drugged. He didn't sense any contradiction there. It seemed only right in this place somehow. The only thing, sensibly, to be and to do.

The next thing he was aware of was that somebody was moaning.

He shut it out.

The sticky concrete floor seemed to soften, to allow him to sink deeper. He slid into blank empty space and shut it out. Shut it all out.

Then he heard the sliding door again, and his name.

The door must have opened at least once before that—the little guy with glasses was gone now too, his bench looking oddly desolate and sad. He hadn't heard anything but that didn't surprise him. Probably it was mostly the sound of his own name and not the door opening that had roused him even now. His hangover was raging. Wine, he thought. You ought to have known better. His head pounded. He was trembling.

He dragged himself outside.

It may have been a different officer, maybe not. In his condition they were all looking pretty much the same.

"This way," he said.

They turned a corner. He dialed at the telephone on the grey concrete wall.

She picked up immediately.

"Ann?"

"My God, Richard! Are you all right?"

"I'm freezing, I'm exhausted, my head is killing me. But yeah, I'm all right."

"Listen. I've been out of my *mind* here. They won't tell me *anything*. I've been calling and calling and . . . all they keep saying is you're not on the computer yet. It's like you're not even *there*, Richard!"

He smiled. "Oh, I'm here. Believe me."

"Have they set your bail yet?"

"Yes. Three hundred sixty-nine dollars. Can you manage it?"

"Of course I can manage it. I'll get down to the bank right now."

"Don't hurry. I'm not getting out of here for a while. According to Johansson they keep you eight hours minimum from the time of arrest—or booking. I'm not sure which. What time's it now?"

"Almost seven."

"Jesus. Four more hours."

"Oh God, Richard. I'm so sorry!"

"Hey, it's not your fault. It was just bad luck, that's all."

"If I hadn't told you to turn. . . ."

"I know. And if I didn't have some squad car behind me. And if we hadn't been drinking all night. And if I hadn't come down here in the first place. Forget that. You can drive yourself crazy."

"Do you regret it?"

"What?"

"Coming down here."

"No. I *regret* being arrested."

"You swear?"

"I swear. Not for a minute."

He could hear her thinking about that. And the truth was he really did have no regrets in her regard. After so many months of separation he'd been surprised to get the invitation in the first place. And even more surprised at how glad he was to see her.

Before she left him there'd been nothing but fighting, for a long while. Probably, the marriage had made them both too . . . passionate for their own good about one another's faults and neglected virtues. He didn't know about her, but he now found himself less frenzied. A year apart had taken care of that. It made for easier sledding. If he missed the sheer intensity sometimes—and he did—he didn't miss the drunken anguish that, all too often, went along with it.

He felt softer now, more flexive.

He hoped that in her own way so did she.

"All right," she said. "I'll try to get a couple hours sleep and set the clock for eight-thirty. By nine-thirty I'll be at the bank and down there by ten with the money. Just in case you can get out early. I just wish they'd get you on the goddamn computer. You've been there four hours! How long does it take?"

"I guess they figure they've got time."

The guard was tapping him on the shoulder, motioning him back inside.

"Gotta go," he said.

"Richard? Is it horrible?"

"Bearable. I'm trying to sleep as much as possible."

"Good. I miss you. I'm sorry. I'll see you soon, all right?"

"Okay."

He hung up. Wondering, strangely, if he'd ever actually see her again.

Get a grip, he thought.

Good God.

Inside the holding cell the fat kid was still snoring, looking bigger and softer than ever, his breasts spread out across the sides of his flabby biceps. The con in prison orange was asleep directly across from him. But the crazy guy was wide awake.

"Cell," he said. "*You're in it now.*"

Right. That again.

The eyes darted warily. The man closed them and lay back down. Seconds later he was snoring too. All three of them were snoring. It would have been funny if it hadn't been so disgusting. Like the toilet sitting there in the middle of the room was disgusting.

The guy whose wife had turned him in was gone.

Richard was glad for the empty bench.

He lay down. The bench smelled of alcohol and aftershave. The scent of the guy who'd been lying there.

As though part of him had bled right into it.

It came without warning.

One minute he was trying to get comfortable, trying to relax against the pounding in his skull—and suddenly he was asleep again.

It was like entering a black empty room without doors or windows, a room that swayed and shifted like the surface of a pond under a breeze, as though he were riding that surface, a place where neither day nor night nor time of any recognizable sort even existed—or if it did exist, could possibly matter—just silent, constant, nearly unnoticed movement, some slow-moving drift that seemed to well up out of the vague internal shiftings of the earth like magma. He had a sense of indifference, not only his own indifference but something in the nature of things which absorbed without judging, without sense of right or wrong, strong or weak, clean or dirty or even yes or no. It was as though the world were a stewpot—on simmer. And he was a scrap of meat.

Breaking down.

The holding cell, he thought.

Holding. Cell.

The words sounded odd in his head.

And then he was the fat kid—no, he was the fat of the fat kid and he was melting, scalding human gravy running all along the bench and over the floor, pooling at the wall, an obscene sticky mess running off over muscle and bone, a surprising lot of muscle for a kid so fat—but who was he to criticize. He was the juice. He was the problem.

He woke. The door clanged shut.

The fat kid—the *real* fat kid—was gone.

The con in prison orange sat up on the bench across from him, waking, rubbing his eyes.

Then staring at him.

"You ever been in a holding cell before?" he said.

Richard's mouth felt dry. "Unh-unh."

"Shit. I'd ask *him* but he's fucking bonkers." He nodded toward the crazy guy, still sleeping.

"Thing is, something ain't right here."

"What?"

"Asshole. If I knew that, I wouldn't be talking to you, would I."

Richard decided not to comment.

"Ought to be more of us, for one thing. Usually you get people parading in all night. Second thing, I never been in this *particular* cell before and I thought I seen every damn one of 'em in the whole damn county. Third thing is, where the fuck's everybody got to?"

Richard shook his head.

"You make your phone call?"

"Yeah. A while before. You were sleeping."

"I been sleeping like the fucking dead. You gettin' bond?"

"Bond?"

"A bail-bondsman. You getting a *bail-bondsman*."

"My wife . . . my ex-wife. She's—"

He laughed. Surprisingly it was not an unpleasant laugh. "You got an ex-wife'll make your bail? Very nice."

He smiled. "That's if they can find me on the damn computer."

"Computer?"

"As of around seven I wasn't on it."

"Bullshit! You're on the fucking computer the minute you step *into* this place. *Before* that. In the fucking *car* you're on the computer. That's bullshit!"

"That's . . . that's what they told her."

"It's a fuckup. It's some fuckup then."

He shook his head again, ran his hand through his thinning sandy hair.

"This fucking *place.* . . ."

"*Cell*," said the crazy guy. "*You're in it.*"

There was an edge to his voice this time, something sort

213

of excited, and they looked at him. He was sleeping, talking in his sleep.

"You're in it," he said. He was tossing on the bench, legs wobbling every which way like they were made of rubber.

"Asshole," said the con. He lay back down again.

Richard's head felt worse than ever—soft, eggshell-thin. He pressed it gently back against the wall.

I swear to God, he thought, *I'll never drink again.*

Not wine at least.

He closed his eyes for a moment.

And it was as though he could see through the eyelids, a thin pale red-veined film over everything, over the con on his bench and the crazy guy on the other, over the gleaming metal toilet in the center of the room and the door with the single small window behind it—as though he were the bloodshot walls of the cell itself. Watching. He could even see himself sitting there with his legs spread wide, shirt and trousers wrinkled, his head pressed to the damp wall.

He presumed he was sleeping again, his access to sleep just that sudden.

It shocked him, that access. Frightened him.

Nobody should sleep like this, he thought.

Nobody.

What was it the con had said?

I been sleeping like the fucking dead.

What kind of sleep was this anyway?

And what kind of dream where he could watch them, both the con and the crazy guy, start to struggle weakly—could see *himself* start to struggle—against the shifting tides that were the room—faces, bodies going soft, growing indistinct and somehow particulate, breaking down, blending *into* the room, *part* of the room, looking like something he'd once seen alive through a microscope, some amoebic protoplasmic bacterial *something*, even the toilet losing its precise form now, dark inside the gelatinous mass, its flowing nucleus.

A *shitter*. The nucleus of a cell.

He almost laughed.

Instead he screamed soundlessly and tried to wake.

The con was on his feet—or on his knees—his feet and calves sinking suddenly into the shimmering floor, absorbed instantly to the knee. For a moment the flesh of his face resolved into an expression of fear and astonishment, then slipped away as the con himself slipped away somewhere in front of what moments ago had been his bench.

The crazy guy was already gone.

An atomic swarm like thousands of tiny dots on an empty tv screen, drifting.

He felt a helpless panic.

He looked down. The silk shirt, the beltless pants, the socks. All sinking into him. His flesh blood and bone sliding gently back into the wall, into the bench, the bench sliding down into the quivering shifting floor. . . .

He fought his assimilation for quite some time.

The Paul Stuart shoes were the last to go—laces and all. He was actually glad to see them.

Inside the holding cell, almost everyone was wearing Reeboks. Thousands of them.

He guessed it didn't hurt to be different.

The Work

"Funny place to meet," he said. He sat across from her at the old formica table, sipping his coffee only rarely, waiting for her to get to it, wrapping an elastic band around his middle finger and forefinger and then releasing it, a nervous gesture, the only one he'd displayed so far, a tic. She could live with it.

"You wouldn't be thinking of trying to take me down, would you?"

She laughed by way of answering him. "Where do most of your clients want to meet?"

"A bar. A restaurant. Neutral territory. Not their kitchen usually, and never in the kitchen of some house out in the woods all alone in the middle of nowhere. That's a new one on me. Aren't you worried I might have something other than business in mind? You're an attractive woman. You obviously realize that. And you don't know me at all, do you."

She shook her head. "I'm not worried. Half an hour ago, before you arrived I was. I admit I was. Because you never know. But I'm a good judge of people. Comes with the territory. And I think you're probably very professional about what you do. I thought that about five minutes after I first laid eyes on you."

"I am. That's true."

"But to get back to your first question the fact is that with what I'm about to ask you to do, I'd be the one more likely to get taken down, as you say, than you. Hang on for just a second."

She got up and walked to the middle of the room to throw two split logs in the big potbellied stove. It was only September 12th but already nights in the Maine woods were chilly though the days were bright and clear. She closed the grate. The stove immediately began to roar, the draw creating a furious wind tunnel inside, a small inferno. She'd always liked the sound.

She sat down. "That's better."

For a moment she just looked at him and sipped her own black coffee, watching him over the rim. She thought that Carey was attractive too in his own strange way though she couldn't call him handsome. His hair was thin and his face too rough for her tastes. She could picture him with a toolbelt around his waist, working with his hands some-how—instead of in the tailored English suit he was wearing now. Strong, efficient. And composed. Very composed. All he did was sit there and wait her out while she took his measure. No pressure to continue. No impatience. As though he trusted that she'd get there when she was good and ready.

"Let me tell you something about myself, Mr. Carey," she said.

"Richard. And I don't usually want to know too much about my clients. Sometimes it gets in the way."

She nodded. "I can understand that but in this case it's important. Without knowing who I am I doubt you'd even take the job."

"Really?" He smiled.

"Really. Trust me on this."

Now it was his turn to look. She waited for his permission.

"All right," he said. "Tell me."

"I'm a writer. A novelist. I do the occasional short story as well. I've published eight books in this country and nine in England. I've published in France, Italy, Japan—even in Russia believe it or not. I have what I suppose you'd call a cult following. Though my sales figures have always been small. If I sell forty thousand paperback copies of any given book I'm lucky. There are fans out there who seem to devour everything I do, even search for the out-of-print novels—and most of them *are* out of print—through mail-order catalogues and used bookshops. But I've never been able to break through with anything. Probably, I never will."

"Why's that?"

He was interested, she could tell by the look on his face. Which probably meant he was a reader. She supposed from a man like this you might expect the unexpected.

"I'm cranky I suppose. I write what I like to write. The kinds of books I like to read. Mostly they're short, a couple hundred pages. And Americans all seem to want doorstops these days, or at least that's what publishers are foisting off on them. Plus it has to do with the kind of things I write. Suspense, horror. I tend to proceed from the dark side, to try to disturb you. Some of it can be pretty brutal. But look at it this way. Stephen King can be brutal. James Ellroy and Thomas Harris can be brutal. And they've all written best-sellers. They also happen to be honest writers. No. Mostly it's the publishers. They check the computer to see what you sold last time and that's the number they expect to run this time. I can't seem to get them to *print* enough copies so that they can *sell* enough copies to get my work out there on any kind of ongoing basis."

"Change your style. Write them a big fat blockbuster."

She opened a fresh pack of Winstons.

"I don't have a big fat blockbuster in me, Richard. Nothing wrong with them if you have the stamina, if you can sustain it. *Lonesome Dove* certainly manages. But I rarely read them and I rarely like them when I do, and I'm damned if I'm going to write something just for the money or so some editor can be flavor of the month with the boys on publishers' row. Anyhow, all that's beside the point now."

She lit the cigarette and held out the pack. He took one and she lit that too.

"Thank God," she said. "A smoker."

Cigarette smoke rode the back of the woodsmoke from the stove and mingled with tonight's earlier cooking smells. Steak. Baked potato and steamed squash.

"More coffee?"

"If it's not too much trouble. The flight. Then the drive here."

"No trouble if you don't mind microwave this time."

"That's fine."

She got up and went to the sink and rinsed his cup, filled it with lukewarm coffee and put it in the microwave. The timer buzzed away the seconds. She watched the moths fluttering at the window over the sink, dozens of them drawn to the light, wanting in. She turned away from them.

"I'm not interested in getting rich," she said. "I make enough to squeak by on and I've long since come to terms with that. The *work's* the thing, Richard. I work hard and carefully at what I do and I think I do it fairly well. I'm no Dostoevski but I'm no hack either. You get themes in my books, you get people, issues—though I try hard not to hammer you over the head with them. You get some decent writing. What you *don't* get I hope is simple, comfortable beach-reading. Tub-reading. Subway-reading. You don't get Jackie Collins. It's the *work* not getting out there—that it's simply unavailable most of the time even if you wanted to read it, even if you're looking for it—that's what gets my goat. That's what I always come back to."

The buzzer sounded. She brought him the steaming mug. She set it down in front of him and then walked to the living room and took a slim black dog-eared paperback off the bookshelves and brought it back with her into the kitchen. She flipped through it for a moment and found what she wanted and then sat down again.

"You mind doing some reading?"

"Not at all."

She held it out to him.

"Pages eighty-two to ninety-four, where the scene breaks. My first novel. It made me some money and it made my reputation. Or maybe I should say notoriety."

She watched him slip the elastic band into his jacket pocket and settle back in the chair and begin reading and saw that he did not break the binding—no more than it was already broken, the book having been lent and lent again. So in fact he *was* a reader. He knew how to treat a paperback.

He was also fast. By the time she'd refreshed her own mug he was almost through.

"You are good," he said, smiling, closing the book. "And you *are* brutal. Unusual for a woman."

"Try some of Joyce Carol Oates. Try Susanna Brown. It can be a brutal world, I figure. Anyhow the scene you've just read and a few other scenes got the publisher so upset he damn near fired the editor. Distributors were furious. So they decided to bury it, pretend it never happened. Pulled all the advertising, window posters, point-of-purchase displays, all that sort of thing—which were already set in motion by the way—and never put it into a second printing. This despite the fact that the book made money for them. That it sold a quarter-million copies, by word of mouth alone. Now I'm told it's a collector's item."

He handed her the book and sat back in his chair and looked at her.

"I know what you're thinking," she said. "You're thinking this is all very interesting and she's paid me a good retainer and flown me out here but now let's cut to the chase please. Let's get on with it."

He nodded. "Something like that. May I?"

He reached for another cigarette, lit it and stared at her through the smoke. The stare did not make her uncomfortable.

"I guess the question in my mind," he said, "is who exactly is it? Who do you want me to get rid of? Your publisher? Your editor? Who's the target?"

She almost laughed. She *did* smile. There were so many publishers, so many editors. So many distributors for that matter. To hire him to get all of them would take millions.

"Me," she said. "I'm the target."

If this surprised him she couldn't see it. He just sat there calmly smoking, watching her. She sighed.

"The disease always strikes me as so damn banal. Bone cancer. I smoke two and half packs a day. It should have been lung cancer at least. Something that has something to do with me, something to do with the way I live. But I'm assured it will be painful enough."

"So you don't want to wait."

"No, I don't want to wait. I do want something else though."

"Which would be what."

"I want it done a certain way. In fact you've just read the way I want it done."

And now she saw that she *had* managed to surprise him.

"You mean an approximation. Some kind of staging."

"No. I want it done as closely as possible to the scene you just read. You see why I told you before that without knowing me you'd probably refuse the contract? But I'm not crazy and I'm not some kind of masochist. Someone is going to *notice* if you do it this way. Any other way and I'm just one more dead writer. But if you do it this way someone is going to refer it back to the book. Plenty of people will, I think. And the book is going to go back into print, big-time. In fact if you do it right they'll *all* go back into print. I know the way this works."

He snubbed out the cigarette and nodded slowly, frowning.

"Give me the book again," he said.

"Page eighty-two."

"I know."

She watched him read for a moment, reading it in a different way now, with a different understanding, then stood and went to the window by the sink. The moths fluttered, tapping with tiny feet and wings. On the hill outside she could see the dark outline of the tree. The rope was already there waiting coiled at its base beside the bucket. The pegs were driven. The kindling and logs all piled for the fire.

"Good God," he said. "You really want this? All of it?"

"I want a good cop or a good forensics man to be able to go over every detail in the book and find it right there, in the flesh, outside. This is about the *work*, Richard, not about pain. I can handle the pain. I have a feeling you're good. I have a feeling it won't last long. Not as long as bone cancer anyway."

"The last line . . . there's no way in hell I could . . ."

"I anticipated that problem. And believe me I wouldn't ask you to. So here's the only area we'll fudge a little."

She opened the drawer in front of her beside the sink and reached in and withdrew what she'd made for him weeks ago and walked over and set it on the table. Two halves of a can of Pepsi. She'd taken scissors to each half and cut into them into two jagged lines.

"Ten years later I did a sequel," she said. "Another attempt to get this first book back in print. It didn't work. But these were in the sequel. Use them instead. Surrogate teeth, not real ones. Use them, take what you need to take and then dispose of them somewhere. Turn to the next chapter. Where it says *1:18 a.m.* That's how it ends for her.

You haven't read that yet. That's how *I* end."

He read. For a moment he actually went pale. He shook his head.

"I honestly don't know if I can do this," he said. "God knows you're paying me well but . . ."

She sat down across from him and reached urgently across the table and gripped his hand so hard her knuckles went white.

"I'm paying you *everything*, Richard. Everything I have. My bank account has exactly fifty two dollars in it. I'll show it to you. That's what this means to me. One last gamble, Richard. All or nothing. Everything riding on the work. Your work and mine. Please. Do it right. I'm begging you."

He stared at her hard across the table, searching for something inside her she thought or perhaps inside himself and then at last he seemed to find what he needed.

"Thank you," she said.

They lay naked side by side in the bed because that was in the book too, that was how it started and Richard had not complained or balked at that, at the wearing of two hats so to speak but now it was time for the rest of it to happen. She had found him alternately a rough and tender lover and her orgasm perhaps because it was to be her last astonished her with its fierce complexity, its rhythms, smooth and jarring, so much like the way she wrote. She watched him rise from the bed and put on his clothes and glance at her bathed in moonlight, taking her in.

"Please. Do it *all*," she said.

"I will."

She lay peaceful in the silence waiting for him knowing that he would not lie to her, wondering if he'd read her now in the days and weeks to come, feeling that probably he would for how could he not be curious to give the work a try after this, thinking this as suddenly shattered glass was everywhere, she felt it spray across her breasts and stomach, her face and hair and felt hands close hard over her wrists and pull her roughly across the broken window-pane raking her backbone, the broken shards of glass cutting deep and then she was out in the cool night air exactly as it should be, exactly as she'd written, and the end of her night began.

The *New York Times* reporter hung up the phone.

My God, he thought, *what he'd done to her*.

He'd promised the Dead River, Maine PD to withhold some information just in case they caught the guy and to eliminate the cranks and crazies but felt pretty certain they were withholding none from him. These cops were so excited with their find they probably would have talked to the *Enquirer*.

Besides, the *Times* was *all the news that's fit to print*.

And a whole lot of this didn't qualify.

He went over the notes in front of him. The writer's name was unfamiliar. Forty-nine years old. Female. Unmarried. No children. He made a mental note to get a photo. It would help if she was a looker. Eight novels under her belt. Her publisher was here in New York.

Then the details.

The writer had been dragged naked through her bedroom window in the middle of the night, punched in the jaw probably to unconciousness, hauled up the limb of a tree by ropes tied to her feet while two more ropes tied off each arm to pegs driven into the ground. There were indications she had awakened at some point and struggled, struggled hard, rope-burns on her wrists and ankles. The guy had taken a knife to her, slit her open from vagina to collar-bone and then slashed her throat, bleeding her into a large metal tub. Then he'd opened her up and took the heart.

And apparently ate quite a bit of it.

He'd taken out the liver and the kidneys and spitted her over a fire. He'd hacked meat off loins and breast, hacked off one of her legs, severed the head and cracked it open on a rock and then scooped out the brains. All these showed signs of having been significantly nibbled too.

His story was going to be a monster.

He dialed information and got the number for her publisher, dialed that and asked to speak to her editor. Then he waited hoping he was going to get to the guy before the police did, hoping for the perfect stunned reaction.

His pencil was hot and ready.

The editor sat at his desk cluttered with notes and books and contracts and unanswered correspondence not to mention the telephone which he felt had just now bitten him like a snake and gazed up at the unkempt rows of westerns, mystery novels, suspense novels, romance novels, spy novels, all of which he had bought with hopes ranging from high through meager to almost none at all, none of which had done him any good within the company, few of which had earned out their advances and thought, *I've got to call the boss, my God I've got to call the boss, Jesus jumping christ I never call the boss but I've got to on this one.*

First, though, he thought.

He pushed up from the swivel chair and away from the desk feeling a whole lot lighter than his two-hundred twenty-five pounds and ran out of the tiny nasty cubicle they called his goddamn office and out into the hall and leaned over his secretary's desk and asked how many books they had of hers. *How many? she said. Copies? Not copies you dummy he said,* contracts! *How many books of hers are still under* contract! *Three, she said, the last three, rights have reverted on the rest. Well we're sure as shit buyin' 'em back!* he thundered so that a copy editor he thought a total incompetent because he actually insisted on reading a book through before he would deign to take a red pencil to the thing looked up at him and scowled because to the copy editor this was some kind of goddamn library not a fucking publishing company and he went back to his office and sat in his chair and calmed himself and laughed and shook his head and thought, *I love this job* and then he made the call.

225

The Best

What remained when the tears were finished was a black column driven straight through her heart.

She decided to let it stay there.

They were in the bedroom. Their fights were always in the bedroom. Now this final one and it was as though they were a pair of boxers breaking to their respective corners. He sat down on the bed. She sat in the chair by the dresser. Both smoking their Winstons. Both in silence. She was the one who broke it.

"You know you're the best I've ever had, Tommy." Her voice was still a little shaky. She supposed that was all to the good.

"I know. You told me."

"I'm gonna miss that. I'm gonna miss a lot of things."

"Yeah."

She looked at him a moment and then stood and began to unbutton her blouse.

He noticed.

"What're you doing?"

"One last time, Tommy. You said you'd always want me. No matter what."

"Hey look, I dunno."

"You said."

She slipped the blouse off her shoulders. She wore no bra. At thirty-five her breasts were still fine and she knew it. So did he. She unzipped the skirt and let it fall. She pulled down the black silk panties. Stepped out of them and walked to the bed.

"Look Shiela . . ."

"You *owe* me. I want you, y'know?"

She leaned over and unbuckled his belt and unzipped his fly and Janine or no Janine she could see that he wanted her too. At least his body did.

That would do.

"Pull up."

"Okay but listen. This doesn't mean anything, Shiela. I'm still outa here tomorrow." He slid out of his teeshirt.

"I know. Pull up."

He lifted his ass off the bed and she pulled down his jeans. The briefs came off with them. The black column in her heart now matched by the angry red fleshy thing rising off the bed. He looked at her.

"Whatever. I still think this is crazy. But if you want, climb on."

"Condom first."

"Awwww, for chrissake."

"Condom first, Tommy. You think I want to get pregnant? *Now*?"

She opened the drawer on the bedside table and took out a Trojan and peeled off the wrapper and slid it over him.

When they were finished she took it off again. Just like she always did.

"Hi, Janine."

The younger woman standing in the doorway looked startled.

"You busy? Am I interrupting something?"

"Jeez, Shiela, it's after midnight."

Janine looked ready to run at a moment's notice. She held the nightgown tight around her. *Guilty as sin.* Shiela smiled.

"Don't worry. It's not as though I wasn't expecting something. Lucy Baskin told me months ago she thought the two of you were into one another. I just looked the other way is all. You know how it is. I'm not mad at you. We can probably even still be friends. I just wanted to talk to you. Tommy said he thought it might be a good idea."

"*Tommy* did?"

Tommy was in bed, snoring. As usual after they fucked.

"Yeah. So what do you say? Can I come in for a minute? Just a minute?"

"Well, I . . . I guess. Yeah. Sure."

She stepped aside and Shiela walked on in and when Janine turned around after shutting the door that was when Shiela planted a good hard right to her chin, an uppercut, still smiling and pleased all to hell about the six months' boxing lessons which Tommy said were unfeminine and basically dumb because muggers didn't box, he said, they mugged you and Janine slid down the door limp as a sack.

Shiela reached into her purse for the blue rubber gloves she'd meant to use for oven-cleaning one of these days and put them on and grabbed Janine by the ankles and dragged her across the piss-yellow carpet into the bedroom and dropped her feet and grabbed her under the arms instead and hauled her onto the bed. She took off her coat and draped it over the fake-brass foot-rail. She took off her sneakers and put them on the floor beside her purse. Then she went to Janine's closet for a belt that would do the trick and found one that wasn't just cheap imitation leather and climbed up on the bed and scattered the pillows so she could kneel comfortably with Janine's head between her knees and looped the belt around her neck.

When she began to pull Janine woke coughing and sputtering and trying to get her fingers in under the belt but it was too late for that and the thrashing didn't help much either. Shiela had twenty pounds on her, easy. When her tongue protruded and her face went from red to greyish blue she unlooped the belt and got off the bed and went to her purse. She put the belt in the purse for later. Then she went back to Janine.

She tore at the nightgown noting that her own boobs were better than Janine's though the rest of her she had to admit was young and dismayingly firm and then ripped off her panties and threw them on the floor. She took a few minutes to give the body a good beating, concentrating on the ribs and head and did that until the face was bloody and her knuckles throbbed. She went back to her purse again. She took out the condom and pin.

The condom was sealed at the end with a coated wire twistie-tie off a loaf of rye bread so she undid that wondering if any of these little guys were still alive in there and if they were whether they'd try to impregnate a dead Janine.

Dead or alive she knew it wouldn't matter to anybody interested in DNA. But it was still interesting to speculate.

And then came the nasty part.

It couldn't be helped.

She had to spread the legs and get up inside her, open her up. It wasn't easy because what she discovered was that the dead don't lubricate much but then she guessed that blood would do just as well and in fact make it look even better. The bruising too. It occurred to her that what it was *actually* going to look like to the cops was that Tommy'd fucked her after she was already dead.

Tommy, one of those necrophiliac-types like Jeffrey Dahmer? Tommy? The idea made her giggle.

When she was through she slipped the condom over her blue-gloved index finger and pricked its well-end with the pin. Then she inserted the condom and pushed until she was certain the condom was pretty much drained of Tommy. Then she withdrew and packed up. The condom

229

and pin went into one ziplock baggie and the rubber gloves into another.

And that was that.

Driving home she tossed first one baggie and then the other and finally the belt out the window along the road a half mile or so apart from each other. When she got home Tommy was still sleeping.

She took off her clothes and got into bed.

She felt the familiar humid warmth of him beside her and thought for a moment how sad it was, really, that he'd be leaving anyway. Not where he wanted to go but somewhere.

She'd been telling him the truth before.

God's honest truth.

He was far and away the best she'd ever had.

Redemption

Dora followed them down into the Forty-second street station, standing well back in the line as he paid for both their tokens.

Big spender.

She watched him take her hand as they went through the turnstiles side by side, then fished a token out of her change purse and followed them down the stairs to the uptown local waiting on the tracks. Her luck was holding— she slipped into the car ahead of theirs just as the doors slid closed in the face of the old black bag lady behind her. The woman howled and swatted at the door like she was chasing flies.

So many of these women. So many flies.

She could see them through the door windows, standing, straphanging, swaying together as the train pulled away. The back of Howard's suit looked wilted with heat and humidity. The woman was smiling.

Dora gave him this much, he'd always had taste.

The woman wore a black silk jumpsuit, possibly Versace—*black*, for God's sake, on a day like this—looking fresh and clean despite the ninety-degree weather. Her skin was pale, drawn tight across the delicate facial bones, her hair long and black, lips stained bright red and teeth very white.

Her body was not unlike Dora's, but built on a different scale. The woman had easily three inches on her and maybe four—five seven or five eight—so that the slim thighs looked even slimmer, the breasts and buttocks fuller by contrast.

Early thirties.

Irish, probably.

And money. The jumpsuit was expensive. So were the heavy silver bracelet and the ruby-studded earrings.

She was the best one yet as far as Dora was concerned.

Good for you, Howard, she thought.

Bastard.

They got off at Sixty-sixth, walked out of the station and up to Sixty-eighth and then eastward toward the park. A homeless woman in front of the Food Emporium was hawking the *Daily News*. To Dora she looked like one of those dust bowl photos by Walker Evans, all gaunt angles and sad hard lines. The teeth in her mouth would be rotten. Her flesh would smell of mildew and old leaves.

She felt a flash of pity for the woman that was not entirely free of pity for herself.

It was rush hour. Yet this far uptown the sidewalk traffic was light, and she had no trouble following them. At Columbus they turned north past Fellini's, and he took her hand again as they stopped for a moment in front of a boutique, gazing in at the lingerie in the window, while Dora ducked inside a store and picked up the latest copy of *Elle*. The *Elle* fit nicely with the light tailored Burberry suit and Mark Cross briefcase.

Just another pretty young career woman on the rise.

The magazine was an accessory.

With the first one it had been glasses. For some reason no

232

one ever worried about a woman wearing glasses, and the girl, some goddamn secretary no less, had opened the door immediately. All Dora'd said was that she was looking for Howard, she was an old friend from school and he'd given her this address in case he wasn't at his own apartment—and since he wasn't here, either, would the girl mind if she left him a note? Sure, said the girl and turned her back on Dora to show her in. She took the six-inch stainless-steel carving knife out of her handbag, reached up into the girl's frizzy red hair, pulled her head back, and slit her throat.

The rest of it was harder. She had to get the body into the bedroom, up on the bed, and strip it naked, making it look like a sex crime and not what it was, an execution, and the girl was heavier than she looked, heavier in fact than Howard usually liked them, so that she had to wonder what it was the girl had— she wasn't all that pretty, really—not like this one—and she supposed it was the sex, it had to be; Howard always did think with his prick. And considering that took some of the unpleasantness out of inserting the handle of the electric broom and then, rolling her over, the bottle.

On Seventy-first street they moved east again. Halfway between Columbus and Central Park West they turned up the stairs of a renovated brownstone. Number thirty-nine. The woman opened the door. Dora crossed the street, staring up at the windows, slowly walking by. It was dusk by then, and the apartment would be dark inside. She watched. Once again her luck was good. The woman had a front apartment. She saw the light go on the third floor, had a brief impression of high white ceilings and plants hanging in the window. She looked away and continued walking.

At Central Park West she turned back the way she came. She glanced at the apartment and saw that the curtains were drawn now, their color indistinguishable. Dark, heavy material. At Pizza Joint Two she asked the waiter for a table by the window and seated herself facing east so she could watch the entrance to number thirty-nine across the street.

She ordered shrimp parmigiana, antipasto, and a glass of wine.

She looked at her watch. Six-thirty-five.

If her luck still held, he wouldn't stay the night.

And then this would be the easiest yet. Easier even—and far less dangerous—than pushing MaryBeth Chapman, budding blond account exec for Shearson, in front of the Seventh Avenue express at Thirty-fourth street. If anyone had noticed her hands on MaryBeth's back, they hadn't said anything. Maybe there was too much shock at the sound of it for anyone to have reacted even if they had noticed—the liquid crack like a huge balloon full of water bursting and a tree-limb snapping, both at once. The enormous red spray.

Easier than both the others because he'd brought the others to his apartment first, and she'd had to wait and follow them once they were alone, planning it, getting to know their habits somewhat—where they lived, who they saw, and where they went.

Here she only had to wait till he left. Then she could go in asking for him the same way she had with the secretary holding the copy of Elle in front of her because it looked right there, a prop. Subliminal. She was neat and fashionable and wasn't any threat to anybody, and the brand-new eight-inch knife was handy in the briefcase. She would cut her a little differently. Rob her this time. Nothing sexual. No connection from a police point of view. Clean and tragic.

The talking heads on television all loved the word "tragic."

An abandoned baby in a dumpster was tragic. A kid caught in a crossfire between crack dealers was tragic. A rising young businesswoman falling in front of a subway train—oh yes. That was tragic, too.

Nonsense.

To be tragic you had to have *stature*. Your suffering—and you—had to be somehow bigger than life. The Electras, the Medeas, the Lears, and the Hamlets. You had to fall from great heights, endure great pain. You had to have all the world to lose—and then you had to lose it.

Take Howard, now. Nothing tragic there.

Though on the surface there were arguments to be made.

A successful corporate lawyer. Yes. *Very* successful. A modicum of stature was implicit in any success.

Then his mother had died two months ago. Sad.

And then the inexplicable, seemingly random loss of two of his lovers. *Each of his lovers following Dora, whom he'd dumped after five long years of practically tying his damn shoe-laces for him.* Pitiable.

And now a third to follow.

All this. But still—nothing tragic.

Because Howard was a worm, essentially. Small. Small enough to tell her that the sex was her fault—though *he* was the one who couldn't get an erection—and small enough to blame her when the bank had laid her off—*along with thirty other people, thank you very much*—to say she wasn't aggressive enough. Wasn't sharp enough.

Small enough to try to make her feel that much *smaller* just because his ego needed boosting. And then to dump her entirely.

No. No tragic figure there.

Just a weak little man with a lot of bad luck when it came to romantic involvements.

And his luck would not improve. Not ever. Not if Dora could help it.

Not one of them would live. Not one.

Until finally, one day, sometime in the future, he saw himself for the evil jinx virus he was and stopped trying altogether.

She knew what sex meant to him. For years, until he developed his . . . problem, it meant plenty.

It would absolutely kill him.

Redemption, she thought. It meant to recover something pawned or mortgaged. What she'd mortgaged to Howard.

To set something free.

Her sense of self. Her own *true* self.

She thought, *I need some damn redemption.*

At eight o'clock he left the building.

She was dawdling over a second cup of coffee, and she almost missed him—he walked right by her seated in the window. Dora thought he looked sort of sad somehow, thoughtful.

Perhaps upstairs things were not going all that smoothly.

It didn't matter.

She finished the coffee slowly and paid the bill in cash. *No records.* A cabbie was picking up a fare—a dapper old man in an expensive suit, wearing a bow tie and carrying a cane—directly across the street from number thirty-nine. She thought of the Walker Evans woman in front of the market. It was still a man's world. Even an old man's. She waited until they pulled away and then crossed the street, walked up the stairs, opened the door, and scanned the mailboxes in the hall. Three F was B. Querida. The name surprised her. She'd been sure the woman was Irish.

She buzzed her.

"Yes?"

"Hello. Yes. It's Janet."

"Janet?"

"Yes. Is Howard there?"

There was a pause.

"Hold on. I'll buzz you up."

The buzzer sounded. She opened the door and went to the elevator and pushed 3.

There were only two apartments on the floor, which said something about their size. And the location was a block from Central Park West. B. Querida was doing rather well for herself, she thought. Probably as well as Howard.

The woman stood in the open doorway, still wearing the black silk jumpsuit—or was that *wearing it again?*—looking poised and smiling and faintly curious.

"Sorry. You just missed him," she said.

Dora stopped just outside the doorway.

"Damn!" she said. She looked momentarily confused and flustered. "I work with him. I've got some papers for him to sign. Oh, God."

"He gave you this address?"

"He said he'd be here till about eight, eight-thirty. And I just now got away. Did he say where . . . ?"

"No. Afraid he didn't."

"Listen. Would you mind . . . ? Do you think I could use your phone and try to call someone on this?"

"Sure. Of course. Come on in."

The woman stood aside.

The room in front of Dora was cluttered, almost Victorian, though spotlessly clean. And not nearly as large as she would have guessed. Overstuffed chairs in front of what looked like a working fireplace. Heavy maroon curtains. Bric-a-brac and vases filled with long-stem roses.

The room was dark. Deep reds. Mahogany furniture.

Even the paintings were dark. Landscapes in storm. Undecipherable forms. One of them, she thought, might be an Albert Ryder.

It was not what she'd expected.

"The phone's in the bedroom. This way."

The woman was walking in front of her now, through a paneled corridor, black-and-white prints and old sepia photos on the walls, their subjects mostly a blur to her. A closed oak door lay directly ahead of them. The corridor was narrow.

Dora opened the briefcase. Her fingers found the hardwood handle.

It was awkward here, the space too tight.

Better to wait until the bedroom, she thought. Even fake the phone call if she had to.

There would be plenty of opportunity. B. Querida had turned her back on her. She wasn't afraid. If she'd do it once, she'd do it twice.

The woman's fingers closed over the cut crystal doorknob, turned it, and gently pushed open the door. And now she was standing in profile, half her face visible to Dora and smiling in the dim hall light, the other half lost in the bedroom's dark.

"I'll get the light," she said. She stepped inside.

Dora stepped in silently behind her, into darkness. And at once felt oddly out of place here, as though she were not in the city at all anymore but in some room in Vermont or New Hampshire, out in the country somewhere on some night when there was no moon and no stars, when the darkness seemed to swallow every shred of light. New York was never *black*. Never. It glowed.

Not now. Her eyes could make out nothing of the woman inside. She could only hear her cross the room with the practiced ease of someone long blind in a wholly familiar darkness.

And stop. And wait.

And she almost turned away then because there was something wrong with that, somehow it wasn't right, there was a trick here somewhere, and she didn't much care to know where or how but this blackness was *all wrong* and something was telling her to get the hell out of there when she heard a *click* and suddenly the dark exploded, flooded her with light.

So that *she* was the blind one for the moment, unaware of the woman moving back across the room until she was already leaning toward her through the beam like some sudden evil angel bathed in light, aware only of heat and scalding brightness until the woman grabbed her arm and her briefcase and shoved her forward into the room, tore the briefcase from her hands and sent her sprawling across the floor.

The door slammed shut.

Dora thought of her father.

The door slammed shut behind him. The lock turned. Whiskey on his clothes and on his breath as he leaned over.

Whose little girl are you?

The woman walked directly toward her out of the klieg light trained on the door.

"Some of my clients want to feel like movie stars," she said. "Or maybe political prisoners." She laughed. "Sometimes a little of both."

The room was strung with track lighting. Out of the beam of the klieg, Dora could see normally. She sat up and looked around, and the woman saw her looking.

She extracted the knife from the briefcase.

As though she knew it was there all along.

"I lied about the bedroom," she said. "That's over on the other side of the apartment. And nobody goes there but me. Sorry."

Dora looked up and felt the hysterical urge to laugh and then the urge to run.

The room was long and narrow, and except for a wooden chair and small oak linen cabinet, empty of conventional furniture. There were no windows. She could see where there had been one, the sill and frame were there but the window itself had been bricked over and painted black. The rest of the room was like the padded cell of an asylum—except that the padding, too, was black. Thick steel rods webbed the ceiling. Chains, harnesses, and manacles dangled from them irregularly, some connected by ropes to pulleys on the wall. There was a wall of instruments made of steel and wood—instruments to clamp and probe, to cut and to pierce and tear.

Another wall displaying masks, belts, whips, some of them tipped with metal balls.

In the center of the room stood two huge eight foot black beams intersecting to form the letter X.

The wall in front of it was a mirror.

She saw what looked like an outdoor grille made of old rusted iron.

A wooden barrel lying on its side, studded with nails.

She saw a scarred butcher-block table arrayed with weights and clamps and knives.

To this the woman added Dora's carving knife, setting it down gently, almost lovingly.

"He comes here, you know? He feels guilty."

"Guilty?"

"Of course he does. Look at what he did to you."

"Me? How do you know . . . ?"

"Oh, I know you all right. I knew you right away. See, Howard always pays cash. You'd think a guy like him, with the kind of job he's got, you'd think he'd go with a credit card just to get the float. Not Howard. Always cash. Did you know he still carries a picture of you in his wallet?"

"I . . . he does?"

"I told you. He feels guilty. I bet you didn't think he had it in him, did you?"

The woman was serious. *Her picture was in his wallet.* Amazing.

"Of course it's not just you. There's the broker and the secretary. He feels guilty about them, too. Though I never could figure out why. Hell, I think he even feels guilty about his *mother* dying. Howard's got a lot of guilt. A lot to answer for. At least *he* thinks so." She laughed again. "Don't look so shocked. In this business you hear a lot of stories. People confess. I make them confess."

She stepped closer.

"Stand up, Dora."

She did as she was told.

"Take off your jacket. Let me look at you."

She hesitated.

"I'm a whole lot stronger than you. Without your little toy there. You know that, don't you?"

Dora looked up into her wide green eyes and nodded. She slipped the jacket off her shoulders. And suddenly felt naked there.

The woman reached out and lightly touched her hair. Her touch was electric.

"So what about you?" she said. "What have *you* got to answer for?"

You've got to get out of here, she thought. *Now*.

The woman turned away, walked to the klieg light and switched it off.

"Let's see if I've got this correct," she said. "Once you had him, you didn't want to fuck him anymore, am I right?" She shrugged. "It happens. For some people, the capture's everything. Once you've proven you can *do* it, once he's yours, it's not so much, is it? Kind of turns to ashes. Especially if you don't really like yourself much. And you don't, do you?"

Dora felt her eyes on her again, probing.

"Of course it took *him* awhile to catch on to that—to catch *up* with you, to become the incredible shrinking dick you really preferred him to be in the first place. And then once he did, he sort of retaliated, he started to belittle you, tried to make you feel like somebody small and stupid and powerless. Which part of you *really thinks you are*. He knew exactly which buttons to push, didn't he."

She walked to the table and picked up Dora's knife again, fingering the edge she'd honed this morning.

"I do, too," she said.

And Dora believed her.

"Did it occur to you that he was only whittling you down to size in a way? So he could finally leave you, get free of you without feeling like something was wrong with *him*, prove to himself that it was really you all along? And it *was* you, wasn't it. Part of you really *is* small. You didn't want to fuck him. You'd already got what you wanted. Simple as that.

The woman walked back to where Dora stood in front of the huge black X and pointed the knife at her, at the top button of her blouse. Dora stood frozen. The woman turned her wrist and the button was gone.

"So," she said. "I'll say it again. What've *you* got to answer for?"

She felt the coolness of the knife as it parted her blouse, its flat edge moving down. Another flick.

Another button falling to the bare hardwood floor.

"I . . . I didn't . . ."

"*Mean to?* Of course you did, Dora!"

She trembled. The knife moved down over her cream silk bra, over her sternum. To the next button.

Flick.

The woman shook her head and smiled ruefully.

"And he still keeps your picture in his wallet. You're standing on the rocks by the shore. You're wearing a halter and jeans and the waves are crashing white foam and you're smiling."

The flat of the blade moved down across her belly. The blade felt warmer now. She could feel the woman's breath on her cheek. It smelled of rain and fresh open air. The woman was beautiful.

They had all, in their ways, been beautiful.

"Dora. Don't you feel *guilty*?"

She couldn't help it. She began to cry.

"Oh. No need for that," said the woman. "Just step back."

She felt the point of the knife in her belly now, pressing her gently toward the wooden structure behind her. But the woman was wrong—there was plenty of need to cry. Whether the tears came out of guilt or fear seemed almost irrelevant now, they were practically one and the same.

The woman knelt and fitted her ankles into the soft black leather manacles at the base of the structure and strapped them tight. When she parted Dora's legs to set second strap she felt all volition leave her, expelled in one long breath.

"Raise your arms."

She felt the manacles tighten over her wrists, smelled leather and rich scented oil. The woman stepped back.

"And the others, Dora. Have you thought about the others?"

She hadn't.

She had.

Of course she had.

She gazed at herself in the mirrored wall, and then at

the woman's long sleek back. I'll see everything, she thought. Everything.

Both of us. All the while.

It was terrifying. Also thrilling. As though she and the woman were part of a single entity and both were Dora— *essentially Dora*—the punisher and the punished.

"You killed them. You were going to kill me."

Her heart pounded. In the mirror she saw the rise and fall of her breasts, nipples hard and aching beneath the thin filmy surface of the bra.

The woman sighed. "You've been a very bad girl," she said. "They didn't deserve it. Certainly not because of you and Howard. I think you've got a lot to answer for. Don't you?"

In the mirror she watched herself respond. She nodded.

And thought, *I was only looking for some redemption.*

She watched as the knife slit through her skirt from waist to hem, the sweat of the day cooling suddenly on her as the skirt fell away, then moved up to the final two buttons of her blouse and trailed up along her arms to slit the sleeves, so that blouse and skirt formed a pool on the floor in front of her like a snake shedding its skin.

The woman paused and stepped away and allowed her a moment to see herself in the mirror.

That was good. She found that she needed to see.

She walked to the linen cabinet, took out two black sheets, and spread them around Dora's feet both front and back. She unbuttoned the jumpsuit and shrugged it off her shoulders. Beneath it she was naked. She placed the jumpsuit neatly on the back of the chair, then took a long pearl-handled straight-edge razor from the table and opened it. The razor gleamed in the track lighting. She thought that it was very much like her father's.

"This is going to take awhile," she said. "And it's going to get somewhat messy. But we'll get to the bottom of you, you and I. I promise you that. Your own true inner self."

When the razor plucked through the straps and center

of her bra and the sides of her panties, she felt a sudden rush of freedom bound tight to a sudden sense of dread. It was perfectly right that this should be so.

"We'll set you free," said the woman.

For the first but not the last time, the razor descended.

The Exit at Toledo Blade Boulevard

The boys in the pickup were traveling north along the dark empty stretch of I-75 near Nokomis, three of them cramped side-by-side in the cab and sweating in the mid-July heat despite the open windows. They could smell each other's sweat wafted in and out by the breeze. They didn't mind. It was Monday night. There weren't any girls around anyhow.

Jimmie who had just turned eighteen the week before and was losing yet another battle in his ongoing war with zits popped a Bud and handed it to Doug who handed it to Bobby. The truck was in the fast lane doing seventy in a sixty zone. Bobby was driving. Having his fourth beer open in his hand was dangerous. Less out here on the highway at nearly midnight than it would have been back home on the streets of Tampa—you were much more likely to get stopped in towns—but dangerous enough.

He didn't mind that either. Hell, the risk was part of it.

He'd been lucky so far.

He tilted back the can. The beer was warmer than he liked but the first pull always tasted good, warm or not.

"Hey. Turn that up," he said to Doug. "Quick."

The song on the radio was Johnny Cash doing *The Tennessee Stud* and it reminded him simultaneously of his uncle's hardscrabble farm in Georgia and of Mary Ann Abbot and Dee Dee Whitaker—and what he, Bobby, knew about life that these other two, Doug and Jimmie, didn't.

He loved this guy. The Man in Black.

And for once Doug didn't complain about Johnny's singing. Truth was, Doug was past complaining. Five cold brews at the Cave Rock Inn in Murdock and one on the road and old Douggie could barely find the volume control. He managed though, leaning forward and studying the panel and then Jimmie started singing along beside him. Jimmie had a pretty good singing voice but he couldn't get the growly low notes that Johnny got. What could you expect? Hell, Bobby still remembered when little Jimmie's voice changed. Wasn't that long ago, either. Jimmie was still a kid.

He thought about Mary Ann again, an image of cool white thighs spread naked in the woods.

He was thinking of that and listening to the wind and the song up loud over the wind and he had the beer can to his lips again when he saw something glint ahead of him and then something loom suddenly in the headlights and way over against the passenger side door Jimmie stopped singing and shrieked and he guessed he did too something like *whathafuuuuck?* and he swerved the pickup and braked and tried to steer and the next thing he knew they were cruising the bumpy dirt shoulder at fifteen miles per hour, amazed to be alive. He was shaking like a cold wet dog and his lap and legs and teeshirt were foul and wet where Doug had thrown up all the hell over him.

*   *   *

Earlier that afternoon George Hubbard stared out the double glass doors leading from his kitchen to the lanai and thought about the dog and how the dog had in some ways been the beginning of the end of it.

The dog had been a gift to her, something to make her stay, a hope against hope that a few furry pounds of warm retriever puppy would be the glue for them that sex no longer was, nor love, nor anything else was able to be.

It hadn't worked. She was gone, the dog with her.

Just like all the rest of them.

His father was gone—dead of a heart attack—and that was all to the good, actually. At least one of them wouldn't be around to play victim to his mother's fucking viciousness any more. His sister, now in her thirties, had somehow without his noticing turned into the lesbian bitch from Sodom, working as a mail carrier for God's sake in Shreveport, Lousiana. They hadn't talked in two years, not since his father died and even then that was mostly to shout at one another. His friends had drifted away into one Sarasota warren or another since he started telling them the truth about what was really going on with him. They'd all stepped back into their own little lives, their own private blind alleys of pseudo-awareness. Good riddance. Sister, friends. Even his sadass father.

The only one he *couldn't* get rid of was his mother.

Ever since he was a kid she'd been trying to kill him and lately she'd been stepping up the pace. In a way, she'd already succeeded.

He stared out into the dimming sunlight on the lanai and pulled at the joint. The joint was one of the few ways he had of escaping her.

They said he was crazy. Paranoid. The doctors at the hospital after his meth OD had the balls to go even further. Paranoid *schizophrenic* they said.

Even Cal and Linda thought he was paranoid and said so to his face. Told him he needed to get help—his best friends since high school. Said his mother couldn't *do* all that. When he knew damn well she was mob connected, knew damn well she'd been harassing him constantly, anyone could see that, getting her friends in the IRS after him, getting her friends in the police force after him for back child-support payments to his first wife and his daughter, trying to put his ass in jail.

He'd had to leave the state. Come here to Florida.

He'd disappeared.

His mother wasn't the only one who knew a trick or two.

Though he knew she was looking for him even now. He could feel it. In his blood he could feel it. His mother had tentacles everywhere. She was psychic as hell and she was looking.

Get help. Shit. Once, years ago, he'd fucked Linda. It had been a good fuck too. Friendly.

And now she denied him.

They all did.

Even Sandy, after three years of loving him or at least saying she loved him, making him think that, making him feel he *knew that*, staying with him even through the relocation because she understood first-hand what a bitch his mother was, she'd had enough run-ins with her herself by then, though even *she* wouldn't believe how connected she was with police and mob and government, his mother was too smart for that, too smart to let on to her. Some things she reserved strictly for him.

He stubbed out the joint and walked absently through the condo, looking at what she'd left behind. It wasn't a whole lot. In the living room, his desk, a shelf full of paperbacks and audio tapes. In the kitchen, some old pots and pans, some silverware and glassware, the toaster and the microwave they'd bought together.

Upstairs in the bathroom she'd even taken the shower curtain.

The worst, for him, was the bedroom. The bed was still there, but stripped of its quilt and the lace hand-made bed-

248

spread. Dirty sheets lay in a corner. She'd left him three out of seven pillows. The television was gone and the night stand by the bed. The dresser was there, but empty of her jewelry boxes and perfumes and toiletries it looked uninhabited, the entire life of it fled. The empty hangers in the big walk-in closet seemed ridiculous, poverty awaiting an abundance that would never occur again.

He crossed the room and sat down on the bed.

His footsteps sounded much too loud to him.

The bed had seen them through three apartments together, one for every year they'd been together. It seemed almost wrong that she hadn't taken it with her—like leaving a child behind or a kitten. A kind of betrayal. He thought of what had happened on the bed, the talking, the laughing, the fighting, *Jesus*, all the joys and sorrows between them that had lasted long into the night sometimes, he thought of making love to her, her intense, amazing passion that was easily the equal to his own and the like of which he'd not only never seen before but never even knew existed in a woman and which hadn't dimmed at all until just recently, until just this last year when he'd begun telling her the truth about what was happening to him, *sharing* with her really, what his mother was doing and the whole damn conspiracy. And finally, a week ago, about what was wrong with him.

He thought of how intimate a bed was. *In the night, before sleep, the soul pours forth its strength.*

He put his hands to his face and cried.

His listened to his sobs echo in the empty room.

When he was exhausted he stood and went downstairs again. One of the dog's chew-bones lay half-eaten on the landing. He picked it up and walked to the kitchen and dumped it in the garbage.

He stood a moment looking out at the lanai, into the fading light. The screens leading out to the small enclosed yard were becoming overgrown with creepers. Normally he'd have wanted to take care of that right away. He made his living as a gardener and it was a matter of his pride as a professional. A few creepers were one thing, even attractive. He liked them there, their graceful abstract patterns. But the way they were going, eventually they'd ruin the screen.

He decided it was time to break his rule. He'd quit because Sandy hated the smell of the stuff on his breath and he wanted to smell good for her for when they went to bed, for the times they made love or even just kissed good night, so that sleeping beside her on the bed, he wouldn't offend. But now that she was gone there was no one to offend anymore and given this fucking little problem of his, there never would be.

He went to the liquor cabinet. He poured himself a drink.

A half hour after Bobby's pickup went off the road and thirty miles south along I-75, Pete and Jan Hoffsteader's white Ford Thunderbird crept along the on-ramp at Peace River, waited for a set of headlights to pass in the slow lane and then pulled out onto the highway.

They were both a little nervous to be out this late. It was after twelve.

That almost never happened.

Normally they'd have been in bed over half an hour now, right after the news and weather.

Pete was weary.

It had been a pretty good evening, though. They'd had dinner with Jan's brother and sister-in-law, ate good German food at the Karl Ehmer Restaurant in Punta Gorda, too much of it really, so much food that they couldn't finish it all. Which at their age seemed to be happening a lot lately. About half his sauerbraten, red cabbage and potato dumplings were in the usual styrofoam container resting in Jan's lap. They'd gone back to her brother Ed's mobile home for a nightcap which then became two nightcaps and he'd lost track of time a little talking with Ed about their

Join the Leisure Horror Book Club and
GET 2 FREE BOOKS NOW—
An \$11.98 value!

┌─── **Yes! I want to subscribe to** ───
   the Leisure Horror Book Club.

Please send me my **2 FREE BOOKS**. I have enclosed \$2.00 for shipping/handling. Each month I'll receive the two newest Leisure Horror selections to preview for 10 days. If I decide to keep them, I will pay the Special Members Only discounted price of just \$4.25 each, a total of \$8.50, plus \$2.00 shipping/handling. This is a **SAVINGS OF AT LEAST \$3.48** off the bookstore price. There is no minimum number of books I must buy and I may cancel the program at any time. In any case, the **2 FREE BOOKS** are mine to keep.

─── *Not available in Canada.* ───

NAME: _____

ADDRESS: _____

CITY: _____ **STATE:** _____

COUNTRY: _____ **ZIP:** _____

TELEPHONE: _____

E-MAIL: _____

SIGNATURE: _____

If under 1 8, Parent or Guardian must sign. Terms, prices, and conditions subject to change. Subscription subject to acceptance. Dorchester Publishing reserves the right to reject any order or cancel any subscription.

respective outfits stationed in France during the War and then Pete thought he'd best have some coffee before heading back.

They were on their way home to the Silver Lakes retirement community in Sarasota.

Forty-five minutes' driving time.

The highway was nearly deserted at this hour.

What if they had car trouble? *Jesus. What if they had a flat*?

At sixty-seven, with a heart that was not exactly in the best shape possible, not to mention with three drinks in him, he didn't feel up to changing a goddamn flat.

What the hell, he thought, you hope for the best.

Jan was nervous, though. He could tell by the way she kept fidgeting with her hands, playing with the tongue of the styrofoam container.

Part of it was that he wasn't really supposed to be driving at night at all and she knew it. The glaucoma. It narrowed his field of vision and the oncoming headlights could be hell. But out here on the highway the headlights were few and far between. And if he stayed over here in the slow lane they weren't that big a problem. It was worse in town actually, where the streets were narrower.

He felt a momentary annoyance with her. *She'd* been the one who made the dinner date with her brother. What did she expect them to do afterwards? *Fly* home? Whether it was eight o'clock or midnight darkness was darkness, headlights were headlights. He used to drive a bus for a living. He'd manage.

He couldn't stay mad at her, though.

He reached over and patted her pale cool hand.

He was lucky. His second wife was a damn good woman. He'd known that when he married her. But if he'd had any doubts, the way she stood by him during the angioplasty, him scared shitless, scared to tears, she a goddamn *pillar*, well, he would have lost them then and there.

Whoever said that men were tougher than woman didn't have any idea.

Now though, she was really pretty nervous for some reason.

Get her talking, he thought. Relax her.

The usual subject was the first that came to mind.

"So. What do you think about the Stockyard for dinner tomorrow? We haven't been there in a while."

She thought about it.

"Oh, I don't know," she said. "It'll be crowded."

"Not so bad this time of year. With all the snowbirds gone."

"It's *always* crowded. Dorothy went there last *week* and it was crowded. What about the Olive Garden?"

He shrugged. He'd rather have a steak from the Stockyard but so what. "Olive Garden's fine."

"It's just that the Stockyard's going to be so *crowded*."

"I don't mind the Olive Garden."

"I don't know."

He glanced at her. "You all right?"

She was frowning, her mouth turned down, tight brows squinting her eyes. He heard her fingernails pluck at the styrofoam container.

"I'm fine."

"I'm driving okay, aren't I?"

He was doing fifty in a sixty zone, riding the straightaway in the slow lane, the Thunderbird on cruise control, not another car in sight in front of him or behind.

"Yes, dear. You're doing fine."

He knew that.

"So? What, then?" he said.

"I don't know. Something's wrong. Something's not right."

"You worried about your brother?"

Ed had prostate cancer. It was still too early to tell if the treatments were going to take.

"I don't know," she said. "Maybe."

252

He glanced at her again. The dashboard lights gave off a pale greenish glow. Her face was set, immobile.

He thought for a moment that this was what she would look like dead and then dismissed the thought.

Hell, she'd outlive him by ten years, if not more.

She's just tired, he thought. Tired and nervous being out this late, with me driving.

We'll be home soon.

He concentrated on the road ahead and did not look at her again.

Five and a quarter miles behind them Annie Buxton held to a steady sixty in the rented red Nissan and thought about how amazingly *clear* her head was.

Three weeks ago by about this time at night she'd have been sipping her sixth or seventh vodka and tonic. Or she'd have switched to Stoli straight up. Either that or she'd have passed out altogether.

She glanced down at the gas gauge and saw she was down to a quarter of a tank. She'd make it home to Bradenton. Barely. Who cared?

The point was she was going home.

She considered turning on the radio but it was entirely possible that anything the slightest bit sentimental—hell, any song with the word *love* in it—would get her crying again. She was weepy these days.

Her sister said that was to be expected. Annie was picking up the pieces of her life and putting them together again and there were so *many* pieces and so *much* putting together it would make anybody weepy now and then.

Anyhow, Madge said, you always cry when you realized that against the odds, you've survived.

Still she decided against the radio.

It was better to have just the silence and the wind and the highway's bleak flat sweep in front of her.

She took a Marlboro from the pack on the dashboard and lit it in the orange coil glow of the lighter. Cigarettes

253

were something she would continue to allow herself, she thought, at least for the time being. She'd quit them too one of these days, maybe get the patch. But first things first. Or as all the literature read, one damn step at a time.

My God, the air felt good pouring in through the window.

For a week and a half she'd seen nothing but the inside of her sister's stuffy bedroom. The first two days of that, she'd spent strapped to the fourposter bed.

Tough love, Madge called it.

You won't go into a goddamn hospital, okay, fine, we'll do it this way.

She saw rabbits on the bed with her and snakes who swallowed the rabbits whole. She floated out to sea on that bed, sunk and drowned and rose again. She howled and sweated and hurt and stained the sheets.

Tough love. That it was.

Three weeks, total, at her sister's house. Most of that time a virtual prisoner, held hostage against her own vices, trapped inside her own feverish sweaty body while she waited for her system and then her mind to clear themselves of the poisons that were killing both her and her six-year marriage to Tim.

Two weeks before Madge would even allow her to light up a smoke.

By then she'd called her sister every name in the book. Early on, even swung at her a couple of times. Even while she knew in her heart that big sister was busy as hell with the nasty job of saving her silly life.

It was only later, when she was sane enough to talk about things, talk until they were both exhausted, endless exhausting exhilerating nights, that she realized she *actually wanted* to save her life, and that some of the *facts* about her life, like Tim's being a respected English teacher while she'd barely finished high school, like the fact that so far they were childless and she was pushing thirty-five, like the fact that at the moment he was busy with his life and she was not, that these kinds of things didn't matter half as much as she was simply *letting* them matter. It was wilfull destructiveness. She was obsessing on the trivial and ignoring one great big *beautiful* fact—that Tim loved her, hell, he adored her. Even adored her when she was drinking.

Though the drinking was poisoning him too.

So many times she'd sent this gentle quiet man into a towering rage.

So many times she'd pushed and pushed at him.

You're just like Mom! Madge said. *You damn fool. You love him to death and he loves you and all you care about is that you're jealous, that at the moment you're fucking bored and unemployed and you feel stupid and useless because he's not. You know how crazy that is? You're exactly like her! You're not just missing the forest for the trees, you're burning the goddamn forest!*

She brushed her cheek with her fingertips and, in the oncoming glare of headlights moving south toward her, saw that her fingers came away glistening and black with mascara.

You really are a fool, she thought. You might as well turn the radio on after all. You're going to be crying anyway. Why not just wallow in it?

She smiled at herself and stubbed out the cigarette and took a deep breath of the warm night air.

It was over. She'd get into a program if she had to—though she'd never been much of a joiner. Anything. There was no chance in hell she'd ever touch a drink again. She suspected there was going to be a lot of coffee around for a while. His voice on the telephone when she called to say she was coming home to him, the *break* in his voice, the sob when he said *thank God*, told her as clearly as her own finally steady voice did that nothing was ever going to be the same from here on in.

Lives were to be made as best you could and then remade if necessary.

Not broken.

Never broken.

When he climbed into the car that night George Hubbard didn't really know what he was going to do.

He was going out for a drive. Going out to shake the blues. Forget about Sandy. Forget about his mother. Get out of the lonely bare condo and drive before he drank too much to impair his judgement or get his ass arrested.

Meandering through the streets of town he was fine. It was only when he turned out onto I-75 that the darkness began to envelop him.

The darkness began in his mind, in some corner of his mind where his mother lived and Sandy lived and mostly, where anger lived and had for a very long time. It reached out from that place to embrace his future, a growing black clot of pain which dimmed his senses and fed itself on ghostly images of future prosecutions by his demon mother, by the authorities, by doctors, images of the long lonely loveless sexless months ahead of him while the AIDS virus ate away at his immunity, of wasting away alone, of bedsores and coma and that single crystal meth spike in his arm so long ago that was also his mother's demon spike, his mother's revenge, his mother's hydra venom, the reality and consequences of which for both Hubbard and for Sandy he had finally admitted to her and which had driven her away from him in horror and in fury.

The darkness inside spread as the AIDS spread, inking his conscience black.

On I-75 it reached out from his fingertips and turned off the headlights.

And then turned him south into the northbound lane.

He was only half aware of the pickup truck going off the shoulder. Only that he was still alive and whoever was inside was still alive and that so was everybody else on this miserable planet and that none of these things would do.

He drove.
Within and without he was only darkness.

It was probably the glaucoma. Pete never would have seen it were it not for Jan, never did see the car really or not much of it, her eyes good and fixed on the road ahead, his wife worried, nervous about being out so late, Jan startling him so much when she screamed his name that he stomped on the brakes and wrenched at the wheel away from the black hurtling mass ahead of him skimmed by light and the Lincoln rolled, skidded on its side and rolled again and for a moment they were weightless and then they were crashing down, air bags suddenly inflated, his door caving in and the front fender throwing sparks across the highway, the shoulder-strap harness biting deep into his chest and thighs and pulling his shoulder out of its socket with a sickening thud of pain, the air bags enveloping them both as the car slid and righted itself and rolled to a stop at an angle across the highway.

He pushed his way free of the air bag and looked for Jan beside him but only the passenger-side bag was there, the brown and red remains of his dinner from the styrofoam container dripping over it. Her harness was empty. *Had she been wearing it? God! had she had it on her?* Her door was wide open, its window shattered. He tasted metal and smoke.

Only then did he panic.

"Jan! Jesus Jan!"

He shoved at his door but it wouldn't move and pain raced hot through his shoulder. He tried again but he was weak and hurt and then he heard her pulling at it from the outside, calling his name.

"Other side!" he said. "Your side. I'm coming! I'm okay."

Thank God, he thought. Not for himself. For her.

He got out of the harness and edged himself across the seat past the air bag to the door. By the time he got one foot out on the tarmac she was already there in front of him, leaning toward him, crying and smiling both, her pale thin arms reaching out to him to ease him gently home.

Maybe this is a mistake, he thought.
People just kept going by me.
Perhaps it wasn't meant to be. It was possible.
Near the exit to Toledo Blade Boulevard he pushed it up to eighty, sightless of the speedometer in the roaring dark.
There were lights out there in the distance.

I'll get flowers, she thought. I'll make dinner.
Candlelight.
No wine.
Everything new, she thought. People could start over. People could forgive and if not forget exactly they could take up life sadder and wiser than they were and make something good of it, they could make love again and find a halfway decent job and maybe even someday make a baby, she wasn't too old, she had her health now that the poison was gone and the dark cloud over her life was gone, she had strength.
I'm coming, Tim, she thought. *I'm coming home.*
I'm alive. I'm fine.

Chain Letter

I'm waiting for the postman again. I promised myself I'd stop that but here I am.

Most days nothing comes. Not even junk. Nothing.

Which is all to the good, I suppose.

I dreamed last night that I'd broken my leg, so I had to take a cab back to my hotel. Which is silly because there are no cabs here and I live in a little house at the end of a long dirt road and there are no hotels here either. Anyhow I took a cab and got distracted, I was looking out the window and I must have let the driver take a wrong turn somewhere because the next thing I knew I was lost. I cursed the driver. I hated that stupid sonovabitch. By the time we found my hotel we were in deadly emnity. I had whined and bullied. For his part he wouldn't say a word to me.

I got out without paying and went directly into the bathroom and found two old sticks to which I'd attached some rusty nails and I whipped myself over the back and shoulders until I'd done myself real harm.

As I say, it's all ridiculous, because I live all alone out

here at the end of this narrow dirt road, it's so wild that I've got a nest of garter snakes just under my doorstep. There's a beaver dam thirty yards away. There aren't any hotels.

Yesterday I waited too. I waited all day long.

Jesus! Shit! Fuck the postman!

Think I'll go to town.

By the side of the road he saw a child long dead, small birds feeding on its entrails. It was impossible to tell if the child was male or female. It stank terribly. There was a horse with a bullet in its brain further on. Just at the town line he stopped to watch some boys nailing a woman to a barn. He watched for a long time. They had put two nails in each hand, one through the palm and another just below the wrist. The woman was naked. Her blood ran down her arms and over her breasts, which were small and tanned. The boys beat her with thin birch switches about the face and head. One of them pushed his thighs against her but he was still too small.

Mr. Crocker was busy with a customer so he sat down at the soda fountain to wait. In the paper's op ed page there was a debate over whether whoever finally was to be at the end of the chain letter was determined by chance or personality. A lot of bullshit. Mr. Crocker poured him a cream soda and they watched the building burning across the street. Leary's drugstore.

"Don't like that," said Mr. Crocker. "Could just as well be me."

"Nobody'd burn you out."

"Hard to say what some people will do these days, Alfred."

"You don't have to worry." He opened a package of potato sticks.

"Postman arrive up your way yet?"

"Not yet."

"Been here already this morning. Henley got his letter, y'know."

"Did he? No, I didn't know."

260

"Got it yesterday."

"What did he do?"

"Passed it on, of course."

"That was sensible of him."

"Wouldn't expect otherwise of Henley."

"No. I guess not."

He finished his soda and paid Crocker his dollar eighty and walked outside. So Henley had got his letter. He wondered how he felt. It was the first time anyone he knew personally had ever got one. He thought about Henley's shy stutter and wondered. Of course now he was a free man. There was no need for him to worry anymore. Though it must have been a shock nevertheless. Alfred himself had taken to worrying far too much these days. It might be better to have it over with. He wasn't sure, but he thought he envied Henley.

Though now you couldn't trust him.

He walked across the street to the cafe. Jamie was sitting there in front of a cup of coffee, squinting at the smoke from the drugstore.

"Damned nuisance," he said.

"It is."

"I saw you come out of Crocker's. He tell you about Henley?"

"Uh-huh."

"Too bad."

"You think so?"

"Sure." He took a sip of his coffee. The mug was all but buried inside his hand. His broad bearded face dipped down to the hand and rose again. You barely saw the transaction. "Henley was a decent enough guy," he said. "Mean drunk sometimes but otherwise he was fine. Now what have you got. Another bloody butcher. Either that or he'll be having second thoughts or regrets or whatever and he'll sit himself in a corner somewhere and wait for the brains to crawl on out of him. Either way we won't be seeing much of Henley anymore. Too bad. I'll miss him."

"I suppose."

"You're a cold one."

"I didn't know him all that well."

261

"Sure you did. Anyway I knew him."

He ordered coffee just to sit with Jamie awhile. It was too soon to go back. He really didn't want to go back.

"You ever hear of anybody the same after the letter?" Jamie said. "Damned right you haven't. They all change. Always for the worse, seems to me. And they call this a religion. Bullshit."

"There's something of a . . . religious nature about it."

"Sure. In the old days they used to rub shit in their hair."

"At least there's the problem of conscience."

"There is that."

The two friends sat silent for a moment. The wind had shifted so it was pleasant sitting there. Alfred wondered if Henley had put his name down. Or Jamie's. The letter might be waiting for either of them.

"See the paper today?" said Jamie.

"Yes. They're wondering what kind of man it will be who stops the letter. Again."

"A saint of course."

"You don't think so?"

"No."

"What kind then?"

He shrugged. "Some fucking lunatic. Somebody tired, disgusted. No promethian, you can bet on that. Somebody without the stomach for it, without the imagination—I figure suicide is about lack of imagination. Somebody missing the urge to make use of all that permission."

"You?"

"Hell, no. I've got a few scores to settle. Enough to keep me busy for a while. I'll take my turn. I expect to enjoy it. The freedom I mean. I don't swallow a word of it but I'll play the game according to the rules and then I'll probably blow my damned fool brains out. Far too late for heroics or sanctity or whatever the fuck they're calling it, but probably it's inevitable. My imagination will just give out on me. What to do next? Followed by instant remorse. Conscience will hit me far too late to do anybody any damn good but it'll hit me eventually. And then of course I've had it. I think of conscience as a kind of pulling of the blinds, you know?"

"I have no desire to hurt anybody. Nobody."

"Sure you do. Just wait."

It was the age they lived in, he thought—but that was hardly an explanation. Somewhere along the line he'd lost the track. It was the age they lived in but how? And why? It was impossible to see an evolution going on from the inside. All you could do was point to its most outlandish deformities, its most hideous incarnations. But the substance of the change lay hidden. Some mystery of the blood.

He walked the same route home.

The woman was still there, bleeding against the barn. He wondered if she was still alive. The boys were gone. The dead horse and the child were gone too. He wondered for what amusement they'd been dragged away. Someone had been using plastic explosive on the second-growth timber along the roadside. Trees cracked and scarred everywhere. No life exempt.

He approached the house as he always did, carefully, soundlessly. By now it was his habit. An old woman had got Wayne Lovett with a shotgun as he walked through his own front door one night.

His letter had fallen through the mail slot.

He opened it.

Just above his own name was Henley's. It amused him to think that such a dangerous world should also be so damn predictable. He read the letter through and then read it again.

The aforesigned pass on to you all responsibility for their actions, past, present and future. We deem this the highest honor, the highest challenge . . .

The colorless language disappointed him. There was nothing here either to inspire or elate. Was that exactly unexpected?

You may of course choose to accept or reject this responsibility . . .

He knew the contents. The contents were a matter of public record. It was the wording, the exact form and syntax which had fascinated him, which remained secret to any who had not

263

already got the letter and now he found that they had no power to stir him.

To reject, merely add a new name to the space provided beneath your own. Be sure to check the list thoroughly to see that you do not repeat any name already entered above . . .

If this was the most important moment of his life he felt no resonance to it. Everything, everything was missing! He felt nothing. Only a great void in which a stranger who looked like himself held an odd but commonplace form letter. Who exactly dreamt this up? he wondered. And where? In what grey office building? At what grim bar?

Its conclusion was worst of all.

Declared by the will of God and the First Congress of Faith, Abraham White, founder. All bless.

His Gethsemane bored him.

I keep standing staring at the thing wondering who to send it on to. Someone in the family, maybe, some uncle or cousin. Maybe one of the kids. No point making them wait as long as I have, getting old waiting, getting more and more nervous. Besides, a lot of kids seem to enjoy themselves at this.

Maybe I should send it to Jamie. Not strange at all that we should talk about it today, as though it were understood between us—first Henley, then me, then Jamie. Or Jamie and then me. Whichever.

I wonder if I can do this. It's as hard for me to choose freedom as it is to choose the other. I should not have got this letter. I'm not cut out for such decisions. Jamie would have been much more suitable. He's smarter, tougher, more thoughtful.

Strange it doesn't say what to do in order to end the chain. Everything else is so neatly and clinically spelled out for you. But I guess that's understood. It's the old, old concept of sin-eater again, only more extreme.

To end the chain you'd have to die. To accept responsibility for all these crimes nothing short of death makes sense. And a hideous death at that. The worst death imaginable. What's needed is a martyr, a brand-new Christ. If it were me I'd start by putting out my eyes.

Do I send the letter to somebody I hate or somebody I love? Do I spare those I love the pain of waiting or take a chance that the letter might miss them entirely, as unlikely as that seems? Henley neither loved me nor hated me. He just knew me. Was it fair of him or even decent to involve me? I wonder what went through his mind, writing down my name.

But I shouldn't try to decide through Henley.

A martyrdom I think is fascinating. I like the idea of putting out the eyes. Without the eyes there would be no going back, you couldn't even see where to sign anymore even if you wanted to, you couldn't see the list of names. The names, the writing, the ordinary symbols behind which all these people hide would be obliterated instantly. All that would remain is crime. Their crimes would enter you free and clear like breath through the nostrils to pollute you through and through.

Next you should break the eardrums. *See no evil, hear no evil.* That's the ticket. A pencil should do it. Break it off in the ear itself. Two pencils, one for each ear. It would take great resolve but that's the idea. A martyr's gestures have got to be big gestures. All these actions would have great importance. Mythic importance. In years to come men would pour over the corpse to discover the hidden meaning to each nuance of the slaughter. A kind of divine autopsy. Every move had to leave a clue and point the way. The key to Paradise from the black mouth of the Savior.

Meat scissors at the root of the tongue. *Speak no evil.* A mouth filled with gore, with the hot brine of life. One's own cup drunk dry. Be careful, Alfred. It would take a poet to see that one. And most of the poets are dead.

Maybe Jamie.

I really should pass it on to him. See if he follows

through as he said he would. Probably he lied, though, or at least exaggerated. A liar under the gun.

I have no faith in anyone.

Let's see. What's next?

If only it were possible to extract the brain without destroying the body. It would be good to add *think no evil* to our new easy-step commandments. If you could tap the skull and drain it dry and then go on from there. But no, you have to stick to what's possible so the brain and heart are out of the question until the very end because clearly it's got to be slow, a death to last forever, a death commensurate with the crime, the one really emphatic death amid all these careless neutral ones.

One should break the legs and smash the bones of the feet with hammers, crush the fingertips and sever the thumbs. Especially important, the thumbs. But first the genitals should be torn away and the teeth smashed and swallowed, one should have to throw oneself against a wall or table until the backbone cracks and the skull is fractured, long sharp knives one should shove up one's ass, the nose must be severed, the nipples burned black.

All this before my brains tumble free down my face and chest and puddle on the floorboards of this old dusty room.

It would be delightful to know before it is impossible to know what the mistake was, the error in composition, the failure of the glands or of the nervous system. I really don't want to hurt anybody, least of all myself. But I think that's asking too much.

I have to get busy.

I have a message to send. A personal message. From the end of the chain.

You're full of shit, every one of you. I'm about to prove it.

Forever

It was many years ago over what was probably a little too much Almaden white wine and marijuana that my wife Rita, *my old lady in those days, remember?* said to me that to her way of thinking the real goal of life was simple—it *was* life, more and more of it, moments to days to years down a long winding path through eternity. That the *ultimate* goal, obviously, was to live forever. She believed that someday we'd master that trick too and was mildly pissed off that ours did not look like the generation who were going to manage it.

I remember she cited our ever-increasing lifespan, our extended years of health and vigor. We were moving, she said, in baby steps in that direction. In the Middle Ages you were lucky to hit thirty. Our parents could probably count on seventy. And then the urge toward procreation. A pretty poor substitute for any single organism's struggle toward eternity but as yet the best we had. Because at least it begged the gene-pool foward, it gave us time, as a species, to get the hang of it.

I said I didn't want to live forever. It would get boring.

No it wouldn't, she said. Think of all there is to *learn*, all the books you could read, the people you'd get to meet, the places you could travel. Moons and planets maybe. The only limit would be your own imagination.

She had me there. Hell, I prided myself in my imagination. What young would-be writer didn't?

So let me get this right, I said. Nobody would ever die?

Sure they would. An accident could get you. A natural disaster.

But aside from that we'd *all* live forever? Even all those right-wing assholes out there? *Kissinger and Nixon?*

It seemed to me there were flaws here.

The way I remember it now she sort of sighed and smiled at me like *you just don't get it, dummy, do you* and said something about time, about time being on *our side* in this. Because if you had all eternity ahead of you, why would you grasp at things and fight for money and fame and land and position, for *protection*, it was all about protection, wasn't it? Why would you feel all this hate and rage toward the other guy? Time would sort that out because it would take away the fear. And it was fear that drove you. Fear of a poverty you could never get out of because you didn't have the time to figure out how, of never having accomplished anything worthwhile because life was too damn short and your daily needs too pressing for you to try to find out exactly what it was you *could* do. Fear of failing health and an ugly painful death surrounded by strangers and tubes and wires in some antiseptic hospital.

Limitless time would stop wars. Global and personal. Time would gut all the purses and distribute the wealth. Time would empty hospitals.

She got pretty passionate, I recall.

We did in those days.

I miss them.

And I miss her passion too.

*   *   *

Until recently I took a lot of walks. Rita and I lived in small two-bedroom hundred-and-fifty-year-old house in the foothills of New Hampshire's White Mountains, in our souls die-hard hippies to the end though we'd long since given up on soy and sprouts and brown rice. Our acre plot of land lay between the State Park on one side and ten more acres of forest owned by a pair of New Yorkers, brothers by the name of Kaltsas, who bought it in the '60s for tax purposes. They'd never intended to build. So there was plenty of space to meander.

There's a place on the Kaltsas property I always found myself going back to. Especially in summer. It's a ledge, a high outcropping of bare rock up a trail thirty feet or so from a fast-running stream. But it's a gradual, easy climb up the eastern slope. Once you're up there you're standing beside a waterfall on the western side which pours down over the rocks into a pool you can wade in up to your waist if we've had a little rain. You can drink the water. It's cold and clean. Beyond the stream is thick forestland, cool even in summer. Turn to the east and you're looking beyond some tall oak and birch trees to the mountains far away across a wide sloping field of grass. No thicket, no scrub, just tall waving grass. Until the treeline at the foot of the mountains halts its gentle march.

Stand here on a hot sunny day and the shade-trees above your head, the breeze and the cool stream comprise a kind of natural air-conditioning.

The smells are wonderful.

Wet rock and sediment. Grass and trees.

And roses.

From up out of the grasslands on the eastern side wild roses creep the rock. I don't know how they got there. You see them more often along the roadsides here.

But roses are hardy. They'll grow practically anywhere. And they'll *keep* growing. They're hellish to unroot.

These are not the kind of roses you'd be likely to send your mom on Valentine's Day. They're prickly as porcupines for starters. The flowers are much smaller than the ones you see in the florist shops and many fail to open. But as I say, roses are a hardy species and these always seemed to want my ledge, my rock. Maybe it's the scent of water that draws them. Maybe they want *over* the rock to the waterfall and the stream. I don't know. But the smell that drifts back and forth on the breeze up here puts most store-bought varieties to shame.

Roses were Aphrodite's flowers.

When Rita started to fail on me I came here quite a lot.

Bed sores bloom too. They open from the center outwards. *Pressure ulcers* the doctors call them. Across the bony areas of the body especially—the spine, pelvis, heels—they appear first as abrasions and then blister up white and then slowly become shallow and then deep craters that need to be drained and packed and peel back healthy skin along with the dead and dying, opening across the flesh like wet red flowers. Their scent is foul. You clean them with saline, moisturize them with corn starch and try to keep the ulcer moist and the surrounding skin dry. And still they spread.

Bone-cancer patients like Rita see a lot of them.

People like me who suddenly find themselves caregivers see a lot of gauze pads and disposable rubber gloves and wet-to-dry dressings and foam wedge mattresses—trying to fight off the twin enemies of bacteria and the sheer press of gravity. Sometimes we win. Sometimes the patient goes into remission, can get out of bed and walk around again and if the ulcers aren't too bad and have been carefully attended-to they disappear with time. The bloom fades, shrivels into scarred puckered flesh.

That first time I mostly remember turning her every two hours, even at night, even in her sleep and I remember waiting for the nurse to arrive in the morning so I could get some sleep myself. I remember changing her bedclothes and dressing the wounds which weren't too bad this time and washing her with warm water and collecting her dry fallen hair off the pillow when she wasn't looking.

Days into weeks. Weeks into months. Scoring dope for her in Plymouth against the nausea, feeling slightly old to be buying pot but determined. Riding with her in the ambulance for her chemo treatments in the city until finally they took and I had some semblance of my Rita back again, a brave pale wife who could walk with the aid of a walker and then later with a cane and who insisted on doing the cooking and light housekeeping even though I'd gotten pretty good at both by then.

I'd be writing in the study—the spare bedroom, never used except by the occasional guest—working on yet another of the Jack Pace mystery novels which were our sole bread and butter now that Rita wasn't up to teaching a mob of third-graders anymore, writing yet one more slim paperback which would earn us fifteen grand if we were lucky, maybe another fifteen abroad and I'd hear her out in the living room, the Electrolux roaring, knowing she was vacuuming the damn rug with one hand while she clung to the walker with the other. I couldn't stop her. The only time we'd fight was when I'd try to stop her.

I lived in dread of her falling. I dreaded it constantly.

But she didn't fall. And I suppose the excercise and the familiar feeling of usefulness were good for her because she got better. Once she switched to the cane we started going for walks together, ranging farther and farther afield until one bright hot August morning she asked me to take her up to the rocks on the Kaltsas property. *You remember the place*, she said. Of course I did. I'd come there so often during her illness I'd practically worn a track there. The ledge always seemed to comfort me.

"You sure you're up to the climb?"

"No." She smiled. "But I'm pretty sure I can make it along the stream. Even just a wade in the pool would be nice. Come on. Let's see what I'm up to."

She was wearing jeans and a faded denim workshirt and

a red scarf wrapped and tied around her head. Her hair hadn't come back the way we'd hoped it would. Her face was still drawn and the lines around her mouth and eyes cut deep. I thought she was beautiful. My hippie-chick at forty-seven.

"Lead the way," I told her.

She was right. She made it upstream slowly but without much difficulty and about an hour later, around ten or so, we were standing by the pool.

"I'm beat," she said. "Let's sit a while."

"Still want to go up top there?"

"Sure. In a while."

We sat down at the edge of the pool and she slipped off her canvas U.S. Keds—no Nikes or Adidas for *us*—rolled up her jeans and slid her feet into the water. She smiled.

"*Mmmmm.*"

"Cold?"

"A little. Feels good, though."

I did the same. The water was icy at first but you got used to it. We splashed our feet a little and leaned back on our elbows into the dappling morning sunlight and watched it play over the water and talked about my latest book. I was having plot-points problems and Rita was always fine at helping. Once we were satisfied that we'd gotten Jack Pace out of his latest jam *somewhat* realistically she sat up and said, *know what? I'm going in.*

"You are?"

"Uh-huh."

"You'll freeze to death."

She smiled and started unbuttoning her shirt. "No I won't."

She slipped it off her shoulders. Old habits die hard. She still refused to wear a bra. She unzipped the jeans.

"Well hell, if you can I can."

"There you go."

She got hold of the cane and stood and used it for bal-

272

ance while she slid one leg and then the other out of the jeans and then pulled her panties down over her hips which were still bony from weight-loss. You could count her ribs and along her backbone were a few pink scars. I got out of my own clothes and she stepped into the water cane and all and turned to me smiling and then glanced up and said *hey*.

"What?"

"Look at that."

I turned to where she was pointing, to the ledge above— *my* ledge—and saw a small white cat looking down at us. Wide-eyed, curious. *Two naked humans about to purposely freeze themselves half to death in cold water*. What's *that* all about? I laughed.

"That's Lily," I said.

"Who?"

"Lily. Liz Jackson's cat. Liz had her along the day she stopped by with that casserole for us, remember?"

"I don't. . . ."

"Yeah, I guess you were pretty out of it. She jumped up onto the bed with you. You petted her for a while. Got her purring. Then you fell asleep."

"I did?"

"You did."

"She's beautiful."

"She's just your basic mutt. Liz got her from the shelter. But you're right, she is."

And perched there high on the lip of rock like some animate Egyptian stone statue, a small white shorthair, poised and slim, she *was* beautiful. Utterly still except for her eyes moving over us, alert to whatever the hell it was we were doing down there.

I stepped into the water. Rita went into a crouch, the waterline sliding up over her breastbone so I did too. We laughed and shivered and then did the only thing reasonable in that sudden cold—held onto one another for dear life, passing body-heat back and forth until finally the temperature was tolerable. I kissed her and stroked her back and she stroked mine and we listened to the stream tumble down off the rocks.

"Love me?" she said.

"Uh-huh. You?"

"Uh-huh."

We kissed again. She tasted the way she'd always tasted. Cancer and chemo had changed that for awhile.

"What a gorgeous day," she said.

"It is."

"You think she'll stick around?"

"Who? Lily? I don't know. Might."

"Be nice to really meet her. Conscious, that is."

She turned and I looped my arms around her waist and we bobbed together in the water. I glanced up at Lily, who had settled down into a crouch and seemed to be gazing at something overhead.

"You still want to live forever?" I said.

I don't know why I remembered that just then. I said it very softly. I think I may have said it as a kind of prayer.

She nodded. "Today I do."

We let ourselves dry in the sun and then dressed and climbed to the ledge. I only had to help her twice. When we arrived at the top Lily was gone, vanished.

We sat and smelled the roses.

I had her back for about five months before it started again. The nurses, the treatments, the bedsores blooming far more fiercely than before. The enemy now was the Stage Four ulcer, where the sore blazes through skin and subcutaneous tissue to the underlying fascia, a fibrous network between the tissue and the underlying structure of muscle, bone and tendon, burns like a self-made acid. And finally to the bones, the muscles and tendons themselves. I turned her, washed her, cleaned and dried her when she soiled the bed. Held her head while she vomited up breakfast into a plastic kidney-shaped pan.

She fought hard and so did I and we beat the rap again. By February she was on her feet moving with the aid of the walker.

But something was different this time.

She didn't come back the way she had before. February turned to March and March into April and she still only rarely bothered to cook or do any cleaning or laundry and left the Electrolux to me—which initially, at least, came as a relief. I didn't have to worry about her falling.

But she seemed suddenly obsessed with money.

Money we *didn't have*.

Jack Pace was still selling steadily, sure. He had his audience. But it was clear that barring a miracle the guy was never going to make us rich. I tried writing a partial-and-outline of a *serious* novel and my agent couldn't sell *that* damn thing at all. It remains in my drawer to this day, testament to two months' wasted energy. In the meantime Rita kept talking about money. She'd got it into her head that the reason she couldn't lay the cancer for once and for all was that we couldn't afford the best doctors, the best-equipped hospitals, the most state-of-the-art treatments.

As gently as possible our own doctors assured us otherwise.

You didn't beat bone cancer at this stage, it beat you.

It was only a matter of time.

"I don't believe them," she said. "They're just watching their asses."

"You believed them before. Why not now?"

"I just don't, that's all. Do you?"

"Yes. Look, Rita, we've both read up on the subject. We know what there is to know. Come on."

"Books! Books and magazines! You're not the one who's dying."

She apologized to me right off. She wasn't trying to make me feel guilty.

She just was.

Guilty and sad and frustrated and fearful. Her own fear

275

passed to me as simply as you'd hand someone a flower.

Over the months I watched her sink into listlessness and a kind of quiet that I knew was simply despair. There was no other word for it. She was quitting the world and she knew it. The world was leaving her behind.

It got so we barely talked. Our walks were usually short and mostly silent.

Like we were both just waiting for another axe to fall.

And I remember lying awake beside her late one night thinking about what she'd said on that other evening so long ago over Almaden white wine and pot, *that what drove you was fear. That limitless time would have the power to take away that fear. That you wouldn't have to grasp for things like money and protection if time was on your side.*

That time would empty hospitals.

I cried myself to sleep that night. Because what we didn't have was time. Not time nor money nor protection of any kind.

Nothing to take away the fear. Her own fear and mine. That it was going to happen again. And worse this time. Much worse. It had to—that was the nature of the disease. And maybe if we were lucky or unlucky a fourth time or a fifth until the bedsores were deep as potholes, until the bones powdered to chalk, until she mercifully gasped and died.

She was groping for protection from all that, from that long slow slide. That was what all the talk about money was about. *It was all about protection, wasn't it?* Something I couldn't provide.

But I think that strangely, mysteriously, somehow deep in the night we tend to work out solutions—or that our dreams work out solutions for us—to problems we can't solve in the light of day or tossing sleepless in our beds at night. You wake up in the morning and sometimes you've got an answer.

That morning I had mine.

It frightened me, saddened me and God help me, it relieved me too.

Against all my expectations I thought that maybe Jack Pace might be able to save us both after all.

I forged the documents carefully.

It wasn't very hard. All I needed was a xerox machine and my word-processor. I took from my files an innocuous letter from my agent announcing the enclosure of royalty statements to *Wild Side*, my third Jack Pace novel and another letter from ABC announcing the same book's rejection as a made-for-TV-movie, pasted plain white paper over the texts of both leaving only the letterheads and signatures and then brought them into Plymouth and copied them onto two slightly different grades of Mail Boxes, Etc.'s best paper stock. I took them home and went to work.

About an hour later I had a letter from my agent confirming that per her phone call we did indeed have a deal for a TV *series* based on the novels at such and such an exhorbitant price and enclosing the letter from the ABC exec which outlined the deal. I tucked them in my drawer under some other papers to await the time.

It didn't take long. It was a morning right after the Fourth of July weekend. Like most people I guess we get the usual number of phone solicitations unless we leave the answering machine on to screen them. And for a week or so I got purposely absent-minded about using it.

I don't know what the woman on the other end was trying to sell me but I must have confused her plenty because as soon as she got started in on *her free trial offer* and *money-back guarantee* I started yelling *you're kidding! I can't believe it!* how *much*? into the handset because the timing was just perfect, there was Rita sitting at the kitchen table with a cup of coffee in front of her watching me acting up a storm, and when I put down the receiver I shook my head like I was dumbstruck and by then she was across the room to me wondering what in hell was going on.

277

"Larry, what *is* it?"

More acting.

Like I was about to tell her. But then thought better of it.

"No. I want to wait," I said. "I don't want to get your hopes up. Let's just say it's good news. It could be really good news."

"*Larry!*"

"Sorry. Call me superstitious. You tell somebody, you might screw the deal. Alice is sending me a memo. It'll only take a couple of days, maybe a week or so."

"A *week*? That's not fair," she said. "No way that's fair!"

But she was smiling.

I let a week go by and then a few days more for good measure and they were happy days for us though I was sleeping very little and badly. She didn't press me any more about the deal. I knew she wanted to but that was Rita— she'd trust me to let her know when the time came. There was no more talk about money and treatments, either. I worked on the novel as best I could and we'd shop in town and go out for our walks and watch TV and read at night as though we hadn't a care in the world nor any limit to our time at all.

"Let's go up to Kaltsas' pool," I said. "I've got something I want to show you."

"I don't know," she said. "It's a kind of a trek."

"Come on. You know you like it there."

We'd just that morning had a series of rainshowers but now at nearly noon the sky was bright as crystal. You could still smell the rain in the grass.

I was afraid to wait any longer. Afraid the strain was showing.

"We'll get wet," she said.

I gave her a look and laughed.

"That never stopped you before. Remember?"

We hiked through our back yard over the hill and

through the trees down to the water and then we walked upstream. The air was cool and still. Her cane clattered against the rocks. Our sneakers crunched the smooth gravel along the banks. We took it very slowly. I didn't want to exhaust her.

The pool was high that day because of the rainshowers, the stream pouring wide and fast from the rocks above. We sat down to catch our breath.

"Can you manage the top?"

"I think so. I got all this way, I might as well give it a try. Just let me sit a few minutes. What is it you want me to see?"

"Show you when we get there, okay?"

"Okay."

We sat until she was rested and then we started up. Midway to the ledge it began to rain again. Heavy at first and then fading fast. We waited under some birch trees until it stopped. A very long wait for me. But I suppose that by then Rita needed the break anyhow. Then the sun burned down again and water steamed off the rocks as we climbed.

I think now that I could not have gone through with it had it not been for the cat.

The cat and the roses.

My heart was pounding too hard, my hands were doing too much shaking.

My confidence was all gone and with it my resolve.

Then, *Shhh. Wait*, Rita said and nodded toward the ledge just ahead.

And there was Lily.

Sprawled across the steaming rock. Basking in the sun.

There's something about the light here after a rain. I'd noticed it before but never so completely, never with such a shock of recognition. The light will plays tricks on your eyes and alter the color of things. Usually you're barely aware of it. A rock will take on subtle shades of blue. There's yellow in the leaves.

Lily was a white cat.

Yet here in this light she was green.

Green as the leaves overhead, as the tall grass in the valley down below us, as the leaves of the wild roses which I saw had finally attained the summit of my ledge and among which she was lying so that from where we stood at some distance it almost seemed that one bright splash of red was growing from the tip of her tail, growing out of her, red echoed in her eyes as though rose and cat and foliage surrounding were all of one nature burst from the earth, out of decay, out of foment and death which I saw in that moment was only the proper way of things after all. Rita was wrong. *Not eternal life, never.* Because only death and decay could breed life in the first place and though, like the roses, Rita and I could strive and climb on and on, the earth was intractable and without remedy and each of us was rooted there, in loam and dirt and crumbled stone.

The light shifted. We made our way.

We got to the top of the ledge and this time Lily stayed. A white cat again lying languid in the sun.

I showed Rita the letters. I watched hope brighten her face and then saw doubt. As though it couldn't be true, we just weren't that lucky. *Look*, I said. *There's the proof. There. It's why I brought you here.* And I pointed down to the valley below. *All that*, I said. *It's ours. I bought it a week ago. Look. We'll build there when you're better.*

She turned and looked.

The rock was where I'd placed it days before.

I took it up and then I brought it down.

Thanks to McPheeters again for telling me about a dream of his, and of course, to Alan.

Gone

Seven-thirty and nobody at the door. No knock, no door-bell.

What am I? The wicked old witch from Hansel and Gretel?

The jack-o-lantern flickered out into the world from the window ledge, the jointed cardboard skeleton swayed dangling from the transom. Both there by way of invitation, which so far had been ignored. In a wooden salad bowl on the coffee table in front of her bite-sized Milky Ways and Mars Bars and Nestle's Crunch winked at her reassuringly—crinkly gleaming foil-wrap and smooth shiny paper.

Buy candy, and they will come.

Don't worry, she thought. Someone'll show. It's early yet.

But it wasn't.

Not these days. At least that's what she'd gathered from her window on Halloweens previous. By dark it was pretty much over on her block. When she was a kid they'd stayed out till eleven—twelve even. Roamed where they pleased. Nobody was afraid of strangers or razored apples or poisoned candy. Nobody's mother or father lurked in attendance either. For everybody but the real toddlers, having mom and Dad around was ludicrous, unthinkable.

But by today's standards, seven-thirty was late.

Somebody'll come by. Don't worry.

ET was over and NBC were doing a marathon *Third Rock* every half hour from now till ten. What *Third Rock* had to do with Halloween she didn't know. Maybe there was a clue in the Mars Bars. But *Third Rock* was usually okay for a laugh now and then so she padded barefoot to the kitchen and poured herself a second dirty Stoli martini from the shaker in the fridge and lay back on the couch and picked at the olives and tried to settle in.

The waiting made her anxious, though. Thoughts nagged like scolding parents.

Why'd you let yourself in for this, idiot?

You knew it would hurt if they didn't come.

You knew it would hurt if they did.

"You've got a no-win situation here," she said.

She was talking to herself out loud now. Great.

It was a damn good question, though.

Years past, she'd avoided this. Turned off the porch light and the lights in the living room. *Nobody home.* Watched TV in the bedroom.

Maybe she should have done the same tonight.

But for her, holidays were all about children. Thanksgiving and New Year's Eve being the exceptions. Labor Day and the Presidents' days and the rest didn't even count—they weren't *real* holidays. Christmas. *That was Santa.* Easter. *The Easter Bunny.* The Fourth of July. *Firecrackers, sparklers, fireworks in the night sky.* And none was more about kids than Halloween. Halloween was about dress-up and *trick or treat.* And *trick or treat* was children.

She'd shut out children for a very long time now.

She was trying to let them in.

It looked like they weren't buying.

She didn't know whether to be angry, laugh or cry.

She knew it was partly her fault. She'd been such a god-damn mess.

People still talked about it. Talked about *her*. She knew they did. *Was that why her house seemed to have PLAGUE painted on the door? Parents talking to their kids about the lady down the block?* She could still walk by in a supermarket and stop somebody's conversation dead in its tracks. Almost five years later and she *still* got that from time to time.

Five years—shy three months, really, because the afternoon had been in August—over which time the *MISSING* posters gradually came down off the store windows and trees and phone poles, the police had stopped coming round long before, her mother had gone from calling her over twice a day to only once a week—she could be glad of some things, anyhow—and long-suffering Stephen, sick of her sullenness, sick of her brooding, sick of her rages, had finally moved in with his dental assistant, a pretty little strawberry blonde named Shirley who reminded them both of the actress Shirley Jones.

The car was hers, the house was hers.

The house was empty.

Five years since the less than three minutes that changed everything.

All she'd done was forget the newspaper—a simple event, an inconsequential event, everybody did it once in a while—and then go back for it and come out of the 7-Eleven and the car was there with the passenger door open and Alice wasn't. It had occured with all the impact of a bullet or head-on collision and nearly that fast.

Her three-year-old daughter, gone. Vanished. Not a soul in the lot. And she, Helen Teal, *nee* Mazik, went from pre-school teacher, homemaker, wife and mother to the three *p*'s—psychoanalysis, Prozac and paralysis.

She took another sip of her martini. Not too much.

Just in case they came.

*   *   *

By nine-twenty-five *Third Rock* was wearing thin and she was considering a fourth and final dirty martini and then putting it to bed.

At nine-thirty a Ford commercial brought her close to tears.

There was this family, two kids in the back and mom and Dad in front and they were going somewhere with mom looking at the map and the kids peering over her shoulder and though she always clicked the MUTE button during the commercials and couldn't tell what they were saying they were a happy family and you knew that.

To hell with it, she thought, one more, the goddamn night was practically breaking her heart here, and got up and went to the refrigerator.

She'd set the martini down and was headed for the hall to turn out the porch light, to give up the vigil, the night depressing her, the night a total loss finally, a total waste, when the doorbell rang.

She stepped back.

Teenagers, she thought. *Uh-oh.* They'd probably be the only ones out this late. With teenagers these days you never knew. Teens could be trouble. She turned and went to the window. The jack-o-lantern's jagged carved top was caving slowly down into its body. It gave off a half-cooked musky aroma that pleased her. She felt excited and a little scared. She leaned over the windowsill and looked outside.

On the porch stood a witch in a short black cloak, a werewolf in plaid shirt and jeans, and a bug-eyed alien. All wearing rubber masks. The alien standing in front by the doorbell.

Not teenagers.

Ten or eleven, tops.

Not the little ones she'd been hoping for all night long in their ghost-sheets and ballerina costumes. But kids. *Children.*

And the night's thrill—the *enchantment* even—was suddenly there for her.

284

She went to the door and opened it and her smile was wide and very real.

"*Trick or treat!*"

Two boys and a girl. She hadn't been sure of the alien.

"Happy Halloween!" she said.

"Happy Halloween," they chorused back.

The witch was giggling. The werewolf elbowed her in the ribs.

"Ow!" she said and hit him with her black plastic broom.

"Wait right here, kids," she said.

She knew they wouldn't come in. Nobody came in anymore. The days of bobbing for apples were long over.

She wondered where their parents were. Usually there were parents around. She hadn't seen them on the lawn or in the street.

She took the bowl of candy off the coffee table and returned to them standing silent and expectant at the door. She was going to be generous with them, she'd decided that immediately. They were the first kids to show, for one thing. Possibly they'd be the *only* ones to show. But these also weren't kids who came from money. You only had to take one look to see that. Not only were the three of them mostly skin and bones but the costumes were cheaplooking massmarket affairs—the kind you see in generic cardboard packages at Walgreen's. In the werewolf's case, not even a proper costume at all. Just a shirt and jeans and a mask with some fake fur attached.

"Anybody have any preferences, candy-wise?"

They shook their heads. She began digging into the candy and dropping fistfuls into their black plastic shopping bags.

"Are you guys all related?"

Nods.

"Brothers and sister?"

More nods.

The shy type, she guessed. But that was okay. Doing this felt just right. Doing this was fine. She felt a kind of weight

285

lifted off her, sailing away through the clear night sky. If nobody else came by for the rest of the night that was fine too. Next year would be even better.

Somehow she knew that.

"Do you live around here? Do I know you, or your mom and Dad maybe?"

"No, ma'am," said the alien.

She waited for more but more evidently wasn't forthcoming.

They really *were* shy.

"Well, I love your costumes," she lied. "*Very* scary. You have a Happy Halloween now, okay?"

"Thank you." A murmured chorus.

She emptied the bowl. Why not? she thought. She had more in the refrigerator just in case. *Lots* more. She smiled and said *happy Halloween* again and stepped back and was about to close the door when she realized that instead of tumbling down the stairs on their way to the next house the way she figured kids would always do all three of them were still standing there.

Could they possibly want more? She almost laughed. *Little gluttons.*

"You're her, right, ma'am?" said the alien.

"Excuse me?"

"You're her?"

"Who?"

"The lady who lost her baby? The little girl?"

And of course she'd heard it in her head before he ever said it, heard it from the first question, knew it could be nothing else. She just needed to hear *him* say it, hear the *way* he said it and determine what was there, mockery or pity or morbid curiosity but his voice held none of that, it was flat and indeterminate as a newly washed chalkboard. Yet she felt as if he'd hit her anyhow, as though they all had. As though the clear blue eyes gazing up at her from behind the masks were not so much awaiting her answer as awaiting an execution.

286

She turned away a moment and swiped at the tears with the back of her hand and cleared her throat and then turned back to them.

"Yes," she said.

"Thought so," he said. "We're sorry. G'night, ma-am. Happy Halloween."

They turned away and headed slowly down the stairs and she almost asked them to wait, to stay a moment, for what reason and to what end she didn't know but that would be silly and awful too, no reason to put them through her pain, they were just kids, children, they were just asking a question the way children did sometimes, oblivious to its consequences and it would be wrong to say anything further, so she began to close the door and almost didn't hear him turn to his sister and say, *too bad they wouldn't let her out tonight, huh? too bad they never do* in a low voice but loud enough to register but at first it *didn't* register, not quite, as though the words held no meaning, as though the words were some strange rebus she could not immediately master, not until after she'd closed the door and then when finally they impacted her like grape-shot, she flung open the door and ran screaming down the stairs into the empty street.

She thought when she was able to think at all of what she might say to the police.

Witch, werewolf, alien. Of this age and that height and weight.

Out of nowhere, vanished back into nowhere.

Carrying along what was left of her.

Gone.

Closing Time

Only the dead have seen the end of war.
—Plato

October 2001

<u>ONE</u>

Lenny saw the guy in his rear-view mirror, the guy running toward him trying to wave him down at the stoplight, running hard, looking scared, a guy on the tall side and thin in a shiny blue insulated parka slightly too heavy for the weather—one seriously distressed individual. Probably that was because of the other beefy citizen in his shirt-sleeves chasing him up 10th Avenue.

Pick him up or what?

Traffic was light. Pitifully light ever since World Trade Center a month ago. New York was nothing like it used to be traffic-wise. And it was late, half past one at night. He had the green now. Nobody ahead of him. No problem just to pull away.

And suppose he did. What was the guy gonna do? Report him to the Taxi and Limousine Commission?

You had to figure that a chase meant trouble. For sure the guy in his shirtsleeves meant trouble if he ever caught up to the poor sonovabitch. You could read the weather on his face and it was Stormy Monday all the way down the line.

Get the hell out of here, he thought. You got a wife and kids. Don't be stupid. 10th and 59th was usually a pretty safe place to be these days but you never could tell. Not in this town. You've been driving for nearly thirty years now. You know better. So what if he's white, middle-class. So what if you need the fare.

He lifted his foot off the brake but he'd hesitated and by then the guy was already at the door. He flung it open and jumped inside and slammed it shut again.

"*Please!*" he said. "That *guy back there* . . . his goddamn *wife . . . Jesus!*"

Lenny smiled. "I got it."

He glanced at the American flag on his dashboard and thought, *I love this fucking town.*

The beefy citizen was nearly on them, coming down off the curb just a couple steps away.

Lenny floored it.

They slid uptown through time-coordinated greens like a knife through warm butter.

"Where to?"

"Take it up to Amsterdam and 98th, okay?"

"Sure. No problem." He looked at the guy through the rear-view, the guy still breathing hard and sweating. Glancing back out the window, still worried about shirtsleeves. Like his ladyfriend's irate hubby had found some other cab and was hot on his tail. It only happened in the movies.

289

"So what's the story, you don't mind my asking? You mean you didn't know?"

"Hell, no, I didn't know. It was a pickup in a bar. She's got her hand on my leg for godsakes. It's going great. Then this guy shows up. Says he's gonna push my face in! Jesus, I never even paid the bar-tab! I just got the hell out of there. Thank God for *you*, man!"

Lenny reflected that nobody had ever thanked God for him before. Not that he could remember. It was a first.

Your Good Deed for the Day, he thought. From the look of the shirtsleeves, maybe for the month.

"So you go back, you pay your tab another time. No problem."

"I don't even know the name of the place. I just wandered in."

"Corner of 58th and 10th? That would be the Landmark Grill."

The guy nodded. He saw it in the rearview mirror.

And there was something in the guy's face right then he didn't like. Something nasty all of a sudden. Like the guy had gone away somewhere and left a different guy sitting in the back seat who only looked like him.

Ah, the guy's had a hard night, he thought.

No babe. No pickup. Almost got his ass kicked for his trouble. You might be feeling nasty too.

They drove in silence after that until Lenny dropped him at Amsterdam and 98th, northeast corner. The guy said thanks and left him exactly fifteen per cent over the meter. Not bad but not exactly great either, considering. The next fare took him to the East Side and the next four down to the Village and then Soho and Alphabet City and then to the Village again. He never did get back to Tenth or even to Hell's Kitchen for that matter.

So it was only when he returned to the lot at the end of his shift that he learned from his dispatcher that the Landmark Grill had been robbed at gunpoint by a tallish thin sandy-haired man in a parka. Who got away in a cab, for chrissake. Everybody was buzzing about it because he'd used a goddamn cab as getaway. Thought it was pretty funny.

That and the fact that the bartender had been crazy enough to chase him.

A guy with a gun. You had to be nuts to risk it.

Or maybe you had to be bleeding from the head where the guy had used the butt end of his gun on you. Lenny hadn't managed to catch that little detail in the rear-view.

There was never any question in his mind about calling the cops. If they didn't have his medallion number then so be it. You didn't want to get involved in something like this unless you had to. But Lenny thought about his fifteen per cent over the meter and wondered what the take was like.

No good deed ever goes unpunished his mother used to say.

He hated to admit it but as in most things, he supposed his mom was right.

TWO

At first Elise was embarrassed by them. No—*for* them.

First embarrassed. Then fascinated.

And then she couldn't look away.

The train was real late—she'd wondered if it was another bomb scare somewhere up the line, it would be just her luck to miss her dance class entirely and it was the only class she could care about at all—so that the platform was crowded and getting more so, mostly kids like her just out of school for the day and *thank God it was over*, nobody but Elise seeming to care if the train was late or not, the noise level enormous with the echo of kids shouting, laughing, arguing, whatever.

For sure these two over by the pillar there didn't care.

She doubted they even noticed the kids swarming around them. Much less the lateness of the train.

291

She had never seen a pair of adults so . . . *into* one another.

But it wasn't a good thing.
It was terrible. And it was going on and on.

They were probably in their thirties, forties—Elise couldn't
tell but she thought they were younger than her mother—
and the woman was a little taller than the man who was
almost as cute, for an old guy, as she was pretty. Or they
would have been cute and pretty if their faces didn't keep
. . . *crumbling* all the time.

They kept hugging and pulling apart and staring at each
other as though trying to memorize one another's faces and
then hugging again so hard she thought it must have hurt
sometimes, she could see the man's fingers digging deep
into the back of her blouse. And both of them were crying,
tears just pouring down their cheeks and they didn't even
bother to try to wipe them away half the time, they mostly
just let them come.

She saw them stop and smile at each other and the smiles
were worse than the tears. *My God, they're so sad.* And smiling seemed to bring the tears on again, like they were one
and the same, coming from the very same place. It was like
they couldn't stop. Like she was watching two hearts breaking for ever and ever.

She was already ten or fifteen feet away from them but
she found herself stepping back without even knowing at
first she was doing it. It was as though there were some
kind of magnetic field around them that repelled instead
of pulling, as though they were pushing out at empty space,
in order to give them space, all the space they needed to
perform this horrible dance.

I meant what I said, you know that, right? she heard the
woman tell him and he nodded and took her in his arms
again and she missed what the woman said after that but
then they were crying again though real silently this time

and then she heard the woman say *I just can't anymore* and then they were crying hard again, really sobbing, clutching each other and their shoulders shaking and she wanted to look away because what if they noticed her staring at them but somehow she knew that they weren't going to notice, they weren't going to notice anything but each other.

They were splitting up, she knew now. At first she'd thought maybe they had a kid who'd died or something. *I just can't anymore.* The woman was dumping him but she didn't want to because they still loved each other. And they loved each other *so much*—she'd never seen two people that much in love. She wasn't even sure she'd ever seen it in the movies.

So how could you do that? How could you just break up if you felt that way? How was it even possible?

She noticed that some of the other kids were watching too and would go silent for a while. Not as intently as Elise was watching and mostly the girls but there on the platform you could feel it pouring out of these people and it was getting to some of the other kids as well. Something was happening to them that she had the feeling only adults knew about, something secret played out right out there in the open. Something she sensed was important. And a little scary.

If this was what being an adult was all about she wanted no part of it.

And yet she did.

To be in love that much? God! So much in love that nothing and nobody matters but the two of you standing together right where you're standing, oblivious to everybody, just holding tight and feeling something, *somebody*, so much and deep. It must be wonderful.

It must be awful.

It must be both together.

How could that be?

So that as the train roared in and kids crowded into the car, Elise behind them, wiping at her own tears which only

293

served to confuse her more now, the woman stepped on a little behind her to the side and turned to the window, hands pressed to the dirty cloudy glass to watch him standing there alone on the platform and somehow smaller-looking without her and Elise looked from one to the other and back again and saw their shattered smiles.

THREE

She put down the paper and washed her hands in the sink. As usual the Sunday *Times* was filthy with printer's ink. She went back to her easel in the living room. Her lunch-break was over. The pastel was coming along.

She had that much, anyway. The work.

What did you expect? she thought. When things got bad they were probably bound to get worse. If only for a little while.

She hoped it was only for a little while.

Because she was seriously doubting, for the very first time ever, her actual survival here.

Everybody in the city was fragile, she guessed. No matter where you were or who you were World Trade had touched you somehow. Even if you'd lost nobody close to you, you'd still lost something. She knew that was part of it.

She could look at a cat in a window and start to cry.

And breaking off with David would have been bad enough under any circumstances—correction, still *was* bad enough. Because he wouldn't quite let go and neither could she exactly. Lonely late-night e-mails still were all too common between them.

I understand you can't see me, I understand it hurts too much to keep seeing me and I'm sorry. But I miss just talking to you too. We always talked, even through the worst of it. E-mails just don't work. I feel like I've lost not only my lover but my friend. Please—call me sometime, okay? I want my friend back. I want her bad. Love, David.

294

I can't call. Not yet. Someday maybe but not now. I'd call and we'd talk and the next step would be seeing you and you know that. Why do you want to make me go through this again, David? Jesus! You say you understand but you don't seem to. You're not going to leave her and that's that. And I need some-body who'll be there for me all the time, not just a couple nights a week. I miss you too but you're not that person, David. You can't be. And I can't simply wish that away. So please, for awhile, just please leave me be. Love, Claire.

She knew he was hurting and she hated that because there was so much good between them and the love was still there. She hated hurting him. But she was alone and he wasn't. So she also knew who was hurting the worst. She was. She was tired of crying herself to sleep every night he wouldn't be there next to her or every morning when he'd leave. It had to stop.

He'd never stop it. It was up to her.

She'd been alone most of her life but that was always basically okay. She liked her own company. She'd always been a loner.

But she'd never felt this lonely.

What was that Bob Dylan line? *I'm sick of love.*

She knew exactly how he felt when he wrote it.

Fuck it, she thought, *get to work*. You're an artist. So make art.

The piece was one of a series, a still-life, an apple core surrounded by chains. A padlock lay open, gleaming, embracing one of the links of chain.

She studied it.

She knew exactly what it meant. Most people didn't. That was fine, so long as they *felt* it.

And bought one now and then.

Which hadn't happened in a while now.

Concentrate, she thought. Focus. Work the blacks. Work the shadows.

But that was the other thing. Money. Cold hard cash.

Financially her life was a mess too. She'd only just started painting again—David was the main one who'd encouraged her, dammit!—had only sold a few pieces for good but not terrific money, and the New York restaurant business, which she'd always counted on as backup, had been hit hard by the Bush economy even before World Trade Center. Tourism was down to a fraction of what it was this time last year and the natives were paranoid about going out to dinner. In the past three months she'd been laid off as a bartender, hired as a waitress, laid off as a waitress, hired as a manager—a job she'd always loathed—and then laid off as a manager too.

She was always assured it was a matter of cutbacks, not her performance. Last hired, first fired. Simple as that.

She'd been making the rounds. Nobody was hiring.

So that at the moment she was jobless, with two months' rent and utilities in the bank and if she didn't find something soon she was going to have to eat this apple core off the canvas.

It's Sunday, she thought. You can't do a damn thing about it now.

So make the art. Later, call your mother.

Get on with it. All of it.

She drew a line, smudged it lightly with her finger. A link of chain sprung suddenly into focus on the canvas. She drew another.

FOUR

What the hell are you doing? he thought.

It was two in the morning. He was standing outside across the street from her apartment. He could see the light burning through the second-floor living room window. Either she was still awake or she'd fallen asleep and left it on but to leave it on was very unlike her.

She was awake.

He could walk up the steps, ring the bell.

No he couldn't.

He had no right to. It would be tantamount to harrassment.

And standing out here was tantamount to stalking.

So what the hell are you doing, David?

A glimpse, he thought. That's all. A glimpse of somebody you love through a brownstone window. What the hell is wrong with that?

Everything. It's crazy, desperate. It's pathetic. You're not Romeo and she's not Juliet. Go the hell home.

Don't want to.

Your wife is waiting.

By now she'll be fast asleep.

You've had too much to drink again.

So? What else is new?

Go home.

A cab cruised past him going west. Northwest was the direction of his apartment. The cab's sign was lit. He could have flagged it down. A simple wave of the hand. He didn't.

He needed something. He wanted to *feel something.*

Now what the hell does that mean?

59th was quiet. No breeze. Nobody on the street but him. There was traffic heading south on 9th half a block away but not here and even on 9th the traffic was light, he could barely hear it hissing by.

So here he was, alone. Staring up at a living-room window and afraid to look away or even to blink for fear that if he did it would be exactly that moment she'd choose to appear and not any other moment and not again, afraid of the perversity of incident and chance, perhaps because it was precisely incident and chance that had got him here in the first place. She a new bartender, he a regular. Quickly becoming friends, far more slowly becoming lovers—two years before that happened—not until a casual date that left them alone in a crowded noisy new dance club they found not to their liking at all, waiting for two other friends to return from the bar so they could get the hell out of there, a single slightly boozy hug turning to a surprisingly lovely kiss and then more and more and before they knew it two more years had gone by and love had trapped them as surely incident and chance could trap anyone.

The window blurred over.

He wiped his eyes.

He was aware of sirens in the distance, somewhere around Times Square.

The window blurred again.

Were the sirens doing this? some fucking *ambulance* making him cry? Somebody else's distress? Some stranger's? It was possible. These days anything was.

But that was too damn ridiculous even for him and no, he saw what it was now, literally saw it in that way that the mind imposes an image it chooses over the eyes so that what the eyes see in the natural world disappears for a moment, unable to compete, utterly sterile compared to the image the brain mandates. He saw it, vividly, sobbed once because he knew that in the natural world he might never see it again and certainly not the way he did now, directed so wholly at him—her open happy smile—and turned and started home.

FIVE

The composite on the nightly news was not great.

They'd got the nose right and the chin mostly but the forehead was way too high and the eyes were completely wrong because the eyes in the composite were bland, they held nothing, while his were full of. . . .

. . . *what?*

Something. He didn't bother trying to go there.

They were off on the numbers too. They had him down for around fifteen, twenty jobs this year. He had to laugh. The number was more like thirty, thirty-five. Roughly one every week and a half. He figured that by the end of his own personal fiscal year which began and ended on his birthday just before Christmas he'd take in fifty, maybe sixty grand. Not as much as if you were robbing banks but bars were a whole lot safer. Bars were vulnerable.

For one thing you didn't work in daylight except to cruise for likely joints to hit. You didn't have much in the way of surveillance cameras to worry about. And you didn't have some retired cop with an attitude, some asshole armed guard willing and stupid enough to start blazing away at you.

It was a pretty rare bartender who was willing to die for the till and his tips.

That guy last week, though. That asshole actually *chasing* him.

He thought he'd put the fear of God in him. Especially that last hard whack on the head. He guessed there had to be a first time for everything.

Usually the getaway was simple. You headed for the nearest subway, didn't matter where you went once you were on it. If there was a bus handy you caught that. You got off and had a beer or two at another bar far away and then you went on home.

They'd worried out loud on the news about his gun. Some police lieutenant mouthing off. Said that seeing as he *had* a gun, sooner or later he was going to use it. That was bullshit. His weapons were surprise and fear. The gun was only window-dressing. Loaded window-dressing but window-dressing all the same.

Then they tried to link him up to a wider trend. All very ominous. Seems that shootings in the City were up 24% over the same month last year—the figure spiked by the thinned ranks of the NYPD who were now on anthrax, security and ground zero duty since World Trade Center instead of manning street crime.

Again, bullshit. He wasn't part of any goddamn trend. He just did what he always did.

Plain old-fashioned armed robbery.

He sat on the sofa and sipped his beer. The composite

didn't worry him. Except for the eyes he was blessed with one of those more or less *basic* faces, a kind of no-frills face, one that set off no bells and whistles in anybody. *Acceptable*—that was how he liked to think about it. Acceptable enough so that guys had no reason either to fear him, be impressed or intimidated by him or even to remember him for that matter. Acceptable enough to women so that he got himself some pussy now and then. Not a hard face and not soft. No scars, no dimples, no cleft palates or cleft chins.

The composite didn't work. His face was far too mutable.

The hair you could cut or color. For the line of forehead, a hat or a baseball cap. You could change the eyes with colored contact lenses or no-scrip glasses or just by trimming down your eyebrows a bit. Or darkening them with eyebrow pencil.

He thought eyebrows were seriously underrated.

You wanted to avoid a good tan. A good tan was memorable to New Yorkers, who were used to pallor. You made the mistake getting of a tan, you powdered it. Physique was changeable as the goddamn weather. You're on the tall side like he was? five-eleven? So you're stoop-shouldered now and then. You flex the knees. Build? Baggy sweaters or business clothes one time, jeans and teeshirt the next.

Backpack on one job, shopping bag or briefcase on another.

He finished the beer and frowned at New York One. New York One was supposed to be about New York City, wasn't it? But now they were going on and on about the fucking anthrax again. If it wasn't the anthrax it was the fucking war in Afghanistan or else the fucking World Trade Center. Who cared if some senator's assistant or postal clerk got anthrax—inhaled, cutaneous, or shot up the ass? Who cared if the towelheads took out skyscrapers?

He strictly worked ground-floor.

They ended with some puff piece about this guy who had to be the most politically correct asshole on the face of the earth—some Westchester dentist who was offering to buy up all the neighborhood kids' Halloween candy so they didn't rot their teeth. Fuck their teeth. He turned the damn thing off and got up and tossed the beercan into the sink.

Time to get.

In the bathroom shaving he glanced down at his various toiletry items and got a really great idea.

"You're lucky," the bartender said. "I was just about to tell my friend here last call. What'll it be?"

"Miller, thanks."

"Miller coming up."

The barkeep's *friend* probably didn't know him from Adam. His *friend* looked to have been on a long night's pub crawl and only one step up from blue-collar, if that, while this was clearly a kids' bar, Barrow and Hudson, pool table and concert posters, *Sweet Home Alabama* on the jukebox and the bartender not much more than a kid himself. Wire-rim glasses, rosy cheeks, spiked hair, good strong build under the teeshirt. Irish maybe.

"Gettin' cold out there?"

The kid poured a half glass of Miller into the beer mug and set it down in front of him.

"Nah. Good breeze, though."

The barkeep took his twenty to the register. The guy next to him downed his beer and mumbled thanks and slid off the barstool and tapped his dollar fifty with his forefinger. He was tipping the bartender one fifty. Big spender. He put his hands in his pockets and headed for the door. Which meant that this was going very nicely indeed.

"G'night. Thank you, sir. You take care now."

The barkeep put his change in front of him. Scooped up his tip and dropped it in the bucket.

He slipped on the surgical gloves.

"*You* take care," he said.

301

"S'cuse me?"

They said that a lot. *You take care*. You said it back to them, it threw them off balance. Maybe even started to worry them right then and there.

But this kid was only puzzled.

He slid the .45 out from behind his sport jacket. Rested it flat on the bar pointed at the barkeep's trim flat belly.

"I said *you* take care. Now, listen real carefully and you'll get to go home tonight to your girlfriend. Let's say I'm an old college buddy of yours and I'm closing up with you, so you do what you do every night, only I'm here. That's how I want you to act. I'm just here having a drink. You lock the door and hit the lights outside and you dim the ones in here. Only difference is after that you go to the register and instead of counting it you empty it into this bag."

He handed the Big Brown Bag from Bloomie's across the counter.

"Open it and put it on the floor. That's it. Very good. Now go about your business. And don't even think about opening that door. I know you really want to but see, it takes too long to open it, throw it back and then go through. You'll be dead by the time you hit the sidewalk, believe me. They've already got me down twice for Murder One"—*it was a lie but it always worked*—"so it doesn't mean a thing to me one way or the other. I'm a very good shot, though. So it would mean a lot to you."

For emphasis he clicked off the safety.

He could smell it then, that faint ammonia smell or something like ammonia. Bleach maybe. Fear-sweat coming off the guy. Fear cleansing the guy, pouring through the fat and skin all the way up from the organs, the organs unwilling to cease their function, unwilling to give up the pulse.

He put the gun between his legs and swivelled on the stool smiling as the guy moved on shaky legs out from behind the bar and fished his keys out of his pocket, locked

302

the door, put them back in his pocket and reached behind a tall brown sad potted cactus and flicked off the outside lights.

"The dimmer's over here, okay?"

The guy was pointing across the room to another half-dead fern or something.

"Why shouldn't it be okay? I trust you. What's your name?"

The guy hesitated. Like he didn't want to say. Like it was getting personal.

"Robert . . . Bob."

"Bob or Robert?"

"Bob."

"Okay, Bob. Let's dim the lights."

He watched him cross the room, not even daring to glance out through the plate-glass window, afraid that even that much might get him shot. Good.

It was always amazing to him. Within minutes—seconds—you could get a guy performing for you like a trained seal. Half the time, like now, you didn't even have to ask.

"You should water your fucking plants, Bob. Know that?"

He nodded, reached up and dimmed the lights.

"Okay, Bob, let's get to the good stuff."

He drank some of his beer. The barkeep moved back behind the bar and keyed open the register.

"Just the bills, now. No change."

He watched him drop the bills into the Bloomie's bag. Bob had had a pretty good night tonight. From where he sat it looked like well over a thousand. He'd read in the paper today that business was down in the City about $357 million since September 11th. Bars and restaurants particularly. You wouldn't know it from where he was sitting.

"Tell you what, Bob. Let's play a little game for your tip bucket. I'm sure you got a couple hundred in there. I'm sure you'd like to keep it. So. I lose, it's yours. I win, it goes in the bag."

"No, that's okay, you can just . . ."

He started reaching for the bucket above the register.

"Hey! It's *not* okay, Bob!"

He lurched to his feet and leaned over and shoved the barrel of the gun against the barkeep's pale high forehead. He could feel the guy trembling right down though to the handle of the gun. Saw his glasses slip half an inch down his sweaty nose.

"Get this right, Robert. I say we play a little game, then we play a little game. Let me tell you something you don't know about me, Bob. I don't like people. In fact it's fair to say that I fucking hate people. Not just you, *Bob*, you spikey-haired little midwest shit-for-brains—though I do hate you, for sure. But see, I hate *everybody*. I'm a completely equal-opportunity hater—Jews, Arabs, Asians, blacks, WASPS, you name it. Some people think that's a problem. You know how many people have tried to help me with this little problem, Bob? Have tried to *reform* me? Dozens! I'm not kidding you. But you know, it never takes. Never. You know why? Because my one real kick in life, the one thing that really gets me off, is to reform all those people who want to reform me. And it is my honestly held belief that the only way to reform people is to hurt 'em or kill 'em or both. Period."

He sat back down again, rested the gun on the bar, his hand spread out on top of it.

Bob was visibly twitching now, mouth gulping air like a fish.

"Jesus, calm down, Robert, or this isn't gonna work. Hand me the bag. And your keys. That's good. Thanks very much. Now slide over that cutting board there and that little knife you use on the lemons."

"Oh, Jesus."

"Just do it. And dump the lemons."

The kid glanced at his hand on the gun and then turned and did as he was told, set the knife and the board down in front of him.

304

"Okay, here's what we're gonna do. You're right-handed, right? Thought so. So you're gonna put your right hand down, *palm-side up*—that's important, palm up—and spread your fingers. Then I'm gonna take this knife here, which I notice you keep nice and sharp—very good Robert—and jab around between your fingers. Slow at first, then maybe a little faster. Not too fast, don't worry. Believe me, I'm good at this. I really am. But if I miss, even the slightest little cut, the slightest nick, you get to keep the bucket. I don't miss, bucket goes with me. Fair enough? Sure it is. All you got to do is hold very still for me now."

"Oh Jesus."

"Stop with the *oh Jesus*, Robert. Try to be a fucking man for a change. Or you can just remember that I got the gun here, whichever works for you. Okay. Spread your fingers."

The kid pushed his glasses up on his nose. They slid back down again. Then he took a deep breath and held it and put his hand down flat on the board.

He took the knife between his thumb on one side and forefinger and middle finger on the other and as promised, he started off slow. *Thump*, beat. *Thump*, beat. *Thump*. Then he picked up tempo and the thumps got louder because the force got greater and he really was good at this, damn he was good, *thumpthumpthumpthumpthumpthumpthump* and the kid kept saying *oh Jesus, oh Jesus*, Bob a Christian through and through now and he knew that for poor Bob this was going on forever, this was an eternity and when he finally got tired of scaring the shit out of the kid pinned the web of his thumb to the cutting board so that the kid gasped and said *aahhhh!!* and he said *don't you yell, Bob, whatever you do, don't you dare fucking yell.*

And Bob didn't. Bob was toughing it out as expected. He just stood there breathing hard, his left elbow propping him up on the bar against the pain and probably against a pair of pretty shaky legs and looked down at the spreading pool of blood between his fingers. He reached into his pocket and took out the envelope and opened it. Tore it down one side and blew a tablespoon of Johnson's talcum powder directly into his face.

Bob looked startled. Blinking at him, confused.

"*Anthrax, Bob*," he said. "It's the real thing, I promise."

He picked up the bag of money. Took four pair of rolled-up socks out of his jacket pockets and unrolled them and spread them out over the money.

Like he'd just done his laundry.

"You try not to breathe now for a while Bob, go wash your face. That shit'll get right down into your lungs. And you know what happens then. Bucket's yours. You won it fair and square. You take care now. And if you think I've treated you badly which I really hope you don't, well hell, you should just see what I do to the ladies."

Whether the kid believed him or not about the anthrax didn't matter but he was betting he'd have a bad moment at least, the City being what it was nowadays.

He keyed the lock, looked right and left, threw the keys in the gutter and slipped off the gloves as he walked on out the door.

SIX

It had taken Claire a while to do this, to work up the will and the courage finally and Barbara had felt the same way. So they'd decided to do it together and that helped.

They stood in front of the Chambers Street subway exit on an unseasonably warm sunny day along with thirty or so other people scattered across the block staring south from behind the police barricades at the distant sliver of sky where only a month and a half ago the Twin Towers had been.

The smell was invasive, raw, born on a northerly breeze. It clawed at her throat. *Superheated metal, melting plastic and something else. Something she didn't like to think about.*

She had never much liked the Trade Center. It had always seemed overbearing, soulless, a huge smug temple to money and power.

And now both she and Barbara were quietly crying.

All those people lost.

She was crying so much these days.

She knew nobody who had died here.

Somehow she seemed to know everybody who had died here.

She stared up into a bright blue sky tarnished with plumes of pale blonde smoke and after a while she turned around.

She had never seen so many stricken faces.

Old people and young people and even little kids—kids so small she thought they shouldn't even know about this let alone be standing here, they shouldn't have to grow up in the wake of it either. It wasn't right. A woman wearing jeans and an *I LOVE NY—EVEN MORE* teeshirt was wiping back a steady stream of tears. A man with a briefcase didn't bother.

She didn't see a single smile.

"Let's walk," she said.

It was a whisper, really. As though they were standing in a church. And that was the other uncanny thing about this—the silence. New York City heavy and thick with silence broken only by the occasional truck rolling by filled with debris and once, the wail of a fire engine hurtling through the streets to ground zero. She had only one memory of the City to compare it with—a midnight stroll a few years back after a record snowfall, a snowfall big enough so that it had closed all the airports and bridges and tunnels. It had paralyzed the City. She remembered standing alone in the middle of the northbound lane at Broadway and 68th Street in pristine untracked snow for over twenty minutes until finally a pair of headlights appeared far in the distance. She could have been in Vermont or New Hampshire. Instead she was standing in one of the busiest streets in the busiest city in the world. She remembered being delighted with the sheer novelty of it, of all that peace and silence.

This was not the same thing.

They walked south down Broadway past shop after shop selling posters or framed photos of the Towers, their eyes inevitably drawn to them. And they didn't strike her as crass or even commercial particularly, though of course they were—New York would always recover first through commerce—they stuck her as valid reminders of what had been. And there was nothing wrong with that.

They stopped in front of a boarded-up Chase Bank filthy with dust, the entire broad surface of its window covered with ID photos of cops and firemen dead, all those young faces staring out at them frozen in time forever. The thick brown-white dust lay everywhere. On the sidewalks, the streets, the surfaces of shops and highrises—canopies and even whole skyscrapers were being hosed down to try to get rid of it.

It was a losing battle. The site was still burning.

She stared at the faces moving past her. She guessed that not one in thirty was smiling.

They passed police barricades strewn with flowers.

Windows filled with appeals for information on the missing. *The dead.*

Their photos.

They passed children's bright crayon drawings—hearts, firemen, cops, flowers, words of grief and thanks.

It had been a while since either of them had said a thing. She'd always been perfectly comfortable with Barbara ever since their days bartending together at the Village Cafe but this was different. Each of them, she thought, was really alone here. Everybody was.

The wind shifted. The stench died down. But her mouth still tasted like steel and dust and plastic. She was hungry. She hadn't eaten. Yet it was impossible to think of eating here. She wondered how the sub shops and sidewalk stands stayed open. Even a Coke or a bottled water here would taste . . . wrong.

They'd stop at each corner and gaze into the empty sky.

Approaching Liberty Street the sidewalks became more crowded and then very crowded and before long they were trapped in the midst of a slow-moving mass of people that was almost frightening, what felt like hundreds of people, tourists and New Yorkers all crowding together at the barricades and straining for what was supposedly the best view of what was no longer there. And here you *did* see smiles and laughter, too damn much laughter for her liking. Almost a carnival atmosphere, fueled by morbid curiosity. And packed too tight together, far too tight, seven or eight deep—so that what if something happened? what if somebody panicked? You could be crushed, trampled. And when a father snapped a photo of his smiling little girl against the horizon and then a teenage boy with his girlfriend did the same she said, *let's get the hell out of here.*

"We can't," said Barbara.

"I don't like this."

"Neither do I."

She was shaking with a mix of fear and fury.

"This way."

It was easier than she'd thought. As they stepped slowly through from the center to the rear of the crowd people were happy to take their place so they could get nearer to the site. Finally they stood at the edge of this crawling human tide, their back nearly scraping the filthy storefronts and climbing over steps leading into other storefronts and soon they found themselves on Park Row leading east so that it was silent again finally and they laughed and shook their heads almost dizzy with relief and that was when they heard it, a small soft mewling sound.

"Is that. . . . ?"

"Shhhh," she said. "Yes."

She listened. In a moment she heard it again. There was a long green dumpster on blocks and packed with rubble, mostly chunks of cement, across the street to her left. The sound was coming from there. They walked over and peered beneath the dumpster, Claire working one way, Barbara the other.

"Nothing," she said.

"Nothing here either."

She looked behind it. A dirty empty sidewalk and the wall of a building.

"We didn't imagine that," Barbara said. "That was a kitten."

"I know. Hold on a minute."

She put her foot down on one of the blocks and hauled herself up to the lip of the dumpster and scanned the rubble. And there it was, far over to her right, a tiny tabby walking unsteadily across a narrow jagged cement-shard tightrope, back and forth, gazing down at something beyond her sightlines to the far side of the dumpster. They heard it cry again. She hopped down.

"Over here," she said.

They walked over to where she judged the cat had been but there weren't any blocks there, nothing for her to step up on. She looked around for a milk crate or a bucket or garbage can. Something.

"Cradle your fingers."

"Gotcha."

Barbara did and her first try failed miserably and Claire fell back to the street again practically into her and they both started laughing and then she tried again.

"Okay. I got it. Hold on."

She took most of her weight out of Barbara's hands when her belly hit the lip of the dumpster and she folded at the waist and she spotted the cat and reached and the kitten turned to look at her, wide-eyed at this new disturbance and she thought it probably would have bolted had it not been perched there so precariously, but as it was, stayed put just long enough for her to put her right hand down

310

and push further at the lip to get an extra foot of reach so that she caught it in her left hand and lifted it away.

The kitten gave one long *meeeeeooooowwwww* in earnest now and glanced anxiously over its shoulder and she looked down to where the cat was looking and saw the much larger body whose markings so nearly matched its own. Its head lay hidden beneath a block of stone. She saw long-dried blood along its bib and shoulder.

"Oh, you poor little thing," she said.

The kitten just looked at her, trembling.

"I've got her," she said. "I'm coming down."

"How did you know?" Barbara said.

"How did I know what?"

"That it was a she?"

She laughed. "I did. I didn't. I don't know."

They were headed uptown and over to the subway and then home. Barbara carried her bag for her. She carried the kitten pressed against her breast and shoulder. The kitten was matted and caked with dust and God knows what else and smelled like the inside of a garbage can and she gripped Claire's shoulder fiercely. Claire didn't mind a bit.

"How old, do you figure? Five, six weeks?"

"God, I doubt that her eyes were *even open* a week ago. She's young. Really young. I'll get her to a vet this afternoon. Check her out and see if she's okay. The vet'll probably know."

They were going back roughly the way they came. Past the dusty shops and into the smell of burning and the strange sad New York silence.

"You going to keep her?"

She lifted the cat off her body and held her up over her head with both hands and the cat looked down and she smiled at the cat and smiled too out into the quiet street.

"Forever."

311

<u>SEVEN</u>

When David finished work for the day—the acrylic for the YA bookcover was getting somewhere, finally—he did what he always did and cleaned his brushes; and covered his canvas and went to the bedroom and pressed MES-SAGES on his answering machine and turned off the mute button and listened.

Sandwiched between a recorded pitch from Mike Bloomberg asking for his support in the coming election and a call from his agent's assistant asking him to phone when he got the chance, she had good news for him, was her voice saying *it's me, just wanted to see how you were doing,* cut off abruptly.

There had been whole days by now that he hadn't even thought of her though they were still few and far between but this had been one of them, he'd been that absorbed in the work for a change, and then her voice, or the ghost of her voice—his machine was an old analog cassette recorder and had the annoying habit of allowing snippets of old buried messages to rise up from between the new ones like withered fingers from a grave—rushed at him with all its force and broke the dam inside him again.

How am I doing?

Some days fine, Claire. Most days, not well at all.

He dialed her number. Something he hadn't done in weeks now at her request.

He got her machine.

"It's me," he said. "Did you phone today? Or is my machine messing with my mind again? I figured I'd better check. Anyway, I'm here, and I hope all's well. See you."

He'd given her plenty of time to pick up. She hadn't, so either she really wasn't there and the call had come in earlier or her voice had been a mechanical glitch and she still wasn't talking to him.

312

Ready to talk to him was the way she put it.

He'd wonded if she'd ever be ready.

His agent was on speed-dial. She wasn't. He'd taken her off almost a month ago. *Too much temptation, far too easy.* His agent said they had a terrific offer for him, cover art for the next six Anne Rice paperback reissues, his agent very enthusiastic about it, and went on to outline the deal. The deal was a good one and he sure as hell could use the money but he'd worked with Rice a few years back and knew she could be difficult, one of those writers who seemed to think they were painters too and let you know it each step of the way, detailing you to death, your art going back and forth for approval like a canvas ping-pong ball.

"Tell them I'll take it," he said.

He hung up and went to his computer and lit his twenty-first cigarette of the day. It was supposed to help him cut down if he counted them but so far it had only made him nervous to know he was smoking so damn much. He went into his e-mail. Half an hour later he hadn't answered any of them. The words wouldn't come.

It was obsessive but all he could think of was her message on the machine. *Just wanted to see how you were doing.* Maybe she really did. Maybe she had just gone out for a while and she'd call back later.

He doubted it.

But he missed her enormously and whenever he allowed himself to realize that, whenever he truly let it through, he'd cling to even the most delicate thread of hope. *She'd changed her mind, it didn't matter that he couldn't bring himself to leave, she missed him too much, all's forgiven, let's try again.*

He knew her far too well to think it was anything but fantasy but he clung to hope as though hope itself might make it so. It wasn't just the sex he missed though God knows it had never been anything but fine between them but his heart had an entire Whole Earth catalog of what he missed about her and his mind kept flipping through the pages. Sometimes almost at random, something striking him hard for no reason. *The gap between her two front teeth, the husky voice, the talk about mutual friends whose names he hadn't heard for weeks now and incidents long past and people long gone in both their lives and art and books and feelings, the tall proud way she walked the street or the feel of her waist beneath his arm or her cheek beneath his hand or the two of them staring up at the darkening New York sky*—it just went on and on. Countless images, moments observed and shared over the heady course of two long years. And the friendship which always lay beneath.

He pushed back away from the computer and turned it off, watched the screen crackle down to neutral grey. The e-mail would have to wait. He wasn't feeling up to the basically cheery voice it always seemed to require of him.

A drink, he thought, that's what was in order. *You got a lot of work done today. You deserve it. Have a scotch and turn on the news for a while. Couldn't hurt.*

Could it?

He was drinking a fair amount these days.

Was it for pleasure the way it used to be? Or just to throw a cozy blanket over pain?

He knew Sara worried about it. Sometimes so did he.

He seemed to have to bludgeon himself to sleep these days.

He got up and poured one anyway. His two tabby cats yawned awake on the counter when he cracked the plastic tray of ice. He scratched them both behind the ears. They fell asleep again. Sara wouldn't be home from work for two hours yet and the cats wouldn't be fed until she did. They knew that as well as they knew every flat surface in the apartment and the exact extent to which it was good for sleeping on. Until that time rolled around, dozing was an appropriate response to life.

He wished he were as sensible and poured himself a stiff one.

He was waiting for a phone call.

It might be a long night.

It was.

Seven hours, five drinks and a leftover chicken dinner later she hadn't called. So it had been a glitch, as suspected. Tomorrow he was getting a new machine, dammit. He didn't need the torment.

And it *was* a torment. He wasn't overstating. He felt like a caged animal in his own apartment. Sara was in the bedroom watching TV and doing paperwork, some homework from the bank but he couldn't join her the way he usually did, not tonight. He couldn't turn it off. It was as though being in the same room with her right now would constitute betrayal—of Sara, of Claire, of all three of them.

He tried to read but that didn't work either. He never painted or even sketched when he'd been drinking and he wasn't about to start now. So that left the computer. He answered his e-mail as best he could and then surfed the net, looking for images, not sure what he was looking for but something to startle him or comfort him. Something. He felt hot-wired to her voice on the phone. Finally he left-clicked on the WRITE MAIL icon and began this long, feverish, idiotic letter to her. A plea for some kind of communication, any kind would do but mostly he wanted to see her and probably he wanted that for the very same reason she did not want to see him. It might start it up all over again, which he was selfish enough to want even knowing it could not be good for her and was honest enough about to make him feel guilty as sin.

He didn't know if the booze was helping or hindering in the sense-making department but the letter poured out of him and when it was finished he began to hit the SEND button but then stopped to read it again. He didn't know if it spoke to his feelings or didn't. If it was self-pitying drivel or not. Fuck it, he thought. *Fuck it fuck it fuck it.* He saved it into the MAIL WAITING TO BE SENT file. Maybe

315

he'd send it off tomorrow when he was more sober and maybe he wouldn't.

Meantime he was not going to sit here staring at a computer screen all night.

He knew where she worked these days.

They still had a few friends in common who hadn't deserted him completely and he'd pursuaded Barbara to give up the address. Hell, she was right here in the neighborhood. Only ten blocks away.

He turned off the computer and got up and walked into the bedroom. Sara looked up at him from the bed. Piles of papers fanned out in front of her in an orderly fashion. She was doing something to them with a red felt tip pen.

"I'm going out," he said. "Feeling restless."

"Okay. Where to?"

"Take a walk, have a drink. We'll see."

"You going to see Claire?"

"I don't know. Maybe. I guess I'll figure that one out once I'm out there. She still doesn't want to see me."

She put down the pen.

"David, are we in trouble? Do we need to talk?"

"No, we're not in trouble. At least not now. I don't know about the long run. I don't know where we're going. But we don't need to talk, not now."

"I worry."

"Don't. It's okay. I just might need to see her. I don't know."

She looked at him and nodded. "All right. Be careful," she said.

She meant it. All that *careful* entailed.

"I will. I love you."

She went back to her papers. He thought how strange this would look to some outsider. As though she really didn't care. But he knew she did care and how much. They had thirty years together and the ties were strong even if sometimes invisible to most people, stretched thin these days because he had fallen in love and she of course knew

316

as she knew everything important in his life—and maybe it was that knowing, as much as the cats they shared or the apartment they shared or the fact that she was his first best critic or even the years themselves of order and easy companionship which was why he stayed and couldn't seem to leave.

Sarah was family by now. He had no other.

He put on his jacket and stepped into the hall and locked the door behind him.

EIGHT

Half-past midnight and Claire was *finally* getting to eat—the ceasar salad with grilled chicken she'd asked the cook to leave for her in the microwave. They'd been slammed all night long for a change but now there was only old Willie in his usual corner, arms folded in front of him and half asleep over his beer. When she finished she'd roust him. Willie weighed in at a good two hundred pounds and he'd already fallen off his barstool once since she'd started working here only a few weeks ago. He was going to crack his head open one of these days. She didn't want it to be on her watch.

Sandi dumped the last of the candles out of its holder into the black plastic trash bag down at the end of the bar, sighed and smiled and untied her waitress' apron and slid it off over her head.

"I'm outa here, that okay?"

They'd already split the tips and balanced out the register. There hadn't been any discrepancies between that and the cash-due printout or they'd have had to go through the checks together one by one to find the error. And Sandi looked dead on her feet.

"Sure. Go. You have a good night."

"What's left of it."

"Give that guy a hug for me."

"Yeah. Hey, listen, I really want to thank you for that. I

317

really appreciate you talking to me. It helped."

"Kenny's a good kid. Everybody screws up now and then. Just don't let him make a habit of it, that's all."

Sandi smiled again and slipped on her jacket and hoisted her shoulderbag.

"I won't. See you tomorrow?"

"I'll be here."

She finished her salad. Hell, she'd wolfed the damn thing down. You got busy, you didn't have time to eat. Then you forgot to eat. Pretty soon you were starving. It was high time she had a shot and a Marlboro. She poured a double Cuervo neat and lit up and let the smoke slide down deep.

"Hey, Willie. Last call."

"Hmmmm?"

She watched the heavy eyelids slide up and then down again—what her father used to call the Long Blink.

"Willie. Hey."

"Hmmmm?"

"Time to go."

"Oh yeah, 'course. Okay I finish this?" He smiled.

"Sure."

She watched his fingers toy with the neck of the Heineken, literally feeling around for the thing, and then grip it and pour. He had about a third of a glass left. She took a hit of the Cuervo and another pull on the cigarette and walked around the service station and then down the bar past him to turn off the central air over by the plateglass window and then heard the sounds of the city rush in to her left as the man opened the door and stepped through. The man nodded and smiled and took off his thin brown leather gloves and she thought, *shit, why does this always happen to me?* because she was supposed to stay open until one if there were any customers at all, that was the rule in this place and here it was twelve forty-five and it would be just her luck and she was just that new on the job that the boss would come around to check up on her if she told this guy she was closed already.

318

The man was tall and wore a good brown three-piece suit and he put his brown leather briefcase down on the bar eight stools back from Willie, just in front of the register and smiled again and said, *evening*.

"Evening," Willie said.

The man just looked at him.

She had to laugh.

"I'm just about to close," she said. "So this'll be last call. But what can I get you?"

If he knew about anything he knew about bars and barflies and he could tell from the way the fat guy was sitting on his stool that he was about to drop, that she sure wasn't going to serve him again so that was when he'd made his move. He'd walked across the street from the flower shop where he'd been pretending to admire the window display and through the door. From where he stood he had a perfect view of the street and the corner of Columbus and 70th. Nice easy monitoring.

"What's on tap?" he said and she told him. He said he'd take the Amstel.

The Amstel came in a frosted mug. He liked that. He took a sip and watched her rinse a few glasses and dry her hands and then walk over to the fat guy in the corner. He liked the way she walked. It was assertive, very New York.

"Hey, Willie. Wake up, Willie."

"Huh?"

"Finish your beer."

"Right. Okay."

He tilted the glass and drank and set it down again.

"Tomorrow's another night, Willie. Finish it up."

"Okay." He did. "What I owe you?"

"You already paid me."

"I did?"

"Yep."

"Tip?"

"You left a good one, Willie. Thanks."

"Pleasure," he said and smiled and waved at her once like he was the goddamn Pope bestowing a drunk benediction and slid off the barstool. He tugged once at the collar of his faded grey raincoat and straightened up and managed not to stagger as he walked out the door.

God, he hated barflies. Fucking disgusting.

She went back to the dishes again.

"He's really a very nice guy," she said. "But with all that weight he's carrying I worry about him. I'm afraid he's going to have a heart attack or something right in the middle of my shift. Then what am I supposed to do?"

"I don't blame you. But say it did happen, what *would* you do?"

She shrugged. "Call 911 I guess. I've seen CPR but I've never, you know, actually done it."

"You've seen CPR?"

"Movies, television. Not in real life."

"Oh. I'm Larry by the way."

He put out his hand. She smiled and dried hers on a towel and took it.

"Claire. Nice to meet you."

"Nice to meet you, Claire."

He looked around while she went back to the glasses in the sink and thought, hell, as good a time as any, slipped on the surgical gloves out of her sightlines beneath the bar, unlatched the briefcase and opened it and pushed it aside with the top open so that it would block any view from the street and lay the gun down softly on the bar.

"Claire?"

She looked at him first and then at his hand spread over the gun and he watched her face change. He always liked this moment. *Revelation-time.*

"Here's what we're going to do, Claire. We're going to pretend we're a pair of old friends, maybe we even dated way back when, who knows? and I'm here closing up with you, so you do what you do every night, only I'm here. You lock the door and hit the lights outside and dim the ones in here. Only difference is that once you've done all that you empty the register into this briefcase. Me, I'm just having a drink. You understand?"

She nodded.

"Okay, now go on about your business. And Claire? Don't even think about trying to run out that door. I know you really want to very much right now but here's the thing, it takes too long to open the door, throw it back and then go through. Believe me, I know. You'll be dead before you hit the sidewalk. And I'm already up for Murder One in New York, New Jersey and Connecticut so it won't mean a thing to me one way or another."

He clicked off the safety.

"Do we have a meeting of the minds here, Claire?"

"Yes."

"Good. You know what you're supposed to do?"

"Yes."

"Then go."

"The keys are in my bag. The door keys."

"So? Get 'em."

He watched her, trying to gauge her reaction as she stooped down to the floor for her bag and set it in front of the speed rack and opened it and fished out her keyring. Her hands were shaking as she fumbled for the right one and that was good. Her color was off and that was good too.

But she kept glancing up at him—just before she stooped to retrieve her bag and then as she set it on the speed rack and then again as she turned the corner at the service station and a fourth time as she passed him headed for the door. He thought, *this one's a wiseass, she's trying to memorize what I look like*, but there were ways to minimize that possibility and ways to wipe it out almost completely.

It was called shock therapy.

The night had turned chilly and David was unprepared for that, dressed only in a light tan jacket and even with it zipped to the chin the wind off the river along West End Avenue was enough to send him immediately east all the way across to Central Park West where the packed-together rows of high-end residentials blocked it. He walked from 63rd all the way up to 78th Street wondering what he was doing, keeping to the west side against the buildings both for the shelter and because you never knew about Central Park and who you might encounter this time of night. It was a lonely stretch though pretty well lit—a few people out walking their dogs or on their way home from some-where or other and light two-way traffic. He supposed the street matched his mood. *Lonely and at least half-lit.*

At 78th he crossed three blocks over to Broadway though her bar was back on Columbus. He meant, he guessed, to describe a wide circle around her and only then, if he hadn't managed to shake this feeling by then, narrow in. He hoped the feeling would just go away. It was stupid, what he was doing. Even just standing across the street from the bar watching her through the plate-glass window would be stupid because if he could see her then there was also the possibility that she'd see him. Never mind that it was easily as humiliating as standing under her apartment window. To go inside and try to talk to her, which was what he really wanted to do, which was what he was aching to do, was bound to cause more hurt for both of them.

There could be no good ending to this.

But he was doing it anyway.

He headed down Broadway, hands shoved into his jeans against the cold. Some of the bars were still packed mostly with kids in their twenties and he heard music and loud laughter and other bars were still and dark, closed already or just about to close and the thought came to him sud-denly that he had no idea how business was over at her place. She could easily have locked up and gone home by now. It was a definite possibility.

The thought filled him with a kind of dread and he

picked up his pace so that by the time he crossed against the red and passed Gray's Papaya at 72nd Street his heart was pounding so he slowed again. It wouldn't be good for her to see him this way, if he was going to be seen at all. He still wasn't sure about that. Wasn't sure what in the hell he was going to do.

But this feeling hadn't been mitigated being out here. The night air hadn't cleared his head or cured him. Not by a long shot. *He was so close*. To seeing her at least. To something.

He turned east at 70th and walked slowly toward Columbus.

She was going to keep this under control. He wouldn't use the gun.

He wanted the money, that's all.

Fine.

"I cashed out already," she said. "The money's in back."

"What's in the drawer?"

"Two hundred startup money for tomorrow."

"Put it in the briefcase. Cash box or safe?"

"Cash box, locked in the desk. They wouldn't trust me with the safe. I'm still new here."

"Oh? You're not trustworthy?"

"I'm new here."

She stacked the money in his briefcase. She watched him sip his beer.

"You already said that. But what I asked you is, are you trustworthy?"

"Y-yes."

Stop that, she thought. *Shit!* You don't want to show him fear. Not the slightest *bit* of fear.

"Should I trust you to go in back there and get the box for me?"

"Up to you."

He smiled and looked her up and down and she wished

she'd worn something a little less clingy than the thin scoop-neck blouse.

"I don't think so," he said. "You're a woman. And I wouldn't trust a woman on a short leash with her fucking legs cut off. Nothing personal. Walk me back. And keep your hands down at your sides. Move."

She walked back through the tables and chairs stacked for the night back to the office and opened the office door and thought of slamming it in his face but that was only a thought and nothing she'd consider for a moment because all he wanted was the money. She found the right key for the drawer and opened it, took out the cash box and put it on the desk beside the printer and computer.

She turned.

And he was so close. The gun only inches from her chest. She lurched back and her hip hit the desk. It hurt. Her mouth was very dry all of a sudden.

"You want me to . . . I mean, should I open it? Or you want to just take it as it is?

"Open it. I like to see what I've got."

He was smiling again and the brown eyes seemed to jitter back and forth and she thought strangely of *ants or bees, of insects.*

And there was no smile in the eyes at all.

It was a relief to turn back to the desk. Not to have to look at the eyes. She used three fingers against the box to steady her thumb and forefinger and finally found the keyhole and turned the key and turned and stepped away a little to her left. He lifted the lid.

"You had a good night, Claire."

He shut it again and took one step toward her, his face only inches from her face, directly in front of her.

"You really don't know CPR?"

"What?"

"You really don't know CPR? Just from what you see on television?"

"I never . . ."

"So what happens if some customer throws a fit or something? I'm just curious. Aren't you supposed to be *in charge* of this bar, Claire? Isn't that you? It's not the waiter who's in charge, it's not the fucking busboy. Is pouring a goddamn beer the only thing you're good for? What about responsibility? *Suppose I pitched a fit or something!* What would you do for me? Call 911 while I'm dying here? Jesus Christ!"

He's crazy, she thought. He's a goddamn fucking lunatic and God knows what a lunatic will do.

Maybe it isn't just the money.

And for the first time now he really scared her.

He had her now, he could tell by the look on her face, time to put the real fear of God into the bitch and see if she remembered anything *but* fear after that. He put the gun against her temple and backed her ass to the desk again.

"Open your mouth."

"What?"

"I said open your mouth. Do it, Claire."

She did.

"All right, now keep it open, understand? I'm gonna show you something. I'm gonna show you how to do CPR."

He reached over and pinched her nostrils shut. Her eyes skittered. He took a deep breath and put his mouth over hers and exhaled hard and heard her gasp when he pulled away and try to catch her breath but he did it again before she could, emptied his lungs into her and this time when he let her up for air she was coughing and her eyes were gleaming with tears.

She tasted like smoke and tequila.

The coughing stopped. She leaned back against the desk, chest heaving.

"There you go. Of course you'd be on your back, normally. But you get the idea. Grab the cash box. Come on."

He marched her back the way they'd come and saw her wipe her cheek with one hand and thought, good start.

David sat on the steps of a brownstone across the street from the ornate blue-and-gold Pythian building, a lit cigarette in his hand, trying to will his heart to stop pounding. He'd gotten halfway down the block when it felt like somebody had put a hand to his chest and said, *asshole, don't you take another step further*. Don't even think it.

He had no business being here.

Not on the steps, nobody would care about that—but *being here*. This close. Thinking what he was thinking.

She'd said she didn't want to see him, period and no hedging this time, that she couldn't see him, that seeing him had become a kind of grief played over and over again and that they simply had to stop, get away from one another and go lick their wounds until maybe in time they could be friends again or something like friends but that now they could be nothing.

It was the act of a willful selfish child to be this close to her.

What he needed to do was go home. Be an adult.

He'd made his choice. He should live with it.

He gasped at a sudden unexpected rush of tears. *That he should have to choose at all*. Not fair.

He wiped away the tears and drew on the cigarette and sat there, slowly calming.

"Pour me another Amstel, Claire. This one's gone flat. Use one of those good frozen mugs you've got there."

She did as he told her to do while he transfered the contents of the cash box to his briefcase, poured the beer and set it in front of him, trying to keep her hands from shaking, trying not to spill it, not to show. The taste of him was still in her mouth. He handed her the empty box.

"Put that on the floor or something, will you?"

She did that too, bent over and set it beside the garbage can and when she stood up again something hit her in the chest and she gasped, something freezing cold sliding down off her chest and over her belly.

He was laughing. The frosted glass was empty.

"Ooops. Little spill there. Gee, sorry."

"*You. . . . !*"

He leaned in close over the bar.

"You *what*, Claire? You *what*? What do you want to call me? You want to call me names? Pour me another beer you dumb little shit and keep your fucking mouth shut. And I want a new glass."

She looked down at herself, arms out to her sides. She didn't know what to do. You could see almost everything through the thin material and the bra was thin too so you could even see her nipples puckered by the cold. *He* could see them, goddammit. If she brushed at it that would only make it worse, plastering the material to her body. She wanted to cry. *She wouldn't cry*. She turned to the freezer to get the glass and that was when she brushed herself off because then he couldn't see.

She drew the beer and set it in front of him on the bar. And almost wasn't surprised when he lifted it and threw it all over her again.

But when he laughed the second time, then she did cry. She couldn't help it. It just happened. Whether it was humiliation or frustration or fear or all of these together she just stood there, eyes closed and quietly sobbing.

"Look at me," he said.

She wouldn't. If she couldn't see him then she could almost pretend he couldn't see her.

"I said, look at me, dammit!"

She opened her eyes. What she saw was a man enjoying himself immensely. She couldn't understand. Why was he putting her through this? Shouldn't he be running away right now? Wasn't he at all worried about the cops?

How could anybody *be like* this?

"You stink of beer, Claire. Clean yourself off. You smell like a slut. Use that hand towel there. Dip it in some water.

327

That's right. You have nice nipples, Claire. Say *thank you, sir*. I'm the customer. The customer's always right."

"Thank you."

She plucked the material out in front of her and wiped at it with the wet rag. The blouse was going to be stretched and ruined.

"Thank you, sir, Claire."

"Thank you, sir."

"Better. Now hand me that spindle."

"The what?"

"Jesus Christ, Claire, you've worked in bars for how long? The spindle. The goddamn spindle. The spike you stack your checks on, for chrissake!"

"I . . ."

She didn't want to do this. Her heart was suddenly hammering. She hated those things. Always had. Even just to look at them. The spike was maybe eight inches long rising straight up out of a thick coil of wire at its base. This one was set at the service station below one of the wine racks and whenever she had to climb up onto the counter to get to one of the more pricey wines up top she had visions of losing her balance and falling right onto it, of being impaled. She could see it. Ridiculous, horrible way to die.

The spike was as sharp and thick as an icepick.

"Please . . . I don't . . ."

"Ah, begging. I like that."

"Those things scare me, okay?"

"Why? You use it every day."

"They just do."

"Maybe I want to scare you."

"What? Please . . ."

"Maybe I want to scare you. Maybe I don't like you one goddamn bit, Claire, and maybe I want to scare you so much I could almost come in my pants just thinking about it? What if the money's only a kind of perk? Maybe this is what it's all about. You ever consider that, you dopey whore?"

"Why . . . ?"

"Why? Because I want to. Because this gun tells us both
I can. You hear me, you ugly fuck? You get ugly when you
cry, Claire, you know that? *You want to know why? Because
after me you'll never feel safe again, Claire. Never. Not at work,
not at home. Nowhere. Because that's my wish for the whole
fucking world and for you, Claire, in particular.* Now hand
me the goddamn spindle!"

She could barely see him through the tears but she could
feel the heat of his anger reach out to her across the bar.
For a split second she imagined him bursting into flame.
Where did all this come from? Why? What had she done?

David thought, *if she hates me for it, so be it. I have to see
her.*

He crushed out the cigarette and stepped down off the
brownstone.

"I want to show you how we're gonna do this, Claire. Stop
blubbering, for chrissake. Take one of those cocktail nap-
kins there. Wipe your goddamn nose. You're gonna do it
once first, just so you can see how hard it is, and then it's
my turn. See, I put my hand on the bar, palm down, just
like this. Then you pick up the spindle. You raise it over
the center of my hand to exactly the level of this beer mug,
no lower and no higher. Lower's cheating. Higher and it'll
never work. Then you try to spike me."

"I can't . . ."

"Sure you can. I'll give you some incentive. You spike
me and the game's over right now and you get to keep
whatever's in your tip jar. I don't think you will, though.
Like I say, it's hard. Assuming you don't, then I get three
tries. I miss all three, you keep whatever's in your tip jar.
I don't miss . . . well, then you're shit out of luck, Claire.
Now pick up the spindle. And remember, the gun's in the
other hand so you don't want to be thinking about doing
anything else with it other than playing our little game."

He watched her eyes. The eyes always flickered when they made their move. The eyes were a dead giveaway. But he didn't even need the eyes this time. Instead of bringing it straight on down she raised it a half inch first so it was an easy thing to pull his hand away. Gave it a lot of force though. She was game, he gave her that much. He freed the spindle from the bar.

"Okay. My turn."

"No. Please. Just take the money. Just leave me alone please? Enough, all right? All right??"

The husky voice had turned into a whine. The eyes were red with tears.

He smiled.

"Not enough, Claire. Not all right. But what are you worried about? You saw how tough it is. I'll probably lose anyway, right? Of course maybe I won't."

"I can't, please . . ."

"You can, Claire. You have to. See the gun? See this tubing at the end? It's called a silencer. I made it myself. That means I can shoot you three or four times if I want to without even killing you, you dumb piece of shit and nobody's going to hear it, the neighbors upstairs will never be the wiser. And *that*, Claire, is a world of pain, I promise you. You want it to go down that way? Fine by me. Different game is all. Nastier."

"Oh, Jesus! Why . . . ?"

"You know the little *pffttt* sound silencers always make in the movies? Doesn't happen. More like car door closing. So what'll it be?"

She thought of her widowed mother in Queens and how in another month it would be Christmas and then of her sister married three months almost to the day and pregnant out in Oregon and that she'd never visited, thought of the paintings just finished and half-finished and of David still not free of her nor her of him and she thought about the kitten who curled between her feet each night and who would feed her and take care of her and apprehended something of what the world would be like without her in it, an almost impossible concept just an hour ago but glimpsed now for a moment and thought *I'm so afraid, I'm so afraid of what I won't get to see* and she put her hand down on the bar.

. . . and now his control is complete. He can see it in her eyes. He can see she knows a truth he's known all along, that there is no help in this world, that what will happen will happen and no amount of pleading to God or Jesus or to the milk of human kindness will get you any goddamn where at all, that in the face of loathing as deep and strong as his is she is just another worker ant in an anthill he can bring down in a second, crush beneath his feet at any time he wishes—her hand on the bar says all of this to him, and the temptation is there to do it to her on the very first plunge of the spike, to bring it instantly into even more stark perspective for her, the perspective of flesh, of spilled blood, of pain.

Yet he resists that. He lets her pull away and listens to her gasp and the dull thud of the spindle against the bar and raises it again and watches her hand slide across the bar to submit a second time and wonders, is she hopeful? does she see an end to this? because he seems to have missed? That this might be true is delightful to him too because he can wipe it all away so quickly, he has lied again and he is very good at this, he has had practice and if hope is not yet there he can place it in her heart on this second try, bait his trap for the hungry animal which is all she is after all—hungry for the truth of what he knows to be.

And this time he can practically hear her heart beating, racing as she pulls away because yes! he can feel the hope there coiled in her like a snake—he has missed by a mile it seems to her and he can smell the stink of hope, its sudden sweet reek as he positions the spike above her hand a third and final time and then, prescient and sly and born of months and years

331

watching his back, trusting his senses, he glances out the plate glass window to the street . . .

"Who the hell is that?" he says.

And at first she can only think it's part of this game he's playing, this insane evil fucked-up game and she doesn't look up at all but only at her hand on the bar waiting for the courage to pull it away if she can a third time but then the words and the tone of the words seem to spill through to her and what she hears is unexpected, wrong in these circumstances, a flat even tone as if he'd said *well that's interesting, it's raining out* and she looks first at him and then at where he's looking and sees David on the corner by the closed dark flower shop across the street. Their eyes meet and he's scowling, puzzled and she thinks, *oh no, oh God no, I was so close, I might have finished this here and now*. She remembers seeing him down on the street across from her apartment building many nights ago and drawing away from the curtain before he glimpsed her at the window and remembers thinking how terribly sad it was for both of them and how wasteful that she could never, ever have come out to meet him and thinks *David, why in hell are you here again? what in hell have you done now?*

She holds his gaze and slowly shakes her head. *Don't even think it.* The scowl disappears. Instead the eyes plead with her, confused and uncertain. Eyes so well known and loved. She needs to deny these eyes. For both of them.

"Who is he, Claire?"

"My . . . boyfriend. Ex-boyfriend."

"Ex?"

"We've broken up."

"So what's he doing here?"

"I don't know."

The man seems to think a moment.

She watches David take a step closer to the curb. She shakes her head again. *No, goddammit! Don't do this! Please, you fucking lovely idiot, stay the hell away!*

"I think you'd better invite him in, Claire."

"No."

"Oh yes. You have to."

"I won't."

"Yes you will. Or it's you first and then him. Twenty seconds is all I need. He'll never know what hit him."

He closes the briefcase beside him and snaps it shut and slides the spindle down the bar well beyond her reach. He's ready to go now. The game is over. All of it over now unless she brings David into this and if she does, won't it just begin again? to what end? Why does he want this? What can he hope to gain? He can walk out the door right now. Free and clear. Just walk away.

Her eyes go back to David. To hold him there. *Don't move.*

"Do it."

"I can't."

"You will."

She thinks—hard and fast as best she can. *She will not do this to him.* And there seems only one way to do that. To convince him that she's furious at him for being there. He ought to be able to believe that. He ought to have anticipated that reaction from her. She has every right to be furious—though she's not. Though seeing him again even under these terrible circumstances feels so tender that what she'd like to do is embrace him, hug him, sob into his shoulder not just for what this man has put her through tonight but for all they've lost and all they had. To do that one more time again. What she'd sworn she'd never do.

She moves out past the service station and turns and heads past the man to the door.

Outside on the corner David sees her long purposeful familiar stride but the look on her face is unfamiliar. It's a look he can't quite read. When he'd thought he knew them all. He's only just arrived here but already something feels wrong about her and he thinks, who's this guy in there?

New boyfriend? Boss? But boyfriend doesn't feel right. Of course it's possible he doesn't want to admit that she might already have one. Might already have replaced him.

But boyfriend doesn't feel right. Nor does boss. Something about her face, the look in her eyes.

A car passes and then another. Claire is at the lock now. He steps out into the street.

Claire looks up from the lock and he's crossing, coming toward her and she feels the blood rush to her face, pulse pounding and she flings open the door because *she will not expose him to this goddammit, she will* not *permit that* and summons the most dismissive angry tone of which she is capable and shouts out into the still night air.

"*DAVID! GO! GET . . .*"

. . . OUT OF HERE! is what she means to say. . . .

. . . but the sheer sudden size of her voice startles the man inside and he thinks . . . *HELP! THE POLICE! she's calling for help the stupid bitch* so he turns and fires and the flower blooms wet in her back and he hears the silencer like a door closing exactly as he's told her it would be and she falls spilled to one side, the glass door wedged open by her hips and he pulls the briefcase off the bar thinking *the fucking cop was right, he's finally had to shoot somebody* and the boyfriend is almost across the street closing the gap between them and as he steps over her body he sees her eyes flutter stunned and wide and the man is yelling *Claire! Claire!* loud enough to wake the dead, the man not exactly understanding yet he thinks but there's no way to know what he'll do once he does so as he turns a sharp right headed toward the subway at 72nd he fires again and watches, for just a moment, a second flower bloom across the man's chest, watches him sink to his knees and fall and reach for her, the man's hand settling in her flung tangled hair along the sidewalk, his hand opening and closing in strands of hair, unable to reach further.

He doesn't know if he feels fear. He might. Maybe he should.

But he knows he feels good.

David lies sprawled along the sidewalk. The sidewalk feels oddly warm to him. It ought to feel cold this time of year. He tries to move but can't. He tries to breathe and barely can. Is this shock? Death? What? He sees her lying near him in the doorway. If he focuses on her, on Claire, he might live, someone might come by.

That he might even want to live disgusts him.

She stares up, blinks into empty sky.
Tears again.
So many tears in this city. So much heartbreak.
Then none.

Thanks to Amy, Mila, and Adonis

The Rose

for Beth and Richard

She was his earth, his ground. He had cast his seed to her again and again.

He awoke feeling that he knew what was necessary, that what she needed was a kind of light both real and metaphoric, that she needed to get out into the world far more than he had allowed himself to trust her to do.

He decided he would take her.

When they stepped off the bus into early afternoon sunlight he saw how the city had changed, none of it for the better. It was only a town, really, that had tried to bloom into a city during the Fifties and arguably had succeeded for a while, but now the war babies who had driven its boom years, who had caused its schools to rise out of the vacant lots and farmland and crammed its movie palaces and soda shops, had fled and left its potholed, littered streets to time and waste.

Still he felt at home here.

He took her to Mabel's Coffee Shop, where as a boy he had sat over Coke and crumb bun waiting for Miss Lanier, his accordion teacher, to finish with the pigtailed little red-head who had the lesson just before his on the third floor across the street. They had lunch there at the counter—she a hamburger from the grill and he a tuna sandwich with a thin slice of pickle.

Miss Lanier was gone. Cancer. Miss Lanier had gone to earth. And he had not seen his accordion in thirty-five years.

The faces in Mabel's were mostly black now. But they seemed to him the same tired faces he had always seen there, working people's faces bent over working people's food.

He realized that Mabel's always had depressed him, even angered him somehow.

It had not just been the accordion lessons.

But the girl didn't seem to mind.

He took her arm and led her past a shoe store, a dress shop, thrift shop, and the Arthur E. Doyle Post of the Veterans of Foreign Wars, to the Roxy.

The Roxy was boarded up. It had probably been closed for years. Graffiti was sprayed across rotted boards thick and colorful as the patterns on a Persian rug. He walked her across the street to the Palace.

The Palace was open.

"How about a movie," he said.

She brushed a clean fine strand of blond hair off her pretty face and nodded.

They sat in the dark, alone but for three other patrons slouched low and scattered in front of them, and watched Jean-Claude Van Damme fight his way through a double feature, and he thought how they were the only couple there.

At intermission he bought popcorn. Midway through the second feature he unbuttoned her blouse and massaged her naked breast and rolled her pale wide nipple between his

337

fingers, letting it harden and then go soft again, feeling the nipple beneath the palm of his hand and thinking, if only I had gotten this thirty years ago. Jesus.

When it was over it was really dark. They had dinner at a place called Rogerio's a few blocks over. He thought the place had served Chinese take-out once, but now it was Italian. He ordered a double scotch for himself and iced tea for the girl and then ordered himself another. They ate pasta and thick, hot crusty bread, and she was very quiet.

They walked out into streetlights shining.

Across the street he saw the sign.

Like so many others the shop had not been there when he was a boy. He would have remembered it. But someone was inside. The place was all lit up.

He felt the flush of pleasure and swelling of his cock inside his baggy trousers.

"Come on." he said.

She sat on the wooden bench in front of him naked to the waist, nipples going hard and then soft just as they had in the movie theater, while the bearded man sat behind her working on her shoulder blade, his needle buzzing like a barber's electric trimmer over the soft rock music on the radio.

The music was meant to be soothing. The man had warned them that there would be more pain than usual because the bone was so near the surface of the skin in this location. He could see the pain skitter in her eyes. She had been under the drill for over half an hour now.

"What's it like?" he asked her.

"Feels like . . . cat scratches," she said. "Hundreds of little cat scratches. Then it's like . . . he's peeling me. And then . . ."

The tattooist smiled. "Like a dentist's drill, right?" he said.

"Yes," she breathed.

He saw the sweat beaded on her upper lip.

338

"Scapula," he said. "Can't be helped. You're a helluva subject, though, you know that? You don't move a muscle. You're like working on a canvas. I'm gonna give you something special. You'll see. A rose is just right for you. Just a few more minutes."

From the hundreds of drawings that lined the walls he had chosen for her a simple red rose no more than an inch and a half in diameter. He thought the rose was beautiful and that the man had quite a delicate hand. You could see veins in the green leaves, the creamy blush of red, the thorns that studded the graceful stem.

The buzzing stopped.

"There now," said the man. "Give me your hand. Hold the gauze here and press. Not hard."

She did as he said. The man stood up from the bench.

"You want to see?"

He got up and walked over behind her. The tattoist lifted her hand away. He was very gentle.

Beautiful, he thought. The rose looked even better than it did on paper, more detailed and more delicately formed, its stem tracing precisely the natural curve of bone as though it belonged there, as though it had grown there in her silky flesh.

The man looked at him, nodding, appraising his reaction. He had a long bushy beard and his greying hair was tied back into a tail as long as a horse's tail and his eyes were unreadable. But he saw no judgement there. Though it was impossible that he had missed the marks along her back and shoulders.

He saw no judgement there at all.

"Anything else I can do for you?"

His eye drifted to the glass display case by the register. There were rings and studs of gold and silver and semi-precious stones.

"Yes," he said. "Yes, there is."

*   *   *

339

She had not sat so well for the piercing.

On the first try she had flinched despite the topical anesthetic, and her flesh slid free of the instrument that was similar to a paper punch just as he had begun to apply pressure. The man had cursed and then apologized to her for cursing. The girl said nothing though it had hurt and tears streamed down her cheeks. The man had reapplied the anesthetic and tried again, holding the tip of the nipple more firmly between thumb and forefinger and pulling so that it was possible to see that that hurt, too, telling her soothingly that it would only be a second, just a second, then squeezed the handles together.

She gasped and then was silent.

He was surprised there was so little blood.

The man threaded her flesh with the thin silver band he had chosen from the display case.

Then bent to the other breast.

The lights went out behind them, and he heard the tattoist draw his shade as they stepped into the street.

He took her arm and led her to the corner.

On the bus trip home he was annoyed with her. It was as though she didn't want the nipple rings. She had shown no reluctance about the rose tattoo. It was as though she accepted that. Whereas to him they were one and the same. Both rose and rings marked her as his—they would for the rest of her life. And if he could not bring her fecundity, if he could not bind her to him by fucking a girl-child into her depths of her womb, he could at least do this. Children were the glue, his mother had said, and he thought it ungrateful of the girl to wish to deny him.

It had been such a good day in the city.

He opened his flask and drank. In the darkness there was no one to see. Towns faded by and dark suburban homes. He drank some more.

The towns grew smaller. Houses yielded to woods and

340

thicket and stands of pale birch trees and old weathered stone fences.

Finally they were home. He got off the bus ahead of her and held out his hand. She took it, and they walked up the unpaved road in the moonlight. He could see the small grey spot on the back of her blouse where the tattoo had bled through the gauze. There were no such spots on either of her breasts, but he thought that the blouse would still need washing before the blood had set, and that annoyed him, too, for some reason he wasn't aware of. He tilted the flask and finished it as they came to the door and he took out the keys and opened it and turned on the lights as they walked inside.

"Get ready," he told her.

"Why?"

"Why? Why are you *asking*?"

Her face looked pained.

"Get ready. And put that blouse in some cold water."

He walked behind her to the kitchen and watched as she ran the water in the sink and stripped off the blouse. He could see the outline of the rose on her shoulder beneath the thin layer of gauze. The man had said it would scab for a few days and then heal. That was fine. He wouldn't touch her there. Nor, for the moment, would he touch the rings.

"Turn around."

He reached for the short leather riding crop on the peg-board behind him on the kitchen wall hanging amid the pots and pans.

"Raise your arms," he said.

He began on her stomach.

He lay across his sheets drunk with too much scotch on top of too little of the greasy Italian food and heard her shift in the box he'd built for her beneath the bed. He knew that it was hard for her to sleep. Her nipples would hurt. Her back would hurt from the tattoo. Her thighs and stomach would still be stinging.

341

It was nothing new. In the four years since he'd found her in the parking lot at K Mart and bluffed her into the car with his toy pistol pain had become something she was used to. There had been a thousand such nights. Tonight was only different, really, in that he'd had hopes again in fucking her. Perhaps his arousal would translate into her own, and arousal into a baby. He wanted the baby because it would be a continuation of her when she was gone. But it hadn't happened. He knew it hadn't.

It was dark as the grave inside the box. He knew that, too. He'd tried it out himself to see if the casters worked and found that it was darker even than the basement where he'd kept her the first two years of her captivity, listening to her whine to please, please set her free—to let her call her parents or go to the toilet or loosen the wire coils around her wrists—until finally there was no more whining and no more talk at all for a long time.

The box was better than the basement and darker. It was what she deserved. To be buried there.

It was a sin that he loved her.

"Barren," he muttered. And finally he fell asleep.

The following day was Monday, and he went to work as usual, leaving her bound naked inside the box beneath the bed. The bonds were not really necessary. The bonds were merely custom. It was over three years ago that she had attempted to escape him twice over the period of a single month and he had discouraged her with the red-hot blade of a kitchen knife and the suggestion that he had contacts everywhere, that he was part of some vast vague criminal machine and that should she try a third time, first her mother and then her father would meet with accidental death, reinforcing this by showing her that he had their address and her father's business address in his Rolodex and even knew the make, model, and year of the car sitting in their driveway.

He told her stories of this criminal network frequently,

mostly of their viciousness in matter of retribution. He told that her name was registered in their central computer and that should anything happen to him, should he die or be arrested, they would be honor bound to find her and torture her to death according to their code. In his stories he described these tortures in loving detail and saw that she soon came to believe them.

She no longer tried to run away.

He returned from work at noon to let her feed herself and use the bathroom and saw that she had her period again. Her first day's flow was always heavy. He had her change the thin grey sheets in the box before he put her back inside again. The period meant that he probably wouldn't want to touch her for a few days. He'd probably just watch cable.

Nights he'd come home to a liter of scotch and "Nick at Nite," and he'd be able to forget that she was there doing the dishes, the laundry, even the vacuuming if he turned the sound up loud enough. He'd be able to forget his phone installation route and his goddamn supervisor and the long-dead woman whose home he was living in even though her ghost was everywhere. He'd get a little smashed and think, Ma, if you could see me now.

On the fourth night he fucked her.

He had to have been blind drunk to fuck her because there was still some bleeding, some residue inside her, but fucking her blind drunk was nothing new either, and he pulled and tugged on the rings in her nipples until she screamed, and he came in her from behind with a power that astonished him. And he must have been pretty blind drunk indeed because as he fell away from behind her across the bed and she stepped away he thought he saw not one rose but two branching off the same central stem that curved along her shoulder blade.

He even thought he smelled them.

The following night, he *was* blind drunk, no question, raging.

"You want to call your parents? We're back to *that* shit? You're giving me that shit again?"

He had all kinds of whips all over the house just for times like these when he needed one instantly and did not want to go looking for one and this one on the living room mantel was long and thin. It was meant to produce pain and it was studded to produce blood.

She knew that about the whip but didn't run away—just stood there looking at him, defiant. He'd thought they were long past the defiance.

"Take off your clothes."

She didn't move.

So he whipped them off her.

She was wearing just a light summer skirt and blouse he'd picked out for her at K Mart, and when he was done they were just tatters hanging off her hips and shoulders, spackled and streaked with blood.

He put her in the bathtub and ran a tub for her and closed the door.

By the time she came out again he'd killed the bottle. He watched her crawl meekly into the box and roll herself under the bed just moments before he fell asleep in the heavy overstuffed armchair in front of the television.

She was naked. The welts across her body looked like runners, like heavy creepers—serpentine, overlapping and intersecting inside her flesh—the ripe red wounds that the metal studs had made like the small blossoms of flowers.

And then it was the weekend again.

On Saturday he left her alone, feeling bad about the beating of the night before. Though she'd provoked him.

The girl kept her distance. She made them lunch and handed him a shopping list, and when he returned with the groceries she was on her knees scrubbing the kitchen floor. She wore an old red sweatshirt and sweatpants which had once belonged to him but which had shrunk with repeated washings so that they were even tight on her now,

344

and because the front of the shirt was wet he could see the outlines of the nipple rings when she stood to change the water.

Still he left her be.

That night they watched a movie together—*Poltergeist*—about a family battling supernatural forces which threaten to drive them apart and winning.

The children were the glue, he thought. He looked at her sadly.

"That could be us, you know."

"What could?" she said.

He drank his whiskey.

By Sunday night he was still feeling tender toward her.

It was partly because she didn't look good. Her face had a grey-brown cast to it that he didn't like. She needed sun. But Sunday was as overcast as Saturday had been. Rain threatened. So there was no point in letting her sit out in the backyard deck sewing his buttons or mending his socks.

Plus she was off her feed. She'd never been one for breakfast, but she usually had a little lunch at least and a fairly decent dinner. Chicken was normally her favorite, but tonight they had chicken and she barely touched it, seeming to prefer the vegetables—though she didn't do much with them either.

He wondered if she were coming down with something.

Or if that beating Friday night had been more extreme than he remembered.

It was possible that she needed a treat, some kind of pick me up. A boost to her morale.

So when it was time to go to bed he told her as she came out of the bathroom in her pajamas that she did not have to sleep in the box tonight, tonight was special, she could be beside him on the bed. She said nothing but crawled in next to him and rested her head in the crook of his arm.

He smiled. The girl smelled of musk and roses. He wondered how she had managed that. He was not aware of having ever bought her any perfume, but perhaps at some point he had. It was considerate of her—even loving—to wear it for him now.

She slept in the moonless night.

He could tell by her breathing.

He almost fell asleep, too. It had begun to rain, and he lay listening to it patter on the roof for a long while, and then he thought about her young girl's body, marked by his hand and bearing his sign, so wet and soft inside; which he had not seen or even touched in nearly two days now, and he felt himself begin to rise.

Perhaps tonight, he thought. He knew nothing about a woman's fertility, only that it was there, and that somehow he might touch it if he were to go deep enough to dig it out of her.

He turned her toward him in the dark. He unbuttoned her pajama top and felt something prick his middle finger as the third button slid through the buttonhole and thought that she would have to replace that in the morning, that it was broken and jagged and might hurt her.

He drew the bottoms down off her legs, felt the welts like thick coils along her thighs. She stirred and in her slide across the sheets he heard a sound like the rustle of leaves.

He heard the distant thunder.

And it must have awakened her, or else his stripping her had, because she put her hands to his shoulders as he parted her legs and entered her, feeling the welts along the insides of her thighs as she gripped him inside her and moved, swaying gently, beneath him.

It was like nothing that had ever come before.

She had never been so responsive to him, pulling herself up onto him, urgently close to him while the thunder rumbled, and he saw flashes of lightning beneath the closed lids of his eyes and then opened them so he could see her, could see this sudden phenomenon that was clawing at him, fingernails scoring the skin of his back and shoulders,

346

this amazing phenomenon as his slave of love in every way now plunged in moonless black, which tore and bit and moaned as though tossed in a savage wind and who suddenly seemed to be everywhere around him at once, her fingers a thousand thorns, her body a billion petals all falling together and himself the author of this destruction, this overflowing flowering.

The lightning flashed twice.

He heard the rings drop off the bed and roll across the floor as her wide soft nipples opened, bloomed, and parted, smelled loam and fresh-turned earth as a strand of briar turned twice around his neck. He felt her cunt like a crown of thorns gripping him tight and tearing and felt himself throb and shoot suddenly deep within her, blood and semen, runners crawling over him, their thorns sinking deep, felt himself bleeding into her, veins, arteries pricked and severed as he looked down at the body which was no longer her body but the tangled garden of wild blood-red roses that he had made of her blossoming and erupting from tortured flesh.

She was his earth, his ground. He had cast his seed to her again and again.

And the creepers grew, nourished.

The Turning

In three years the City had changed again.

You could almost smell the blood in the air.

Bad blood.

He walked down Riverside from 82nd. For six blocks no one had passed him. The cool night breeze drifted off the Hudson. Across the street the park was grey and empty in the moonlight.

This area was one of the loveliest in New York. It still was. Old, newly-renovated townhouses along one side, the park along the other. The residents, who were extremely well-off, saw to it that the sidewalks were kept mostly clean. At night there was little traffic.

But look. Here.

He had to walk around her. Her filthy skirt hitched up to her fat pasty thighs. Cap pulled down over dull brown matted hair. She lay asleep, her toothless mouth wide open—a foul, black hole beneath the streetlight.

He walked by.

It occurred to him that this had been coming for a very

long time. The wealthy—or almost wealthy—and the poor living in wholly separate camps, paths barely intersecting. The middle class, such as they were, little more than badly disguised servants to the rich. Insulated by the same cloak of privilege that draped the shoulders of their masters.

You could no longer refer to the "growing numbers" of the poor. The poor were multitudes.

Even here. On this quiet street.

And not surprisingly, he heard them before he saw them.

Ahead of him. Not far.

He walked slowly, with a measured stride. He was in no hurry to see.

They were across the street in the park at 78th Street, the old man helpless against a tree, the four boys going at him with fists and stones. The homeless man pleading, the sense of his words lost in broken teeth and blood and bone because the tall boy was shoving a rock into his mouth at the same time—no, a piece of jagged macadam from the street—while two others hooted their encouragement and the smallest of the boys, thin and blonde and wiry, twelve maybe, crushed his left kneecap with three rapid blows from a metal bat. The bat gleamed in the moonlight. The man collapsed, shrieking, the chunk of macadam tumbling from his mouth out onto the grass.

He did not need to watch more.

There were many of these groups now.

Not all of them children.

At 72nd Street he turned East toward Broadway. As always in the City, a single turn, a different block, and you were in another world entirely.

Here there was plenty of traffic. Horns blared. Fire engines sudden in the distance. People passed by without a glance. While he studied faces. Hard young women, soft young men. Both with money. Barely able to conceal their fury that they did not have more. Shopowners stern and forbidding standing in doorways, defending their mercantile fortresses. And the elderly. Barely hanging on, having lived too long. Fear etched deep into pale brows and faces.

As though they knew. Knew in their ancient bones.

What was coming.

And knew they had helped create it.

And everywhere the homeless. Standing at banks like hopeless sentries, on streetcorners like whores, sprawled, squatting, kneeling on broken limbs and no limbs at all, strong and crippled and drunk and crazy, young and old and impossible to guess how old.

Too cowed, most of them, even to beg anymore.

He felt the turning.

There. That one.

He crossed Broadway, walking toward Columbus.

That one, yes, but not this.

She was beautiful. Perhaps that was why the owner of the bar allowed her to sit there. Perhaps her beauty offset her situation and could be counted upon to not overly offend the owner's patrons. Perhaps the man retained a shred of pity.

There was a dirty white cast on her right leg. A taped wooden crutch across her lap. Her clothes were too small but they were relatively clean. An empty fast-food coffee cup stood on the sidewalk beside her.

She could not have been more than twenty. Her skin was the deep rich black of the islands, tight and soft-looking over her whippet-thin frame. Her eyes were wide, brown and luminous. The eyes of a doe trapped in headlights. Permanently startled, and fearful.

They looked fearfully at him now as he stopped beside her.

He saw that she was afraid to speak. Knew she would not speak. That it was necessary for her to be careful. He could already feel the stares of passersby, their disgust with him for stopping. He crouched down.

"Are you hungry?"

"Yes, sir. I am."

350

Her voice was soft and tired. It reminded him of the voice of someone who has just lost a loved one and now, finally, has no more tears left, who has been crying for days and who is now exhausted.

"Your leg. What happened to it?"

She almost smiled. She didn't quite dare.

"Stupid thing. I fell right off that curb here."

She pointed.

"Right into. . . . whaddya call it? The bars. Over the . . . ?"

"The grate? Over the sewer?"

"That's right. I guess I wasn't looking. Fixed me up at Emergency. But they wouldn't let me stay."

"You have no place to stay?"

"No, sir. There's a place down on West End will keep me for a week, but you need twenty dollars for that and I ain't got twenty dollars. If I had a place, even for a week, then I got an address. Can't nobody get a job without an address. Me, I got nothin'."

He reached for his wallet.

He was certain. Not her.

Maybe she'd even survive this. Maybe. Who knew.

"Here's twenty."

Her smile alone was worth the twenty. He thought, what beautiful teeth.

She squealed over the twenty like a little girl. It was as though he'd given her a hundred.

"Thank you! God, thank you!"

She leaned over and wrapped her arms around him, hugged him, and kissed him on the cheek.

Behind him a woman's eyes stabbed hard at them both. They ignored her.

"Bet you never been kissed by a black girl before," she laughed.

"You'd be wrong," he said. "Now I want you to get out of here, all right? Go to that place you were talking about. I don't want to see you out here again. You understand?"

351

"Yes, sir. You know I will. God! Thank you, sir, thank you."

He helped her up. Stood watching her hobble toward West End Avenue. She didn't look back.

"Asshole," someone muttered behind him.

The man walked by and shot him an angry glance over his shoulder.

Not even a man yet, he thought. *A boy. A boy who thinks he's a man because his job pays him $100,000 a year plus bonuses.*

The boy would be lucky to survive exactly what and who he was about to pass, there on the corner of Columbus.

That one.

He lay up against the streetlight. Babbling madly to whatever voices babbled back inside him.

He was already changing.

There were more and more who were changing now.

And not just the crazy ones.

He had seen it happen once before. A long, long time ago. When the collective will and consciousness of an entire people had grown intense enough, black enough, angry enough, fearful enough and focused enough to rend deep into the nature of human life as it had existed up till then, all that dark cruel energy focused like a laser on an entire class, transforming them in reality into how they were perceived and imagined to be almost metaphorically.

In the past it had been the rich—the ruling class who were perceived as vampires. Feeding off the poor and destitute.

Now it was the poor themselves.

And it wouldn't be long at all before everyone in the City and in half the world for that matter would be seeing what he'd been seeing for quite a while from his own unique perspective, recognizing exactly what was happening because it had happened to him.

Because last time it had *been* him. Him and a handful of others. Nobles, kings, princes.

This time, of course, they would not be merely a handful.

This time they would be legion.

He could see them everywhere.

Turning.

Changing.

He hoped the girl with the beautiful smile and the fine, warm skin would not be one of them.

He had always enjoyed walking in New York. He would have continued walking, but it was late by now and he was hungry. At Columbus he hailed a taxi.

A taxi was safer than a limousine.

Limousine drivers always felt the need to be ingratiating. To talk to you.

Whereas cabbies almost never bothered to glance back at anything other than traffic through their rear-view mirrors—and that was important.

You almost weren't there.

"The Four Seasons," he said.

He had a reservation.

To dine with a beautiful recently-divorced real-estate heiress and then return to her East Side penthouse apartment filled with drawings by Vlaminck, Emile Nolde, and Gauguin, originals, all of them, twenty-one stories above the East River, with a built-in steambath and sauna.

Unlike most of the world, he preferred to feed upon his own.

To Suit the Crime

"I think you've done a remarkable job," said Dugas. "Really."

Morgan leaned back on the red leather-studded sofa and lit a Camel, unfiltered, enjoying the first passage of smoke over his palate and up through his nose. It was wonderful to him that these old appetites were back in favor.

"Thank you," he said. "But it's hardly my doing. Not even that of the Court, entirely." He smiled. "We have all those Republican Presidents to thank—Reagan, Bush, Quayle—"

"Not Quayle," said Dugas. "Dear God. Not Quayle."

Morgan laughed. "All right. Not Quayle. His man Beavers never did amount to much. But Denninger, certainly. And Harpe. All the nominations were theirs."

"True."

"Obviously, we were abetted by history. The will of the people. It only remained for a single Democratic judge to fix upon the people and understand their will as it applied here. And we've always been best at that."

Dugas watched him raise the cigarette to his lips and

draw smoke down into his lungs. It occurred to Dugas that the lips were too thin to be attractive to anyone other than a public figure—for some reason the American people like their politicians lipless—the hands too perfectly manicured and delicate. There was not an ounce of sensuality to the man. Though by reputation he was no less debauched than anyone in Washington.

No less than himself, perhaps.

Dugas thought, though, that had they not both been members of the same Club—empty, now, but for the two of them—he'd never have wasted his time sitting here talking to Morgan. Despite Morgan's power, despite his undeniable accomplishments, and despite their political and career affiliations, there was something smug and distasteful about him. But here, courtesy demanded his attention.

"It was a feeling I'd maintained since law school," said Morgan. "That the punishment, very simply, should suit the crime. That something fundamental had been overlooked in the very structure of our adversarial system— *that* being the suffering of the victim. The *condition* of the victim at the time of his or her victimization."

Dugas watched him warm to his topic. Here we go, he thought. He owned a television set, after all. He'd heard this dozens of times. Still. . . .

He nursed his single-malt whiskey and listened.

"You, as a lawyer, understand, I'm sure. Take a boy, for instance, struck down by a drunken driver. The boy is in the prime of his life, struck unexpectedly. One moment he's alive, perhaps happy—the next he's dead. Is it wise and correct to sentence the driver to a given number of years in prison, to allow him the luxury of counting the days toward his release from prison, feed him, clothe him, allow him time in the yard for exercise and time in the dayroom for television, and then, finally, release him? When, over the intervening years, the bars have not disappeared, the liquor stores have not disappeared? He can even apply for a driver's license again."

He doesn't like me, Morgan thought. But he's reasonably attentive. That will do.

He went on. He had a point to make here, so that Dugas would thoroughly understand what followed.

"Many years ago, when I was still on the State Court, I had a case I will never forget. A man had walked in to a college dormitory, shot the aged housemother in the forehead with a .45 caliber Smith & Wesson fitted with a silencer, and then stalked upstairs and picked a room at random. Inside were two students, young women, very pretty. The man forced them to strip at gunpoint, then forced one of the girls to tie the other to the bed and gag her. Then he tied and gagged the second girl, pushed her down on the same bed—and forced her roommate to watch while he *ate her friend alive*.

"He began, I believe, with her buttocks.

"The law being what it was back then, the usual jury of his peers sentenced him to life imprisonment in a State facility for the criminally insane. While, of course, he should have died."

Morgan stubbed out his cigarette.

"Died horribly."

"Excuse me, gentlemen."

It was the waiter, Woolbourne, carrying a tray and picking up Morgan's empty wine glass.

"Will you be wanting another? The workmen, I'm afraid. . . ." Impertinent bastard, Dugas thought. Woolbourne addressed them both but looked only at Morgan—as though he, Dugas, didn't matter.

Dugas glanced toward the workmen, two large muscular types, laying down a plastic tarp across the far corner of the library. Apparently renovations were in order, though he couldn't see the need of any.

"What are they doing, Woolbourne?" he asked.

"The wallpaper, I believe, sir. They're replacing a section." The man still didn't look at him. Merely picked up his glass, which was not even quite empty.

356

He'd've liked to smash that glass against Woolbourne's well-bred patrician face.

A goddamn waiter, for God's sake.

"Another," Dugas said. "One more."

"Yes," said Morgan. "One more would be fine."

"Very good, gentlemen."

Dugas lit a Camel and ran his gaze over the gold and red fleur-de-lis wallpaper near the window. Perhaps the damaged section lay behind the heavy Utrecht velvet curtains.

Morgan sighed.

"It changed my life, that case. From that point on I knew what I wanted to do—what needed to be done. And, thank God, times have come exactly 'round to that."

"Yes."

The toady in Dugas could easily have said, yes and *you've* brought them 'round to that. Career-wise it was the intelligent thing to do. It would even have been true. But shoptalk with this old magistrate was boring him. His career was fine as it stood. He wasn't even sure he cared about a career anymore. He had other interests. He said nothing.

Insolent or not, at least Woolbourne was efficient. He brought their drinks. Sherry for Morgan, another single-malt for Dugas.

Morgan raised his glass.

"To the law," he said smiling.

"To the law."

They touched glasses. Then the old bird was off again.

"I've had a case culminate just recently," he said. "An interesting one, actually. An excellent problem in . . . appropriateness. The accused was a young adoptive mother who had murdered her three-and-a-half-year-old son, whom she had adopted when he was only one year old. Somehow her systematic abuse of the child had gotten by the welfare people for over two years."

"It happens."

"Yes, unfortunately it does. Her explanation was that the

child had fallen down a flight of stairs. Said he was generally a clumsy child. But that was patently false. For one thing, the bruises, some of them, were months old. For another, there were burn marks all over him."

He held up a cigarette.

"These, no doubt. There was evidence of severe malnutrition. Neighbors reported that she had, on at least one occasion, fed the child his own feces. Finally, the rectal passage was severely scarred and lacerated and abnormally distended.

"As usual, we accepted her explanation and then investigated, charged her and convicted her of murder. Her husband, by the way, was also charged and convicted—of negligent homicide. We had no evidence he'd ever touched the boy. And probably he hadn't. But he'd watched.

"For two years the wife was burned, beaten, neglected, starved, and upon occasion, fed her own bodily wastes, and abused with the broomstick from her own home—I believe they found it in the basement—while the husband, of course, was forced to watch. I'm told he's quite insane now, by the way.

"Then only last week she was pushed down the stairs. She died, as did the child, of a broken neck. We were really quite pleased with it. Rarely, in my experience, has a punishment so closely fit the crime. Nearly a duplication of it."

Dugas smiled. "Ah," he said. "But the boy was just a child. An innocent, so to speak. What about that?"

Morgan shrugged. "After a few months or so of deprivation and abuse, so was the woman. For all practical purposes."

Dugas thought about it, then nodded.

"Elegant," he said. "Quite elegant."

"We thought so," said Morgan. "The only thing missing," he added, "was possibly some of the element of surprise."

"Surprise?"

The workmen by the window had unfolded their plastic tarp and were taking a break, standing there smoking, oc-

casionally glancing in their direction. Dugas thought it typical of the lower classes these days. From secretaries to
waiters to craftsmen.

"Of course," said Morgan. "Go back to our boy on the
bike, run down by a drunken driver. Well, he's *surprised*,
isn't he? Shocked! One moment he's fine, riding along, and
the very next moment is filed with some *sudden* blinding
agony. Or the two young girls I mentioned, sitting in their
dormitory, chatting over boyfriends or schoolmates or family or whatnot, when, suddenly, life becomes an utter horror, a nightmare, all pain and death and helplessness.
Unthinkable. Unimaginable. And quite surprising."

Morgan saw he had Dugas' full attention now. Better late
than never.

He sipped his sherry.

"The element of surprise. It's the entire reason we inves-
tigate, try, and sentence completely out of the public eye
these days. Why those early experiments in televised and
print-medium reporting, and even with juries and open
courtrooms, are over. Because most, if not all, violent
crimes definitely include that element. The sudden shock.
So, to be fair to the victim, to come as closely as possible
to the *experience* of the victim, any punishment which
hopes to suit the nature of the crime must come as a shock
to its perpetrator, as it did to his or her victim at the time.

"And here this last case, *on the surface*, falls slightly short
of our ideal. Since her punishment lasted over such an
extended time—two years—one must assume that this
woman realized, at some point, how it all would end. But
look deeper and it's really not so far off the mark. Her initial
arrest surprises her. The nature of the punishment—so
closely mirroring her adopted son's—*that* must have surprised her, and on an absolutely fundamental level. That it
can *hurt*, for instance, to be forced to eat your own shit."

Morgan's use of the word "shit" was enough surprise for
Dugas so that he choked on his single-malt whiskey.

"Sorry," Morgan said. And then went on.

"Then look at the end. Isn't death *always* something of a surprise? Doesn't it always come as something of a shock? Maybe not the how—but certainly the when? Heart patients, cancer patients, even patients in daily, agonizing pain who *pray* for death, must finally be somewhat surprised when it actually comes. Even if it comes . . . as relief.

"And who is to say that even a three-and-a-half-year-old cannot realize his own mortality, his growing frailty, his own approaching death?"

He settled back slowly and finished his wine.

"Your mirror may have been a very good one, then," said Dugas.

"Yes," said Morgan, smiling. "I think we've all been doing our jobs quite adequately. Even on that one."

My God. You *are* a smug sonovabitch, thought Dugas.

"Even on you," said Morgan. He stood up, straightening his dinner jacket.

Dugas saw that it was a signal. The two burly workmen approached from the corner of the room and stood close by. Woolbourne appeared in the mahogany paneled doorway, blocking his exit.

"Emil Dugas," said Morgan. "You stand accused, tried, and convicted by this Court of the murder of Lynette Janice Hoffman, aged 23 years old, your one-time lover and one-time secretary, on January 23rd of the year 2021, one year, one month and three days previous. Your sentence to be carried out immediately, and your punishment to suit the crime."

Dugas' brain reeled. It was impossible. *Literally* impossible. All this talk. All this hypocrisy. All this crap about punishment to "suit the crime," this tedious prefatory lecture, when in fact they were going to kill him in some fucking phony novel way and that was all they could possibly do. Because the rest was impossible.

He almost laughed. Instead he exploded.

"You're a fool, Morgan! A buffoon! Or a goddamn lying hypocrite. Or all three. How are you going to make this punishment 'suit the crime?' You know damn well you can't *begin* to. If you know what I did to that girl, then you must know *how* I did it. It is not something you can mirror. So what am I going to get here? Some *approximation*?"

He spat the word out in disgust.

Morgan smiled. Dugas still didn't understand. Well, he expected that he wouldn't.

He nodded to the workmen. They took Dugas' arms and led him to the plastic dropcloth. Dugas struggled, but it was like struggling with someone three times as strong as he was and three times his size. Which, he guessed, these two were. *Exactly as he'd been three times as strong and nearly three times as heavy as Lynette when he'd. . . .*

And now he was laughing, hysterically, as they stripped off his clothes. Laughter mixed with fury.

"You can't do it!" he screamed. "You can't fucking do it because I've got no *hole* there! You see? No fucking orifice you dumb goddamn asshole! She saw me when I did it to her, do you understand that? You know what that means? You see the goddamn difference? To see the face of your murderer? To see his *pleasure*? What are you going to do, stick it up my ass, you goddamn hypocrite? You fucking *loser*! You can't even begin to know what I made that little bitch suffer! Right up to the moment I decided to wring her fucking neck! That entire goddamn time she was looking right at me, right into my *face!*"

"We understand that," said Morgan. "Perfectly."

He nodded again and one of the workmen dew an object out of his clean white overalls. To Dugas it looked like a combination garden trowel and apple-corer. Made of surgical steel. With a two-inch diameter. And a sharp serrated edge.

When the man applied it to his groin, sunk it deep and twisted, and then withdrew, Dugas screamed and screamed.

"Will *my* face do?" Woolbourne asked politely.

Through blinding pain, Dugas watched the waiter's trousers fall down around his ankles.

Almost as Dugas' own had been, Woolbourne's was quite an erection.

Lines: or Like Franco, Elvis Is Still Dead

It was the greatest opening line I'd heard in years. I was on my way back from the juke and the first song I'd played, "Suspicious Minds," was already on when I passed her at the bar. Elvis singing and this good-looking woman sitting all alone.

She turned and gave me a glance and said, "*so, seen him lately?*"

I laughed and walked on past her to where my scotch was and got it and then came back to her and said, "I think I saw him on the beach today. It could have been a whale though. Hard to say."

Not nearly as good as hers but enough to get us talking. She had a low husky voice which I always like in a woman and big brown eyes and long curly hair. She was slim and pretty. Wore jeans and workshirt. Nothing fancy.

363

I found out right away she was not all that crazy about Cape May. Personally I thought it was a welcome change from New York. But she was a local while I was only in for the weekend. What did I know. It was possible to see where after a while maybe the quiet would get to you. Where all the painted gabled corniced bay windowed turn-of-the-century Victoriana might get to you. Where you could get pretty tired of the tourists and their beach-gear and the quaint little shops.

I could see my friends Liam and Kate were amused with me down at the other end of the bar. Liam and Kate were married and always seemed to be amused when I picked up a woman. Or, as in this case, when a woman picked up me. I think they thought I got a whole lot more action than I did and they liked the notion of having this lounge lizard as a drinking buddy. Plus it was Sunday, the last night of my stay here with them and they knew that Tess—that was her name—had the potential to make my weekend.

Which in a weird way, she did.

The talk was nothing unusual. She seemed to like the fact that I was a writer who had once actually spoken on the phone to Stephen King and that Liam was a paint and cover artist and that Kate was a teacher at the Professional Children's School back in New York. I avoided talking about my ex-wife and the two kids. It wasn't hard. It was clear to me that she was a little bored with herself, with her own life here, and it was easy to sympathize. Here she was, thirty—she looked a lot younger, mid-twenties I thought—back home living with her parents and helping to manage their Bed-and-Breakfast and that was about it.

"A glorified maid," she said. "Sometimes not even a fucking *glorified* maid."

She was kind of vague about how it got that way. She said she'd been living in Boston for a while. Going for her Masters in business at B.U. and waitressing to make ends meet. It was obvious she'd much rather still be doing that. What wasn't obvious was why she quit. She volunteered

364

the fact that there was a guy in the picture. Somebody she was no longer with but who was somehow involved in the retreat back home to Cape May.

What she didn't say was who or how or why.

I figured she'd give it up when she wanted to. I wasn't going to pry.

Meanwhile I liked the scent of her. I liked the crinkle around the soft brown eyes when she smiled. I liked the boyish body and the long tangle of hair.

I wanted to get her out of there.

It was late. The bar was going to close soon anyway. People had begun to drift away. I could see Liam and Kate showing signs of wear.

"Let's take the drinks outside," I said. "I'd like to get some air. That okay?"

"Okay."

We were barely out the door when the bartender, name of Phil, appeared in the doorway.

"Can't do that," he said. "The drinks. It's against New Jersey law."

"Sorry," I said. "I didn't know." It was just as against the law in New York City but I suppose I figured this being a vacation town they might be looser here. I wondered why Tess hadn't stopped me. She was local. I guessed she didn't mind breaking a law or two once in a while.

Neither did I. My child-support was two months behind.

The bartender was okay about the drinks though.

"No problem," he said, "Just give 'em here and I'll take them back to the bar for you."

We handed them over. My scotch and her Stoli cranberry juice. Phil went back inside.

There was nothing to do then except what I'd been wanting to do all along.

"Mind if we try something?" I said.

That was a line too. I'd used it before. But it usually worked to get this part of it out of the way one way or another.

I leaned over and kissed her.

She hesitated and then she kissed me back and then she pulled away.

"Hell. You don't even remember my name," she said.

"Sure I do. Tess."

"After tonight I'll probably never see you again."

"I'm coming back here the end of next month, in July. Maybe for a week this time."

"Really?"

"Really."

It was true. Or half true. Liam and Kate and I had already talked about my returning. They were here for the entire summer and I was welcome pretty much whenever I wanted. But it depended on the work, how much time I'd have.

I kissed her again. This time she didn't pull away.

And the kiss was just what you always want a kiss to be.

And usually isn't.

"Let's walk," I said.

I slipped my arm around her waist. I didn't know where we were exactly or where we were going. But it was hard to get lost in a town as small as Cape May. I'd find my way home or else if I was lucky Tess would find it for me.

It was well after two in the morning and the streets were quiet. Nobody walking but Tess and me. No cars at all.

We talked some more and every so often I'd turn and kiss her, hugging her tight, still walking, hardly even slowing down. I felt that intense sense of well-being that you get when the woman on your arm is the woman you *want* on your arm and she's new and you've both had just enough to drink but not too much and you have no idea where all this is leading but so far it's fine and dandy.

"How about the beach?" I said.

She laughed. Like I'd said something really funny.

"The *beach*!" she said.

I thought it was a good idea. It wasn't too cold. In fact the night was warmer than the day had been.

366

Probably I was showing her what a tourist I was, I thought. To her the beach was probably a cliche.

I still liked it. I thought about lying on the sand. Nobody round but the two of us. Moon on the water. Booming urf and big sky. It was a cliche but I liked it anyway. It's ot something you get to do in Manhattan, lying on the each and necking with a pretty woman.

I smiled. Like I was in on the joke but so what. "Why ot?" I said.

She kissed me and then her voice went low again.

"*Sure. Why not,*" she said.

I don't think we were there ten minutes before we heard he gunshot.

I'd thought we were alone. But then I'd been concen- rating on her, on the soft warmth of her mouth on mine nd the warmer breasts beneath the denim shirt and the vay the nipples rose silky smooth under my fingers.

I looked up and I could see this dark heavy figure the quivalent of maybe three city blocks away running up the each toward Atlantic Avenue. There was a rifle or maybe shotgun in his left hand and judging from the loudness f the echo still hanging in the air I was thinking shotgun.

I expected sirens, police pulling up, people rushing out om inside the hotels across the street. But we sat there vhile the man ran the last few steps up the ramp off the each onto the high concrete walkway and then started trolling down the opposite ramp toward a car parked just ff the walkway—we could only see the top of the car— nd then got in and drove away.

Not another soul in sight. Just Tess and me kneeling in he sand. Staring down the beach at another dark figure ving still as driftwood far above the tideline.

Tess got to her feet.

"Let's go," she said.

"You sure?" I said. "Maybe we should just find a phone. all the police."

She stopped and turned and seemed to consider this and

somehow I thought she was studying me too. Both at th
same time.

"He could be hurt or something," she said. "You can
just leave him. We have to see."

I knew I didn't want to see.

But she had a point. I went along.

The man was lying flat on his back and one of his le
was curled under him, the opposite arm flung high. Lil
he was running, waving to somebody except he was lyir
in the sand and he wasn't going to be doing any runnir
or waving any more. It had been a shotgun, all right. B
neath the outflung arm there was a chunk of him missir
as big as a baseball. The chunk was nowhere around th
I could see. But the sand was dark all down under his che
and his chest was glistening bright in the moonlight.

Mid-thirties, I thought. Slim and dark and well-muscle
Wearing jeans and a Dallas teeshirt. One eye open wid
the other half shut. Jaw dropped and mouth open. Th
sand-crabs would love him.

Crawl in, crawl out.

I felt my stomach roll and tasted acid.

"Well, it's not Elvis," she said, her voice soft and low.
took me a second to realize she was remembering th
dumb-ass line of mine in the bar. "This guy couldn't eve
carry a tune."

And that took a second to sink in too.

"Jesus, Tess. You *know* this guy?"

She nodded. "Yes. I do."

I waited for her to explain. She didn't explain.

But I saw that there were tears in her eyes.

"I think we'd better find a phone," she said and turne
and started walking.

"Wait a minute. Who is the guy?"

"Look, right now we need a phone. Later, okay?"

She was trudging across the sand, headed for a ram
Not the ramp the man had used but one further on dow
the beach.

We hit the broad concrete walkway and I could see a lighted phone booth a few blocks away in front of a closed dark arcade. I was aware of the sea-smell of the beach and the lonely sound of our shoes against the concrete.

She got in the booth. Dialed 911.

"There's a man on the beach. He's dead," she said. "Across from Franklin Street. We found him. My boyfriend and I. We saw a man with a shotgun. He was running away and then he got into a car. We didn't see the car. You'll find one set of footprints leading up to one of the ramps and two sets leading up to another." There was a pause. "No, of course not. Why would you need our names. That's all we saw. Goodbye."

I thought, *boyfriend*. I'd arrived there fast. I wasn't sure to be pleased or worried about it. I was leaving around noon today, about nine hours away. I wouldn't be back for over a month. If at all. I hardly knew her and I wasn't sure what it was she expecting.

She stepped out of the phone booth and took me by the arm and pushed me back into the shadows of the arcade and kissed me. I wasn't prepared for the kiss and certainly not for its ferocity. I returned it, though. Willingly.

"I'm scared," she said. "What if he comes back? Could you take me home? To your friends' house, maybe?"

Her eyes glittered, reflecting back the moon. The only light in that dark place.

"Sure," I told her.

On the way back to Queen Street I didn't push her about the guy. I figured, let her open up to me in her own good time.

The walk didn't take long. We met no one along the way.

When we were nearly there she said, "his name was Tommy Brookwalter. He was a year behind me in high school. I knew him a little then but you know, a year's forever when you're in high school. Then he moved to

369

Boston while I was working on my Masters. He looked me up and we had a thing for a while. It didn't work out."

I put my arm around her. She sounded sad and I knew she'd cared for him. And then we were home.

We poured some drinks downstairs and crept quietly up to my room so as not to wake Liam and Kate—and that was the second pair of drinks we never got round to drinking that night because as soon as we sat down on the bed we were both all mouths and hands, we were suddenly nothing but flesh, trying *against* flesh to stifle the moans, the hisses and gasps of pain that came of the sheer steady violence of it, her fingernails gouging my back urging me to violence of my own, sex like the pounding weight of surf strong enough to break the shell and polish the stone, the two of us like a pair of sin-eaters devouring the crimes and guilts of the dead and of our own.

We had all that. And then we rested.

And then we had it all once again.

In the morning she was gone. Of course she was.

It was the cops who awakened me, talking downstairs to Liam and Kate.

Two ordinary-looking men in shirtsleeves and ties. She had given them this address and she had given them my name.

They wanted to establish that I was with her. All night. I said I was. I told them it was the two of us who had heard the shot and seen the body and that of course it was Tess who called it in. But I was curious. How had they arrived at *Tess* as being the woman on the phone? They said they hadn't. That Tess had just admitted it to them an hour ago when they questioned her.

I didn't understand.

The cop I was talking to sighed and told me that Tommy Brookwalter was pretty much the reason Tess was back in town in the first place. That they'd been all set to open up a business together, a restaurant and raw bar coupled with

370

a fish store that would contract directly to local fishermen and wind up selling the best damn seafood in town. They knew Cape May and they knew there was room for a place like that. Meanwhile they'd been engaged to marry. Until Brookwalter took up with another woman. And not long after that Tess got the boot. The woman was now his wife and the restaurant belonged to them and Tess was out of the picture completely and working for her parents at their little Bed & Breakfast.

It was common knowledge that Tess had taken all this badly. She drank. And when she drank she talked.

Not to me, though.

She hadn't talked to me.

I was trying to take this in. I asked them if that meant she was a suspect, if they were saying they thought she'd *arranged* it somehow.

Not at this time, they said. Right now they were only asking questions.

And I was her alibi.

A pretty damn good one at that.

I got the train back to Manhattan. I stood in the cool misty rain at Penn Station wondering which was likely to be more dangerous—going back there and calling as I'd promised her I would or never going back there again and never ever calling her at all.

The answer would have been obvious. Except for the last thing she'd said to me.

The last thing she said before I fell asleep.

Well, she'd *sung* it, actually.

And me, I'd smiled.

You're caught in a trap. You can't walk out. Because I love you too much, baby.

I thought she had a really good voice. A nice husky alto.

It didn't surprise me.

The Visitor

For Neal McPheeters

The old woman in bed number 418B of Dexter Memorial was not his wife. There was a strong resemblance though. Bea had died early on.

He had not been breathing well that night, the night the dead started walking, so they had gone to bed early without watching the news though they hated the news and probably would have chosen to miss it anyway. Nor had they awakened to anything alarming during the night. He still wasn't breathing well or feeling much better the following morning when John Blount climbed the stairs to the front door of their mobile home unit to visit over a cup of coffee as was his custom three or four days a week and bit Beatrice on the collarbone, which was not his custom at all.

Breathing well or not Will pried him off her and pushed him back down the stairs through the open door. John was no spring chicken either and the fall spread his brains out all across their driveway.

Will bundled Beatrice into the car and headed for the hospital half a mile away. And that was where he learned that all across Florida—all over the country and perhaps the world—the dead were rising. He learned by asking questions of the harried hospital personnel, the doctors and nurses who admitted her. Bea was hysterical having been bitten by a friend and fellow golfer so they sedated her and consequently it was doubtful that she ever learned the dead were doing anything at all. Which was probably just as well. Her brother and sister were buried over at Stoneyview Cemetery just six blocks away and the thought of them walking the streets of Punta Gorda again biting people would have upset her.

He saw some terrible things that first day.

He saw a man with his nose bitten off—the nosebleed to end all nosebleeds—and a woman wheeled in on a gurney whose breasts had been gnawed away. He saw a black girl not more than six who had lost an arm. Saw the dead and mutilated body of an infant child sit up and scream.

The sedation wore off. But Bea continued sleeping.

It was a troubled, painful sleep. They gave her painkillers through the IV and tied her arms and legs to the bed. The doctors said there was a kind of poison in her. They did not know how long it would take to kill her. It varied.

Each day he would arrive at the hospital to the sounds of sirens and gunfire outside and each night he would leave to the same. Inside it was relatively quiet unless one of them awoke and that only lasted a little while until they administered the lethal injection. Then it was quiet again and he could talk to her.

He would tell her stories she had heard many times but which he knew she would not mind his telling again. About his mother sending him out with a nickel to buy blocks of ice from the iceman on Stuyvesant Avenue. About playing pool with Jackie Gleason in a down-neck Newark pool hall just before the war and almost beating him. About the time he was out with his first-wife-to-be and his father-in-law-to-be sitting in a bar together and somebody insulted her and he took a swing at the guy but the guy had ducked and he pasted his future father-in-law instead.

He would urge her not to die. To try to come back to him.

He would ask her to remember their wedding day and how their friends were there and how the sun was shining.

He brought flowers until he could no longer stand the scent of them. He bought mylar balloons from the gift shop that said get well get well soon and tied them to the same bed she was tied to.

Days passed with a numbing regularity. He saw many more horrible things. He knew that she was lingering far longer than most did. The hospital guards all knew him at the door by now and did not even bother to ask him for a pass anymore.

"Four eighteen B," he would say but probably even that wasn't necessary.

Nights he'd go home to a boarded-up mobile home in an increasingly deserted Village, put a frozen dinner into the microwave and watch the evening news—it was all news now, ever since the dead started rising—and when it was over he'd go to bed. No friends came by. Many of his friends were themselves dead. He didn't encourage the living.

Then one morning she was gone.

Every trace of her.

The flowers were gone, the balloons, her clothing—everything. The doctors told him that she had died during the night but that as of course he must have noticed by now, they had this down pretty much to a science and a humane one at that, that once she'd come back again it had been very quick and she hadn't suffered.

If he wanted he could sit there for a while, the doctor said. Or there was a grief counselor who could certainly be made available to him.

He sat.

In an hour they wheeled in a pasty-faced redhead perhaps ten years younger than Will with what was obviously a nasty bite out of her left cheek just above the lip. A kiss, perhaps, gone awry. The nurses did not seem to notice him there. Or if they did they ignored him. He sat and watched the redhead sleep in his dead wife's bed.

In the morning he came by to visit.

He told the guard four eighteen B.

He sat in the chair and told her the story about playing pool with Gleason, how he'd sunk his goddamn cue ball going after the eight, and about buying rotten hamburger during the Great Depression and his first wife crying well into the night over a pound of spoiled meat. He told her the old joke about the rooster in the hen yard. He spoke softly about friends and relations, long dead. He went down to the gift shop and bought her a card and a small potted plant for the window next to the bed.

Two days later she was gone. The card and potted plant were gone too and her drawer and closet were empty.

The man who lay there in her bed was about Will's age and roughly the same height and build and he had lost an eye and an ear along with his thumb, index and middle fingers of his hand, all on the right side of his body. He had a habit of lying slightly to his left as though to turn away from what the dead had done to him.

Something about the man made Will think he was a sailor, some rough weathered texture to his face or perhaps the fierce bushy eyebrows and the grizzled white stubble of beard. Will had never sailed himself but he had always wanted to. He told the man about his summers as a boy at Asbury Park and Point Pleasant down at the Jersey shore, nights on the boardwalk and days with his family by the sea. It was the closest thing he could think of that the man might possibly relate to.

The man lasted just a single night.

Two more came and went—a middle-aged woman and a pretty teenage girl.

He did not know what to say to the girl. It had been years since he had even spoken to a person who was still in her teens—unless you could count the cashiers at the market. So he sat and hummed to himself and read to her out of a four-month-old copy of *People* magazine.

He bought her daisies and a small stuffed teddy bear and placed the bear next to her on the bed.

The girl was the first to die and then come back in his presence.

He was surprised that it startled him so little. One moment the girl was sleeping and the next she was struggling against the straps which bound her to the bed, the thick grey-yellow mucus flowing from her mouth and nose spraying the sheets they had wrapped around her tight. There was a sound in her throat like the burning of dry leaves.

Will pushed his chair back toward the wall and watched her. He had the feeling there was nothing he could say to her.

On the wall above a small red monitor light was blinking on and off. Presumably a similar light was blinking at the nurses' station because within seconds a nurse, a doctor and a male attendant were all in the room and the attendant was holding her head while the doctor administered the injection through her nostril far up into the brain. The girl shuddered once and then seemed to wilt and slide deep down into the bed. The stuffed bear tumbled to the floor.

The doctor turned to Will.

"I'm sorry," he said. "That you had to see this."

Will nodded. The doctor took him for a relative.

Will didn't mind.

They pulled the sheet up over her and glanced at him a moment longer and then walked out through the doorway.

He got up and followed. He took the elevator down to the ground floor and walked past the guard to the parking lot. He could hear automatic weapons-fire from the Wal-Mart down the block. He got into his car and drove home.

After dinner he had trouble breathing so he took a little oxygen and went to bed early. He felt a lot better in the morning.

Two more died. Both of them at night. Passed like ghosts from his life.

The second to die in front of him was a hospital attendant. Will had seen him many times. A young fellow, slightly balding. Evidently he'd been bitten while a doctor administered the usual injection because the webbing of his hand was bandaged and suppurating slightly.

The attendant did not go easily. He was a young man with a thick muscular neck and he thrashed and shook the bed.

The third to die in front of him was the woman who looked so much like Bea. Who had her hair and eyes and general build and coloring.

He watched them put her down and thought, this was what it was like. Her face would have looked this way. Her body would have done that.

On the morning after she died and rose and died again he was walking past the first-floor guard, a soft little heavy-set man who had known him by sight for what must have been a while now. "Four eighteen B," he said.

The guard looked at him oddly.

Perhaps it was because he was crying. The crying had gone on all night or most of it and here it was morning and he was crying once again. He felt tired and a little foolish. His breathing was bad.

He pretended that all was well as usual and smiled at the guard and sniffed the bouquet of flowers he'd picked from his garden.

The guard did not return the smile. He noticed that the man's eyes were red-rimmed too and felt a moment of alarm because he seemed to sense that the eyes were not red as his were simply from too much crying. But you had to walk past the man to get inside so that was what he did.

The guard clutched his arm with his little white sausage

fingers and bit at the stringy bicep just below the sleeve of Will's shortsleeved shirt. There was no one in the hall ahead of him by the elevators, no one to help him.

He kicked the man in the shin and felt dead skin rip beneath his shoe and wrenched his arm away. Inside his chest he felt a kind of snapping as though someone had snapped a twig inside him.

Heartbreak?

He pushed the guard straight-arm just as he had pushed John Blount so long ago and although there were no stairs this time there was a fire extinguisher on the wall and the guard's head hit it with a large clanging sound and he slid stunned down the face of the wall.

Will walked to the elevator and punched four. He concentrated on his breathing and wondered if they would be willing to give him oxygen if he asked them for it.

He walked into the room and stared.

The bed was empty.

It had never been empty. Not once in all the times he'd visited.

It was a busy hospital.

That the bed was empty this morning was almost confusing to him. As though he had fallen down a rabbit-hole.

Still he knew it wasn't wise to argue when after all this time one finally had a stroke of luck.

He put the slightly battered flowers from his garden in a waterglass. He drew water in the bathroom sink. He undressed quietly and found an open-backed hospital gown hanging in the closet and slipped it on over his mottled shoulders and climbed into bed between clean fresh-smelling sheets. The bite did not hurt much and there was just a little blood.

He waited for the nurse to arrive on her morning rounds.

He thought how everything was the same, really. How nothing much had changed whether the dead were walking or not. There were those who lived inside of life and those who for whatever reason did not or could not. Dead or no dead.

He waited for them to come and sedate him and strap him down and wished only that he had somebody to talk to—to tell the Gleason story, maybe, one last time. Gleason was a funny man in person just as he was on TV but with a foul nasty mouth on him, always cussing, and he had almost beat him.

Snakes

What she came to think of as *her* snake appeared just after the first storm.

She was talking on the phone with her lawyer in New York. Outside the floodwaters had receded. She could see through the screen which enclosed the lanai on one side, that her yard, which an hour before had been under a foot of water, had drained off down the slope past the picket fence and into the canal beyond.

She could let out the dog, she thought. Though she'd have to watch her. At one year old the golden retriever was still a puppy and liked to dig. Ann had learned the hard way. Weather in south Florida being what it was she'd already gone through three slipcovers for the couch due to black tarry mud carried in on Katie's feet and belly.

The lawyer was saying he needed money.

"I hate to ask," he said.

"How much?"

"Two thousand for starters."

"Christ, Ray."

"I know it's tough. But you've got to look at it this way—he's already into you for over thirty grand and every month the figure keeps growing. If we get him he'll owe you my fee as well. I'll make sure of it."

"*If* we get him."

"You can't think that way, Annie. *I* know you're starving out there. I know what you make for a living and I know why you moved down there in the first place—because it was the cheapest place you could think of where you could still manage to bring your kid up in any kind of decent fashion. That's *his fault*. You've got to go after him. Just think about it for a minute. Thirty grand in back child support! Believe me, it will change your life. You can't *afford* to be defeatist about this."

"Ray, I *feel* defeated. I feel like he's beaten the shit out of me."

"You're not. Not yet."

She sighed. She felt seventy—not forty. She could feel it in her legs. She sat down on the couch next to Katie. Pushed gently away at the cold wet nose that nuzzled her face.

"Find the retainer, Ann."

"Where?"

I'm trapped, she thought. He's got me. I barely made taxes this year.

"Trust me. Find the money."

She hung up and opened the sliding glass door to the lanai and then stood in the open screen doorway to the yard and watched while Katie sniffed through the scruffy grass and behind the hibiscus looking for a suitable place to pee. The sun was bright. The earth was steaming.

She couldn't even afford her dog, she thought. She loved the dog and so did Danny but the dog was a luxury, her collar, her chain. Her shots were an extravagance.

I'm trapped.

Outside Katie stiffened.

Her feet splayed wide and her nose darted down low to

381

the ground, darted up and then down again. The smooth golden hair along her backbone suddenly seemed to coarsen.

"Katie?"

The dog barely glanced at her, but the glance told her that whatever she saw in the grass, Katie was going play with it come hell or high water. The eyes were bright. Her haunches trembled with excitement.

Katie's play, she knew, could sometimes be lethal. Ann would find chewed bodies of ginkos on the lanai deposited there in front of the door like some sort of present. Once, a small rabbit. She watched amazed and shocked one sunny afternoon as the dog leapt four feet straight up into the air to pluck a sparrow from its flight. She was thinking this.

And then she saw the snake.

It was nose to nose with Katie, the two of them fencing back and forth not a foot apart, the snake banded black and brown, half-hidden behind the hibiscus bushes, but from where she stood, six feet away, it looked frighteningly big. Definitely big enough, she thought, whether it was poisonous or not, to do serious damage if it was the snake and not Katie who did the biting.

She heard it hiss. Saw its mouth drop open on the hinged jaw.

It darted, struck, and fell into the black mud at Katie's feet. The dog had shifted stance and backed away and was still backpedaling but the snake was not letting it go at that. The snake was advancing.

"Katie!"

She ran out. Her eyes never left the snake for an instant. She registered its fast smooth glide, registered for the first time actual *size* of the thing.

Seven feet? Eight feet? Jesus!

She crossed the distance to the dog faster than she thought she'd ever moved in her life, grabbed her collar and flung all seventy-five pounds of golden retriever head-

382

first past her toward the door so that it was behind *her* now, *shit*, head raised, gliding through the mud and tufts of grass coming toward her as she stumbled over the dog who'd turned in the doorway for one last look at the thing and then got past her and slammed the screen in the goddamn face of the thing just as it hit the screen once and then twice—a sound like a foot or a hammer striking—hit it hard enough to dent it inward. And finally, seeing that, she screamed.

The dog was barking now, going for the screen on their side, enraged by the attempted intrusion. Ann hauled her away by the collar back through the lanai and slid the glass doors shut and even though she knew it was crazy, even though she knew the snake could not get through the screen, she damn well locked them.

She sat down on her rug, her legs giving out completely, her heart pounding, and tried to calm Katie. Or calm herself by calming Katie.

The dog continued to bark. And then to growl. And finally just sat there looking out toward the lanai and panting.

She wondered if that meant it was gone.

Somehow she doubted it.

She was glad it was President's day weekend and that Danny was with his grandmother and grandfather at Universal over in Orlando. The trip was a present to him for good grades. She was glad he wouldn't be coming home from school in an hour as usual. Wouldn't come home to *that*.

The dog was still trembling.

So was she.

It was two o'clock. She needed a drink.

She could pinpoint the moment her fear of snakes began exactly.

She had been eight years old.

Her grandparents had lived in Daytona Beach, and Ann and her parents had come to visit. It was Ann's first visit

383

to Florida. Daytona was pretty boring so they did a little sightseeing while they were there and one of the places they went to was a place called Ross Allen's Alligator Farm. A guide gave them a tour.

She remembered being fascinated by the baby alligators, dozens and dozens of them all huddled in one swampy pen, but seemingly very peaceful together, and she was wondering if maybe the reason they weren't biting one another was that they all came from one mama, if that were possible. She stood there watching pondering that question until she became aware that the tour had moved on a bit and she knew she'd better catch up with them but she still wanted an answer to her question about the alligators so when she approached the group she did what she'd been told to do when she had a question, never mind how urgent.

She raised her hand.

As it happened her tour guide had just asked a question of his own. *Who wants to put this snake around his neck?* And Ann, with her hand in the air and thinking hard about the peaceful drowse of baby alligators found herself draped by and staring into the face of a five pound boa constrictor named Marvin, everyone smiling at her, until her father said *I think you'd better take it off now, I don't know, she looks kinda pale to me,* and she'd fainted dead away.

There had been green snakes in the garden by her house and they had not bothered her in the slightest and there were garter snakes down by the brook. But nothing like a five pound boa named Marvin. So that afterwords she avoided even greens and garters. And shortly after that she had the first of what became a recurrent dream.

She is swimming in a mountain pool.

She is alone and she is naked.

The water is warm, just cool enough to be refreshing, and the banks are rocky and green.

She's midway across the pool, swimming easily, strongly, when she has the feeling that something is . . . not right. She

384

turns and looks behind her and there it is, a sleek black wa-
tersnake, lithe and whiplike, so close that she can see its fangs,
she can see directly into the white open mouth of it, it is un-
dulating through the water toward her at stunning speed, it's
right behind her and she swims for dear life but knows she'll
never make it, not in time, the banks loom ahead like a giant
stone wall bleeding gleaming condensation and she's terrified,
crying—the crying itself slowing her down even more so that
even as she swims and the water thickens she's losing her will
and losing hope, it's useless, there's only her startled frightened
flesh driving her on and the snake is at her heels and she can
almost feel it and

She wakes.

Sometimes she's only sweating. Twisted into the bed-
sheets as though they were knots of water.

Sometimes she screams herself awake.

Screams as she's just done now.

Goddamn snake.

Seven feet long and big around as a man's fist. Bigger.
The snake in her dream was nothing compared to that.

She got up and went to the kitchen and poured herself
a glass of vodka, added ice and tonic. She drank it down
like a glass of water and poured another. The shaking
stopped a bit.

Enough for her to wonder if the snake were still outside.

The dog was lying on the rug, biting at a flea on her right
hind leg.

The dog didn't look worried at all.

Take a look, she thought.

What can it hurt?

She unlocked the door, opened it, and stepped out onto
the lanai, then slid the door closed behind her. She didn't
want Katie involved in this. She picked up a broom she
used to sweep up out there. Behind her Katie got to her
feet and watched, ears perked. She scrabbled at the door.

"No," she said. The scrabbling stopped.

She peered through the screens.

Nothing by the door.

Nothing in the yard either that she could see, either to the left, where the snake had first appeared and the hibiscus grew up against the picket fence, nor to the right, where a second, taller plant grew near the door. The only place she couldn't see was along the base of the screened-in wall itself on either side. To do that she'd have to open the door.

Which she wasn't about to do.

Or was she?

Hell, it was ridiculous to hang around wondering. There was every chance the snake had gone back through the fence the way it had come and was rooting around for mice down at the banks of the canal even as she stood there.

Okay, she thought. Do it. But do it carefully. Do it *smart*.

She opened the dented screen door to just the width of the broom and wedged its thick bristles into the bottom of the opening. She peered out along the base of the longer wall to the left.

No snake.

She looked right and heard it hiss and slide along the metal base near the hibiscus and felt it hit the door all at once, jarring its metal frame.

She slammed it shut.

The broom fell out of her hands, clattered to the concrete floor.

And then she was just staring at the thing, backing away to the concrete wall behind her.

Watching as it raised its head. And then its body. Two feet, three feet. Rising. Slowly gaining height.

Seeming to swell.

And swaying.

Staring back at her.

It was nearly dusk before she got up the courage to look again.

This time she used a shovel from the garage instead of

386

the broom. If it came after her again with a little luck she could chop the goddamn thing's head off.

It was gone.

She looked everywhere. The snake was gone.

She took another drink by way of celebration. The idea of spending the night with the snake lying out there in her yard had unnerved her completely. She thought she deserved the drink.

If she dreamed she did not remember.

In the morning she checked the yard again and finding it empty, let Katie out to do her business, let her back in again and then went out the front door for the paper.

She took one step onto the walkway and hadn't even shut the door behind her when she saw it on the lawn, stretched to its full enormous length diagonally from her mailbox nearly all the way to the walk, three feet away. Head raised and moving toward her.

She stepped back inside and shut the door.

The snake stopped and waited.

She watched it through the screen.

The snake didn't move. It just lay there in the bright morning sun.

She closed the inner door and locked it.

Jesus!

She was trapped in her own home here!

Who the hell did you call? The police? The Humane Society?

She tried 911.

An officer identified himself. He sounded young and friendly.

"I've got a snake out here in my yard. A big snake. And he . . . he keeps coming right at me. I honestly can't get out of my house!"

It was true. The only other exit to the condo was through the kitchen door that led to the garage and the garage was right beside the front door. She wasn't going out that way. No way. No thanks.

"Sorry, ma'am, but it's not police business. What you want to do is call the Animal Rescue League. They'll send somebody over there and pick it up for you. Get rid of it. But I gotta tell you, you're my third snake call today and I've already had four alligators. Yesterday was even worse. These rains bring 'em all out. So the Animal Rescue League may make you wait awhile."

"God!"

He laughed. "My brother-in-law's a gardener. You know what he says about Florida? '*Everything* bites down here. Even the *trees* bite at you.'"

He gave her the number and she dialed. The woman at Animal Rescue took Ann's name, address and phone number and then asked her to describe the animal, its appearance and behavior.

"Sounds like what you've got is a Florida Banded," she said. "Though I've never heard of one that big before."

"A what?"

"A Florida Banded watersnake. You say it's seven, eight feet? That's big. That means you've got maybe thirty pounds of snake there."

"Is it poisonous?"

"Nah. Give you a darn good nasty bite, though. The banded's aggressive. He'll hit you two three four times if he hits you once. But again, I never heard of one *goin' after* you the way you're saying. Normally they'll just defend their own territory. You sure you didn't go after *him* in some way?"

"Absolutely not. My dog, maybe, at first. But I pulled her away as soon as I saw the thing. Since then he's come at me twice. With no provocation whatsoever."

"Well, don't start provokin' him now. Snake gets agitated, he'll strike at anything. We'll be out just as soon as we can. You have yourself a good day now."

She waited. Watched talk shows and ate lunch. Stayed

purposely away from both the front door and the lanai.

They arrived about three.

Two burly men in slacks and short-sleeved shirts stepping out of the van carrying two long wooden poles. One pole had a kind of wire shepherd's crook at the end and the other pole a v-shaped wedge. She stood in the doorway with Katie and watched them. The men just nodded to her and went to work.

Infuriatingly enough, the snake now lay passive on the grass while the crook slipped over its head just beneath the jawbone and the v-shaped wedge pinned it halfway down the length of its body. The man with the crook then lifted the head and grabbed it under the jaw first with one hand and then the other, dropping his pole to the grass. Its mouth opened wide and the snake writhed, hissing—but did not really seem to resist. They counted three and hefted him.

"Big guy, ain't he."

"Biggest banded I've seen."

They walked him across the street to the vacant lot opposite into a wide thick patch of scrub.

Then they just dropped him, crossed the street, got the pole off the lawn and walked back to the van.

She stood there. She couldn't believe it.

"Excuse me? Could you hold on a moment, please?"

She walked outside. The bald one was climbing into the driver's seat.

"I don't understand. Aren't you . . . moving him? Aren't you taking him somewhere?"

The man smiled. "He's took."

"That's supposed to keep that thing away from here? That *street*?"

"Not the street, ma'am. See, a snake's territorial. That means wherever he sets down, if there's enough food 'round to feed on, that's where he's gonna stay. Now, he's gonna find lizards, mice, rabbits and whatever over there in that lot. And see, it leads back to a stream. When he's

389

finished with this patch he'll just go downstream. You'll never see that guy again. Believe me."

"What if you're wrong?"

" 'Scuse me?"

She was angry and frustrated and she guessed it showed.

"I said what if you're wrong! What if the damned thing is back here in half an hour?"

The men exchanged glances.

Women. Don't know shit, do they.

"Then I guess you'll want to call us up again, ma'am. Won't happen though."

She wanted to smash furniture.

She talked to Danny in Orlando that night and told him about the snake. She must have made it sound like quite an adventure because Danny expressed more than a little pique at missing it. By the time she finished talking to him she almost thought it *was* an adventure.

Then she remembered the hissing, racing through the grass. Rising up to stare at her.

As though it knew her.

She fell asleep early and missed the evening news and weather report. It turned out that was the worst thing that happened to her all day.

The following morning she cleaned house from top to bottom, easier to do with Danny gone, and by noon had worked herself up into a pretty good mood despite thinking occasionally of her lawyer and the money. She had considered how she might raise the cash for his retainer but had come to no conclusion. Her ex-husband had seen to it that her credit was shot so that a loan was out of the question. Her car was basically already a junker. And her parents barely had enough to get by on. *Sell the condo?* No. *Everything in it?* Dear God.

Once in a while she'd go out and check the yard. And maybe those guys were right, she thought. Maybe they knew their business after all. Because the big banded watersnake had not appeared again.

She showered and dressed. She had a lunch date for Suzie over at the Outback set for one-thirty.

Suzie, too, had missed the weather the night before and when they came out of the restaurant around three—aware that it was raining but not for how long nor nearly how hard—the parking lot was ankle-deep in floodwater. Hurricane Andrew be damned. Here they are, standing in the midst of the worst damn rainstorm of the year.

"You want to wait it out?"

"I was cleaning. I left the second story windows open. I can't believe it."

"Okay. But be careful driving, huh?"

Ann nodded. Suzie lived nearby, while her house was over a mile away. Visibility was not good. Not even there within the parking lot. Sheets of rain driven by steady winds gave the grey sky a kind of thickness and a warm humid weight.

They hugged and took off their shoes and ran for their respective cars. By the time Ann unlocked hers and slid inside her skirt and blouse were see-through and her hair was streaming water. She could taste her hair. She could see almost nothing.

The windshield wipers helped. She started the car slowly forward, following Suzie out through the exit to the street where they parted in different directions.

Happily there was almost no one on the usually congested four-lane street and cars were moving carefully and nobody was passing. The lane-lines had disappeared under water. She was moving through at least a foot and a half of it.

Then midway home she had to pull over. The windshield wipers couldn't begin to cope. The rain was pounding now—big drops sounding like hailstones. The wind gusted and rocked her car.

She sat staring into the fogged-over rearview mirror hoping that some damn fool wouldn't come up behind her and rear-end her. It was dangerous to pull over but she hadn't had a choice.

She looked down at herself wished she'd worn a bra. It was not just the nipples, not just the shape and outline of her breasts—you could see every mole and freckle. The same was true of the pale yellow skirt gone transparent across her thighs. She might as well be naked.

So what? she thought. Who's going to see you anyway? In *this*.

The rain slowed down enough so that her wipers could at least begin to do their job. She moved on.

The water in the street was moving fast, pouring toward some downhill destination.

Curbs were gone, flooded over.

Lawns were gone. Parking lots. Sidewalks.

The openings to sewers formed miniature whirlpools in which garbage floated, in which paper shopping bags swirled and branches and bits of wood.

In one of them she saw something that chilled her completely.

A broken cardboard box was turning slowly over the grate. The box was striped with black and brown and the stripes were moving.

Snakes. Seeking higher ground and respite from swimming.

She had heard about this happening during storms in Florida but she'd never actually seen it. *Everything bites,* said the man.

This goddamn state.

She turned the corner onto her street.

And she might have guessed if she'd thought about it, might have expected it. She knew the street she'd turned off was slightly elevated over her own. She'd noted it dozens of times.

But not now. Not this time. She was too intent on simply getting there, on getting through the storm. So that her car plunged into three and a half feet of water at the turnoff.

She damn near panicked then. It took her totally by surprise and scared her so badly that she almost stopped. Which would no doubt have been a disaster. She knew she'd never have gotten it started again. Not in this much water. She kept going, hands clutching at the wheel, wishing she'd never dreamt of having lunch with Suzie.

The water was halfway up the grille ahead of her, halfway up the door. The car actually felt *lighter*, as though the tires had much less purchase than before.

Almost crawling, expecting the car to sputter and die any moment, she urged it on. Talking to the car. Begging to the car. *Come on, honey.* Her condo with the open second-story windows was only four blocks away.

You can do it, honey. Sure you can.

One block.

Going slowly, the car actually rocking side to side in the current like a boat, her foot pressing gently on the accelerator.

Two blocks.

And her home just ahead of her now, she could see its white stucco facade turned dull grey in the rain, seeing the wide-open window to Danny's bedroom like a dark accusing eye staring out at her, the front lawn drowned and flooded with water.

And as she passed the third block, going by the overpass to the canal, she could see the roiling.

At first it wasn't clear just what it was. Something large and black moving in the water ahead like some sort of matter in another whirlpool over another sewer grate only bigger.

Then she came closer and she almost stopped again because now she saw what it was clearly dead ahead but she didn't stop, my God, she couldn't stop, she inched along with her foot barely touching the accelerator, letting the idle do the work of moving the car forward like a faintly beating heart somewhere inside while she desperately tried to think how to avoid the writhing mass of bodies and what the hell to do.

There must have been dozens of them. All sizes.

All lengths.

The water was thick with them.

They moved over and through one another in some arcane inborn pattern, formed a mass that was roughly circular in shape and maybe six or seven feet in diameter, thickest at the center, lightest at the edges, but all in constant motion, some of them shooting like sparks off a sparkler or a catherine wheel and then swimming back into the circle again that formed their roiling gleaming nucleus.

Driving through them was unimaginable. She had to go around them but it was impossible to see where the street ended and lawn began and like every street in the development the curbs were shallow—she would feel very little going over them.

But she had to try.

And in fact felt nothing as she passed to the right onto her neighbor's lawn and into her neighbor's mud and she tried not to see them out the driver's side window as the car lurched once and shuddered and stopped while her wheels spun uselessly on.

Her first response was to gun the thing but that was no good, all it did was dig her deeper into the mud on the passenger side.

Well. Not exactly all.

It also stirred them, seemed to annoy them all to hell. She heard them hit the front and back doors on her side. *Bump. Bump. Bumpbumpbumpbumpbump.* She dared to glance out her window and saw that the circle had become and oblong figure stretching the entire length of the car—as though something protoplasmic were trying to engulf her.

She put the car in park and let it idle. Fighting a growing panic. Trying to consider her options.

She could sit there. She could wait for help. She could wait for them to disperse.

But there wouldn't be any help. There was practically nobody on the main road let alone this one, no one but her dumb enough to be out on side streets in a storm like this.

And they wouldn't be dispersing either.

That much was obvious. Now that the car was quiet the circle formed again. Almost exactly as before.

Except for these two. Crawling up over the hood.

A black snake. And something banded yellow and brown. Crawling toward the windshield. Looking for higher ground.

And she could feel them with her inside the car. She could hear them on the seat in back. Crawling up to her seat. Crawling up to her neck and over her neck and down across her breasts and thighs.

She had to get out of there. That or go crazy. There was one option she simply could not tolerate and that was just to sit there listening to them slither across the roof and over the hood. She could imagine them, see them, thick as ropes, blocking her view through the windshield, crawling, staring in at her. *Wanting* in.

She had to get out.

She could run. She could run through the water. It wasn't that deep. Go out the passenger side. Maybe it was free of them.

She shifted seats.

It wasn't. Not completely. But there weren't many. Just sparks on the catherine wheel. Darting back and forth beneath the car.

The black snake was at the windshield. Another yellow and brown appeared just over the headlight, moving up across the hood.

How long before the car was buried in them?

Her heart was pounding. There was a taste in her mouth like dry old leaves.

You can do this, she thought. You haven't any choice. The only other choice is giving up and giving in and that

will make you crazy. When you have no choice you
what you've got to do.

Don't wait. Waiting will make it worse. Go. Go now

She took a deep breath and wrenched at the door han
and pushed hard with her shoulder. Warm floodwa
poured in over her feet and ankles. The door opened a f
inches and jammed into the mud. The spinning tires h
angled the passenger side down.

She pushed again. The door gave another inch. She tr
desperately to get through.

It wasn't enough.

She threw herself across the seat onto her back, grabb
the steering wheel above with both hands for leverage a
kicked at the door with all her might, kicked it twice a
then got up and rammed her body into the gap. Butto
popped on her blouse. She screamed and kicked as
brown snake glided over her leg above the ankle and in
the car and she pushed again and then suddenly she v
through.

Mud sucked at her feet. The water was up to mid-thi,
Her skirt was floating. She slogged a few steps and alm
fell. A green snake twisted by a few feet to the left—a
what may have been a coral snake, small and banded bla
yellow and red swam back toward the car beside her: S
lurched away. Corals carried poison. She turned to ma
sure it had gone back to the swirling hell it came from a
that was when she saw him.

Her snake.

Perched atop the roof of the car. Coiled there.

Looking at her.

And now, beginning to move.

The dream, she thought, *it's the dream all over again*
she saw the snake glide off the roof and into the water a
she hauled herself through the water, making for what s
knew was the concrete drive in front of her house, its firn
footing, but now she was still on the lawn next door, h
feet slapping down deep into the soft slimy mud, l

plashing through the water so that she was mud from head
o toe in no time and not turning back, not needing to—
he snake gaining on her as real in her mind's eye as it had
een in her dream.

When she fell she fell flat out straight ahead and her left
and came down on concrete, the right sunk deep into
ud. She gulped water spit it out. Scrambled up. The torn
lk blouse had come open completely and hung off one
houlder like a filthy sodden rag.

She risked a glance and there it was, taking its time,
liding, sinuous and a graceful and awful with hurt for her
st a few feet away.

A black snake skittered out ahead but she didn't care,
er feet hit the concrete and suddenly she was splashing
ward the garage because its door was kept unlocked for
anny after school, there were keys to the house hidden
y the washing machine, there were rakes and tools inside.

She hit the door at a run and turned and saw the snake
aise its head out of the water ready to strike and she bent
own and reached into the warm deep muddy water, her
ead going under for a terrible moment blind as she clawed
t the center of the door searching for the handle and found
and pulled up as the massive head of the thing struck at
er, barely missing her naked breast as she lurched back
nd fell and it tangled itself, writhing furiously, in her torn
ylon blouse.

Floodwater poured rushing into the garage, the thick
uscular body of the snake turning over and across her in
s tide, caressing the flesh of her stomach and sliding all
long her back as she struggled to free herself of the blouse
nd twist it around its darting head. She stumbled to her
et and ran for the washing machine, found the keys and
ipped them tight and ran for the door.

The snake was free. The blouse drifted.

Ann was standing in two feet of water and she couldn't
e the snake.

She fumbled the key into the lock and twisted it and flung open the door.

The snake rose up out of the water and hit the lip of the single stair just as she crossed the threshold and then it began to move inside.

"No." she was screaming. "I don't let you in I didn't *invite* you in. Goddammit! You bastard!" Screaming in fear but fury too, slamming the wooden door over and over again against the body of the snake while the head of the thing searched her out behind the door and she was aware of Katie barking beside her, the snake aware too, its head turning in that direction now and its black tongue tasting dogscent, womanscent, turning, until she saw the vacuum cleaner standing by the refrigerator still plugged in from this morning and flipped the switch and opened the door wide and hurled it toward the body of the black thing in the water.

The machine burst into a shower of sparks that raced blue and yellow through the garage like a blast of St. Elmo' Fire. The snake thrashed and suddenly seemed to swel Smoke curled puffing off its body. Its mouth snapped ope and shut and opened wide again, impossibly wide. Sh smelled burning flesh and sour electric fire. The cord crack led and burst in its wallsocket. Katie howled, ran ears bac and tail low into the living room and cowered by the sofa

She grabbed a hot pad off the stove and pulled the plug She looked down at the smoking body.

"I got you," she said. "You didn't get me. You didn' expect that, did you."

When she had hauled the carcass outside and closed th garage door and then fed Katie and finally indulged in wonderful, long, hot bath, she put on a favorite soft cotto robe and then went to the phone.

The lawyer was surprised to hear from her again so soo "I'm having a little garage sale," she said.

And she almost laughed. Her little garage sale would r

doubt relieve her of everything she was looking at, of practically everything she owned. It didn't matter a damn bit. It was worth it.

"I want you to go after him," she said. "You hear me? I want you to get the sonofabitch."

And then she did laugh.

Rikki-Tikki-Tavi, she thought.

Snakes.

Firedance

Frisco Hans shifted the Remington over-and-under to his scarred white-knuckled left hand and nervously adjusted his hat. A night as cold as this, they all wore hats. A night like this you could feel the body-heat rise off your head like steam out of a sewerpipe. For eight and a half years Hans had worked as a merchant seaman. Then one morning he jumped off a lifeboat made fast high over the leeward rail onto the deck of the *Curlew*, hit the deck too hard and lost his sense of taste. Couldn't tell salmon from a plate of liver and onions. It never came back. When he realized it was not going to come back he quit the merchant marine before he lost some other of his senses and took a job as a security guard in a frozen-fish factory way up here in Maine. Hans knew about loss. He kept his hat on.

The little guy beside him, Homer Devins, considered that he knew about it too. But that was because Devins' wife had run away with the Chinese dry-cleaner last winter while Devins was out hunting rabbits. He bagged one rabbit and Chin Feng Chi made off with his wife of thirty years.

Devins was still a little uncomfortable with the deal.

Hans shook his head. "What I still want to know is, how the hell does this kind of thing just happen? Did I just wake up one morning and all the rules're changed?"

Devins pulled hard on his Camel Light, a tiny glow in the dark. "Damned if I know. You come up with the answer to that, you tell me."

Devins glanced down the line of bare scrubby trees that encircled the field. Other cigarettes glowed. A kitchen-match flared. Half the town was out, standing around the perimeter, watching. He threw his Camel Light into the snow.

"Damn! Animals are s'pposed to be *afraid* of fire."

Hans nodded. He'd been hearing the same puzzled wisdom for over two days now, ever since Ray Fogarty and Dot Hardcuff rushed into the Bar None Grill Wednesday night just after one in the morning all red-faced and out of breath and babbling about animals in the clearing up by Zeigler's Notch. To which he and most of the sixteen or eighteen gathered there responded bullshit. And what the hell were the two of them doing up there in the first place? kidding them, knowing full well what they were doing, but knowing also that Ray's wife would skin him alive if *she* knew and so would Dot's husband.

Not one of them believed them. Not for a second. But it was Wednesday night and nobody in the joint had much to go home to—damn few even had work to go to in the morning given what was happening with the economy. So they piled into half a dozen trucks and made the run up the mountain to the Notch, their tire chains grinding up the dirt beneath the snow like one long open wound.

They pulled over where the road stopped dead and even from the base of the trail through the thicket you could see the glow up ahead over the hill so that they knew the part about the fire was true enough. But the rest? Bullshit. Ray and Dot were having a little fun with them was all.

It was only at the rim of the clearing that the cigarettes

started falling out of incredulous wide-open mouths and beer bottles started dropping down into the snow—because what they were looking at wasn't possible. Wasn't natural. Wasn't *right*. It flew in the face of everything.

You didn't have to be a genius—you didn't even have to have finished high school for godsakes—to know that it was not just brainmatter and the almighty opposable thumb that set people apart from the animals, certainly set them apart from the animals in nature, in the wild, you were not talking about some fat old yellow hound or bone-lazy housecat lying all curled up and comfy on the sofa, you were talking about wild things, and it was not just brain and thumb that made humans different. It was *fire*.

An animal saw a fire in the hearth, it stayed the hell outside. Saw fire in a cave, it hung well clear in the dark. Saw fire in the woods, it panicked. It ran like the beejeezuz.

What kept us warm and comforable was for animals a source of terror yet here they were, seven of them, basking in its warm red glow.

And not even all the same species.

Yet another impossibility.

You had mice, two of them.

You had snakes, big ones, impossible to tell exactly what kind from this distance but a pair of those too.

You had a big red cardinal, a goddamn *bird* no less.

You had a wolf. You had a lynx. Both of them rare as hens' teeth around here.

But basically, you had a bunch of natural enemies. Wolf. Lynx. Bird. Snakes. Mice. Nobody eating nobody. Lying instead by a good hot fire enclosed by a fieldstone circle maybe three and a half feet in diameter. Easy as you please, staring into the fire, listening to its crack and sizzle.

The first thing Hans realized was that it would not be a good idea to fuck with them. Other than the occasional half-empty beer bottle they were all unarmed out there. A wolf could get nasty. A lynx was practically *bound* to get nasty.

So the patrons of the Bar None Grill stood in the cold perimeter and at first it was as though they were standing in the presence of something as miraculous and awe-inspiring as the Second Coming, as Lourdes for chrissake, they could have been watching little green men stepping wide-eyed out of a saucer, they could have been watching Nessie poke her head from beneath the waters of a Scottish lake.

Then one man stepped back, and then another. In the crackle of the flames and the silence which surrounded them they seemed to have heard something ominous, felt the dark chill of a moonless Maine winter night move from outside to in.

Later, many would admit to having pretty much the same thought.

It was as though the natural way of things had reversed itself.

Humans in the shadows, wild things in the light.

"*Not right,*" someone said. "No-fucking-way *right!*" and suddenly they bolted, pounding down the mountain, running like kids from the bogeyman, half of them ignoring the trail entirely and battling their way through the thicket as though the woods itself had all of a sudden turned on them and was barking, snapping at their heels, racing after them like cobras, diving from the skies like hunting birds.

The drinking lasted till dawn.

By noon that day the whole town knew.

Something was happening with the animals.

It was Gert McChesney talking. Who, because she was old and lived alone in an ancient ramshackle house on top of Cedar Hill and walked with a rolling limp, refusing the indignity of hospital gown and bedpan the hip replacement would have called for, the local kids dubbed the Witch. But who in reality was Dead River's one and only Rhodes Scholar—Yale University, Class of '31—and only marginally a drunk.

They were sitting at the Bar at the Tip Top Lounge and

Gert was on her second Heineken and Musiel and Schilling and Frisco Hans were each on their third. It was only one o'clock—a cold, grim grey day that seeped across the floor of the bar and over their feet even with the door closed tight behind them.

"You think about what fire is," she was saying, "and what do you come up with? Fire's a *breaking down* of things. You start with a hardwood log, you end up with a pile of ash. You get the fire hot enough, same goes for flesh and bone. See, the *form's* gone. All you're left with's minerals and gasses and the temporary release of energy. That's what scares the animals. The destruction, the breaking down of all those old familiar forms. Trees, grass, nests—and whatever's unlucky enough to be trapped in 'em. Animals got enough sense to run like hell when things are falling apart around them. Us on the other hand, we love it. We love the smell of a fire, the look and sound of it, the nice warm glow. To us fire's a comfort. We're the only animal on earth who takes *comfort* in the breaking down of things."

She sipped from her beerglass, a little foam clinging to the long steel-grey hairs of her upper lip.

"Maybe that's changed now."

"Now how the hell could that be, Gert? The fire ain't changed any." Frisco Hans slapped his bottle down and pointed at it and Teddy Panik swept it away and uncapped him another and set it on the bar. He didn't ask if anybody else was ready. He never did have much to say.

She shrugged. "I dunno."

Hans looked at her, frowning. He'd been following her pretty well he thought. Now he'd run head-first, tires screeching into a mental brick wall. *Maybe that's* changed *now?* He thought Gert had more sense than the whole town council combined on the very best day of their lives but what the hell did that mean? Musiel and Schilling were looking at her like they were puzzled too.

Hans was a man of action though. Given the roadblock he'd skirt around it.

"Okay," he said. "So what do we *do* about it?"

She smiled. More often than not Gert's teeth had a lip-stick stain on the uppers. Today was no exception.

"Call up the evening news? Get somebody in from the University? I suppose you could. If it was me, I'd just leave well enough alone. See what happens. Long as they don't burn the woods down, what's the difference?"

Hans thought on that. Maybe there was a difference and then again maybe there wasn't. Leave that for awhile too, he thought.

"Okay, then explain to us how come we got snakes not eating mice, we got cats not eating birds, we got cats, *lynxes* for godsakes and wolves not tearing the living shit out of each other. Explain that."

She smiled again. "Peaceable Kingdom," she said.

"Huh?"

"Old testament passage, a kind of prophecy, it might be Isaiah. A lot of nineteenth-century *naif* painters favored the subject. Edward Hicks, Henri Rousseau. There's this bucolic scene, a lion sniffing at the muzzle of an ox, a wolf lying down with a lamb, leopards lying next to a goat, that sort of thing. I only remember one line from it. 'And a child shall lead them.' There were usually some kids in the paintings too. Peaceable Kingdom. Interesting."

Hans wondered what *naif* was and what *bucolic* meant. It sounded to Hans like a disease.

He wished he could taste his Heineken.

That was yesterday. Nighttime fell and they'd gone up the mountain, little after midnight, and instead of half a dozen trucks parked where the road left off and the trail began there were cars and trucks all over the place and he and Homer Devins had to walk about a quarter of a mile from where they left the Dodge.

This time some of them, the original crowd from the Bar None Grill and a handful of others, were armed with shot-guns, rifles. Despite their embarrassment and efforts to conceal what they'd done word had got around about their headlong flight down the mountain. Even Hans had his over-and-under.

His neighbors and friends were already standing two-deep in the shadows along the perimeter by the time they arrived. Women and children too this time. He and Homer moved in close beside Gert and Dot Hardcuff and Jack Musiel where they could see. The hush was the same as the night before. The inexplicable made flesh. Nobody could believe their eyes.

There were a lot more animals this time. A big wild black-and-white dog. Another wolf, smaller, a female, maybe the mate of the first one. Two more cardinals and a half dozen sparrows. A pair of bullfrogs. A bluejay. An owl and a rooster. A pair of water moccasins from down by the river. A hawk.

And they weren't just basking by the fire either. They were moving in a slow irregular circle in either direction *around* it. Frisco Hans watched the lynx brush shoulders with the she-wolf and a mouse crawl right on up over the back of a water moccasin sliding in the opposite direction. The moccasin didn't even turn its head, didn't blink an eye.

"What in the Lord's name are they *doing*?" whispered Dot. Hans noticed that her husband wasn't there. But then again neither was Fogarty. He wondered if they'd up and shot one another. By now half the town knew it was Dot and Ray Fogarty who'd barrelled down the mountain last night, bursting in with the news to the Bar None Grill.

"They're moving," said Gert, as if to say, *how in the hell do you expect me know what they're doing, you damn fool?* which with a few more beers in her she might have. You could almost hear the click in Gert's head sometimes when she'd been drinking and then she wasn't so polite anymore.

It didn't matter much what they were doing though because whatever it was, they stopped. It was as though some prearranged signal had passed between them. They

406

stopped on a goddamn dime and they did it all at once.

And that was truly scary. You could hear safeties click and bolts thrown on rifles all along the periphery. Everybody thinking, *you gotta bet they know we're out here*. Everybody nervous as a virgin in a whorehouse, wondering if the animals wouldn't turn and move against them. Even tame animals reverted. These were wild.

But what they did was, they sat down.

Just like the night before. As though the people in the shadows didn't matter one damn bit. As though they weren't even there. They just curled up in front of the fire. A wing fluttered. The she-wolf sighed. You could hear the soft raspy coil of a blacksnake.

And it was strange then, Hans thought, even he was aware of it, as the fear passed off them there was something maybe about the way these creatures who were supposed to be frightened of men with guns were *ignoring* them instead, or maybe it was just them all being out here in the first place, to what end nobody could say, scaring *them*, scaring *humans*, but a feeling passed through the crowd that felt like a kind of collective shame or guilt or something, as though the animals had made them smaller somehow, humbled, a damn sight less significant. You were aware of a dull resentment of that. It moved across the crowd like a pale moon rising.

And there was a moment when he knew, just *knew* it was going to get ugly. In all his experience with people of every nation on the face of the earth there was a link between pride and humiliation and an aftermath of bloody violence. He'd seen it in Singapore bars and Polish whorehouses, on docks and freighters, over and over, everywhere. You could almost feel the bodies tensing, fingers tightening on triggers.

"Guess the show's over for the night," said Gert—loud, so everybody could hear. "You can't help but wonder what in the world they got for us tomorrow, though."

People laughed here and there. The tension eased.

In front of them by the fire not an animal stirred.

They got their own business, Hans thought, not even sure what he meant by that but pretty certain it was true.

Then one by one they filed down the mountian.

And now they watched for the third night.

Gert wasn't with them. What with standing out in the cold last night her authritis had kicked into overdrive. She'd called Natty Horner and said she could barely walk. He felt bad for her but worse for the rest of them.

Because the mood was getting ugly again.

This time it was the sheer size of the damn thing that had them spooked.

To Frisco Hans it looked like the entire forest was there.

Squirrels, chipmunks, birds, 'coons, moose, bears, weasels—there were even plenty of farm animals this time. Pigs, chickens. He recognized Tom Mullins' old black goat Henrietta from the tufted white spur on her forehead. The flames were taller too, the circle of stones which enclosed them widenened out to maybe six feet across. The entire snowy clearing was brightly lit and shimmering. Only the trees fell gradually into darkness.

The trees and them, standing there.

It was as though they were hiding *in the trees.* As only nights before the animals might have done. There was that same sense of reversal again. Now they were doing it. Humans, hiding.

While the animals, packed four and five deep and lying close together, stared deep into the shifting flames.

And what bothered Hans was this. *What's gonna happen if they got up on their feet again like they did last night and began to move, fifty, maybe sixty of them this time, enough, spread out, to fill the whole damn clearing, and practically everybody armed this time except the women and children— too damn many children to Hans' way of thinking—and no Gert around to crack wise and ease the tension?*

408

"I don't like this," he said. "I think we should just get out of here. Gert was right. Leave 'em be."

Homer Devins looked up at him. "You know better'n that, Hans. Hell, you can't just leave 'em be. This is . . ." He struggled with the idea. "This is just . . . *plain unnatural.*"

How do we know? he thought. Who in the hell knows what's natural in a world up to its butt with poisoned lakes and streams, with poisoned *air* for chrissake, with normal-looking guys not a whole lot different from Homer here walking into a K-Mart and shooting up the customers with some fancy thousand-dollar automatic weapon, guys who like to kidnap and murder little children, a world where you get a doll for Christmas and it eats your hair, a world so crazy and nonsensical that you can jump off a goddamn lifeboat and lose your sense of taste forever? Who says what's natural and what's not?

He was thinking this when they began to rise, spread out across the clearing, and *dance.*

It was not, God knows, like any dance he'd ever seen but he still saw it for what it was, a dance, pure and simple, at the center of it the original seven—two mice, two snakes, the cardinal, lynx and wolf—the mice on hind legs skittering around the fire, the snakes risen high and skating across the hard packed snow, the cardinal's wings spread wide, his beak pointed to the winter stars the same as the muzzle of the wolf was and the black flat nose of the lynx, both of them up on their hind feet too with their front paws spread wide and heads thrown back in abandon— and similar scenes all around them, as though the forest had suddenly come alive with a music only they could hear and which was denied those standing black and shadowy amid the trees.

"Jesus H. Christ!" Homer whispered.

It was as though they were watching some dark unholy magic unfold and it stunned and frightened. You could feel waves of fear sweep the crowd. They took an instinctive, collective step or two back into the brittle tangle of trees. Women gasped. An infant cried. He could hear a shotgun pump a cartridge, triggers cocked all around.

A bloodbath, Hans thought. It's going to be a goddamn bloodbath.

Because we're scared. Nothing more than that.

Damned if it'd be the first time but it was wrong—wrong and incredibly stupid. He got it now, what Gert was saying. Maybe everything *was* changing. What was scaring hell out of all the rest of them was filling him with wonder.

They're like us, he thought. Like what we must have been thousands and thousands of years ago. We must have crawled out of caves on nights like this and done just the same.

He was witnessing the dawn of a whole new time, a whole new nature.

He saw Ray Fogarty a few feet away raise his double-barrel shotgun and aim and thought, *no no, please* but others were rising in the darkness, other weapons glinting in the firelight, while the dancers in the clearing whirled around the flames in some bright joyous rapture of celebration that was impervious to danger, oblivious to harm, and Frisco Hans stood frozen in a fundamental horror at what his species was capable of doing here tonight so sudden and sad and profound that it would not even permit him to shout out a warning, yet another sense gone and him left wondering if it would ever return and if he'd give a damn when it did.

Which was exactly when little Patty Schilling broke free of her mother's arms, ran to the fire and joined them.

You couldn't very well shoot a little girl—not even one who had the habit of stealing crullers from Manger's Bakery when Tillie Manger wasn't looking. And pretty soon some other kids broke away and joined in too and you had kids out there dancing with mice and squirrels and whatnot and then some of the women. He saw Dot Hardcuff dancing around with a big brown bear and not even her husband

410

or Ray Fogarty was going to argue with *that* choice of partners.

Hans stood his over-and-under against a tree and turned to Homer Devins.

"Hey, Homer," he said. "I just got a helluva notion. I bet you never seen the hornpipe."

Afterword

People will often ask a writer, where do your ideas come from? The answer for me is just about anywhere. Everything from a nosebleed to a love affair to a TV ad can trip the wire to a story. But some come unbidden from deep memory. And memory like writing can be an odd and mysterious thing.

It's well over a year since I wrote the introduction to this book and over five years since I wrote the final story but I just a few nights ago had a kind of well . . . what the hell, *call it an epiphany*.

I was watching a good, highly annoying documentary on PBS about Elvis' gospel music—good because the documentary was good, annoying because it was one of those godawful pledge weeks where every twenty minutes they interrupt for *ten* minutes and the damn thing just goes on and on. I'd give them a hundred right now not to *have* pledge weeks.

Anyway. The film spent a good deal of time on the first gospel EP, relased in 1957. I'd been a boy of only eleven

413

when I first heard it and one song in particular has remained one of my favorites ever since. For my money it's as good as "Lawdy Miss Clawdy" or "Money Honey" and a billion times better than, say, "Hound Dog."

But you know how it is sometimes that when you know the lyrics to a song as well as you know your mother's maiden name you somehow stop actually *hearing* them for awhile? Well, listening to this one again on this fine and tedious special I *did* hear them for a change and thought, my God, that's where it all came from.

The song was Thomas A. Dorsey's haunting, bluesy "Peace in the Valley," written in Georgia in 1936. The lyrics go like this . . .

> Well the bear will be gentle
> And the wolves will be tame
> And the lion shall lay down by the lamb
> And the beasts from the wild
> Shall be led by a child
> And I'll be changed
> Changed from this creature that I am

By now you've presumably read "Firedance." Sound familiar?

When I was working the story it certainly wasn't the song I was thinking of—it was that Alan M. Clark's painting, on which I was basing it, reminded me so much thematically of a darker version of the nineteenth-century *naïfs'* "Peaceable Kingdoms" I'd first seen easily twenty-five years before. Because I'd enjoyed them so much at the time I'd searched out the passage in Isaiah. And then enjoyed the passage so much because it had clearly inspired "Peace in the Valley," something I'd never known before.

Then I proceeded to forget all about it.

But I have to think now that going back in time through the twists and turns of mind, the title of the book you are holding derives from a story written about a painting, then

414

a school of paintings viewed many years before, inspired by a passage in the Bible and finally to a *blues and gospel lyric which captured the imagination of an eleven-year-old suburban kid who loved his Elvis early on.*

So here's the epiphany.

Do the math.

I'm fifty-six.

And I think that I've been waiting for, gradually coming to and then writing down the title of, this book for forty-five years. If that's true, could be that child is still in here somewhere, leading on the beasts in me.

—Jack Ketchum, 2003

RED
JACK KETCHUM

Fans and critics alike hailed Jack Ketchum's previous novel, *The Lost*, for its power, its thrills and its gripping style, and recognized Ketchum as a master of suspense. Now Jack Ketchum is back to frighten us again with . . . *Red*!

It all starts with a simple act of brutality. Three boys shoot and kill an old man's dog. No reason, just plain meanness. But the dog was the best thing in the old man's world, and he isn't about to let the incident pass. He wants justice, and he'll make sure the kids pay for what they did. They picked the wrong old man to mess with. And as the fury and violence escalate, they're about to learn that . . . the hard way.

The Lost

Jack Ketchum

It was the summer of 1965. Ray, Tim and Jennifer were just three teenage friends hanging out in the campgrounds, drinking a little. But Tim and Jennifer didn't know what their friend Ray had in mind. And if they'd known they wouldn't have thought he was serious. Then they saw what he did to the two girls at the neighboring campsite—and knew he was dead serious.

Four years later, the Sixties are drawing to a close. No one ever charged Ray with the murders in the campgrounds, but there is one cop determined to make him pay. Ray figures he is in the clear. Tim and Jennifer think the worst is behind them, that the horrors are all in the past. They are wrong. The worst is yet to come.

___4876-0 $5.99 US/$6.99 CAN

Dorchester Publishing Co., Inc.
P.O. Box 6640
Wayne, PA 19087-8640

Please add $1.75 for shipping and handling for the first book and $.50 for each book thereafter. NY, NYC, and PA residents, please add appropriate sales tax. No cash, stamps, or C.O.D.s. All orders shipped within 6 weeks via postal service book rate. Canadian orders require $2.00 extra postage and must be paid in U.S. dollars through a U.S. banking facility.

Name_____
Address_____
City_____ State_____ Zip_____
I have enclosed $_____ in payment for the checked book(s).
Payment <u>must</u> accompany all orders. ☐ Please send a free catalog.
CHECK OUT OUR WEBSITE! www.dorchesterpub.com

THE INFINITE
DOUGLAS CLEGG

Harrow is haunted, they say. The mansion is a place of tragedy and nightmares, evil and insanity. First it was a madman's fortress; then it became a school. Now it lies empty. An obsessed woman named Ivy Martin wants to bring the house back to life. And Jack Fleetwood, a ghost hunter, wants to find out what lurks within Harrow. Together they assemble the people who they believe can pierce the mansion's shadows.

A group of strangers, with varying motives and abilities, gather at the house called Harrow in the Hudson Valley to reach another world that exists within the house. . . . A world of wonders . . . A world of desires . . . A world of nightmares.

DOUGLAS CLEGG

NAOMI

The subways of Manhattan are only the first stage of Jake Richmond's descent into the vast subterranean passageways beneath the city—and the discovery of a mystery and a terror greater than any human being could imagine. Naomi went into the tunnels to destroy herself . . . but found an even more terrible fate awaiting her in the twisting corridors. And now the man who loves Naomi must find her . . . and bring her back to the world of the living, a world where a New York brownstone holds a burial ground of those accused of witchcraft, where the secrets of the living may be found within the ancient diary of a witch, and where a creature known only as the Serpent has escaped its bounds at last.

___4857-4 $5.99 US/$6.99 CAN

SIMON CLARK

Darkness Demands

Life looks good for John Newton. He lives in the quiet village of Skelbrooke with his family. He has a new home and a successful career writing true crime books. He never gives a thought to the vast nearby cemetery known as the Necropolis. He never wonders what might lurk there.

Then the letters begin to arrive in the dead of night demanding trivial offerings—chocolate, beer, toys. At first John dismisses the notes as a prank. But he soon learns the hard way that they're not. For there is an ancient entity that resides beneath the Necropolis that has the power to demand things. And the power to punish those foolish enough to refuse.

___4898-1 $5.99 US/$6.99 CAN

BEDBUGS
RICK HAUTALA

From the subway tunnels of Boston to the rain-swept streets of Quebec City to the deepest snow-filled forests of Hilton, Maine, no one in these chilling stories by horror master Rick Hautala is safe from the darkness or the dangers that lurk in the shadows. Waiting for us. Reaching for us . . .

Over the years, Rick Hautala has terrified and captivated millions of readers around the world. *Bedbugs* is a career-spanning collection of stories that whisks you away on a guided tour of the darkest reaches of the human mind and soul.

EDWARD LEE
CITY INFERNAL

Hell is a city. Forget the old-fashioned sulphurous pit you may have read about. Over the millennia, Hell has evolved into a bustling metropolis with looming skyscrapers, crowded streets, systemized evil, and atrocity as the status quo.

Cassie thought she knew all about Hell. But when her twin sister, Lissa, committed suicide, Cassie found that she was able to travel to the real thing—the city itself. Now, even though she's still alive, Cassie is heading straight to Hell to find Lissa. And the sights she sees as she walks among the damned will never be in any tourist guidebook.

___4988-0 $5.99 US/$7.99 CAN

SHADOW DREAMS

ELIZABETH MASSIE

Meet the folks in Elizabeth Massie's world. They're normal, everyday people, living mostly in small towns, growing up or growing old and handling all life's problems just like you and me. Except for one thing—these people are about to be touched by the cold shadow of fear, enveloped by a dark nightmare laced with dread.

Elizabeth Massie has twice won the Bram Stoker Award and has been nominated for a World Fantasy Award for her brilliant horror fiction. This chilling collection, containing her best stories from the past ten years, is proof positive that Elizabeth Massie can see the terror lurking in the familiar and the darkness waiting in our dreams.

FACE
TIM LEBBON

When a family picks up a hitchhiker during the worst blizzard in recent memory, they think they're doing him a favor. But he becomes threatening, disturbing, and he asks them for something they cannot—or will not—give: a moment of their time. They force him from their car, but none of them believes that this is the last they will see of him.

The hitchhiker begins to haunt the family in ways that don't seem quite natural. He shows them that bad things can sometimes feel very good. He infiltrates their relationships, obsesses them, seduces them and terrifies them. Bit by bit he shows them that true horror can have a very human face.